An Acceptable Time
Many Waters
A Cry Like a Bell
Two-Part Invention
Sold into Egypt
A Stone for a Pillow
A House Like a Lotus
And It Was Good
Ladder of Angels
A Severed Wasp
The Sphinx at Dawn
A Ring of Endless Light
A Swiftly Tilting Planet
Walking on Water
The Irrational Season
The Weather of the Heart
Dragons in the Waters
The Summer of the Great-grandmother
A Wind in the Door
A Circle of Quiet
The Other Side of the Sun
Lines Scribbled on an Envelope
Dance in the Desert
The Young Unicorns
The Journey with Jonah
The Love Letters
The Arm of the Starfish
The 24 Days Before Christmas
The Moon by Night
A Wrinkle in Time
The Anti-Muffins
Meet the Austins
A Winter's Love
Camilla
And Both Were Young
Ilsa
The Small Rain

Certain Women

Certain Women

MADELEINE L'ENGLE

Farrar Straus Giroux

NEW YORK

Published simultaneously in Canada by HarperCollinsCanadaLtd
Printed in the United States of America
Designed by Victoria Wong
First edition, 1992
Second printing, 1992

Library of Congress Cataloging-in-Publication Data
L'Engle, Madeleine.
Certain women / Madeleine L'Engle.
p.   cm.
I. Title.
PS3523.E55C47   1992   813'.54—dc20   91-34048   CIP

This is a work of fiction.
Any resemblance of the characters
to individuals, living or dead,
is purely accidental.

For my grandmothers,

Emma and Caroline

Barbara Cohen first put the idea of a book about King David and his wives into my mind and generously suggested that I try it, and I thank her.

What happened when I started to write was, of course, very different from the original idea. The story in somewhat its present form began on a fifty-foot boat called the P.S., which is the model for the Portia, *and my thanks go to Phil and Sylvia Duryee; their daughter, Cornelia; and her husband, Terry Moore, with whom I have spent happy times on the P.S.*

M.L'E.

Contents

Certain women made us astonished.
LUKE 24:22

DAVID: *You sound so certain.*
ABIGAIL: *I am.*

Certain Women

Norma

✿ ✿ ✿

And David said to Saul, Let no man's heart fail because of him; thy servant will go and fight with this Philistine.

And David put his hand in his bag, and took thence a stone, and slang it, and smote the Philistine in his forehead, that the stone sunk into his forehead; and he fell upon his face to the earth.

I SAMUEL 17:32, 49

THE PORTIA, a shabbily comfortable fifty-foot boat, was tied up at the dock of a Haida Indian village a day's sail out of Prince Rupert. Emma Wheaton perched on the side of the bunk in the pilothouse, where her father lay propped up on pillows.

"I see Death as somewhat like Goliath," David Wheaton said, "but I am not allowed even a slingshot as I go to meet him." The old actor's voice was still clear and strong. He looked at Emma; at Alice Wheaton, his wife, sturdy in jeans and a red flannel shirt; at Norma Hightree, regal, over six feet tall, seated on the revolving chair by the wheel. Even seated, Norma nearly reached the brass rails installed under the ceiling for use when the sea was rough and the *Portia* was rolling. "King David is a role I would dearly love to have played."

Norma spoke, her voice calm and deep. "You have more than a slingshot, David. You have your entire life."

"Eighty-seven years." He nodded slowly. "Full years. Full of my work. I have been a good actor."

"You *are* a good actor, Papa." Emma regarded her father. Despite his age and his loss of weight, he looked like an actor, with his tawny hair still not completely white, his dark green eyes, his fierce nose.

"That is one pebble," David said. He reached out a hand to Alice, who turned slightly toward him, her blue eyes crinkling

· 3 ·

into her warm smile. "I have been unwise in love—except at the end. All those wives—one more than King David—all my children—and so few left."

He shook his head. "Enough of looking back. It's been an interesting script if nothing else, and I've had the joy of ending my career as King Lear, with my daughter as Goneril—" Now his hand reached toward Emma's, and she took it. "A young Goneril. How old are you?"

With all his children, Emma thought, no wonder he can't keep track of our ages. "Not that young."

"You're a fine actress."

"It's all I know how to do." Her voice was level.

"We're good, the two of us," he said with satisfaction. "Very good. Perhaps that's another pebble."

"Lots of pebbles." Emma squeezed his hand lightly.

"But I never had a chance to play King David. Nik never finished the play."

Niklaas Green. Emma's husband—that was. "No." Emma looked out the windows to the soft wrinkled grey of water, past a couple of weathered fishing boats, one with large black eyes painted on the prow. Her gaze moved on to the land where a small beach was brooded over by great dark trees rising into the cloudy sky. An eagle sat on a high branch, looking down at them.

"Sorry, Em, but it's the only role I've longed to do that never worked out. King David lived a long life, too, and he had more wives than a man should have, and he made every mistake anyone can make. But he danced with joy before the Lord and he made being human a rich and splendid endeavor."

Norma said, "As you have, David."

"Ah, Norma, you know only the best of me."

Norma shook her head slowly. "Oh, no, David, I have a good idea of the worst of you, too."

David's laugh boomed out, still strong, the famous, joyous laugh that had charmed audiences for decades.

Norma rose, looming large in the small pilothouse. "Goliath is only a monster who mimics death, David. You need not fear him."

David looked up at her. Smiled. "I know, Norma. I am not afraid. I have some work still to do, and I hope I will be given time to do it."

"I'm going now," Norma said. "I will see you again."

In the soft light of afternoon David's fine bones pushed sharply against the skin. "That is hardly likely. You know that."

"I will see you again," the Indian woman repeated. She held up her hand in a gesture that could be either greeting or farewell, gave Alice a quick, fierce hug, then took Emma in her arms. "You are good, you and Alice. Good women." She turned and went down the steps to the main cabin and out onto the dock.

Alice's younger brother, Ben, who ran the *Portia*, met Norma there and walked with her along the dock toward the island. Alice followed them. Emma stayed in the pilothouse with her father.

"I know very little about Norma's life in her village," he said. "Only that she is a personage of great importance. She knows little of my life as an actor. And yet we are close friends. We cut through what we do to who we are."

Emma knelt by the bunk. "I'm glad." She had met Norma Hightree and her husband, Ellis, many years earlier when she had first come to spend a week with her father on his boat, between the end of school and the beginning of summer camp. Ellis had been even taller than Norma, and heavy. They made a formidable pair. They had taken Emma late at night up the mountain that rose behind their village to a lookout where they showed her the stars, brilliant against a black sky. They had pointed out the star that was her guardian, making her feel incredibly protected. When Ellis died, Emma's father continued his friendship with Norma, and whenever Emma was with him on the *Portia* she looked forward to seeing the Indian woman.

Emma took Norma seriously when she said that she would see David again. But how? They would be leaving the village in a few minutes, going north. David was dying.

Emma rose and turned down the volume on the two radios constantly broadcasting on both the Coast Guard and the open channels, and to whose static-filled buzz her father was addicted.

Alice could let the noise slide off her; she had been communicating from island to boat to mainland by radio for most of her sixty-plus years. Emma could not tune out the repetitive sound. "Bald Eagle, Bald Eagle, Bald Eagle," the radio summoned. "Greenhigh Sound, Greenhigh Sound, channel six eight." On and on it went, constant messages from boat to shore to boat. Occasionally there came a *"M'aidez! M'aidez!"* or May Day, as it was more commonly thought of, and her father's eyes would brighten. Half a dozen times over the years the *Portia* had been in the vicinity of the call, and once had even rescued a careless teenager from his overturned sailboat.

The *Portia* looked more like a fishing boat than like a yacht, and was more welcome in villages like Norma's than a yacht would have been. Over the years David Wheaton had made many friends with the inhabitants of the various islands and coves in the Pacific Northwest waters the *Portia* plied.

The old man's hand, still strong, but thin, stripped of flesh so that it looked like an eagle's claw, came down over his daughter's.

"Papa, do you need anything?" Papa—the childish pronunciation, Poppa.

"Just to know that you are here."

Emma folded her hands so that the ring finger of her left hand was covered. She knew that her father had noticed the absence of the rings, but for these first few weeks on the *Portia* he had said nothing, and she was not yet ready to talk about Nik, or why she had taken off his rings.

Ben had noticed, had shyly spoken. "Something wrong between you and Nik?"

"Oh, Ben, that's the least of my worries right now, with Papa—he's already so much weaker—my own problems are unimportant."

"Em, if you need me, I'm here for you. You know that."

"Yes, Ben. I know that. Thank you."

But she could not talk about Nik to anyone yet.

Alice returned to the pilothouse with a prepared hypodermic needle. "Time for a shot."

"The pain's not bad."

"Good. Remember, it takes far more medication if you wait till the pain's intolerable. Better to keep on top of it this way, so that you remain alert and your own curmudgeonly self."

Alice was a physician, trained at Johns Hopkins in the States, but her practice until she married David Wheaton had been in northwest Canada, her patients mostly loggers, natives (Alice had known Norma long before David had), or fishermen like Ben, her brother. It was because of Alice and Ben that the old actor could have this summer on the *Portia*.

Emma saw Ben untying the boat. "I'll go help," she said, and went out to the narrow deck. Ben threw her the line and she secured it. When Ben had the little boat safely in deep waters and Alice was at the wheel, she returned to the main cabin. It was time to start dinner. Methodically she rolled flounder in bread crumbs she had seasoned with onions and herbs. Preparing dinner was familiar, understandable.

On the counter was a basket of eggs and a batch of wild greens Norma had brought them. Under the windows of the port side were a worktable, a wood stove, the undercounter fridge, the stove, a sink, and a cupboard. The galley was part of the main cabin. Under the starboard windows was a long, padded seat where, this summer, Ben put his sleeping bag. In front of the seat was a table that could comfortably seat six, maybe eight. Emma and Alice slept in the forward cabin under the pilothouse, where they could hear the old man when he snored, coughed, occasionally moaned. Alice knew when to get out of her sleeping bag to go to him, and when to leave him alone. Emma was unutterably grateful to her stepmother. Alice was far more to Emma than her father's latest wife, Alice with her shock of curly hair which still glinted with touches of gold despite the predominant grey. Her eyes were bright and young in a face finely wrinkled by wind and weather.

Emma stood by the galley watching as the *Portia* slid through the water, away from the village. She had taken over the cooking when she joined her father and Alice and Ben on the *Portia*, having made the long train trip across the continent to Vancouver and then traveling the last leg by seaplane. Her presence freed Ben to take care of the boat, and Alice to concentrate on her husband.

Emma slid the flounder into the oven and turned on the gas. The propane-gas tank lay on the roof of the *Portia* in front of the crow's nest, with copper tubes that fed the stove. She put in half a dozen potatoes—Ben would want more than one; like Nik, he could eat anything and never gain a pound—and was making salad dressing when her father called.

Alice was steering the boat across a placid stretch of water in Queen Charlotte Sound, looking intently ahead of her for deadheads, those great sunken logs which bob along, only a foot or so showing above the water, seemingly innocuous but potentially dangerous for small craft. Then she turned the boat and nosed into an inlet where Ben had put out crab traps, hoping to get enough for at least a crab cocktail before dinner. The long shafts of afternoon light touched Alice's hair, gilding it almost to its original color.

Emma sat down beside her father. He stroked her hair, slightly dank from the salt air. "You shouldn't have turned down an entire summer season," he rebuked.

"I wanted to be with you."

"I'm selfish enough to want you here. But that's sentimentality, and an actress cannot afford that. You could have had a whole season of Shakespeare—Rosalind, Beatrice, Kate, Portia—"

"Papa." Emma held up her hand to silence him. "I've just had nine months of playing Goneril to your Lear, the greatest Lear ever on Broadway." Was that an exaggeration? Perhaps. But there was no denying that David Wheaton's Lear was electrifying.

The old man smacked his lips, as though tasting something pleasant. "At least I'm the oldest. Eighty-seven and still able to hold my lines. I'm happy we did that TV special of it, and in full color, too. It's been a good run, a splendid run. I'm glad you played Goneril and not Cordelia."

Emma nodded agreement. Cordelia, she thought, was a prig. Goneril's pride and ambition made her willing to turn against her father; she was a far more interesting and challenging role.

"Emma, did I push you onto the stage?" he asked. "When my marriage to your mother broke up—I never should have married her. We were too much in competition. You haven't had a mother."

"Hey, Papa. One, no, you didn't push me onto the stage. Acting's in my blood. Two, I had Bahama"—the beloved grandmother she called Bahama when her baby tongue couldn't manage 'Grandmother.' The name stuck; somehow it suited her grandmother, who was large and rawboned and nurturing and forbearing, lavish with embraces. If baby Emma was held, loved, dandled, kissed, touched, played with, it was by Bahama. Emma had been premature and had survived only because Bahama, recently widowed, had come to take care of the baby, and kept her warm between her ample breasts. Elizabeth, Emma's mother, had shuddered. 'She's so little and scrawny I can't bear to touch her.'

Bahama was to all intents and purposes Emma's mother. Once it seemed that Emma was going to live, Elizabeth and David went back to Hollywood to make their famous movie of *The Mill on the Floss*, far more successful than their *Madame Bovary*, the movie they had been making when Emma was conceived, and for whose heroine Emma had been named. Bahama, who had expected to go home to Seattle, stayed on in New York to take care of the tiny creature whose life she had saved.

"I let you do all those glossy magazine ads," David said. "It was not a normal life for a child."

"Papa, stop fretting." Emma had not been a cuddly, golden-haired cutie or beauty. Rather, her hair was a light chestnut in color but so fine that it tended toward limpness. She was thin, too thin, despite milkshakes and eggnogs. But her eyes were an amazing gentian color, totally incongruous in her wistful little face, and her smile, when it could be coaxed out of her, lit up the page.

At eleven she had played the child princess in a Broadway production of *Pavane*, a play based on Ravel's music, and at twelve had been a charming adolescent Celia in *As You Like It*. Then she sat out most of the years of high school and college, eight years of delight in study: literature, astronomy, philosophy, history, even some physics. Then she was ready to make the transition to the roles for which she was best suited. Offstage she knew herself plain. She knew that many theater children were not able to make it as they grew older. It had not been easy for Emma. Perhaps it was a blessing that she had none of the qualities that make a starlet. Her first real role after college was Viola in an Off-Broadway production of *Twelfth Night*. She had read the famous "willow cabin" speech for her father.

'Make me a willow cabin at your gate, and call upon my soul within the house; write loyal cantons of contemned love, and sing them loud even in the dead of night . . .'

He had looked at her as though in acute pain. 'Emma, this is Viola's big speech. It is what keeps Viola from being an ingenue role.'

'I think the director wants an ingenue.'

'Bullshit. Viola's not a simpering idiot. Why did he cast you?'

'I don't know. Papa—'

'Do you want me to work with you on it?'

'Yes. Sure.'

Over an hour later he was satisfied. And the director was intelligent enough to recognize that the depth Emma was now giving Viola was far better than the coyness he had looked for before. Emma's father was her best teacher, pushing, shoving, never satisfied until he had taken her further and deeper into a role than she had thought she could go. Of her father's eleven children, she was the one who was closest to him, the one who had lived with him through childhood, and her Goneril and his Lear had been a superb collaboration. Emma's Goneril had been no flat villain, but a complex, distorted woman, as caught up in her own tortured vanity as Lear was in his.

She closed her eyes against the pain of knowing that they would never work together again.

"Tea?" Alice suggested. "Fresh camomile?"

David nodded without enthusiasm.

"I'll make it," Emma said.

"Ah, Em, if only we could have done Nik's David play together—"

.

Even though her father had actually never played David, Emma still thought of the ancient king as one of his roles. Some of his identification of himself and his wives and children with the characters in the King David story was excruciatingly painful to Emma. Some of it she viewed with wry amusement. David Wheaton saw Emma's maternal grandfather as the twentieth-century equivalent of the prophet Samuel, who played such a large role in King David's drama. The Reverend Wesley Bowman, Emma's grandpa, was familiarly known as Wes the Wise, Georgia cracker, popular preacher, visionary. Indeed, he resembled an Old Testament prophet, with his wild greying hair and beard, which looked as though he trimmed them with pruning shears. Half hidden by bushy eyebrows were the amazing gentian eyes Emma had inherited. When his daughter, Emma's mother, went to Hollywood, he was devastated, until he had a vision of a dozen grandchildren. But Elizabeth had only the one child, Emma, and Emma loved Grandpa Bowman almost as much as she loved Bahama.

.

"Emma!"

The camomile tea. She had almost forgotten. The lid of the kettle was gently lifting and falling. She prepared a mug of tea and took it to her father.

"It was you I wanted, not this hogwash." He smiled at her as he took the cup.

"Alice thinks it's good for you. You need to keep your kidneys flushed out."

"I can think of better ways," he grunted.

"Emma—" She looked up as Ben came into the cabin.

He leaned over the chart stretched out on a table which folded down from the wall, and pointed to the upper-left-hand corner. "We're here. 'Scuse me, Em, I need to get the next chart." His hair, streaked yellow and white like Alice's, fell across his face and he shoved it back.

Under David Wheaton's bunk were shallow drawers that held dozens of charts of the waters the *Portia* plied. Emma moved out of Ben's way so that he could open one of the drawers. He riffled through several charts and selected one.

"What's this?" Emma picked up a much folded piece of blue paper from the open chart drawer.

Her father smiled. "A letter from you while you were at college."

Carefully, Emma opened the fragile paper, skimmed, read: *The thought that I must, that I ought to write, never leaves me for an instant.* Chekhov. She had crossed out *write* and substituted *act.*

"You've always had the passion," her father said softly.

"Passion alone isn't enough," she said. "There has to be the gift."

"Yes," he agreed. "But neither is the gift alone enough. It must be served, and with passion. Listen, this is Chekhov, too—I think I can quote it accurately: *You must once and for all give up being worried about successes and failures. Don't let that concern you. It's your duty to go on working steadily day by day, quite quietly, to be prepared for mistakes, which are inevitable, for failures.* In work, and in life. I've had a few abysmal flops, such as my *L'Aiglon.* And God knows my life has been full of spectacular mistakes."

Emma put her letter back in the chart drawer and saw a manuscript that was slipped in among the charts.

"Some stuff of Nik's," her father said. "I was going over it a while ago."

Emma pulled the pages out. They were in Nik's strong handwriting, on a lined pad, not legal-sized, because Nik liked to have his work fit in a typewriter-paper box. Forgetting her father, Ben, Alice, she sat back on her heels by the bunk, holding the manuscript loosely, letting it drop to her lap.

Some of the pages were typed, and Emma pulled the first one out, remembering when Nik had first shown it to her, the very beginning of his play about David.

A PLAY IN THREE ACTS
BY NIKLAAS GREEN

Act I, scene i

The light comes up slowly. It should be a desert light, so strong as to be almost white. The entire back of the stage is filled with a projection of Goliath, an enormous figure, 'an helmet of brass upon his head, and he was armed with a coat of mail . . . and he had greaves of brass upon his legs, and a target of brass between his shoulders.' He is far larger than life-size, ferocious and fearsome.

In the center of the stage is David, a small figure, holding his slingshot in one hand.

It was a good opening scene, Emma thought. It would catch the audience's attention, remind them of the familiar story of young David and Goliath, and lead them into the far less familiar story of the mature king. Nik had spent well over a year on that play, writing individual scenes that were exciting, but bogging down over the historical information. The year had been for Emma one of the happiest in her life, despite the war, the brown-out on Broadway, the terrible bombing of England with Hitler ready to invade that small green island.

Despite Emma's constant awareness of the war, with two of her brothers overseas, once she met Nik, war was on the periphery of her life. She had a featured role in Niklaas Green's first Broadway comedy; she was in love, and part of that love was irrevocably connected with Nik's writing of the King David play.

Nik admitted candidly that it would be a wonderful boost to his career if he could write a play in which David Wheaton would star, and that it also gave him a chance to pursue Emma. Working on the David play with Nik was, for Emma, not only falling in love with him, but finally believing that he loved her, that he loved Emma the human being, not Emma the actress. The part of the David story that touched her own life she tried to set aside. Most of the time she succeeded. If Nik's work on the play kept him in her life, that was what mattered. She was in love, and she was willing to pay for that love by encouraging Nik with the play if that was the price.

.

If Nik had finished the David play . . . But ultimately their own complex problems kept slipping into the script. He would tear up whole scenes in a rage when he was angry with himself. With her.

She did not want to think about Nik's anger. As Ben left the cabin, she turned back to her father.

"Papa, remember that English drawing-room comedy we did together?"

"Anyone for tennis? How could I forget it?" David smiled.

"Summer stock," she said. "I was playing a character role."

"An eccentric spinster"—her father grinned—"and you had some wonderful business with a cigarette, blowing the ashes off the end."

"I hated smoking," Emma said. "It was one way to have a cigarette and not make my mouth taste vile. It was fun, coming back to the theater after all those years of school and college. And Etienne was stage manager."

Etienne was one of her half brothers. That summer they had thought he would be David Wheaton's stage manager forever. She laughed. "Those ten red raspberry sherberts that never even got eaten! How Etienne hated getting them every evening, melting, making a mess for him to clean up."

David laughed, too. "Only Etienne would have thought of replacing them with red tennis balls and not telling us what he'd done."

"They looked fine," Emma said. "I remember noticing them on the tray by Etienne's table, and thinking how he hated dripping raspberry sherbert."

"And then"—David's face was alight with pleasure—"the actor playing the butler tripped ever so slightly as he entered and—" Laughter stopped him.

Through her own laughter Emma chortled, "Red tennis balls bouncing all over the stage!"

Alice turned from the wheel. "I love it when you two reminisce."

"I've got some good memories," David said, "and I'm glad that Emma shares some of them."

She was smiling. "What about that night when you almost forgot to make an entrance, and you'd started to change costume, and you'd stripped to the skin when Etienne rushed into your dressing room to tell you that you were almost on, and you flung your cloak about yourself, and I couldn't understand why you kept clutching it to you and didn't want me to take it off, the way I usually did."

"You're a joy to work with, my daughter," David Wheaton said. "How I wish we could have done the David play together."

Emma did not reply. That was long ago. It was too late. Much too late.

Her father gave her a long look. "Emma. You're unhappy."

"I'm fine, Papa, fine."

But he reached for her left hand. "What's wrong?" He took her hand, looking at the faint, pale circle. "You've taken off your rings."

"Yes."

"Why?"

Emma shook her head. The tears were close.

David's voice was gentle. "I haven't wanted to hurt you by prying, but—Abby is coming, and she's going to want to know. You're her godchild. She loves you." Abby Wheaton was David's second wife and still a good friend. Abby was coming to say goodbye.

Much as Emma loved Abby, her coming was a potent reminder that her father was dying.

"Emma?" David prodded gently.

Emma bowed her head, spoke in a whisper. "I've taken off my wedding ring because I'm no longer married."

"Take the wheel for a few minutes, Em," Alice said.

"But, my darling, you're not divorced," David continued as Alice left the cabin.

"There really hasn't been time. I don't know, Papa. I'm not willing to put up with the things your wives have put up with."

David grimaced. "Or haven't put up with." He reached toward her, then dropped his hand. "I was so happy when you met Nik." Emma steered the *Portia* between two islands. "It was such good timing. Getting cast in his play was the best thing that could have happened to you."

She kept her hands on the wheel, turning it slightly.

"Fascinating history," her father said, "full of confusions and oddities. Does it hurt you if I talk about him—King David?"

"No, Papa. Go on." It should have stopped hurting by now. Enough water had gone under the bridge to make a great river.

"David, King David, of course is the protagonist and the leading role. But King Saul and the prophet Samuel would be featured roles. And then there are the women. Nik's rendering of the women was extraordinary." He paused, looking at Emma.

"Michal," she counted on her fingers. "King Saul's daughter and David's first wife."

"Abigail," her father continued. "He truly loved Abigail."

"Bathsheba, too, of course—but she was the last wife, the eighth one."

"There were other women besides the wives," David said. "Zeruiah, for instance, David's sister. She'd be a featured role."

"Zer-u-i-ah," Emma said thoughtfully.

"Nik had a terrible time with the Scriptural names."

"Not only Nik, Papa. We all did."

Just then Ben poked his head into the pilothouse, grinning. "Five keepers." Five crabs the legal size limit or above. He limped away.

David had met Ben one year when he had dropped anchor at Whittock Island, where Ben and Alice had grown up. Ben had come out onto the beach to see whose boat was nosing into his small bay, and invited David in for coffee and conversation, and thus began what was to become an enduring friendship, which was cemented the year David arrived at Whittock with an agonizing pain in his belly. Ben had taken one look at David, moved to the wheel of the boat, and had run, as fast as the little craft would go, to Prince Rupert, where Alice had taken out an appendix ready to burst. And David, who had thought never to marry again, and Alice, who had thought never to marry at all, had fallen in love. 'It was crazy,' Alice said. 'I was set in my ways, much too old for romance, and there I was, like a silly schoolgirl.'

The year after David and Alice were married, and Alice had uprooted herself and moved to New York, Ben shattered his right femur, alone, fishing for salmon. How he got the troller into dock no one ever knew. The leg was set inadequately, and the bone knit slowly, and not well.

So it was natural for Ben to take over the *Portia* when David could no longer manage it and Ben, with his lame leg, could not spend weeks alone on his troller, fishing. He kept the house on Whittock Island, but the *Portia* became his real home. Normally, he slept in the forward cabin, where he had his odd collection of books: Shakespeare, Blake, the Bible, *Water Prey and Game Birds*, Webster's Collegiate Dictionary, *Emma*, *Pride and Prejudice*, Thoreau's *The Maine Woods* . . . Emma could see them from her bunk, contained in a high-lipped shelf with an elastic cord.

Ben's lack of formal schooling did not bother him. He had an unselfconscious but firm self-esteem. He was a good fisherman. An adequate logger. He was also perforce a navigator, meteorologist, astronomer, electrician, carpenter, mechanic, shipwright—there was nothing Ben could not do, Emma thought. Occasionally he came up with plans for a kelp farm. The Pacific Northwest was in his blood. He was not happy anywhere else. Nor did he feel the need to be anywhere else. He had married when he was in his mid-twenties and within a few years his young wife had died of cancer. After her death, his life had been solitary and, ultimately, contented. He was nearly fifty now, but he looked younger.

"Emma, Emma," David said. "I'm glad you're here, glad we can share memories. I've hardly had time to give Alice my memories, my stories, and I want her to have them."

Emma looked around at the white salt-washed stones of the shore, the dark green of firs predominating. She looked with loathing at the brown scars, acres of land where the trees had been indiscriminately logged, with only a small fringe of evergreen left at the waterline to disguise the carnage. David was indignant, pointing out ways that logging could bring in a good living and not unbalance the precarious ecology. Some of the scars, Ben had observed calmly, were not man-made, but had come from slides, great roarings of trees and rocks and mud, started by wind and rain. Nature can be as brutal as her creatures, Ben said.

After dinner they sat in the pilothouse with David, letting the long twilight wash over them like water, listening as David talked about his life in the theater, until he was ready for sleep. Alice could mimic the call of a loon, and sometimes she was answered, the long, lovely sound carrying across the water. David sipped a cup of vervain, watching the shadows of the great Douglas firs on the nearby islands deepen and darken. This was the time when he was most ready to talk, to unburden himself to the two women and Ben.

"The world changes," he said. "Behavior which is taken for granted now, in the sixties, which is socially acceptable, would not have been tolerated when I was a young man."

Emma sat in the revolving chair by the wheel and swiveled so that she could look at her father.

"If I'd had affairs, rather than marrying, I'd have been just another immoral actor. Because my wives were legitimate, I get a lot of grief that I could have avoided if I'd merely bedded instead of wedded. Not to excuse myself. I *have* been an immoral actor."

Alice was sitting beside him on the bunk. She put her hand lightly on his knee. "Not an immoral actor, Dave. You have been a most moral actor."

He laughed again. "An immoral man, then. Self-indulgent. Living all my fantasies instead of being satisfied with acting them on the stage. If I'd just had affairs, it would have been more practical as well as—in some cases—more honest. Forgive me, my dears, I maunder."

Ben folded the chart table to its closed position against the wall. "Tell us more theater stories, Dave. When did you get your big break?"

"I don't think I had a big break," David said. "I worked into my career gradually. My first featured role was in a series of French one-act plays when Existentialism wasn't even a word. I played a very young Cyrano de Bergerac who didn't much resemble Rostand's hero except in the size of his nose. But the plays made a modest splash and so did I. Some critical acclaim but not very good box office. I met Meredith, who was to be the first of my wives, at the opening-night party. She wanted to know what had happened to my nose. I spent a long time explaining makeup to her, not just how I put the putty nose on and off. She was considerably older than I and had that strange kind of assurance that comes with being born very, very rich. She thought I was adorable, and I didn't understand that she saw me as some kind of exotic animal she could buy and keep on a leash. I loved the clothes she bought me, especially the wildly expensive Chinese robe I still wear in my dressing room. I didn't realize that the clothes came with the purchase, the way some women buy diamond-studded collars for their poodles."

Then he laughed. "But I exaggerate, as usual. We were in love like two animals. No, that's not fair, either. It is a human tendency to rewrite the past. What is true is that after we were married Meredith wanted me to leave the theater. She had more than enough money for us both, she told me. I could not make her understand that I wasn't an actor for money. For money I'd have stayed in Seattle and worked in my father's bank."

He handed his empty cup to Alice, who put it on the wide

shelf above the bunk, and continued. "If Meredith couldn't understand why I was an actor, I didn't understand that, for people in her social class, acting was still unacceptable work, but she liked to be avant-garde. We were obviously not suited, but Meredith was a stickler for the proprieties, so she took me to the altar. I was young and didn't know what I was doing. My mother, bless her, your Bahama, Emma, begged me not to marry so hastily, to wait. My father threatened. They were right, but I was impetuous and thought I knew everything. Poor Meredith. She had too much money. Her family was terrified that I was going to try to get some of it when we divorced. She never married again." He yawned. "I'm tired now, my dears."

Emma had asked Alice, "Did you know about all the wives?"

"Of course. Dave was painfully careful about making sure I knew what an old roué I was marrying. But he's filling in all kinds of spaces now."

It was to Emma alone, however, that David continued to talk about his wives. Alice and Ben had taken the dinghy and gone ashore to pick berries after dinner, and Emma sat in the pilothouse with her father.

"I'm glad you told us about Meredith," she said.

"Ancient history. Dull."

"No, Papa. It helps me to understand."

"As divorces go, ours was simple. All I wanted was out. Not too much to understand there."

"And then you met Abby."

"Yes. I met Abby."

"She was a painter."

"No, not then." David warmed his hands around the fresh cup of vervain Alice had given him before leaving. "Abby didn't start to paint until after our babies had died and our marriage was broken to bits. She was a teacher when I met her, quiet and shy, except with her students. She brought a group of sixth-graders to see me in a matinee, and they all came backstage after. She was a born teacher, giving her students wonderful gifts she didn't even realize were unusual. They wrote, they painted, they acted. They even did a play in Latin, which she wrote for them, and afterwards cooked them a Roman banquet. But I'm getting ahead of myself."

"Go on. Please."

"When she brought the kids backstage, all I saw was a quiet mouse of a girl with grey eyes that held secrets like the sea." He looked out at the gentle light touching the water. "One of the bolder kids told me they were going to the Lafayette for dinner, and asked if I would join them. I hated the Lafayette, and I told them I'd rather go to Joe's Saloon on Ninth Avenue. It was quieter than the Lafayette. Theater people went there to talk, not to be seen. I took you there a couple of times, didn't I?"

"I think so. The building it was in got torn down while I was away at school."

He smiled. "Once I'd made the offer to the kids, I thought I was out of my mind. But something of Abby must already have reached me without my knowing it. The kids were thrilled, and I was able to point out a few celebrities to them. Abby talked intelligently while we ate, understanding what I was trying to do with my role, but not fawning over me. I asked for her phone number, and she was pleased and blushed, though I never expected I'd call her. She came to the play again, this time in the evening, and sent a note backstage. So I asked her out to supper and we talked away half the night. After that, I saw her every week or so, all winter. She had a kind of innate dignity. She still has, though it's deeper now. I nearly destroyed her, but there's something in Abby that's indestructible." He looked across the water in the direction in which Alice and Ben had gone in the dinghy. "Alice has that quality, too. It doesn't come free. But it's worth it, Emma. It's what I want for you. I can see it in you, too."

Emma looked down at her feet in worn, stained sneakers. "Abby and Bahama?"

"Loved each other from the start," David said. "I hurt my

parents when I divorced Abby. But they remained friends. It was Bahama who suggested that I ask Abby to be your godmother. That was healing, for all of us."

Still looking at the grass stains on her sneakers, Emma said, "But Myrlo—"

"You don't understand Myrlo, do you?" David asked wryly. "Neither do I."

No, Emma did not understand Myrlo, the wife who followed Abby. "You met Myrlo in a play when you were still—" She broke off.

"Still married to Abby. Yes. I would leave Abby, and our twins, and death, because I knew our babies were dying long before either Abby or I accepted it, and went to the theater, and there was Myrlo and life. How greedy I was for life." He let out a long, slow breath. "Abby and I might have worked through everything if Myrlo hadn't become pregnant. She told me she was taking precautions and I believed her. Maybe she was. I wasn't. I am ashamed, bitterly ashamed, of what I did to Abby. The babies terrified me. Tiny, scrawny, wailing all night long until I thought my eardrums would be pierced by that feeble, constant crying. I didn't know how to be a father to those fragile creatures, or a husband to a mother who was in agony."

"Where was Bahama?" Emma asked.

"My parents were in England for a year. But I was a grown man. I should not have needed my mother—or anybody else—to teach me fidelity and courage. Emma, this is not a conversation I should be having with you."

Emma took the cup from him. "If you can talk about it, Papa, it helps me to understand."

David hitched himself up slightly on the pillows, reaching out toward Emma as she put the cup down on the shelf. "There's a lot to explain, isn't there? Myrlo wasn't—isn't—a bad woman. Greedy, yes. But so am I. And with less excuse. She was shallow. Never read a book. Or a newspaper. What went on in the world had little relevance for her. It wasn't really her fault. Her mother was a tart. Myrlo didn't even know who her father was. But she wanted to make something of herself. Myrlo manipulated me by getting pregnant, and I knew I was being manipulated, but I didn't have the strength to say bugger off, your trick isn't going to work. I was a step on the ladder. We never loved each other. Not love. But we had Billy. Unlike Abby's and my twins, he was healthy. My first child to live. My first grown child to die." Tears slid down his cheeks. "We won't talk about Billy. There's too much pain, for all of us."

Emma took David's empty cup and started toward the steps. "I'm just going to rinse this out. I'll be right back."

"Emma—I'm sorry—" His voice drifted after her.

She rinsed and dried the cup, put it away, and returned to the pilothouse. Through the windows she could see the dinghy returning to the *Portia*, Ben at the oars. "Ben and Alice are back," she said.

"Good. That you and Alice are friends is a great joy to me."

Emma sat on the revolving chair, listening as the rowboat bumped gently against the solid bulk of the *Portia*. In a moment Alice came to the pilothouse and sat on the side of the bunk, taking David's hand.

"I've been telling Emma about Myrlo, my third wife." David's voice was strained. "Our marriage was a bust. Billy was all that kept us together. He was beautiful, and Myrlo liked showing him off, though she didn't enjoy caring for him, so we had a sort of nanny. He didn't get the loving attention he should have had from his mother any more than you did, Emma. Or from me."

"Dave, you're tired," Alice interrupted. "Enough for tonight."

"Enough. Too much is enough. Emma, I'm—did I upset you?"

"You're upsetting yourself," Alice said. "Em, will you help Ben with the dinghy?"

"Sure." She rose.

"Come back and say good night to me," David called after her.

"I will, Papa."

While they were getting ready for bed in the cabin under the pilothouse, Alice said, "I think Dave needs to do this, go over the past, come to terms with it."

"He's got a lot to come to terms with." Emma pulled on a flannel nightgown.

"Did he upset you?"

"Yes."

·

"Bear with me," David said the next night. "Meredith. Abby. Myrlo. Then Marical. I saw her picture in *Vogue* and fell in love with her then and there. Myrlo was already pleasuring herself with another actor, withholding what she called her favors from me as a way of punishing me. For what, I don't know, because I was trying in my own way to be a good husband. Am I rewriting again? trying to let myself off the hook? I used to look at pictures of Marical, who was one of the most photographed models of the year, and dream lovely dreams about her, not necessarily erotic, just beautiful. She had that effect. It was the secret of her success. And she seemed not even to realize it. It never went to her head."

Alice was sitting on a stool near David's head. "But how did you meet her?"

"Through a mutual friend. He arranged it, after the theater. Marical had not liked the play; she thought it was shocking. But she liked me, and the way I played down the more obvious bad taste. It wasn't, for its day, as bad as Marical thought, or I wouldn't have done it. Despite the fact that the sex was pretty overt, it was not gratuitous. We talked and I invited her to go to Carnegie Hall to the Bach B minor Mass. It was all very chaste. She knew I was married to Myrlo. But by then Myrlo had met an insurance executive who could give her diamonds and servants and an apartment on Park Avenue. She wanted the divorce, and had lawyers who were able to facilitate things by basing the divorce on adultery. Mine. Fortunately, Marical's name was never mentioned, and there had certainly been no adultery—except mine and Myrlo's, and nobody seemed to remember that. However, I let it go. I wanted out as badly as Myrlo did.

"When I married Marical, I thought the fairy tale had really come to pass and that we'd live happily ever after. We almost did. Our children were healthy and beautiful. Etienne. Everard. Adair. And finally our little girl, Chantal. I had everything any man could want. We were a gorgeous couple. Wherever we went, our picture was taken, people stared, admired. We were happy. Marical did not enjoy the stresses that are an intrinsic part of a model's life, and she loved being a mother. My career was going well. And then I blew it. Marical had taken the children up to Maine, out of the summer heat. I met Harriet, my ballerina, all cool and beautiful as an ice princess, and I was simply curious, wanting to know if there was flame under the ice. Her dancing was pure and perfect and I wanted to know what fired it. We had a one-night stand. A flicker. That should have been it, would have been it, except that Harriet got pregnant. She offered to have an abortion, but we both felt—reasonably or not—that a life had been started because of our impetuousness and we had a responsibility toward that life.

"Harriet was quite willing to go ahead and have the baby and bring it up herself, and in a sense she did, because she didn't want to be married, to be tied down to a husband. But I told Marical. Maybe I should have kept my mouth shut, I don't know, but I told her, confessed, and she insisted that we at least legitimize Jarvis, and then, even after Harriet and I separated, Marical would not have me back. I can't blame her, and yet her punishing me hurt all of us."

Ben came up the steps to the pilothouse and sat on the top one, elbows on knees, listening.

"That's it, I thought," David said. "Then I went to Hollywood and met Elizabeth. Your mother, Emma. Marrying was a habit with me, a bad habit. We played well together, and Elizabeth knew all the right people, and we were stars. Jealousy is a terrible thing. She was good—oh, Elizabeth is a good actress, but I got better reviews. Most of the time. The green-eyed monster stalked back and forth between us. And ultimately split us. I came home to New York, to you and Bahama, Emma, and this time I was certain I would never marry again. It took ten years before I fell into the old pattern of self-indulgence and lust. Edith was a disaster."

"Tomorrow," Ben said, as though not changing the subject, "I'll pull up anchor early and we'll head for Bella Bella."

"Bella Bella and Abby." Suddenly David looked anxious. "Emma—"

"Yes, Papa?"

"It *is* tomorrow that Abby is coming?"

"Tomorrow."

Ben pointed to a framed pencil sketch of two loons which Abby had drawn many years earlier.

"She's not a great artist," David said, "and she knows it, but she's a good one. And a great person. Only a great person could have forgiven me, could have become friends once again. We didn't see each other until after you were born, Emma. She came to New York, where she had an opening. It went quite well, and I saw the reviews in the papers. I'd just come back from Hollywood, knowing my marriage to your mother was a mistake, and I went to the gallery to see Abby's paintings, and she was there. And I loved her. It wasn't a romance this time. I may be an incurable romantic, but I knew that with Abby what I needed, and what I hoped she needed, was friendship. It was—am I repeating? Sorry."

Yes, Abby had always been a warm and loving part of Emma's life, and it did not seem strange to her that her godmother was coming to the *Portia*. "I've made up the bed in the lower cabin for Abby," Emma said. It was the only real bed on the *Portia*; the rest were bunks. Emma thought of her godmother as being wise, but Abby had been young and untried when she married David Wheaton. Only Alice, Emma thought, had been fully mature at the time of marriage, an experienced physician and a woman who had long since come to terms with her own humanness and that of those she loved. Alice's beauty was of the spirit, and this had attracted David, rather than what Bahama had called 'youth and pulchritude.' Alice and Bahama would have loved each other, Emma thought.

Abby Wheaton was good about staying in touch with her god-child. Even during the years when Abby was married to a Yugoslavian count and was living in France, she managed to spend a couple of weeks each year with Emma. The marriage was a happy one, and ended with the count's death. Abby always seemed to bring with her a sense of proportion, and that was something Emma badly needed.

This was the first full summer she had spent on the *Portia*. When she was a child, Bahama had taken her to Seattle for as much of the summer vacation as possible, sent her to camp, tried to keep her life normal. Emma's times on the boat were a few days between school and camp.

Once she was grown and living on her own, Emma had little free time to make the long journey to the West Coast. When a play closed, Emma seldom knew when or what her next job was going to be, so she stayed close to the phone: if an agent or producer called and she was not there, the next person on the list would get the call.

Occasionally, when she had a secure job in summer stock ahead of her, she would plan a few days on the *Portia*, away from the phone, away from the stresses of the city. This became particularly important after her father married Alice and Ben took over the running of the boat. Alice was far more Emma's friend than she was another of her father's wives.

What would happen to the *Portia*? Emma blinked tears away quickly so that her father would not see them.

But he did. "Don't weep for me, my Em." His smile was gentle. "This is simply part of the journey that comes to us all."

Bahama

❦ ❦ ❦

Then Samuel took the horn of oil, and anointed him in the midst of his brethren: and the Spirit of the Lord came upon David from that day forward . . .

But the Spirit of the Lord departed from Saul, and an evil spirit from the Lord troubled him. And Saul's servants said unto him, Behold now, an evil spirit from God troubleth thee. Let our lord now command thy servants . . . to seek out a man, who is a cunning player on an harp: and it shall come to pass, when the evil spirit from God is upon thee, that he shall play with his hand, and thou shalt be well.

And it came to pass, when the evil spirit from God was upon Saul, that David took an harp, and played with his hand, so Saul was refreshed, and was well, and the evil spirit departed from him.

I SAMUEL 16:13–16, 23

AT LEAST once a year Bahama took Emma on the overnight train to Georgia to visit her maternal grandfather. Sometimes Bahama stayed for a few days and then left Emma, returning later to take her back to New York. Emma loved her visits to Georgia, the warmer winter climate, the great Spanish-moss-hung oak trees, the food, hominy with every meal, spoon bread, black-eyed peas.

The year Emma was ten, when she returned to New York after a month-long visit with Grandpa Bowman, she felt that something was different about her father, that somehow he was not entirely there, and she was not sure where he was. She sat up in bed and thought, —He'll be back.

Bahama did not say anything, but she, too, seemed distant.

'What's wrong?' Emma asked.

'Life changes,' Bahama said, unwontedly cryptic. 'Things don't stay the same, my Em.'

Emma turned to Marical's children, the brothers and sister who took her into their lives, loved her, advised her, never made her feel plain in comparison to their beauty; they were lean and long of limb, with apricot-colored skin, straight, silky black hair, and large, luminous eyes. They called their father Papa, the French way.

Chantal was a loving older sister who treated Emma like a

favorite doll. Etienne and Everard played with her, read to her.
Adair, the youngest of the three brothers, she worshipped. Adair
looked like a young god; he shone like burnished copper, drawing people to his light. In Emma's eyes he could do no wrong.
Adair was her protector, her St. George who would slay any
dragon that threatened her.

Jarvis was a dearly loved if definitely bossy older brother.
Emma could not imagine being without Jarvis, who spent more
time with Marical and her children than he did with his mother,
Harriet. It was Jarvis who ended up being the producer of David
Wheaton's *King Lear.*

·

Harriet and David were from different worlds. Harriet was
not interested in the theater. David enjoyed ballet but did not
see it as an entire way of life. Their marriage was brief, their
parting amicable.

'Why didn't Papa go back to Marical?' Emma had asked Adair
when she was old enough to wonder about such things.

He smiled ruefully. 'She wouldn't have him, little sister. Maman has some very strict ideas.'

'Don't you?' Emma asked.

Adair had sighed. 'Yes, I do. But I also believe in forgiveness.'
Then he had laughed. 'However, if Maman had gone back to
our father, you would never have been born.'

'My mother was another mistake, like Harriet, and so was I.'

'No, no.' Adair had reached for Emma's hand. 'You were
wanted, never forget that.'

'Who wanted me?' Emma asked bluntly.

Adair replied thoughtfully, 'I think both your parents wanted
you, but when things didn't work out between them, you would
have slipped through the cracks if it hadn't been for Bahama.
Bless Bahama, she's a wonderful grandmother to us all.'

It happened to many children, Emma knew. It had happened
to some of the children of divorce in her school. She herself felt
no want of love, not only from Bahama and her father, but from

Marical, and from Abby on her annual visits. Any feeling of sadness she had because of her mother's disregard was unconscious until her father married Edith when Emma was ten. For ten years Emma had had her father and Bahama as the center of her universe. Somehow it had never occurred to the child that David Wheaton would marry again.

One day after school she came home to find Edith in the living room, drinking a dry martini.

Her father introduced them, a little hesitantly, and told Emma that Edith was going to be her new mother. Edith, sophisticated, elegant, looked Emma up and down appraisingly. Her look said, 'She's not beautiful.'

David said, 'She's like Duse.'

Edith was a lawyer with a big Wall Street firm. 'Who?'

'Eleonora Duse, the great, the sublime actress.'

Emma stood and looked back at Edith. Edith was beautiful. Where was Bahama?

It soon became apparent that Edith's presence was going to be Bahama's banishment. Edith made it quite clear that she planned to be mistress of David Wheaton's house, and that it was going to be her house. She moved David—and Emma—from the apartment which had been Emma's home all her life, across town to a much larger apartment on Riverside Drive, with a magnificent view of the Hudson River. Bahama went off to do some long-deferred traveling with a group of friends.

·

Edith was not particularly pleased to see Emma until after the baby, Inez, was born and Edith discovered that Emma was a convenient baby-sitter during the nurse's time off. Emma adored the baby. She was embarrassed by Edith. Edith purred like a cat when she was with David, and like a cat twined herself about him. She gave dinner parties for important clients of her law firm; there was a cook in the kitchen, and a maid, as well as Inez's nurse.

One night Emma woke up from a nightmare. Always when

she had a bad dream she ran to Bahama's room for comfort, but Bahama was not there. Emma sat up in bed, shivering with terror, then slipped out of bed and walked quietly down the hall to David and Edith's room. From within she heard strange sounds that sounded like pain, Edith's voice rising and rising until it seemed to break; her father letting out a groan of what Emma thought was anguish. This was worse than the nightmare. She backed away and ran to her bed, where she lay awake for hours. In the morning she was surprised to see her father and Edith sitting at the breakfast table, reading the papers.

Emma determined to protect Inez from the ugly sounds she had heard; that was the only thing she could do. Edith was not affectionate with Emma, but neither was she affectionate with the baby, Inez. She did not like being drooled on, and she seldom picked the baby up except when she was showing her off to guests, and then she held her clumsily. When Edith entertained, or when she and David were out, which was frequently, Emma had dinner on a tray in her room.

One day, when Edith was expecting guests, both the cook and the nurse came down with an intestinal virus and Edith was beside herself. Emma retreated to her room to do her homework. The baby began to cry. Emma, carrying the three-ring notebook she was greatly proud of, walked toward the nursery, intending to pick Inez up and see if she needed changing. Edith, frantic, rushed in and slapped Emma. Emma, startled, dropped her notebook. Edith bent over the crib so that she was on a level with Emma, and Emma returned the slap.

Edith gasped and put her hand to her cheek. 'You hit me!'

'You hit me first,' Emma said.

Inez howled.

No one noticed that Adair, who was now a student at Columbia, had let himself into the apartment, until he stood in the doorway, asking, 'What's going on?'

'She hit me!' Edith began to cry.

'The nurse and the cook are sick,' Emma explained to Adair, 'and she's having company for dinner.' She picked up the baby, held her over one shoulder, and patted her bottom. 'She's soaking. I'll take care of it. You go see about your dinner,' she told Edith. 'The maid's okay. She can help.' Edith, weeping, left the nursery. Emma set about changing the baby.

Adair picked up her notebook and smoothed out the crumpled pages. 'Did you really hit Edith?'

'She slapped me, so I slapped her.'

Adair laughed. 'Good for you.' Then, 'But, Em, love, hitting people back isn't the best thing to do.'

Emma sat in the rocking chair by the crib and rocked, patting Inez gently between the shoulder blades, and the child slid into a contented sleep. 'Sure.' She kissed Inez on the fuzz on top of her head and put her back in the crib.

'I came to see if you wanted to go for a walk.'

'I have a lot of homework to do, and I think I'd better stay with Inez. Edith isn't used to getting dinner.'

'There are a lot of things Edith isn't used to,' Adair said. 'Emma, you do not have to stay here with Edith, you know.'

Emma looked at him in surprise. That she had any choice in the matter had not occurred to her.

'Think it over,' Adair said. 'Okay, pet, see you soon.'

Evidently Adair called his father, because David came into Emma's room that night and sat on the edge of her bed. She could hear the voices of the guests in the living room. 'Emma, is Edith in the habit of slapping you?'

'No, Papa, only a couple of times. And this time I slapped her back.'

'She is never to slap you again.' He took Emma in his arms, rocking her. 'I'm going into rehearsal for a new play. We'll get into a better routine. I know it hasn't been easy.'

'Papa.' Emma pressed her cheek against the tweed of his jacket. Her voice came out muffled. 'I don't want to stay here with Edith.'

'But, my darling—'

'I want to go to my mother.' Now that Adair had given her a choice, she was firm. Adair had probably been thinking that

Emma should go to Marical. But Emma wanted a mother, not a stepmother.

There was a long silence. Then David said, 'I thought you might ask to go to Bahama.'

'I think it's time I went to my mother.' Her voice was flat, adamant. David's arms tightened about her and he kissed the top of her head, gently, over and over, until at last he moved away from her, saying, 'All right, I'll work on it.'

A dancer friend of Harriet's was going to Hollywood and was willing to let Emma travel with her. David had long conversations on the phone with Elizabeth.

'Darling.' He looked at Emma gravely. 'Your mother says of course, come. But I did not hear great enthusiasm in her voice.'

'She doesn't know me,' Emma said. All she knew was that she could not stay in the house with Edith and that she needed to know her mother.

The trip to the West Coast was tiring but uneventful. Harriet's friend delivered Emma in a taxi to Elizabeth's house in Beverly Hills. It was not one of the great mansions, but it was, to Emma, elaborate enough, with a swimming pool and a small guest house.

Elizabeth looked at Emma, who was pale with exhaustion. Held out her hand, awkwardly, to shake Emma's. 'Come in. Sit down, and we'll talk for a few minutes. Do you want anything to eat?'

'I'm thirsty.'

Elizabeth rang a bell and a Filipino servant came into the room, making no sound on the thick carpet. 'She's thirsty, Harro,' Elizabeth said. The servant nodded, disappeared. Elizabeth looked at her daughter with somewhat the same critical gaze with which Edith had regarded her. 'You don't resemble me. Or your father, as far as I can tell. He says you're going to be an actress.'

Emma sat next to her mother on the couch, trembling with fatigue.

Elizabeth laughed with embarrassment. 'Emma, I don't know how to be a mother. I don't think it's one of my talents. I never had a mother of my own. She died when I was four.'

'I'm sorry,' Emma said.

Harro came in with a glass of lemonade for Emma, smiled at her, and left.

Elizabeth looked at her daughter. 'This isn't going to be easy for either of us. I have a very busy life.'

'Papa said you're not making a movie right now.'

'I'm seeing people. Looking into things. I'm out a great deal. What about school?'

'I don't need to go to school. At least, not for a while. I can catch up whenever I need to. Shall I call you Mother or Mama?'

Elizabeth put her hand to her mouth. Took it down. 'Elizabeth. Call me Elizabeth.'

'Can I see my room?'

Elizabeth said, 'I think you'll be happier in the guest house. You don't mind being alone, do you?'

Emma felt as though a fist had clenched in her stomach.

Elizabeth continued, 'There's a bell. One of the servants will come immediately if you need anything. Rudy—one of my friends—bought you some books and some dolls. You do play with dolls?'

'I think I'd like to see my room,' Emma said.

It was large and pleasant, with pale peach walls and bright chintz. A small bookcase was filled with picture books. There were stuffed animals on the bed, and several dolls in little chairs.

'Am I going to eat with you?' Emma asked.

'Of course. Whenever I'm home. I have a dinner party to-night.' There was no rebuff, but there was no warmth, no welcome. When Elizabeth left her, Emma sat down on a chintz-covered stool, too numb even to weep.

She'd had dreams, built from seeing Marical with her children, dreams of Elizabeth bright as a butterfly and loving as the mother in *Little Lord Fauntleroy* or *Peter Pan*. She sat with her shattered dreams.

Emma stood it for two weeks, seeing Elizabeth only in glimpses, cared for by Harro, who was solicitous, who made her feel that she mattered to someone. From the main house at night, bright lights streamed onto the lawn, and so did people, laughing in high voices, glasses in hand. One night a man in a tuxedo came to the guest house and knocked. Emma opened the door. The man was pleasant, curious, and at least a little concerned about the waif who was Elizabeth's daughter.

He sat down on the foot of Emma's bed, a glass in his hand. 'If you looked like Shirley Temple, she'd be showing you off to all her guests,' he said, his voice slightly slurred. 'She's making a mistake about you, you know. You might be an actress, after all, a real one. You have that kind of face that's nothing until the camera—or the stage lights—hit it. Would you like me to talk to somebody?'

'No, thank you,' Emma said.

'You have something special, little one,' the man said, and reached out to pull Emma to him. She wriggled out of his grasp.

'No. Please.'

Suddenly Harro stood beside her.

The man took a sip of his drink and laughed. 'No harm meant, little one. I thought you were lonely.' He left the guest house, walking a little unsteadily.

The next day Harro helped her call home. David said, 'Oh, my darling, we'll get you out of this. Bahama's away with friends, but Grandpa Bowman—you'll go to Grandpa Bowman.'

Then she wept.

When she got to Georgia, Grandpa Bowman held her in his strong arms, tickled her with his beard, fed her, tucked her in bed, waited with her until she fell asleep.

They did not speak of Elizabeth for two days. Then, one evening after dinner, which Emma had helped Grandpa cook, he took her into his dusty library, sat in a cracked leather chair, drew her into his lap.

'You haven't had enough lap-sitting.' He put his arm comfortingly around her, and she leaned against him. 'Child, I'm sorry,' he said.

She did not move, hearing the steady thud-thud of his heart.

'How far people can move apart.' The gustiness of his sigh shook her. 'Your mother was a beautiful child, curly hair. A mouth like yours.'

'She said I didn't look like her.'

'You don't. But the mouth is the same. People adored her and she was cute, too cute.'

'Like Shirley Temple?' Emma remembered the slightly drunk man in the tuxedo.

'Maybe. She was a natural-born actress, your mother, and one day when she was no more than a mite of a thing, she came up to the pulpit and started to speak, and the congregation was quieter than a winter's night and I let her go on talking about how Jesus loved her. God help me, I encouraged her, simple-minded that I was, not heeding that it was the applause that excited her, not Jesus' love. She had heard me, she had learned the words, but they were empty for her except for the responses, the "Yes, Lord!" the "Amen! Hallelujah!" I should have known that she fed on the thrill. Her mother, my beloved wife, was dead. She would have seen the terrible hollow at the heart of our child's preaching. I did not.'

Emma continued to lie against him, listening to his heart beat, half hearing his words.

'When she went to school the preaching stopped, but she was queen of whatever they were queen of in those days, and when she was in high school there was a scout from Hollywood and I lost her. But I blame myself. I should have seen, I should have—'

She wriggled against his chest. 'No, Grandpa. She didn't want me. She didn't love me—' She began to cry and the words were lost.

'Or anybody,' he said. 'There's the tragedy. Not anybody. There are women who cannot—should not—be mothers. My daughter is one of them.'

'Do you love her, Grandpa?'

He rocked her. 'Yes. I love Lizzie.'

'Lizzie?'

'That's what we called her. I am anguished, child, anguished, by her inability to be a mother for you. But yes. I love her.'

'Do you love me, Grandpa?'

Again he rocked her, rocked, rocked. His heart beat, thud-thud. 'You are the child of my heart. You are the blessing God has given me in my old age.'

Leaning against his solid chest, she relaxed in the firmness of his love.

•

The days flowed past, warm, gentle. One morning at breakfast he looked at her, a long, thoughtful gaze. 'Emma, child.' They were sitting out on the porch, basking in the morning sun.

Emma put down her glass of milk. 'What, Grandpa?'

'Edith has left.'

'Left Papa?'

'Yes. Edith is a lawyer, and has clever lawyer friends. She has managed to stick your Papa for a ferocious amount of alimony.'

'What's that?'

'He has to pay her an inordinate—a great deal of money—until she marries again. Let's hope that's soon.'

'Does Papa have an inor—a lot of money?'

'A reasonable amount, but not a lot. He's going to have to take any job he can get, in New York, in Hollywood, on the road. It's not going to be easy.'

'Bahama?'

'Bahama's back in New York. As soon as she heard what happened, she left the friends she was traveling with and came back to your father. But he's going on tour for several weeks, and we all agree that it might be best if you stay with me until things get pulled together.'

'Is that okay with you, Grandpa?'

'Very.'

'It's okay with me, too.'

'But we're going to have to do something about school.'

'No, please, Grandpa, no—' She did not know why she suddenly felt panic. School had never been a problem in New York.

He took a drink of his coffee. 'I will teach you. Not what you might learn in school, but I think that at this point in your education that doesn't matter too much.'

Visibly, she relaxed. 'Grandpa. Thank you.'

Bahama sent her long, chatty letters. 'We're playing three nights in Buffalo—your father is playing, that is. He's quite depressed, so it's best if I travel with him. Tomorrow we have some free time, so we're going to Niagara Falls.'

David sent her funny postcards, with lots of naughts and crosses.

She was happy. Grandpa's schooling was fun and very different from ordinary schooling. Grandpa had decided to give her instruction in the world of the Old Testament, especially the period of King David, who was the old man's favorite character. Grandpa Bowman had been the first to suggest to David Wheaton that King David was a role he ought to play.

'So, child, when did David, the sweet singer of Israel, when did he live?' They sat at the round library table in the cluttered room filled with thousands of books.

'Nearly three thousand years ago, I think.'

'That is a reasonable answer. Who was David?'

Emma replied dutifully, as she might have done in school. 'David was the second king.'

'The second king of what?'

'Israel and Judah.'

'Who was the first?'

'Saul. But Saul had evil spirits inside him and he wasn't very nice. Anyhow, having a king was—'

'Go on.'

'The Jews hadn't ever had a king. They had patriarchs—Abraham, Isaac, and Jacob. And then there was Joseph, and Moses leaving Egypt and going to the Promised Land.'

'You learn well, child. You retain. Go on.'

'Well, the Jews wanted a king. God was all they needed, but they wanted to have a king like other peoples, and they asked

Samuel, who was their prophet, to go to God and find them a king.'

.

'Never should there have been a king in Israel,' Wesley Bowman thundered. 'When the people demanded a king, they were showing that they had lost faith in the Lord.'

Wesley Bowman's voice rolled across the filled pews. Emma sat in the front row, where she had been firmly placed, looking at her grandfather with his white beard blowing as though in a strong wind from the force of his words. ' "Now also when I am old and grey-headed, O God, forsake me not; until I have shewed thy strength unto this generation, and thy power to every one that is to come." God's powah. God's forgotten powah.' Grandpa Bowman's Georgia accent was strong when he was vehement.

'Remember, O my people, it was the Lord who brought your fathers to this place and gave it to you for a dwelling, and your fathers forgot the Lord, yea, they forgot, forgot! And God sold them into the hands of the Greycoats and the turncoats and the carpetbaggers. Beware, my people, lest you forget! Repent! Repent! For you, too, have turned from the Lord, and have forsaken him, and worshipped instead at the place of the corner drugstore, and the disembodied voices coming through the radio, and singers crooning into their microphone as though they held the body of the beloved. You, too, ask for someone outside to save you when it is the Lord, the Lord only, who is king.'

And Wesley Bowman looked like the prophet Samuel, and he dropped his voice to a whisper, and the people slowed the waving of their palm-leaf fans.

'There shall be a sign.' Wesley Bowman paused, sniffing the heavy, humid air. It was summer, and it was hot, but the people had jammed the pews to hear him and their palm-leaf fans swished back and forth with a sound like many wings, but Wesley Bowman's voice could be heard above them. 'Now therefoah see this great thing, which the Lord shall do befoah your eyes. I will call unto the Lord, and he shall send thunder and rain; that ye may perceive and see that your wickedness is great, which ye have done in the sight of the Lord.'

Brilliant light struck through the windows and was followed by a booming of thunder. Outside the church the wind lifted suddenly and whipped around the frame building, and thunder came again, even louder than the preacher's voice, and Emma Wheaton and all the people cringed in their pews.

How did he do it?

While they were eating their evening meal, rice with red beans and chopped onions, Emma asked him. Through his beard she saw his wolfish smile.

'I listen to the weather forecast. I smell the air.' Then, waving those words away with a dismissive gesture: 'I listen to the Lord.'

'Does he talk to you the way he talked to Samuel?'

'On occasion, which is the best anyone gets.'

'Is it true?'

'What, child?'

'About the people wanting a king instead of God?'

'It's always true. Over and over.'

'Did David?'

'David was a child, not that much older than you. He was off in the hills with his sheep. He played his harp to the sheep and the birds, and he sang, and he knew as little as you know.'

'When I'm grown up, I'll know more.'

'Let us hope.'

'Grandpa?'

'Yes, child?'

'Why did the people want a king instead of God?'

'Why did your mother choose greasepaint and footlights and want that small idol of an Oscar?'

It was a rhetorical question. But Emma prodded, 'She's a good actress, isn't she?'

He huffed his beard out. 'I should not have mentioned her. We've talked enough.'

'No, Grandpa. Go on.'

He closed his eyes. 'People make different choices in life. Perhaps Lizzie's choice was the right one for her.'

'But you think acting is wicked?'

His eyes opened wide, a deep, startled blue. 'Where on earth did you hear that?'

'Just some people talking.'

'Where?'

She said, reluctantly, 'After church yesterday.'

He scowled ferociously, his bushy eyebrows almost covering the gentian of his eyes. 'Gossip is ugly. Uglier than acting. Your father is a fine actor and he has integrity. Am I not in my own way an actor, too? Is it not how both your father and I try to bring truth out of the darkness and into the light?'

Now Emma smiled. 'Yes, Grandpa.'

'Your father and I understand each other.'

Emma put down her fork. She could not help prodding, not yet understanding that her grandfather's pain about his daughter was as great as hers about her mother. 'But you do love my mother.'

'I love her. I will always love her.'

'No matter what?'

'No matter what. But you cannot serve God and Mammon.'

'Who is Mammon?'

'A false God. All the things of this world.'

'Bahama says we are supposed to enjoy the things of this world, because God made them for us to enjoy.'

'Bahama is an Episcopalian. Nevertheless, she is right. It is when the things of this world become more important than the One who made them that problems arise.'

'So maybe that's what's wrong about kings?'

'Explain, child?'

'Well, Grandpa, like when somebody puts the king ahead of God.'

Grandpa Bowman was triumphant. 'I have not preached in vain!'

Emma loved Grandpa Bowman. He could call up thunder-
storms. He was larger than life, but with Emma he could be
infinitely tender. At bedtime he sang to her as though she were
a small child, Gospel hymns, *Blessed Assurance; Just as I am,
without one plea; Jesus, tender shepherd.* If he could not assure
her that her mother loved her, he could assure her that he did,
and that God did. 'Be thou my strong habitation!' he sang to her
in a melody of his own devising, 'My strong habitation, where-
unto I may continually resort: thou hast given commandment to
save me; for thou art my rock and my fortress.'

Emma relaxed in Grandpa Bowman's care. She thought less
about her mother, and more about her father and Bahama. In
the early autumn Bahama came for her and brought her back to
the apartment on Riverside Drive.
'Your father is working too hard,' Bahama said, 'but we are
happy.'
David brought Sophie to meet Emma, and Sophie was gently
loving. Sophie was nothing like Edith.
Sophie was an actress David had met on location during the
shooting of a movie. It was apparent that she and Bahama also
liked each other. It seemed natural when a few months later
David married Sophie and she moved in.
'It's your house,' she assured Bahama. 'I'm a terrible house-
keeper, but I do like to cook.'
With Emma she was tentative, not pushing herself, but always
available, affectionate, ready with milk and cookies and conversation after school, more like a playmate than a parent. And she
was soon pregnant. She called Emma into the kitchen one morning, put her arms around her, and whispered, 'You're going to
have a baby brother or sister.'
David glowed with pleasure at the happiness in his household. Sophie bloomed with her pregnancy. 'I never had a real
mother'—she gave Bahama a hug. 'I lived with three maiden
aunts who didn't believe in coddling. I'm happier than I've

ever been in my life.' And she giggled, a sweet, throaty chortle. 'You know what? Marical and I are friends! Isn't that something!'

As soon as Edith remarried and David could stop his alimony payments, he completely did over the kitchen for Sophie. Sophie did not want the cook or the maid Edith had demanded.

'My aunts never let me into the kitchen. They said I'd make a mess. I love making messes.' Sophie turned to Bahama. 'You don't mind?'

'I'm delighted,' Bahama assured her. 'I'm an adequate cook, I suppose, but I don't really enjoy it. I like to sew.'

'Let's have Marical and the children over for dinner,' Sophie suggested. 'Jarvis, too. I'll cook roast beef and Yorkshire pudding.'

'But that's so much work—'

'I do it *mit Liebe*.'

The next few years were the happiest of Emma's childhood. Sophie created a family for her, a strange family perhaps, but a family. Marical and her children were often around, and Sophie encouraged Adair to teach Emma to roller-skate, to ice-skate. Etienne and Everard were called in to help Emma with homework. Chantal and Sophie played with Emma's hair, washing it, rolling it up and setting it with bobby pins, and finally agreeing with Marical that the best thing to do with Emma's hair was to leave it clean and straight.

Sophie was lavish with love, and when Marical's children were not around, she played with Emma, games of make-believe and let's pretend, in which Sophie was quite happy to be the wicked witch to Emma's princess. For Emma, Sophie was an older friend who seemed, if anything, younger than Chantal. Sophie gave parties for Emma, birthday parties, for which she decorated a special cake with Emma's name on it; Valentine parties, with red paper-and-lace doilies and crayons and glue for the making of valentines; Halloween parties, with pumpkin carvings and apple bobbings and pumpkin pie.

'I didn't give you enough parties,' Bahama said.

Emma was quickly loyal. 'Yes, you did. You gave me a birthday party every year.'

Bahama sighed. 'I'm grateful for Sophie. She can do all the things I'm too old to do. She thrives on them and she always manages to make me feel she couldn't do without me.'

'She couldn't,' Emma said. 'You love her, and Sophie needs to be loved.'

Bahama patted her hand. 'Words of wisdom, my grand-daughter.'

Sophie told Emma, 'I want Bahama to live forever, so my baby will know and remember her.'

Emma had never thought of the possibility of Bahama's death, and it struck cold against her heart. Sophie swept her up, holding her against her bulging belly so that Emma could feel the baby kick. 'Don't worry, pet, Bahama's going to be with us for a long, long time.'

Occasionally Sophie did a play or a TV show, but she refused to go to Hollywood when she was offered a big contract. 'I don't like it out there. People have affairs and get divorced. But I trust Davie if he has to go to the West Coast.'

Perhaps it was because of Sophie's childlike trust that David was trustworthy. The marriage was stable. The household was happy. When Louis was born, all ten pounds of him, Emma was filled with joy. She was allowed to hold the baby, to help Sophie bathe him. She loved him even more than she had loved Inez.

When David and Sophie were not involved in a theatrical production, they often went to the opera or the ballet, and Sophie would call Emma to her closet to choose her evening dress. David wore tails and a top hat and sometimes carried an ebony cane with a silver handle. To Emma they were the most glamorous and handsome couple in the world.

If Sophie or David were in a play, they had an early supper with Emma and Bahama. Both David and Sophie took great care to see that Emma did not feel displaced by Louis. Louis was for Emma a gift; he was a happy, healthy baby. On the rare occasions when he woke the household at night, Sophie made a game of it. She would put records of Strauss waltzes on the record player, and if Emma was awake she would follow Sophie and David into the baby's room, and the three of them would dance around Louis's crib until he laughed, drank his bottle, and fell back to sleep.

One night Emma woke from a nightmare. Sat up in bed, shivering. She was afraid to go to Sophie and David's room, where she had heard David and Edith make terrible noises. Finally she called out, 'Papa! Sophie!'

Fortunately Sophie heard, came running. 'Emma, lovey, what's the matter?'

'I had a dream, I had a horrible dream.'

'Emma, Emma.' Sophie put her arms around the child. 'I just happened to be awake; otherwise, I wouldn't have heard you. Whenever you have a bad dream, just come, come to Davie and me.'

Emma started to weep uncontrollably.

'Emma, lovey, what is it? What's the matter? Was the dream so terrible?'

'No, no, not the dream—' Sobs choked her.

Sophie rocked, coaxed, drew it out of her.

'Ah, Emmelie, those weren't bad noises. You just didn't understand them.'

'But Edith—'

Sophie said, 'Little one, how can I tell you—'

'Papa—it was a dreadful groan, as though something terrible was happening. Oh, Sophie, what was it?'

'Emma, you're too young to understand. You'll just have to trust me. Emma, do you know how babies are conceived?'

Emma shook her head, pressing her face against Sophie's soft, sweet-smelling shoulder.

'When a man and a woman love each other, they—they—oh, lovey, how can I explain? They hold each other tight and they —well, sometimes they make noises like the ones you heard—'

'Not you and Papa,' Emma protested. 'Sophie, you wouldn't ever make noises like Edith, would you?'

At that, Sophie started to laugh. Her arms about Emma, she rocked back and forth, laughing and laughing. Finally: 'Oh, *Liebling*, I might put Edith in the shade!'

'What?'

'Let it go for now. Don't worry about it. It's something you'll understand when you're much older. And remember, any time you have a bad dream, you come right in to your father and me.' Sophie knew how to dispel fear.

.

Sometimes when Marical's children came to the Riverside Drive apartment for dinner, they would roll back the great Chinese rug in the living room, left there by Edith because it did not fit in her more modern penthouse. Sophie and David danced well together, but Adair was the best dancer of them all.

'You're better than Fred Astaire,' Sophie would gasp. Emma was quick to catch on to his lead, and ultimately the two of them would dance alone, with the rest of the family applauding. David urged Adair to dance professionally, but Adair only laughed and said he'd wait at least until Emma was old enough to be his partner.

They were good years. Whatever Sophie did, she did *mit Liebe*. When Emma played Celia in *As You Like It*, the family was in the front row for opening night, her father, Sophie, Bahama; Marical, with Etienne, Everard, Adair, and Chantal, with an excited Inez; Harriet with Jarvis; only Myrlo and Billy were not there, and Emma hardly noticed. David and Sophie sent her a corsage. She was made to feel like a star. Adair sent a dozen roses: 'To my beloved sister, Emma, the Duse of the twentieth century.'

Adair knew who Duse was.

.

That year Sophie bought her a box of sanitary napkins and a belt. 'Emmelie, you are an innocent, but it's time you learned some of the facts of life.'

Emma wriggled uncomfortably. 'I know them, Sophie.'

'No, you don't,' Sophie said, and explained the workings of both male and female reproductive organs. 'I read it all in a book, so I know the scientific part is right. Marical told me I should prepare you.'

Emma looked at Sophie, whose face was slightly pink. 'I'm prepared. What do you think we talk about at school? I'm nearly ready to wear a bra. I'm not a child anymore.'

'Did they get it right?' Sophie was sitting on the foot of Emma's bed. 'When I was your age, some kids told me the baby comes out of the belly button.'

'I know where it comes from. You told me, remember? before Louis was born.'

'I guess I did, more or less. The important thing, honey, is that you not be scared the way you were scared when you heard your father and Edith.'

'I'm not scared. I just don't think it sounds very enjoyable.'

'Oh, lovey, it is! When you're older, and there's a man you love, and who loves you, well, Emma, sex is maybe only a third of a marriage, but it's a mighty important third.'

'Sure,' Emma said.

'When it's more than a third, well, that doesn't make for marriage, that makes for an affair.'

Emma looked into Sophie's big brown eyes. 'Is that what happened with some of Papa's wives?'

'I don't want you criticizing your father.'

'I'm not criticizing, Sophie, but—'

'Your father is a great man and a great actor and I love him madly.'

'And I hope you stay married to him forever,' Emma said.

.

Grandpa Bowman gave his instructions to Emma publicly, from the pulpit, demanding of his congregation:

'Do you not understand that our concept of sexuality is as far below our Maker's as that of the amoeba is below ours? Yes, my people, the amoeba. For the amoeba knows little of the pleasures of love. The amoeba propagates by dividing and subdividing. Does that sound like fun? Does that sound like love? Does that not sound egocentric? Would you like to be like the amoeba? I doubt it very much. But understand, my people, understand that we know as little about what love truly means as does the amoeba, in comparison to the one who loved us so much that he sent his only Son to live with us to teach us about love. Not sex, as the advertising world would have us think. The advertising world knows only about sex and nothing about love. And now the people of God are emulating the advertising world and trying to diminish God with human sex. We are not interested in God's genitals!' he roared, looking out over the pulpit and waving his forefinger at the congregation so that for a moment there was a total hush as the palm-leaf fans were stilled.

.

Bahama was more down-to-earth. One evening when David and Sophie were at the theater and Louis was in bed, she sat with Emma in the living room, smocking a yellow summer sundress for her granddaughter.

'Well, Sophie told me,' Emma said, 'but mostly it was stuff I already knew.'

Bahama, embroidering two small green frogs on the dress, began to reminisce about her own marriage. 'My time with your grandfather was sweet. Sweet. We were good together.'

'How?' Emma asked. She could not conceive of her grandmother in sexual terms. Her father, yes. She had heard David and Edith. Talked with Sophie. There was no avoiding David Wheaton's sexuality. But Bahama?

'Oh, yes,' Bahama said, smiling. 'I enjoyed my marriage bed. Or the beach. Or lying on a carpet of moss in the forest. There is a lot to be said for a single, faithful love. It takes a lifetime to learn another human being.' She sighed. 'Emma, I do not want you to be like your father, or to be dazzled by—' She stopped.

'My friends at school,' Emma pronounced, 'say that the idea

of a separate standard for men is Victorian. Men and women are alike.'

Bahama threaded her needle with more green silk. 'Your friends are right and your friends are wrong. A separate standard probably is Victorian. But men and women are not exactly alike. I have extremely strong hands for a woman'—she held them out, long and strong of finger, wide of palm and wrist—'but they are not as strong as a man's. My pelvis is made for bearing babies, my breasts for milk. Like it or not, there is a difference.'

'My friends wouldn't like that.'

'It's a fact. Maybe they should choose the sea horse as an emblem. The female sea horse lays her eggs in the male sea horse's pouch, and he has to carry the babies to term and then give birth.'

Emma pealed with laughter.

'But it's not the way it is for human females. Not, my dear Emma, that I think women are a hundred percent female and men a hundred percent male. We're a rich mix of both. Your father has an amazing tenderness that is often thought feminine, though I believe it can come only from great strength and self-assurance.'

·

David was indeed gentle with Emma, talking to her about the theater like a fellow actor, but hugging her at bedtime like a little girl, praising her for her care of Louis whenever Sophie was away for a few hours and let Emma baby-sit.

Adair often took Emma to concerts. He was in graduate school now, majoring in business, but equally interested in music.

'I'm not an artist,' he told Emma, 'but I can recognize great art when I hear it. Music will always pull me out of my moods. I want you to love it, too.'

'I do.' Emma loved music partly for itself and partly because Adair taught her. He brought her records, played them without showing her the albums, and made her guess the composer.

'Schubert!' she said triumphantly. 'You can always tell Schubert by that sadness that's under everything he writes, even the merriest stuff.'

'Good,' Adair praised. 'Hey, Em, did I see Billy leaving as I came up the street?'

'Yup. He wanted Papa to introduce him to some producer. Do you think Billy's a good actor?'

'Not in Papa's league. But ask Jarvis. He's the one who can pick the stars.'

'But what do you think?'

'Billy's okay. He's handsome. Papa's pull does him no harm.'

Emma made a face. 'He kisses me goodbye whenever he's here.' Adair looked at her sharply. 'I don't like it. I mean, it's not like when you or Ev or Etienne kiss me.'

Adair's voice had an edge. 'Don't let him kiss you.'

'He's bigger than I am. All brawn and no brain, as the kids at school say. I know he's my brother, Adair, but I don't much like him, and I think he uses Papa.'

'He does,' Adair agreed. 'But that's the way of the world. I'd probably try to use Papa, too, if I wanted to make it in the theater.' He put on another record. 'Okay. Now, who's the composer?'

.

Emma sat with Bahama one afternoon after school, playing some special new records Adair had given her, Solomon's interpretation of the *Well Tempered Clavier*. But her mind was not on the music, but on some gossip she had heard at school. She went at her subject in a roundabout way.

'Bahama—' Emma was fourteen, though she still had a child's body.

The old woman let her mending rest in her lap as she looked up at Emma.

'My godmother Abby—she still loves my father.'

'Yes. And David loves her.'

'Even though they're divorced, and he's been married to

Myrlo and Marical and Harriet and my mother and Edith and now Sophie?'

Bahama picked up the school blazer she was mending for Emma, and carefully slid the needle in and out. 'Your father is my son and I love him, but I do not understand him, and I do not applaud his behavior.'

'You think it's wrong?'

'It has hurt many people. It has hurt David, himself. Certainly, it has hurt your godmother.'

'But he loves Abby.'

'Yes, he does. Abby was very young when they were married. She did not have the wisdom then that she has now.'

'And Papa?'

'My dear, your father's charm is a wound as well as a blessing.'

'How can it be a wound?'

'When it causes pain, as it so frequently does, it is a wound. David does not turn on his charm, it is not a willful effort. It simply flows from him like his breath.'

'So, what about Myrlo?' Emma asked. Bahama was not often willing to discuss her son.

'Why do you ask?'

'Some of the girls at school have shown me stuff about Papa in magazines.'

Bahama put down Emma's blazer. 'I should have known that would be inevitable. Did something happen today?'

'There was a movie magazine with pictures of Papa and Myrlo.'

'A new magazine?'

'Last month. There was a feature article about Myrlo. And Papa.'

'I see.'

'Was it true? That Myrlo left Papa because he committed adultery on her?'

Bahama pricked her finger. 'Your father did not commit adultery while he was married to Myrlo.'

'Oh! Did you hurt yourself?'

Bahama sucked her finger. 'Just a prick. Nothing.'

'Bahama?'

Bahama sighed.

'But Papa has—'

'Has what, Emma?'

'Committed adultery.'

'Emma—'

'I know about Harriet. Adair told me.'

'Adair should not have—'

'Adair knew if he didn't tell me someone else would. And I'm not stupid, Bahama. I mean, how else do you explain Jarvis?'

Bahama put down her sewing with a sharp exclamation.

'I'm sorry, but—' Emma broke off as she saw a tear slip down her grandmother's cheek. She knelt swiftly and put her head on Bahama's lap. 'Oh, Bahama, don't—don't—I'm sorry—'

Bahama stroked Emma's head. 'I'm sorry, too, Emma. Sorrier than I can say.'

．

One night, while Emma was alone in her room doing homework, Bahama knocked. Emma looked up and greeted her with a questioning smile.

Bahama sat on the foot of Emma's bed. 'Homework going all right?'

'Sure. I'm almost finished.'

Bahama was silent for a long moment. Then, 'Emma, how would you like to go to boarding school next year?'

'Boarding school? Me? Why? I like it here.'

Bahama looked at Emma's open notebook, then at her granddaughter. 'Abby and I have been consulting, via the mail. Next season your father and Sophie are going on tour with *Hamlet*.'

'But Sophie isn't in Papa's *Hamlet*!'

'On tour she'll play Ophelia.' Bahama's voice was carefully neutral.

Emma looked at her. 'But Sophie's a soubrette! She isn't a classical actress.'

'She's never had a chance to be,' Bahama said. 'She wants to try. They'll take Louis with them, with a nurse. And I would like to go back to Seattle.'

'With me?'

'No, Emma. Alone. My heart has not been behaving well, and the doctor wants me to have a time of real peace and quiet.'

'Bahama!' Emma's voice rose in a wail, and she flung herself on her knees at her grandmother's feet. 'I'll take care of you. I can cook and everything, you know that. And I love Seattle.'

'No, Emma, darling.' Bahama took the girl's face in her hands. 'Abby writes that she was very happy in her boarding school in New England, and she thinks it would be a good place for you.'

Tears began to flow down Emma's cheeks. 'You're just sending me off, like a parcel.'

Bahama caressed Emma's fine hair. 'Never. Everything has been happening at once, and I—oh, Emma, it's not the end of the world. You'll come to me for holidays, and your father and Sophie and Louis will be back in the spring. And if the school doesn't work out for you, we can discuss that later.'

'I could stay with Marical,' Emma suggested.

'Darling, Chantal's in college. Marical's children are grown. She's living in a very small house in Connecticut. You know that.'

'But she'd take me.'

'Yes, Emma, I know she would. We have even discussed it.'

'Behind my back—'

'Hush. You are not being sent to prison. If you do not like the school, we can make other arrangements. But, darling, I want you to try to like it.'

'Sure.'

'I want you really to try.'

'Okay.'

'That's my good Emma.'

'But suppose—suppose something comes up for me in the theater?'

'There are not that many roles for you at this point. Your Celia was enchanting. There is no question that you can act. But now you need to wait until you grow up into yourself.'

Emma had completely stopped thinking about her father's wives and was thinking of herself. She nodded. 'I'm not sure Sophie can play Ophelia, but I'm sure I can't. What's the matter?' She stopped as Bahama began to laugh.

'You did play Ophelia once,' Bahama wiped her eyes.

'Me? I? When?'

'When you were six. You found an old straw hat that had a wreath of flowers on it, and you took the wreath off and put it on, and you wore a white summer nightgown and filled the tub with a couple of inches of water and lay back in it. Your father and I couldn't find you anywhere, and when we looked in the bathroom and saw you lying there in the tub as though you'd been drowned—'

Emma giggled. 'I'd completely forgotten that!'

'I never have. You almost gave me a heart attack right then and there. When your father yelled at you and asked you what the hell you thought you were doing, you sat up, dripping water, and told us you were Ophelia.'

Emma reached out and took her grandmother's hand. 'Is there any theater in Abby's school?'

'She says they have an excellent drama department.'

'I hate it,' Emma said. 'I hate it. I don't want everybody to go away. Bahama, are you sure you'll be all right?'

'I'll do my best,' Bahama said. 'But I do need to get away from this city to where I can get some peace and quiet.'

.

Rather to her surprise, Emma was happy in Abby's school. She made friends, was appreciated by the teachers; there were at least two productions each year, and Emma played good roles.

She went to Bahama for Christmas and Easter, and she loved the water and the great snow-capped mountains that ringed Seattle. She enjoyed being alone with Bahama in the comfortable old house that overlooked the Sound and the Cascades.

Her sophomore year in boarding school, with David and Sophie and Louis back in New York, she spent Christmas at the Riverside Drive apartment, because Sophie would have been devastated without her, and was with Bahama for Easter. She saw with a pang that her grandmother was older, was, indeed, frail, with an odd little cough. She tried not to hear it. She could not imagine life without Bahama.

One evening they were sitting on the porch watching the last rosy rays of sun touching the snow on the mountains. Emma was relaxed in the moment. 'Bahama?'

'Yes, lamb.'

'Right after your husband died, I was born, wasn't I?'

'Shortly after.'

'And you came to take care of me.'

'You were my greatest joy.'

'Why didn't you ever marry again?'

'I had other things on my hands. You, for one.'

'Bahama! I wouldn't have stopped you from marrying!'

'Who would you have wanted me to marry?'

Emma swallowed, then answered boldly, 'Grandpa.'

Bahama laughed.

'Why is it funny?'

Bahama continued to laugh, rocking backwards and forwards, finally gasping, 'One of us would have murdered the other.'

'But—'

'And our backgrounds are so different we might as well come from different planets.'

'Does that matter?'

'Yes, lamb, it does. Marriage is hard enough at best. Your other grandfather—my husband—and I came from the same world. He was a banker, but he was also a great lover of music, and played the cello quite creditably.'

'And Grandpa—Grandpa Bowman?'

'He grew up in the Georgia backwoods. As far as I know, he's never been properly ordained. He's self-educated, and well ed-ucated, I grant you, but we have no roots in common. We can be friends, delightful friends. I've missed my trips to Georgia these past two years.'

'Grandpa has missed you, too.'

'But as much as we're friends, good friends, we wouldn't be good companions, day in and day out. There are too many differences.' She turned the subject. 'I'm glad you're doing well in school. Your report cards have been marvelous.'

Emma laughed. 'School's good, really good. I like the work, the teachers, the kids. I know I fought going, but I do love it. I get to play roles I'll never have another chance to do. I wish you could have seen my Prospero.'

'I wish I could have, too.'

'I'm a good actress, Bahama. I'm lucky to know what I want to do. I'm a classical actress. Sophie didn't get very good reviews as Ophelia. They didn't demolish her, but she says she's through with Shakespeare. I'd like to play Kate, and maybe Beatrice and Portia. You know who I'm going to play next term?'

'Who?'

'Oedipus. Don't you think you could possibly come?'

'Isn't Oedipus a little ambitious for high school?'

'Where else could I do it? Don't you want to see me?'

'Of course I do, lamb. But New England is far, far away from Seattle.'

'Well, you and Abby chose the school for me. And I do love it.'

'Good. I'm glad Abby chose well.'

.

When Emma was a sophomore in college, Bahama's heart gave out. It was in December, just a week before the beginning of vacation. Emma took the train to New York, to Chicago, to Seattle. David and Sophie joined her there, with Louis. Emma did not cry until, unannounced, Grandpa Bowman arrived. Grandpa Bowman hated travel, but he came. Emma buried her face in his beard and sobbed, while her grandfather held her close.

The small Episcopal church, which for years had been Bahama's church home in Seattle, was full for the funeral. Grandpa Bowman and David Wheaton flanked Emma, each one gently

touching her with hand or knee. Louis pressed up against Sophie, almost in her lap, and she enfolded him with her arms,
making no effort to hide her own tears. The funeral service was
strong, affirming, the words of Cranmer and Coverdale prom-
ising that Bahama would be one of the mighty cloud of witnesses,
that she would go from strength to strength. There was an enormous spread of food in the parish house afterwards, provided
by Bahama's many friends.

'No eulogy.' Grandpa Bowman scowled. 'I understand that
your funeral service is the same for the Queen of England and
the lowest street cleaner, but I would have liked to have said
something about my friendship with a great woman.'

Bahama was dead. Grandpa Bowman was no longer young.
Emma felt an aching in her physical heart so strong that she
thought it would break.

Then came the long journey back to New York, and Christmas,
which they tried to keep merry for Louis. Marical, Etienne,
Everard, Adair, Chantal, all came. Jarvis was there; Harriet was
dancing that day, but Jarvis brought Inez with him. Myrlo sent
a telegram that she was sorry but she and Billy were going to
Florida with Billy's father.

She was referring to the insurance executive she had married.
David handed Emma the yellow Western Union paper. She read
it, scowled furiously, then put her arms tightly around her father,
trying to hold his hurt.

The rest of the vacation was cold, with heavy snow. She took
Louis to the park with his sled, and they slid down the hills,
and rolled into the snow, and laughed, and Louis hugged her
and begged her not to go back to college.

'I have to, Louis, dear, I have to finish school.'

'But you're an actress.'

'Yes, but I have to wait for the roles that are right for me.'

Louis reached for her hand. 'I miss Bahama.'

'I know, Louis. We'll miss her forever.'

'Do you think I could go with you to Georgia to see Grandpa
Bowman?'

'Why not? I'd like you to get to know him.' Emma brushed snow off Louis, wiped his face. 'We should start walking home.'

'I love you, Emma.'

'I love you, baby brother.'

'I'm not a baby. I'm nearly eight.'

'You'll always be a baby to me, Louis, you're stuck with it. And I'll always be your big sister.'

.

Yes, Louis was special to Emma, though not as Adair was; her feeling for Louis was protective, whereas Adair was protector.

David Wheaton tried, after Bahama's death, to go to church with Emma when she was home, to St. John the Divine, where he enjoyed the music, the great organ, and the choir of men and boys. He went to church, Emma thought, much as he went to the theater. Except that he did not receive communion, because he believed himself to be unworthy.

.

'Pride,' Grandpa Bowman had bellowed. 'No one is worthy.'

'You're a Baptist!' David Wheaton had shouted. 'Baptists don't go in for communion.'

'Wrong!' Grandpa Bowman's voice matched David Wheaton's, decibel for decibel. 'Every meal I eat is a Eucharist. If you don't believe me, ask—well, you can no longer ask Bahama, alas, but she would have understood. Did understand. It is pride on your part, pride.'

David's voice dropped. 'Perhaps.' He hit himself on the chest. 'Mea culpa. Mea maxima culpa.'

'What play is that from?' Grandpa Bowman demanded.

David bellowed with laughter. 'You old fox. Don't tell me you have no pride yourself.'

'I have plenty,' Grandpa Bowman said. 'It's just different from yours.'

'Oh, God,' David had said, 'I miss my mother.'

'I miss her, too,' Grandpa Bowman said. 'She was a great lady.'

·

Emma would always miss Bahama. Grandpa Bowman talked about her with loving remembrance, somehow always managing to get Emma laughing.

She took Louis down South with her to see him, not really wanting to share her grandfather but simultaneously wanting Louis to have a chance to know the old man.

On Sunday, Grandpa preached about Samuel and his anger when Saul, after a successful battle against the Amalekites, did not kill all the enemy, as the Lord—and Samuel—had commanded him to do.

She and Louis walked home to Grandpa's house through the heat of a Georgia summer.

'I didn't understand,' Louis said. 'I mean, I like the way Grandpa preached, it was really terrific, but there's this guy, Saul, and he's king of the place, right?'

'Right.'

'And then there's Samuel, and he's a prophet, right?'

'Right.'

'And he tells this king, Saul, he has to kill all the Amalekites, and all their animals, too. Why did Saul have to kill everybody?'

Emma dropped Louis's hand. It was so hot that their hands were slippery with sweat, and she wiped her palm on her cotton skirt. Louis reached for her hand again, and she pressed his fingers lightly. 'It does seem pretty blood-minded of Samuel,' she told Louis, 'wanting Saul to slaughter everybody, women and children and old people.'

'Yeah, but Grandpa said Saul didn't kill them all,' Louis argued. 'Saul spared Agag, the king of the Amalekites, and the best of the sheep, and all the best animals.'

'Right,' Emma agreed. 'This made Samuel angry, and Saul said he'd spared the animals so they could be used as a sacrifice to the Lord. But Samuel said that Saul had rejected God's word, and therefore God rejected Saul from being king of Israel.' They had reached the old frame house now, and Louis let go Emma's hand and ran up the steps to the porch.

Emma pondered while she and Louis and Grandpa Bowman were sitting out on the porch eating their midday meal. 'What kind of a god washes people's feet in the blood of the enemy?'

'A local, tribal god,' Grandpa Bowman replied calmly. 'Remember, children, these were still a primitive people. Samuel served the tribal god who wanted everybody except his own people demolished in order to keep them from worshipping other gods. But there were also occasions when Samuel had a vision of a God of the universe, who created the stars, and it was this vision he passed on to David, who was ready to receive it.'

'You mean,' Emma suggested, 'when David moved himself and his people out of the Bronze Age and into the Iron Age, he also moved in his understanding of God?'

'What an educated grandchild I have!' Grandpa Bowman rolled his eyes heavenward. 'Knowing all about Bronze Ages and Iron Ages. But yes, I think you are right. David's understanding of God was wider and richer than Samuel's or Saul's.'

Louis finished chewing a bite. 'You mean, Grandpa, people saw God differently?'

'Through a glass, darkly,' Grandpa Bowman said.

'But, Grandpa, I thought there was only one way to see God, and all other ways were wrong.'

For a long moment Grandpa Bowman was silent, blowing his beard. Then: 'I take it you go to Sunday school.'

'Yes. Mom wants me to.'

'Does your mother get up on Sundays to take you?'

'She and Papa sleep late.'

'Um. Theater hours. Who takes you?'

'Sometimes Emma does. And I'm old enough now to go on my own.'

'Hm.'

'Grandpa?'

'Yes, Louis?'

'About God?'

Grandpa huffed. 'All I can tell you is that God is love, and where there is no love, there God cannot be. For all his faults, King David loved God. That was his redeeming quality.'

Emma asked, 'Did Saul love God?'

'Can one be consumed with jealousy and love God? I think Saul loved himself more than he loved God.'

'And Samuel?'

Grandpa Bowman huffed again. 'Samuel loved his own opinion. So, because Saul spared Agag, Samuel rejected him.'

'And Samuel said God rejected Saul, too?' Emma said. 'What you said in your sermon, Grandpa, it's horrible.'

Louis nodded. 'You said Samuel asked Saul to bring him King Agag, the one Saul spared, right, Grandpa?'

'Right.'

'And this Agag came, all unsuspecting—'

'And Samuel hewed him in pieces,' Emma finished.

.

As usual, Grandpa Bowman answered them in a sermon.

'. . . after Agag's death Samuel came no more to see Saul ever again. Never.' Grandpa Bowman leaned over the pulpit, almost whispering. 'Never. But even in his anger, Samuel mourned for Saul. And the Lord repented that he had made Saul king over Israel.

'Will the Lord repent that he has made this a great and free country? Yes! Well may the Lord repent unless we repent. I tell you the story of Samuel and Saul, my children, but what about our own story? Do we remember our story? Do we remember our fathers, Washington, Franklin, Jefferson, as Samuel and Saul remembered Abraham, Isaac, and Jacob? Do we remember that we, too, are people of a covenant?

'What did the Lord mean? Why did he want Saul to kill all the Amalekites? Is it the Lord, or is it Samuel? How do we look at our own slaughter of the Indians, to whom this land belonged long before we set foot on it? How do we look at the marketplace where we bought and sold slaves as though they were cattle? Were we, too, told to kill the Amalekites? To whose voice did we listen? To whom does the Promised Land belong? Children, my children, let us fall upon our knees, upon our faces, and let us repent for all that we are doing right now in preparation for war. Do we know what we are doing in selling great quantities of scrap iron to Japan? Do we not even suspect that Japan will turn and use it against us? Will the Lord not turn against us in our arrogance?'

.

Grandpa Bowman had prophesied war with Japan when Emma and Louis were visiting him. She was a senior in college when the Japanese bombed Pearl Harbor. It was Sunday, and she and her roommate, a music major, had been relaxing in their room with the radio on, listening to the Philharmonic, when an announcer's voice broke through the music and told them what had happened, or at least as much as was known. Every few minutes the music was interrupted, and Emma's roommate said irritably, 'Why don't they just let us listen to the music and not bother us till they know more!'

.

Did Wesley Bowman really preach that prophetic sermon? Emma was proud of her memory, and her grandpa was unpredictable and paradoxical. Sometimes he angered his congregation, but they kept coming.

.

'Hey, Grandpa,' Louis said. 'You really like King David, don't you?'

'Yes,' Grandpa said. 'I do. I like his *joie de vivre*, his *panache—*'

'Grandpa, is that French?'

'Yes, son. King David had flair. Like your father. It's probably a judgment on me that my daughter married a David.' Then he waved those words away.

Emma looked at him, but the lids had gone down over the smoldering eyes. She sighed. 'Well, Grandpa, to get back to King Saul, he must have spared more than Agag, because wasn't it the Amalekites who killed him and Jonathan in the end?'

'The narrator is not always consistent,' Grandpa Bowman said. 'Perhaps we should learn something from that?'

Emma had taken their dishes to the kitchen and washed them, and they were on the porch, Emma and Grandpa Bowman in the two rockers, Louis on the steps.

'Was Samuel a good man, Grandpa?' Louis asked. Mosquitoes came in through the holes in the screen, despite the cotton stuffed in to keep them out, and Grandpa Bowman swatted at them.

'Come up on the porch, so we can shut the screen door,' Grandpa said, and Louis came and sat at Emma's feet. 'Good and great are not necessarily the same thing.' He slapped at a mosquito which had lit on his brow. 'You two, of all people, ought to know that.'

'You mean like you, Grandpa?' Louis asked innocently.

'No!' Grandpa roared. 'I do not mean like me!'

Emma asked, straight-faced, 'Who on earth can you be thinking of, Grandpa?'

'Your father, child, your father, of course. He is indubitably great, but he is not good.'

'My father is a good actor. He is good to me.'

'And we have just had a good dinner which thank you very much for cooking. But is that the kind of good you're talking about?'

'No.'

'No,' Louis echoed sleepily.

'What, then?'

'Maybe being good has something to do with God?'

'Such as?'

'Maybe being, well, being in tune with God?'

'And that means?'

'Well, not being separated from God. Grandpa, are you being like Socrates?'

'My child, I am an illiterate country preacher.'

'But you know who Socrates is?' Emma thought she had seen a volume of Plato in her grandfather's musty library.

'I am not that illiterate. Nor do I think that either of us is going to succeed in defining good, nor do I think your college professors will teach you to do so.'

.

It was a happy visit. And when they returned to New York in early July, David surprised Emma by telling her that he was trying out a new play in summer stock, and that there was a role for her.

It was the first time she had worked with her father, and she was both nervous and excited. The play concerned a novelist whose work was brilliant but unrecognized; the playwright compared him to van Gogh. Emma played his daughter. Although David Wheaton was successful in his art and the novelist was not, Emma still felt that she was beginning to understand her father as they worked together. The first scene for them was at Christmas Eve in a New York brownstone house; Emma's role was that of a twelve-year-old talking with her father.

Christmas music blared out, and the father exclaimed, 'Why can't they turn the damned radio down? How is anyone expected to sleep? God damn God. Damn him.'

Emma's breath came shallow. She backed away from her father, from his pain, from his blasphemy.

'You still pray? You still say your prayers at night? The nuns see to that?'

'Yes, Father.'

'You don't forget? Even when you're away from the convent?'

'No, Father.'

'And what do you pray for, hah? Now that you're too old to ask for dolls and toys.'

Emma made her voice low. 'That we may be together for Christmas. That we may be happy.'

'But that's not in it, child. That's not part of the bargain. Pray all you like, ask anything you want, but don't forget he never promised he'd say yes. He never guaranteed us anything. Not anything at all. Except one thing. Just one thing.'

Emma waited a beat. Etienne, who was the stage manager, started to throw her a cue, then stopped. She asked, her voice breaking, 'What one thing, Father?'

'That God cares about what he has made. Never forget that, child. That is enough. It is why I write what I write . . .' David Wheaton's voice faded as he asked, 'It is enough. Isn't it?' And then, as Emma drew back, his voice rose to a shout. 'Why don't you answer? Haven't those damn nuns taught you any manners? Why do I send you to a convent school if they aren't going to teach you anything?' He left the room and slammed the door.

With Emma staring after him, her hand to her mouth, whispering, 'Father—'

.

They talked about the scene after rehearsal, sitting at night on the porch of the inn where they were staying, a long porch with green rocking chairs. It was late, and they were the only ones there, sitting and rocking, light from a streetlamp moving over them in shifting patterns as a breeze tossed the leaves.

Emma had had a hard time moving into the role. The atmosphere of professional stock was completely different from college theater, where Emma still had tended to play the leading men's roles in plays by Molière, Chekhov, Shaw.

'Emma, Emma,' her father said after the first rehearsal. 'You're acting like a twelve-year-old.'

'Well, she *is* twelve years old.'

'Ah, there's the difference. She *is* twelve years old. You're acting *like* a twelve-year-old.'

'I don't understand.' Flatly.

'Emma, not so long ago you were twelve years old. As long as you're acting *like* a twelve-year-old, you're not going to believe that you are twelve, and the audience isn't, either. You have to *be* twelve years old. Come on, Emma, you can do it.'

They had two weeks of rehearsal. It was not until well into the second week that David Wheaton and the director were satisfied with Emma's performance.

'I'm vindicated.' David laughed with delight, reaching out to touch Emma's hand.

She clasped his. 'Oh, Papa, thanks. I know everybody thought casting me was a mistake . . .'

'But now,' David interrupted triumphantly, 'you walk on the stage and you *are* a twelve-year-old girl.'

'I work slowly, Papa, even when I have you to direct me. But I do identify with her.'

'Because her father isn't the kind of father most girls would like to have?'

'No, Papa! You make him lovable; sad, but lovable. I guess I mean because she didn't have a mother.'

'Like you?' His smile was wry.

'I have Sophie now,' Emma reminded him gently, 'and she loves you, and she's made a family out of all of us . . . most of us.'

'Most?' His green wooden rocking chair squeaked as it moved back and forth.

'Billy doesn't come very often. I suppose because he's older, and Myrlo's married a man with lots of money. And Edith hardly ever lets Inez get away. But the rest of us—we're a real family, Papa.'

'Marical's kids and Jarvis. Louis is lucky to have such brothers and sisters. Sophie makes me happy.'

'We all love Sophie.'

'With Sophie I have the kind of stable marriage I expected to have with—well, no point hindsighting. My mother—'

Emma smiled. 'Bahama.'

'She gave you at least a semblance of stability, didn't she?'

'More than a semblance.'

'When that poor sod I'm playing asked his daughter about God, I thought of you. I left it to Bahama and your Grandfather Bowman.'

'They were probably a lot better than convent schools would have been.' Emma rocked, slowly. Her skin prickled slightly. This was the first time her father had ever talked to her in this way, revealing himself, admitting frailties.

'Tomorrow, Em, we'll try that scene with the girl and her father in the kitchen. It's tough, but it will be moving. The thing we have to convey to the audience is the real love between the man and his daughter. She's older in this scene, isn't she?'

'Yes. Sixteen, about.'

'That'll be easier for you than twelve.'

Emma laughed. 'Less of a transition. Thank you, Papa. I couldn't have done this without you.'

'You're good to work with, my daughter.'

'I love it.' And then, 'I love you, Papa.'

.

In the morning, while the director had David Wheaton work on a scene with the actress who played his wife, Emma climbed a steep ladder to the grid, which ran the width of the stage, above the proscenium arch, and lay down on it, watching the scene from above, and yet feeling a wonderful part of it. This was her world, and she was happy.

In the afternoon she and her father worked on the scene in the kitchen, over and over, until not only the director but David Wheaton was satisfied.

'Take it from the top,' the director said at last, 'and run it through.'

The scene started with the stage dark, a big basement kitchen lit only by the light from the street outside. Emma came in, looked around, turned on a lamp on a small table, and saw her father sitting slumped in a chair. A half-empty glass of whiskey was on the table by him. She went over to him, touched him on the shoulder. 'Father.' He did not move. 'Father. Come on, Father, please.'

A small tremor went through David Wheaton's body. Emma urged, 'Come on, Father. I'm home.'

David stirred, moving his entire body, then stretching his arms up and out. It was apparent by his movements that he was returning from some place deep inside himself. 'Hello, my darling,' he said, and held his arms out to her, and she gave him a hug.

'Father, I'm hungry.'

David Wheaton gave Emma a big, beautiful smile. 'So am I. What time is it?'

'A little after eleven.'

'Shall I make us an omelette?'

'That would be lovely.'

He rose, taking his glass, went to the refrigerator, and from a basket on a nearby shelf took imaginary eggs, got a pitcher in which was supposed to be cream, and some herbs, and arranged everything on a big, marble-topped table. He took a drink from his glass (filled with iced tea for the stage), then put it down by the cream pitcher. 'My dear, where were you tonight?'

'At a friend's, doing homework.'

He broke the imaginary eggs realistically into a blue bowl. 'I didn't know you were in the habit of lying to me.'

'I'm not. In the habit, that is.' Emma looked at her father's hands as he took a whisk to the imaginary eggs.

'But you were lying when you said you were doing homework with your friend.'

'Yes. How did you know?'

'That is beside the point. I happened to have occasion to call you during the evening and discovered that you were not where you said you were going to be.' He looked at her, then continued with the making of the omelette ('As bad as raspberry sherbert,' Etienne had said), put the frying pan on the stove. 'Please, daughter, don't lie about anything again. Is that what the nuns taught you, along with your charming manners? I've always thought I could trust you. I'd rather have you defy me, tell me you're going to do something anyhow, permission or no, than be underhanded about it.'

'It was just—it seemed simpler this way.'

'I've always told you anything easy isn't worth a damn.' He dished out the imaginary omelette with sharp, angry gestures.

Silently Emma sat at the kitchen table, looked across it at her father.

He sighed, heavily. 'I haven't given you a proper life for a child.' He pushed the untouched omelette away from him.

She reached across the table toward him. 'Oh, Father, I'm sorry I lied to you. I won't do it again.'

'Fight me if you must, but don't lie to me.'

'I promise.'

Her father pulled his plate back to him and began eating. They ate in silence, until her father said, 'I'm tired. So tired.'

She looked across the table at him.

'There is nothing more physically exhausting than a sense of failure.'

'But you're not a failure, Father!'

'Oh, my dear, let's not fool each other any longer. Why do I go on groping in the dark? Why can't I accept the absurdity of existence and laugh, as the absurd ought to be laughed at?' He stood up, took his plate, and put it in the sink. 'Why does all of me reject this? Why must there be beauty and meaning when everything that has happened to me teaches me that there is none.'

She left her plate on the table, went to her father, and put her arms around him in a totally protective gesture. 'But there is.'

He clasped her tightly. 'Why do I do this to you, child? Why do I try to drag you into the pit with me?'

'You don't, you don't, Father.'

'My sweet, go on up to bed and don't worry.'

'I don't want to leave you when you're feeling this way.'

'I'm all right.'

'You're not all right.'

'This will pass, too. Do you know how applejack is made?'
She tilted her head to look up at him, wonderingly. 'No.'

'You put apple juice in a keg and leave it outdoors all winter
and let it freeze. Almost all of it will turn to ice, but there's a
tiny core of liquid inside, of pure flame. I have that core of faith
in myself. There's always that small searing drop that doesn't
freeze. Don't worry about me, my darling, I'm all right. And
you must get some sleep.'

'And you, too, Father. I won't wake you when I come down
for breakfast. I'll try to miss the squeaky stair.' Emma kissed
her father and left the stage, putting her hands over her mouth,
hurrying, so that he would not see her cry.

'Good, good!' the director said. 'Emma, you've really come a
long way.'

Etienne came in from the wings where he had sat at his table
with the script in front of him. 'You nearly made me cry, Em.'

'Okay,' the director said. 'We'll break for today. Tomorrow at
10 a.m. We'll use real props, Etienne.'

Etienne grunted. 'Eggs. Ugh. Okay.'

.

They ate dinner at the inn, talking generally until the other
actors had left their table.

'It's not a terribly good play,' Etienne said. 'I don't think it'll
make it to Broadway, but there are some marvelous scenes, and
that one we worked on this afternoon is one of them.'

'A lot of it might be about Emma and me.' David Wheaton
swirled the ice in his glass of lemonade.

'Oh, come on, Papa,' Etienne said. 'You don't get drunk, and
you're hardly a failure.'

'Not in my work, perhaps.'

'Hey, Papa,' Emma said, 'you've already taught me more than
I've ever learned with anybody else. That's more important to

me—learning to be a good actress—than having an ordinary childhood.'

'Maybe I shouldn't have let you do all that modeling work when you were little—'

'Bahama would have put an end to it if it weren't okay.'

'Bahama. Not your mother.'

'Hey, Papa, I have Abby, and Marical,' She smiled across the table at Etienne. 'And of course Sophie. A plethora of mothers.'

Etienne spoke to his father through a mouthful of meatloaf and mashed potatoes. 'We're not dumping any guilt on you, so don't take any on yourself. You may be an unusual pa, but your kids love you, and so do several of your wives.'

David put down his glass with a thump. 'Yes, I'm an unusual pa, indeed.'

'Unusual pa, indeed,' Emma repeated, 'but if you weren't, I wouldn't have the brothers and sisters I love.'

David said, rising and stretching out his arms, 'I haven't deserved my children, but I'm grateful. I'm off to work on my lines. Don't be too long, Emma.'

'Just long enough to finish this gingerbread and milk.'

When he had left the dining room, Emma turned to her brother. 'Etienne, what is Papa looking for?'

He leaned back in his chair, finished chewing. 'Someone to understand his art, maybe.'

She looked at him questioningly.

'Papa's a fine artist. He wants to be even better, to transform, awe, inspire.'

'Yes, Etienne, I understand that. But—?'

'What I said. He's looking to be understood.'

'I thought Abby understood him.'

'I think she did, as much as anybody. The thing is, Em, there's no tragedy too terrible for Papa to comprehend on stage. Remember his Oedipus? But it has to be transformed. He can't take it raw.'

'Abby's twins?'

'His twins, too, remember. Abby's exhaustion. Abby's grief. Her focus was on the babies. Papa was lost in grief, and there was nothing left for each other.'

'But—'

'Those are the facts, Em, facts which carry neither blame nor merit. The fact was that Abby's twins were born without the strength to survive. We tend to want to blame or praise, but life doesn't divide itself that neatly. You're going to be looking for someone to understand you, too.'

'Papa understands me.'

'Some. He can shape you as an actress, but you don't want him to be a Pygmalion.'

'I want to learn.'

'You'll learn. From Papa. From others. But that's not going to be enough. I've worked with a lot of artists, Em, and they all have a need that cannot be met by another human being. That's why the affairs, the one-night stands. It takes greatness of spirit to understand that the need is not meetable, and just to get on with life.'

'Who—' she started, but he shook his head.

'No one I've met, at least not yet. It's not a good thing to investigate any artist's private life too closely. Papa has Sophie now, and while she doesn't understand him, she accepts him, totally.'

'What about Marical? Did she understand Papa?'

'My mother? No, Em. She loved him, but had quite reasonable expectations of fidelity.'

'Harriet. And Jarvis.'

'Yes. Jarvis.' Etienne finished his glass of iced tea. 'Time for bed.'

She asked, 'Why do we need so terribly to be understood?'

'Some artists settle for adulation instead. It's a trap Papa has not fallen into.'

'Okay, but what about all his wives, Etienne. Isn't that pretty inordinate? Most people don't have to have their needs met that way.'

'You're angry, aren't you?' Etienne asked.

'I suppose so. He's made life a lot more complicated for us than if we'd had one mother.'

'One mother for all of us?'

'Why not?'

'Why not, indeed. The fact is, little sister, that we're stuck with the way Papa is, not the way we'd like him to be, and on the whole I think we've come out amazingly well.'

'A lot of that's thanks to Sophie. The way she makes friends with the other wives—as much as she can—and pulls us all into one big circle.'

'Blessed Sophie,' Etienne agreed. 'She's given Papa a wonderful kind of balance. And while he does like admiration and appreciation from his public, he shuns adulation.'

'I suppose.'

'What about you, Em? How do you feel?'

'At school—in college—people thought I was super. Onstage, that is.'

'And how do you feel about being thought super?'

'It's nice. I like it. But then it feels empty.'

'Good. Don't let it become addictive.'

'I've figured that out. But I would like to meet someone who understands.'

'It's not going to happen. I understand, to some extent, but I'm Papa's son, I'm your brother. It's not enough.'

'What about love?'

'I'm all for it. But—as you can see from Papa's record, it's not enough. Papa wants the moon, and he more or less had it with Abby. On the other hand, Abby didn't start painting until everything went wrong in her life. Maybe she understands Papa now better than she did then. We weren't around, so we don't know. Em, have you been in love?'

'No. Not yet. I had a crush on one of my professors, but he was married, so it didn't count.'

'That doesn't stop a lot of people. I'm glad it stopped you. You've been around the theater all your life. You've seen a lot —or maybe you haven't seen it. Be careful, Em.'

'Sure.'

'I mean it. Be careful.'

Zeruiah

❦ ❦ ❦

And [Samuel] said . . . I am come to sacrifice unto the Lord:
sanctify yourselves, and come with me to the sacrifice. And
he sanctified Jesse and his sons, and called them to the
sacrifice.

And it came to pass, when they were come, that he looked
on Eliab, and said, Surely the Lord's anointed is before
him.

But the Lord said unto Samuel, Look not on his countenance, or on the height of his stature; because I have
refused him: for the Lord seeth not as man seeth; for man
looketh on the outward appearance, but the Lord looketh
on the heart.

And Samuel said unto Jesse, Are here all thy children?
And he said, There remaineth yet the youngest, and behold,
he keepeth the sheep. And Samuel said unto Jesse, Send
and fetch him . . .

I SAMUEL 16:5–7, 11

WHILE DAVID was sleeping after lunch, Emma sat on the floor by his bunk, carefully pulling out one of the chart drawers so it wouldn't disturb him, and lifted one of Nik's scenes from under a chart. The *Portia* was anchored. Ben was puttering in the engine room, and Alice had taken the dinghy and gone ashore.

Emma read a scene between David's older sister, Zeruiah, who had had a hand in bringing him up, and her youngest son, Asahel, still a child. Asahel, like Louis, had been curious about Samuel's anointing of two kings.

Nik had Zeruiah snorting impatiently. "Of course I'm worried. Samuel said God should never have chosen Saul."

Asahel asked innocently, "God made a mistake?"

Zeruiah was folding linens and she snapped, "God does not make mistakes. It's just like Samuel to blame it on God. Samuel made the mistake. It will cause nothing but trouble." And then, with the touch of prescience Nik had given her, Zeruiah shuddered. Asahel would die young.

Zeruiah was a good role for a character actress, Emma thought, acerbic but loving, funny but shrewd.

David stirred slightly, and Emma put the scene away, thinking that for a man who'd professed total disinterest in God, Nik had put a lot of God-talk in the mouths of his characters. She shut

· 81 ·

the drawer quietly and went to the galley to make David a cup of tea. He was awake, pushed up against the pillows, when she returned. He took the mug and set it down on the small table at the head of his bunk. "I want to see my children, all of them."

Adair . . . Etienne . . . Billy . . .

Inez . . .

Everard and Chantal were in Mooréa. Jarvis and Louis were in New York. Emma looked at her father and wondered if he realized how many of his children were no longer alive.

"And Nik," David said. "I want to see Nik."

"Papa—"

"Ah, Emma, don't you see that your old father just wants to fix everything for you?"

"Some things get too broken to be fixed."

"I would like to see Nik once more before I die. Would it be terribly hard on you?"

"I don't know."

"Child," he probed tenderly, "I don't know what happened between the two of you."

Emma interrupted, unsteadily, "I'll go fix some crab cocktail for us for dinner, if Ben has the crabs ready."

"Emma, wait. Please."

She paused in the doorway, turned back toward him.

"Emma. I want to help."

"It's okay, Papa."

"It's not okay. It's my fault Nik's King David play never worked out. I was kidding myself that because the old king and I had many wives I was like him."

"In some ways you are."

David sipped at his tea, looking at Emma over the rim of the cup. "David was a man after God's own heart, the Bible says, specially loved by God, and I, arrogant bastard that I am, felt that I, too, was beloved."

"You are." Emma sat at the foot of the bunk and put her hand gently against her father's foot.

"I couldn't unite my own kingdom," David said heavily.

"Neither could David."

"Ah, Em, I'm just being a foolish old man, suddenly remembering how often I've forgotten God. And David never did that. That was something Nik showed beautifully in his play, remember?" He sighed, but lightly. "I can die knowing that you're going to carry on after me."

·

Yes, she would try to carry on. Her return to the theater after eight years out for high school and college had not been easy. She wanted to make it on her own, not on her father's name and influence. But if directors remembered her from her childhood performances they were suspicious of her ability to be a mature actress. She got a small role in a new play, which reactivated her Actors Equity card. The play was a disaster, panned by all the critics. Emma, rather to her relief, was not even mentioned.

Having her Equity card was, she discovered quickly, both blessing and bane. She was offered several good roles with small, experimental groups, but according to Equity regulations she was not allowed to act with a non-Equity company. She managed to wangle permission to play Viola in *Twelfth Night*, and she rehearsed with a group once a week; although they were all serious about being professional, it was too much like college workshops for her liking, but better than nothing. She had a small but juicy role in an Off-Broadway production which was liked better by audiences than by critics and lasted only a few weeks. She respected the director, who pushed and prodded her in much the same way that her father did, and she knew that he had been pleased with her performance.

It was through him that she met Nik, the autumn of her second year back in New York. She was called to audition for Nik's play, which was both witty and deep, and the leading female role seemed to be right for her. She knew the director and that she could do well under his guidance.

But she did not audition well. She read intelligently but not flashily; it took her time to work into a role. She was thin, and her particular beauty did not emerge until she had worked out of herself and into her part. She could tell that Nik had been disinterested, and she did not get a call-back. She liked her one glimpse of Nik, with his undisciplined black curls and sparkling dark eyes. She was deeply disappointed because she knew that, given time, she could have done well in the role. And she needed to work, not only for the money for her rent, but for her self-esteem. She went home and cried and forgot all about it.

Early one morning, a month after the audition, the phone woke Emma up. 'Emma, love, remember that play of Niklaas Green's you read for?' It was the director.

She was groggy with sleep. 'Um.'

'Rehearsals have finally started.'

'Um,' she grunted again.

'We hired—' and he mentioned the name of an actress she knew slightly. 'She gave a brilliant reading, granted, but she reached her peak with that. She hasn't grown an inch. We're exercising the five-day clause and letting her go. Can you come to rehearsal at eleven this morning and give it a try?'

.

Emma moved tentatively into the role, but it was apparent by the third day that she brought a needed tenderness to it, that she was going to make people cry as well as laugh. She was nervous until those first five days, during which a performer can be dropped, were over. But she knew she was good, and that Nik knew she was good.

'You're marvelous,' Nik said. 'Why didn't I see that when you read?'

'Because I'm not good at first readings. It takes me time.'

'I'll give you all the time in the world,' Nik said.

She loved the rehearsals, once she was confident in her ability to bring life to the part. Even after the successful opening, she continued to look for ways to deepen and brighten her characterization. She had learned from her father never to 'set' a play, but to keep it fluid and alive.

Nik came back to her dressing room at the end of the first week. 'Want to have supper with me, and talk?'

'Sure. Love to.' She hoped she sounded calm and sophisticated and as though she was used to going out with rising young playwrights.

He waited while she finished taking off her makeup, carefully covered her tray with a linen towel. It was the first time she had had a dressing room to herself, and she gloried in the privacy. She was tidy about her makeup, placing it carefully on a tray—liners, lipsticks, pencils, neatly aligned. Some of her dressing-room mates had been casual, if not careless, spreading makeup onto Emma's space, using her mascara, soiling her Albolene.

She put on her coat, turned to Nik.

'Here.' He took her dressing-room key and gave it to the stage doorman to put on the board. Then Nik led her to a little restaurant around the corner from the theater and reached across the table in the dark booth to hold her hands. 'You bring something to my play, a quality of infinite tenderness and longing—it's not in my lines, Emma, you have written your role even more than I have.'

'It's all there, Nik,' she said. 'All I had to do was bring it out.'

'It's more than that. You have a quality onstage that I can't explain. I just know how lucky I am to have you in this role which could have seemed merely funny without the dimension of—of loving tolerance you give it.'

'It's a good play,' she said, 'and a wonderful role. I love the way the audience laughs—'

'With affection,' Nik finished for her. 'And never with derision. They leave the theater feeling good about themselves. That's what I was hoping for, and that's what you've helped me get.'

·

Despite her theater background, Emma felt herself to be inexperienced and naïve in ordinary social situations. For the first time she thought it might have been better if she had gone to coed schools. She did not know how to make light conversation, and she was grateful that Nik did not expect it.

She rode home on the subway alone, and a young sailor sitting next to her fell asleep leaning his head on Emma's shoulder, and she saw that tears were barely dry on his stubby blond lashes. She resolved to go more regularly to the Stage Door Canteen, where players served food to servicemen, danced with them, talked with them.

When she went there after the theater she found that she was able to reach out to their need as she could not with an ordinary date. Sometimes she talked with them about Adair and Etienne, who were both overseas. She was able to forget her shyness in reaching out to men she would see for an evening and probably never again.

On her Canteen nights, Nik often came for her, not wanting her to make her way home alone in the dark and early hours of the morning.

'No wonder they all love you,' Nik said, 'all these guys waiting to be sent overseas. You make each one of them believe that he's the most important person in the world. That's a gift.'

Was he flattering her? She was uncomfortable with praise, even when it came spontaneously from Nik and she believed it was heartfelt and not the superficial gushiness she distrusted. She wanted to be a good actress because that was the purpose of her life—not to be praised, but to bring life to her roles and joy to the audiences. She was grateful for Nik's faith.

He had taken her to their usual small restaurant, and ordered his favorite liverwurst-and-onion sandwich on rye. 'Em?' He looked at her questioningly as the waiter put down their plates. 'I want to show you something.'

'Okay.'

'My next project—' Nik started. 'Want to hear about it?'

'Of course.'

'Well—' He bent down and picked up his old and battered briefcase and took out a sheaf of typed pages, handing her a couple. 'Here. Read it. I don't think it's the first scene. The first scene will be a huge projection of Goliath with a tiny David standing, his back to the audience.'

'David?'

'Yes. King David from the Bible. I want to write a play for your father. Is that audacious of me?'

She tried to keep her voice light. 'Sure, but why not?'

'So this may be the second scene with David, and it may have to be played by a younger actor, though most of the play will be about the mature David.' He sounded simultaneously eager and unsure. 'Read it.'

She looked at the page.

The scene is Saul's palace, and the old king is sitting on his throne, writhing, beating the air with his arms and legs. David comes in with his harp, a diffident lad with nevertheless a joyous spring to his step; Scripture describes him as 'ruddy, and withal of a beautiful countenance, and goodly to look to.' He approaches the king and sits on a stool at his feet, not afraid of the old man's violence, and begins to sing. As he sings, the king quietens, leans his head back against the throne, closes his eyes in peaceful sleep.

Nik leaned toward her, singing the next lines, softly. ' "O God, thou art my God; early will I seek thee: my soul thirsteth for thee, my flesh longeth for thee in a dry and thirsty land, where no water is"—that's from the Psalms.'

She nodded. 'It's beautiful, Nik.'

'You really like it?'

'I think it's lovely—David's singing to drive away Saul's madness.'

'This is just a beginning. I wanted to know what you thought of the idea. See, I think David would be a perfect role for your father.'

She drew in her breath sharply.

'Your father and I talked about it at the party, opening night. He says he's always wanted to play David.'

'Yes.' Her voice was low.

'He says your grandfather suggested it to him years ago, told him it would be a perfect role for him. Emma, he was really pleased when I mentioned it. What I want to emphasize is David's humanness, his unwiseness in love, for instance, rather than the battles. I want to bring his wives and children to life —Emma, is something wrong?'

'No—no—Grandpa does love David, and Papa's always wanted—'

'Something's upset you. What's the matter? Have I done something, said something?'

'No, sorry, it's something else. Go on, please.'

'You don't think my play stinks—I mean, my idea for it?'

'No, Nik, I think it's a wonderful idea.' She was breathing normally. Back in control.

'What I want is an ensemble piece.' Nik signaled the waiter to bring him another sandwich. 'King David had eight wives and God knows how many unnamed wives and concubines, but contrary to what comes across in the Bible, where the women are merely names—I want them to be real people—Abigail, for instance, and maybe Maacah, and Bathsheba. I'm really going to want your input here, Em.'

'You're welcome to any input I can give you." Her voice was carefully level.

"Thank you. Can we do a quick rundown of King David's wives? Michal, his first wife. Cold. Very aware of being a king's daughter—she was King Saul's daughter, remember. Do you know King David's story?'

'Yes, it was one of Grandpa's favorites. I told you about my Grandpa Bowman, the preacher?'

'Yes. Okay, Michal was aware of being a king's wife. She cared about her position. Snooty. So. Who's next?'

It was a rhetorical question, but Emma answered. 'Abigail.' Grandpa had taught her well.

'Abigail. The one wife he truly married for love.'

'Not Bathsheba?'

Nik grinned. 'That was lust, more than love. And then, immediately after Abigail, came Ahinoam.'

'Ahinoam caused a lot of grief.' Emma's lips tightened briefly.

'A lot,' Nik agreed. 'I'll want to talk to you about that when we get to her, chronologically. Right now I just want to list them. Maacah, who was a king's daughter, and who had two unnamed sons, and Absalom, and Tamar.'

Emma let out a breath.

Nik moved on to David's next wife, Haggith. 'She's important, because she had Adonijah, and he's one of the contenders for the throne at the end of David's life, a real threat to Solomon. Then there's Abital, and we don't know anything about her, or her son, Shephatiah. Then there's Eglah, who had Ithream: ditto. And, finally, Bathsheba.'

'Is she going to be the juicy role?' Emma asked.

'Juicy enough, but not the best role. Who I have in mind for you is Abigail. She probably won't come in till the second act, but I want her to be almost as important as David. Before we get to her, there's a whole lot of exposition needed. I'm using Zeruiah, and Asahel, and I hope I can bring some laughter into their scenes.'

Emma nodded. 'Good. So you'll use Zeruiah and Asahel sort of like the butler and the maid in English drawing-room comedies?'

Nik shook his head. 'My play is going to be anything but a drawing-room comedy. There'll have to be humor to lighten it, of course, but I want to write a really serious play, something very different from this piece of fluff you're acting in now.'

'It's not fluff.'

'Thanks. Of course I wanted you to say that. But I'm really excited about this new play.'

The waiter sidled up to their table and put the bill in front of Nik.

'What's my share?' Emma asked.

Nik laughed. 'Sweetie, you've eaten half a sandwich and I've had three. My treat.' He paid the bill. 'I'll walk you home.'

In the doorway of her apartment on West Fifty-fifth Street he paused, took her face in his hands, kissed her gently. 'See you tomorrow.'

It was good. It was enough. If he wanted to write a play about King David and his wives and children, then that was what he should do. He had kissed her. Beautifully. She sang while she bathed, got ready for bed.

·

What had happened to their love?

She took her father's cup to the galley and washed it, looking at the sky shading from a hazy blue down to a soft grey as it met the darker grey of water, thinking of the scenes from Nik's David play which had lain for all these years in the *Portia*'s chart drawers.

"Em—"

She jumped, startled out of her memories. Ben had come in to the main cabin from the deck and was standing behind her.

She reached for a tea towel and began drying the cup.

"Can I help?"

She shook her head, put the cup away.

"Em, I couldn't help hearing—"

"What?" She was still barely back in the present.

"Your father asking you about Nik."

"Oh, Ben, he's my father, and he loves me. I'd like to protect him, but I realize I can't." Her voice galloped unsteadily.

"I hate to see you hurting this way."

"Thanks, Ben, but life's full of hurt, you know that."

"I wish I could help."

"You do help. It means a lot that you care. And you're giving Papa a last summer on the *Portia*. Right now that's what matters."

"We love him. We love you both. Where's Alice?"

"She's taking a nap. She was up with Papa a good bit last night."

Ben scowled. "It's hell. It isn't right. What should happen to us is that we should grow to whatever is our peak, and then blow up in a blast of fireworks."

"That sounds good, Ben. But Papa's reached several peaks as

an actor. I'm not sure when he should have blown up." She smiled. "I'm going up to him."

"Okay. And it's okay, Em, in the long run of things. It's all part of a cycle and I don't know what got into me." He turned on his heel and went back out on deck.

Emma returned to the pilothouse. Pulled David's pillows up so that he could sit more comfortably.

"If I'd left Nik alone—if nothing had happened—"

"But a lot of things happened, Papa."

"If Nik had finished his play—"

"It wasn't really Nik's kind of play. He's better at comedy."

"It could have been good," David said. "It's one of my few real regrets, that I never played David."

.

Amazing that her father could speak of having few regrets. She riffled Nik's pages, remembering going with him after the theater to have supper with her father and Sophie. Sophie always had them sit at the oval dining table, with the candles lit, as though for a formal meal, and then laughed with them as David turned on the overhead lights so that he could see to read the small print in Nik's Bible, brought milk in a bottle to the table, spurning the silver pitcher she offered him.

'This Zeruiah, David's sister,' David Wheaton said. 'What's she like?'

Nik laughed, a little ruefully. 'I visualize her as being somewhat like my mother, old for her age. Living with my father was enough to age anybody. As for Zeruiah, I guess most women back then aged early. Short, dumpy, worn by work and worries. Greying brown hair. A bit of a gossip. I think my mother's happiest times were schmoozing with the neighbors as they swept their stoops. I see Zeruiah as calmer than my mother, more in control of her life. But I'd like to honor my mother in Zeruiah.'

'That's nice, Nik!' Sophie exclaimed. 'I like that.'

'You've obviously thought about this a lot,' David said.

'I've had this idea for a play ever since I first saw you in *The Road to Rome*. You were superb as Hannibal.'

'My Davie is always terrific,' Sophie said. 'But I agree with you about Hannibal.'

Nik smiled at her. 'And right then I thought, Someday I'll write a play for him, and what role more obvious than David? Okay, we've established that Samuel anointed Saul king.' He opened his Bible to a place he had marked with a slip of paper. 'And here it says that Saul shows his strength by hewing a yoke of oxen in pieces, and gathers himself an army—' Nik stopped short as he saw Emma's eyebrows shoot up.

'Hewing a yoke of oxen? Onstage?' she asked.

David and Sophie burst into laughter, and Nik joined in.

'What a thought. No, I think I can just refer to some of the things that happen before David comes into the picture.' Nik hungrily finished the bowl of black-bean soup Sophie had made.

Sophie asked, 'If David was meant to become king, why did Samuel anoint Saul first?'

'Looks.' Nik smiled at Sophie, nodding thanks as she refilled his soup bowl. 'David was an unknown stripling, up in the hills with his sheep, and Saul was a movie-star type, strong and gorgeous to look at.'

'Gary Cooper,' Emma suggested.

'Robert Taylor,' Sophie said.

'Gregory Peck. Whoever.' Nik shut his Bible. 'And old Samuel made the obvious choice.'

'Saul's going to be a marvelous role for an older actor,' David said. 'I see him first as shy and almost uncouth, surprised when Samuel chooses him. And then it will take real ability to show this strong man's disintegration into jealousy and madness, until he's almost like Lear at the end. If you don't finish this play soon, Nik, I may be too old for David, and then I'll have to play Saul.'

'You'll play David, Dave,' Nik said. 'The play won't be anything without you.'

'Emma's grandpa thought Saul was full of pride,' Nik said.

'But it still seems strange to me, God refusing to talk to Saul ever again.'

'Do you think God speaks to President Roosevelt?' Sophie asked. 'Or that he listens?'

'Who knows?'

Emma said, 'Grandpa says it comforts him to remember that God never uses perfect people.'

'Some people think Roosevelt is perfect,' Sophie pursued.

'Do you?' Emma asked Nik.

'No. Probably the leader we need right now, but far from perfect. And I suspect that, like Samuel, he listens to himself and thinks it's God.'

'You must meet Emma's Grandpa Bowman,' David said. 'He can tell you whatever you need to know about Samuel, Saul, and David.'

'Someday.' Nik's voice was wistful. 'Anyhow, I have a real problem with knowing how far back I have to go. I mean, I'd like to start with David, but I have to get over a certain amount of exposition, such as Saul making a thank offering to God without waiting for the prophet to do it, and Samuel is furious with Saul for . . .

.

. . . upstaging him.' Grandpa Bowman often used theatrical terms. 'You see, my dear children, that the people God has chosen to use throughout history, and still today, are never the good and moral and qualified people. They're faulty and flawed and complicated enough to be fascinating and infuriating.'

'Like you.' Emma sat with Louis on her grandfather's porch.

'Saul or Samuel?' Grandpa Bowman asked.

'Samuel, of course.'

The old man laughed. 'I came to the Lord late, after I was fully grown and working on my own. I was walking in the woods when the Lord came to me in a vision.'

'Grandpa,' Emma asked without guile, 'have any of your visions come true?' She froze, as he turned on her, shouting.

'Many of them. Many, many. Your mother turned away from my visions and refused to fulfill them.'

'Okay, Grandpa, okay. I didn't mean to upset you.'

'Only the Lord can upset me,' he bellowed.

'Hey, Grandpa,' Louis said eagerly, 'have you ever had any visions about me?'

'You, child? No. I have had no visions about you. Are you disappointed?'

'It would depend on what the visions were.'

'You're a good boy. Your mother has brought you up well.'

'You do like my mom?'

'She's a pet lamb, like you.'

'Grandpa, would it have been better if my papa hadn't married all those other wives?'

Grandpa Bowman huffed softly. 'I'm not comfortable with better or worse. It is simply a fact, Louis, that he did. He is a human being.'

'And human beings make mistakes?'

'Inevitably.'

'Grandpa, do you think God ever makes mistakes?'

Grandpa Bowman turned to Emma. 'How would you answer that question?'

Emma thought, frowning. 'Well. We often think God makes mistakes because we'd rather blame God than blame ourselves.'

'Heah, heah! So go on.'

Emma paused and scratched a mosquito bite. 'Well. Human beings make mistakes because we have free will.'

'And?'

'It was pretty risky of God to give us free will.'

'Very risky,' Grandpa Bowman said.

'Do you think it was a mistake?'

'I am not God,' Grandpa Bowman said. 'But I am happy that I am a human being who can make mistakes, and not an insect, who cannot.'

Louis asked, 'Have you made mistakes, Grandpa?'

'A great many.'

•

'Your grandpa,' Nik said, 'doesn't sound like the ordinary fun-
damentalist preacher.'

Emma smiled and reached for her glass of ginger ale. Nik had
called for Emma after the theater and taken her to their usual
restaurant, where the dark wooden walls of their booth made
them feel private and protected. 'He's wide open. He and my
Episcopalian grandmother were great friends.'

Nik looked up at the waiter who was hovering over them.
They were the last people in the restaurant. He reached for the
bill. Emma no longer asked about her share. In their world of
theater, Nik's picking up the tab meant that he thought of her
seriously as his girl.

She rose, and the waiter, who had come to regard them be-
nevolently, helped her on with her coat.

They walked to Emma's apartment. Despite the late hour,
the streets were crowded with servicemen on leave, looking for
respite and amusement.

Nik startled Emma by asking, 'Does your grandpa ever come
to New York?'

'No. He hates to travel.'

'Would he come to New York if, for instance, you were to get
married?'

Emma felt herself tremble slightly, and hoped that Nik did
not feel it. 'I don't know.' She paused in the doorway. 'Thanks
for walking me home.' She reached for her keys.

He put his hand over hers and put his arms around her to
kiss her.

•

Grandpa Bowman would surely come if Emma got married.
She could not imagine being married by anyone except Grandpa
Bowman.

•

"Too bad Alice and Ben never had a chance to know your Grandpa Bowman, Emma." David Wheaton looked at his wife, who was at the wheel.

Alice turned, pushing her fingers through her short curly hair. "We never knew our own grandparents, either. Our loss. Hey, this is a lovely inlet, and there aren't any other boats. How about stopping here for the night?"

Emma looked around the sheltering cove. Climactic fir trees, old enough so that they would grow no higher, came down to the rocky cliff that plunged deep into the water. Cedar trees added another shade of green. At the top of a dead, bare tree sat a bald eagle, ignoring them.

Emma saw a flash of brown and something slid into the water. "What's that?"

"An otter, most likely." Alice swiveled off the high stool in front of the wheel. She called out, "Ben, okay if we anchor here?"

Ben came up the steps from the main cabin to the pilothouse and consulted his chart. "Sure. I'll go let down the anchor." He slid open the door to the narrow deck that ran along the side of the *Portia*, and went to the foredeck.

"Take the wheel, please, Em." Alice went out onto the deck, running lightly to the much wider foredeck. She still moved like a young woman. Ben was there ahead of her, and then Emma heard the mechanical whirring of the anchor being lowered.

·

Alice and Emma brought a folding table out to the pilothouse so that they could be with David for dinner. Clouds had gathered over them and rain began to fall, slowly running down the windshield, a soft, summer rain. The *Portia* sat sturdily at anchor, its slow rocking barely perceptible. The red limbs of the madrona trees gleamed wetly. Misty clouds hung between the trees and the water, drifted against the mountains.

David was propped high on pillows, with a hospital table swung across the bunk for his dinner tray.

While they ate, Ben kept the conversation going. They were

anchored across from one of the many small islands in the inlet, islands which were green circles of trees ringed at the base with a crown of white rock. On the ground of the nearest island were weathered boxes, and Ben explained that the island was sacred, an Indian burial ground, not to be profaned by those who did not belong to the tribe. "Those boxes are coffins which originally were placed high up in the trees, with the lower branches cut away so that wolves or other animals couldn't climb up and get at the bodies."

"Birds?" David suggested.

"Yes," Alice agreed, "but birds were thought to be better than animals."

David put down his plate. "When I was in Bombay I saw the vultures sitting on pilings by the Temple of Silence. After the funeral service—quite beautiful—it would take the vultures about an hour to strip a body clean. The theory was that the dead body should go back to the planet as ecologically pure as possible. I've never quite understood why that's more pure than the funeral pyre. After all, vultures have to shit."

Emma turned away. Ben helped himself to more stuffed flounder. Alice buttered a slice of bread Emma had baked that morning. Death was a daily neighbor in this harsh part of the world where a meager living had to be eked out of the forests, pulled from the sea. In large cities, death is less visible, less accepted, is rushed off to the anonymity of hospitals, where it somehow seems less contagious.

"Cremation for me," David said, "and my ashes here in these waters I've loved for so long."

—Not yet, Emma pleaded silently, —please, not yet.

·

'Ben and I were born on Whittock Island,' Alice had told Emma one night in New York when the two women had sat up talking, sharing intimacies, becoming friends, long after David had gone to bed. 'Whittock's a desolate and lonely place. It was once a thriving community, but at the time of the First World

War two hundred men went off to war together, as a group. Nine came back.'

Emma let out a long breath. 'How terrible.'

Alice nodded. 'My father and mother stayed, but everybody else drifted off. When Ben and I were children, we lived there alone with Papa. He loved us.'

'What happened to your mother?'

'She died when Ben was a baby and I was nearly twelve. There's over ten years between us, and after Mom died I was Ben's mother. Dad was a dreamer, full of projects which never came to anything. But we were happy, running wild, living off the land and with what Dad made from logging and fishing.'

Alice's story fascinated Emma.

'I've never talked about myself this way before,' Alice said. 'I took my life for granted. As a child, and after I became a doctor.'

'When your mother died—you were so young for all that responsibility—'

'Kids tend to accept what happens. Your mother didn't die, but didn't she—'

Emma, too, smiled. 'Abandon me? More or less. But I had Bahama.' Saying this to Alice made the almost unacknowledged pain over her mother's indifference easier to acknowledge, and to forgive.

'Do you go see her movies?'

'Yes. Sometimes.'

'How does it feel?'

'When I was a kid it felt awful, seeing this stranger. Papa and Bahama didn't want me to go, so I sneaked off to the movies when I was staying with school friends. Sophie understood that I needed to go see my mother on the screen, see Elizabeth Bowman and respect her as an actress, but not expect more of her than she could give.'

'You accepted what was.'

'I guess so. Kids do. You did.'

Alice nodded. 'We were alone on the island, so there were no comparisons to be made. Dad built our house, but he never quite finished it. He did put in bookshelves, and it was full of books. Whatever else he didn't give us, he gave us books. I don't remember learning to read or write, but Dad must have taught me. Whenever a pleasure craft pulled into the cove, the way Dave first came to see Ben, dropping anchor and rowing in, Dad would come through the woods to meet it and he always asked for books. One family came with their yacht almost every summer. I think they were intrigued by Dad, the strange, blue-eyed dreamer, and his two wild kids. I was an innocent then,' Alice said. 'But I was bright, and the people with the yacht said I was brilliant—'

'They were right.'

'They—the Browns, the family with the yacht—saw to it that I took a high-school equivalency test, and then they sent me to college in Vancouver, and from there to medical school. I got scholarships, good ones, but they paid for everything else, and never made me feel in debt.'

'That's wonderful.'

'They were. Wonderful. But I felt like an alien life form from another planet.'

'How did you manage?' Emma asked.

'I didn't. I was awed by a world of people, but I didn't have any idea what to say to anybody, out of class. One of my professors called me "our wild little savage," and flattered me, and seduced me in his office. I didn't understand what was happening, but I felt that I was being treated—oh, not as a person, but as a thing.'

Emma sighed. 'Oh, God.'

They were in the big living room, curled up on the huge couch, which Sophie had filled with bright pillows made from colorful molas from the San Blas Islands. Alice had brought in an eiderdown from the guest room and it was tucked around them. The wind was blowing shrilly across the river, battering against the windows so that it sounded like waves of water hitting the glass. Emma clutched the quilt more closely around her, shuddering.

Alice looked at her sharply. 'Emma. What's the matter?'

Emma let out her breath in a long, slow sigh. 'There's no reason it needs to go on being a deep, dark secret, at least from you. When it happened, I didn't want it talked about.'

Alice reached under the quilt for Emma's hand, clasped it firmly. 'Dave told me.'

.

Emma walked home, grateful for the deepening friendship. It freed her to talk to Alice as she had never talked to another woman, not even Sophie. Emma often felt older than Sophie. But Alice was old enough to have been Emma's mother, and Emma trusted her as—perhaps—Marical's children trusted her. Emma went to the Riverside Drive apartment at least once a week, as winter deepened, snows came and went, and the harsh winds of March whipped across the river.

.

'Well. It happened.' Emma's voice was flat and dead. 'It happened to you. It happened to me. We survive.'

'Emma . . .'

'It's degrading and humiliating and dehumanizing. You stop being real. You lose your reality and it shatters your faith in other people's reality. Rape is a kind of murder.'

'Yes, rape is murder, spiritual murder. Except that your spirit can't be killed, Em. No one can kill it except you.'

Emma pulled her hand away. 'I know that. But I let it be killed.'

'For a while . . .'

'For a while. I had help—Chantal and Adair—Grandpa Bowman and Norma. And I survived.'

Alice said, 'We need to do more than that. It's obvious we're both survivors. But we need to—to be reborn. That's what happened to me when I married David. Rebirth.'

Emma rubbed her fingers over the flesh of her forearm. 'Alice, it must have taken a lot of courage for you to marry Papa—a man who'd married so often and made such a mess of his marriages.'

Alice laughed. 'David was, to put it mildly, forthright. He told me he'd married for lust, committed adultery, run away from problems instead of trying to solve them. He told me that women were dazzled by the public man and said yes to him, and forgot there was a private man underneath the glitter.'

Emma sighed. 'Yes.'

'But I didn't see the public man till long after I'd fallen in love with the private one. And when I knew he loved me, Alice, grey-haired spinster, it was rebirth. Truly.'

Emma said, 'I heard somewhere that after seven years every single cell in our bodies has changed, been renewed. Does it happen to spiritual cells, too?'

'Perhaps. But I don't think you can put a chronological limit to that kind of renewal. Did it help, when you married Nik?'

'It helped. It helped a lot. But maybe not enough water had gone under the bridge. A lot of those spiritual cells hadn't been renewed, and that was hard on Nik, put demands on him I didn't even realize.'

'Was he sensitive to the demands?'

'Far more than I gave him credit for. We had wonderful times together. We laughed, we played, we enjoyed each other. But we were so different; we came from completely different worlds. My life has been theater, but Bahama and Grandpa helped form me. Bahama was an Episcopalian; Grandpa was a Georgia cracker; and Nik was half Dutch Catholic and half Russian Jew, but he and Grandpa liked each other because they both loved to talk about God. Nik's mother was deeply devout. His father was equally devout, though an atheist. One morning Nik overheard his father while he was shaving, raising his razor aloft and shouting into the mirror, "I thank you, God, Lord of the Universe, that I do not believe in you." Nik was often a battleground for the two of them, and he found my grandfather's robust theology refreshing.'

'Did you like them? Nik's parents?'

'I didn't know them. They died in an accident a few months before I met Nik. They were odd and possessive. If Nik wanted to do something unscheduled after high school, he had to call and get permission. Even after college, when he moved into his own apartment, they still wanted to know where he was at all times. Once he was spending the weekend with friends, and when he hadn't called home by dinnertime, they tracked him down to make sure he was okay.'

Alice laughed. 'I can't even imagine parents with that kind of concern.'

Emma frowned. 'I don't think it was concern. It was obsession. They were immigrants. They didn't speak English very well. They evidently had all kinds of fears. I think I'm glad I never knew them.'

'Different worlds, indeed,' Alice said thoughtfully.

'When I met Nik, I was going through the actions of life, and on the surface I was happy, but my scars were still healing.'

.

Often Emma urged Alice to talk about her slow emergence from the solitary child on Whittock Island. She was almost like a child saying, 'Tell me a story about when you were growing up.'

'When I finished college,' Alice said, 'I got a scholarship to Johns Hopkins for medical school. The Browns gave me whatever else I needed—respectable clothes, for instance, some tweed skirts and warm cardigans and a string of cultured pearls. Medical school wasn't really that much different from college. I was always at the top of my class, but I felt devalued, that nobody saw me as real. So I was isolated. I didn't know how to talk to anyone. I was just a brain.'

Emma asked carefully, gently, 'Did it go back to that professor in college who seduced you?'

Alice was silent for a moment. Then, 'Probably. I can't blame the professor entirely. I was part of it. I let it happen. It wasn't the ugly violence that happened to you.'

'Maybe it was even uglier,' Emma suggested, 'because it mas-queraded as something else. The intent for violence was there.'

'I suppose. Yes. Using people for your own lusts is always violent. We may be different generations, you and I, but that hasn't changed. I saw a lot of it when I did my internship and residency, a lot of the result of that violence, I mean. It was shocking to me, more shocking than it should have been. Whittock and isolation had kept me incredibly innocent.'

'Was that all bad—the innocence?'

'No, Emma. You have it, too.'

Emma frowned. 'Even after—how can there be any innocence?'

'There is, Emma, I promise you. I recognize some of myself in you when I was your age. That's why we can be so honest with each other.'

'Yes. It's amazing and marvelous. How was the residency? In Washington, wasn't it?'

'Yes, at NIH. I knew that once I came back to Whittock and the islands I'd need to be able to do anything, emergency sur-gery, for instance. In some weather a specialist can be flown in, but often the islands are isolated by snow and fog.'

The wind had dropped, and small tendrils of fog further soft-ened the trees in the park. The horizon was a pinkish grey from city lights that were never extinguished, shading from the pink up into a dull grey. If there were any stars, they were not visible.

Emma touched Alice's hand. 'What an unexpected gift Papa brought to me when he came home with you!'

Alice's smile lit the pale blue of her eyes. 'I was the one who received the gift. I was a good physician and that was all I knew about myself. Until I took out your father's appendix.' The smile deepened with remembrance.

·

In the pale light of the long evening that came in through the *Portia*'s portholes, Emma looked at Alice and breathed a sigh of relief that Alice was a doctor, and a good one. She looked at Alice's tired face, and marveled at her ability to care so tenderly for a husband she was going to have to lose, and wondered how she had come to be as sane and centered as she was.

Alice reached up as though to turn on her small reading lamp, then dropped her hand and stared out the porthole; the northern sky would not become dark enough for stars for another couple of hours. "Dave is obsessed by King David. And Nik's play. Is it because it's too late and he can never play King David now? I knew Nik had written a rough draft of a play about David years ago, but Dave has never—" She broke off, sighing. "Isn't it hard on you, the way he keeps bringing it up?"

Emma, too, sighed. "But that doesn't matter. At least I try not to let it matter. If it helps Papa—if his mind is on King David, then it's not on pain. Or fear. Alice, is Papa afraid?"

Alice shook her head. "It's not fear of dying, not more than the normal fear of letting go. I think it's fear of dying with his life unresolved. Despite his age, Dave has always thought in terms of the future, as though he had all the time in the world. While *Lear* was running, he was reading new plays, he was looking ahead to his next show, never turning back. Until this summer, he seemed immortal."

Emma nodded. Agreed. The idea that the vitality that was David Wheaton could be snuffed out had always seemed absurd.

"*King Lear.*" Alice smiled. "We had such fun talking about it before and during rehearsals."

"We had the best of Papa—of David Wheaton," Emma agreed.

Alice was propped up on one elbow in her bunk, her sleeping bag not yet zipped up. "Being David's wife opened an entirely new world for me. I've been *the doctor*, and that's isolating. Too often in my life, I've had to let the masculine side dominate. Or men who have seen me as a woman have seen me only as a sex object. But you know something about that."

Emma laughed and sighed. "People do tend to place actresses in some kind of special category, as though we're not quite real, either. Doctors are supposed to be gods, curing all illnesses. And actresses are all Liliths. I'm exaggerating a little, but not a lot."

"David sees *me*. He treasures me. What he's given me can't ever be taken away. I have a sense of my own value, and that is a priceless gift."

"Dear Alice, you seem to me so totally valuable I can't imagine you not valuing yourself."

"I didn't. Not until Dave. Ben was afraid David was too old to—well, make love."

Emma burst into laughter. "Papa!"

Alice, too, laughed. Then said, soberly, "David is a birth-giver." She put her fingers to her cheeks, and even though Alice's light was not on, Emma could see the deep, slow flush. Then she said, "Last winter in New York was difficult. I was worried about Dave, and knowing you were there for him, for me, made all the difference. Dave has been so present that I've not spent much time thinking about the rest of the family, but this summer I'm going to have to. Abby's coming is the beginning. Dave knows it's a long distance from the East Coast, but he wants to see everybody who can come. It's part of his reconciling leftover pain and misunderstanding, isn't it?"

"Yes," Emma agreed, "I think it is. At first it seemed sort of Victorian and theatrical, deathbed scenes. But I think you're right. He needs to try to—well, as you said—reconcile."

"And—" Alice sighed. "I suppose I ought to know more about David—the Biblical one—if he's that important to Dave. I'll check him out in Ben's Bible. Do you know where the King David stuff is?"

"Samuel I and II, mostly. I remember a good bit because of Nik's play and Grandpa Bowman. I'm sorry you never had a chance to know my grandpa."

"I'm sorry, too. We haven't talked enough about your family, Em, have we?"

Emma moved her hand in a dismissing gesture. "After—after Adair and Etienne were killed we didn't get together, the whole family, the way we used to when Sophie was with Papa."

"The war changed everything, didn't it?"

The Second World War that killed Adair and Etienne. And a

great deal that had nothing to do with the war. "Papa's older. He doesn't like big gatherings anymore. And you make him happy. Happier than I've ever known him."

Alice smiled gratefully. "Thanks. Dave and I do our duty; we go to parties Jarvis thinks he ought to go to, and to openings. Jarvis insists that Dave be seen, and I suppose he's right. But we're happiest alone, or with you and Nik. And maybe that's how I wanted it. I knew things weren't going well with you and Nik during the run of *Lear*, and I didn't know what to say, and I knew Dave didn't want to talk about it—or know about it, for that matter. I'm sorry. I did know, but—well, I was remiss."

"Forget it," Emma said. "There wasn't anything to say or do. You were there, and that's what mattered."

"But I wasn't," Alice said. "I was worried about Dave, and that was foremost in my mind. I was pulling myself into a tight little shell with just room for—"

"It's okay, Alice," Emma said. "We've all done the same thing, I know I have."

·

Alice had known when Emma moved out of the apartment, away from Nik. The two women's time to talk was always after David had gone to bed, when it was just the two of them together. They sat in the living room of the Riverside Drive apartment. It was spring, or should have been, but an April storm was blowing across the Hudson, and the wind slashed against the windows. Emma curled up on one corner of the big couch, a shawl pulled over her shoulders.

Alice sat to her left, in a wing chair. 'Oh, Emma, is it really over, with you and Nik?'

'I don't know,' Emma said. 'I just don't know. I haven't been feeling well, and after that last explosion with Nik I threw up. I caught an intestinal bug which was going through the company. Everybody says it hangs on and on. It hasn't helped me to think rationally.'

Alice looked at her questioningly, but Emma continued.

'I wish I could speak to Grandpa. I wish Nik could.'

'Did Nik know your grandfather?'

'Grandpa came to New York to marry us, and we visited him once, and he gave us his bed, that great, glorious oaken monstrosity I love—so I know he approved of Nik.'

'Emma, I wish I could help.'

'You do help, just by caring.'

The wind beat against the windows and both women jumped. Yes, Alice cared, but her focus was on her husband, not on her friend. Alice, Emma understood later, already knew that David Wheaton was dying.

Michal

᪻ ᪻ ᪻

And Michal Saul's daughter loved David: and they told
Saul, and the thing pleased him.

And Saul said, I will give him her, that she may be a
snare to him, and that the hand of the Philistines may be
against him . . . And Saul said, Thus shall ye say to David,
The king desireth not any dowry, but an hundred foreskins
of the Philistines, to be avenged of the king's enemies. But
Saul thought to make David fall by the hand of the
Philistines.

And when his servants told David these words, it pleased
David well to be the king's son in law . . .

Wherefore David arose and went, he and his men, and
slew of the Philistines two hundred men; and David brought
their foreskins . . . and Saul gave him Michal his daughter
to wife.

And Saul saw and knew that the Lord was with David,
and that Michal Saul's daughter loved him.

And Saul was yet the more afraid of David; and Saul
became David's enemy continually.

I SAMUEL 18:20–21, 25–29

EMMA GOT READY for bed, then climbed into her bunk and picked up a scene between King David and his wife Michal. Odd. Michal was referred to as King Saul's daughter or King David's wife, but never as princess or queen. Nik, she thought, had given Michal short shrift, calling her, casually, 'spiritually constipated.' Emma had pointed out Michal's reputation for beauty; Grandpa had told her that the four most beautiful Hebrew women were listed as Sarah, Rahab, Michal, and Esther.

She let the pages drop, and bent to retrieve them as her memory flicked up Grandpa Bowman telling her that Saul had been called Cush, or Ethiopian, and his dark beauty contrasted with David's 'ruddiness.' Michal, Grandpa said, was referred to in some of his sources as 'daughter of Cush,' so her beauty, like her father's, would have been dark.

Emma skimmed a scene where Zeruiah was defending Michal to the servants. 'She doesn't mean to be rude. It's just her manner. Saul taught her to be arrogant. It's not really her fault. If you have any problems, bring them to me.'

There was no indication in Nik's play that King David's first marriage was a happy one.

.

The wind gently blew the light curtains that covered the *Portia*'s portholes. Alice leaned on one elbow, looking at Emma in the opposite bunk. "Dave doesn't want me to dwell on his past. I think he'd like me to feel I'm the only wife. Not that he wasn't honest with me, giving me a brief rundown on them all."

"We had eight showers in my dorm at college, and I named them after Papa's wives. Meredith, Abigail, Myrlo, Marical, Harriet, Elizabeth, Edith, Sophie," Emma intoned. "Of course, I could equally well have named them after King David's wives, because Papa's always made a lot over the similarities.'

"The first wife—"

"Papa's, or King David's?"

Alice closed her eyes briefly. "Either."

"Meredith was rich and I guess selfish, and Jarvis is the only one who keeps up with her. King David's first wife was Saul's daughter, Michal, and I feel sorry for her, because I think she loved David, at first, at any rate, but for David she was just a very big step up the ladder. Nik certainly didn't think David felt any love for her. Funny, we don't know anything at all about the wife who comes in the right chronology for my mother. And we don't know much about my mother, either."

"Are you bitter about that, Em?"

"Not really."

"She's still in Hollywood?"

"Yes. She's a good actress," Emma said.

"As good as your father?"

"No. She doesn't have his reach. In the revivals of movies I've been able to see that they did together, the two of them have a tremendous combined vitality, but it's Papa who gives the depth."

Alice said, "Ben's the moviegoer. I'd rather read."

Emma smiled. "Not a bad choice. I'm sorry you haven't met Abby before."

"I've seen her work, of course. Dave takes me to galleries and museums. But she was never in New York when we were."

"Now that she's older she doesn't come to New York every spring the way she used to."

"I'd like to have met her before—it might make it easier when she comes tomorrow. She's a good painter, and—wasn't she married for a while to someone in Europe?"

Emma smiled. "To a Yugoslavian count with an unpronounceable name. There were a lot of them in Europe after the First World War, some of them phony. Yekshek was for real—that's what I called him, and it's a small part of his whole name. Abby'd already been painting for a while as Abigail Wheaton when she married Yekshek, and Abigail Wheaton is who she is when she's in the States. I think in Europe she's quite often 'the Countess,' and she has a kind of royal quality. You'll notice it in her bearing and in her manner. I liked Yekshek. He adored Abby. I cried a lot when he died."

"Why didn't she come home to the States?"

"Yekshek left her a house in the Auvergne. And there are servants, old family retainers she feels responsible for. She says it's a wonderful place to paint. And they had a tiny flat in Florence, which she keeps. It's another world, Alice, and mostly it vanished after the war. You'll like Abby, truly. I'm glad she's coming. It's hard for me to remember Sophie's the only one of Papa's wives you know."

"Sophie's so friendly she put me at ease right away. She didn't seem to think there was anything strange about being friends with her husband's new wife."

Emma laughed. "Dear Sophie. She and Marical were good friends, too. She's an extraordinarily generous person. She and Papa were happy together for a good many years."

"I think she still loves him," Alice said.

"She does," Emma agreed. "Ulysses was a mistake. He was the director of a gym where she exercised and they—well, I guess they fell in love. They lost a child, a little girl, and nothing worked out for them after that."

"Dave told me she had a rough time."

"She asked Papa if she should marry Gino—though she didn't take Papa's advice. Gino ran one of the most posh and expensive restaurants in town. Did you ever eat there?"

"Yes, Sophie insisted that we go, as her guest, and we went

a couple of times, but it was obvious Gino was uncomfortable."

"If it weren't for you, I'd be sorry she left Papa."

"Why did she? Was it just this health-club guy?"

"No. Ulysses was the least of it. She got involved with him only because Papa got into a terrible depression after Billy and Adair and Etienne died. That's a lot of death, even in wartime. Sophie stood it for as long as she could, but finally she left. You've never experienced one of his depressions—"

"No. He was very honest with me about them, and I was afraid when he got cancer—but, Emma, he's been marvelous, brave, not complaining, completely himself."

"Papa's depressions are never over anything that happens to him. They come when bad things happen to someone he loves. Abby's exhaustion and grief—the poor little twins—and then he was in this comedy with Myrlo—oh, Alice, Papa's more centered now in his old age than he used to be. He's an actor, and he's vulnerable to—what I'm trying to say is, Papa thrives on sunshine. When those around him aren't shining on him, he turns to someone else."

"And Myrlo shined?"

"I guess. Don't ask me to explain Myrlo. I don't think Myrlo can explain herself."

Alice nodded. "It takes a lot of maturity to acknowledge our real selves."

"Can we ever, all the way?"

"Probably not. But it's worth a try."

·

Sophie's love of David had been not only lavish but tolerant. She had made the apartment on Riverside Drive into a warm, hospitable home, full of color and comfort. Her delight in preparing after-theater suppers for David, and at least once a week for Emma and Nik, was genuine.

'Come often,' David urged. 'It means so much to Sophie. And Louis misses his sister.'

'I miss Louis. But he's in bed when we get to you in the evenings.'

'Come, anyhow. For Sophie. For me. After all, I have a certain interest in this play Nik is writing.'

.

Emma and Nik walked briskly uptown, bent slightly against the wind that was blowing in from the river.

Emma said, 'Your coat's not warm enough.'

Nik laughed, squeezing her hand. 'My play's a success. I can afford a winter coat! That's hard for me to realize!' He swung her hand high in his pleasure.

'Nik, get one tomorrow. Take care of yourself. Please.'

'Come with me and help me choose and we'll buy me a coat. Whoopee!' Nik was normally serious, if not solemn, and Emma rejoiced at this lightheartedness.

As they started to cross Broadway, a group of laughing soldiers ran into them; one caught Emma by the waist and twirled her around, and then they turned the corner, still laughing, and whistling appreciative wolf calls.

Nik was indignant. 'Hey!' and he started after the men.

'Whoa!' Emma put a restraining hand on his arm. 'It's okay. They don't mean any harm. They're on leave and they all know they could be dead in a month or so.' Nik relaxed. Then she dared ask, 'Nik, what about you? Are you going to be called up?'

He shook his head. 'Right after my parents died, I applied to the Air Force and I was turned down. In fact, I was turned down by all the services because I have a slight heart murmur.'

Instinctively, Emma reached out to touch his arm.

'Don't worry. My doctor says it isn't serious. As long as I live a reasonable life, I could easily make it to the Biblical threescore and ten. But war isn't reasonable, and none of the services will take me. For a few weeks I was in a total funk.'

'No, no—'

'I got over it. Like Jarvis.'

'Jarvis tends to asthma.'

'That's what he told me. We sort of apologized to each other for being 4-F.'

'There's no need to apologize.'

'It's just the climate. I'll do my part in other ways.'

'Making people laugh is no small way.'

'It's okay. But you have two brothers in the war, and Everard's a conscientious objector working in that army hospital in New Jersey.'

'Nik, relax. Be happy your play's still drawing packed houses. Work on the new play.'

'Okay. Thanks. The David play. I eat, sleep, dream the David play. Music. I do want to have a lot of music in this play.'

Oklahoma! was playing on Broadway. Emma began to hum one of the hit songs, then stopped as she realized it was 'People Will Say We're in Love.'

'What's the matter?' Nik asked.

'Oh, the music in David's day would have been totally different from ours. I think even the scale wasn't the same. Much more Oriental.'

'David played the harp. Do you think Abigail was musical? We haven't anywhere nearly got to her yet, but she was David's second wife.'

Emma nodded. 'I know. Yes, I think Abigail would play the harp, too. She and David could play together—wouldn't that make a nice scene?'

Nik asked, 'How's your singing voice?'

'Okay. I've taken voice lessons off and on, and right now I'm studying with Madame Estavik.'

Nik was impressed. 'If she's taking you, you've got to be good.'

Emma shrugged. 'Just good enough to sing a small song with the harp. The lessons are good for my breath control. I'm not aiming for musicals, much less opera.'

They had reached David and Sophie's building and went into the marble lobby, greeting the doorman, the elevator man. Sophie was waiting for them.

'Angels. Sit at the table. I have a treat for you, don't I, Davie?'

'A treat, indeed.' David Wheaton led them into the dining room, where Sophie already had the candles lit in the brass sconces and in the silver candlesticks on the oval cherrywood table.

When they were seated, Sophie proudly brought in a silver dish of lobster Newburg. How did she manage it, in wartime?

'Sophie, you're a marvel,' Nik said, 'feeding the starving so miraculously.'

Sophie heaped his plate full. 'You're even scrawnier than Emma.'

'I won't be, if I go on eating like this.'

'I'm going to go double-check on Louis,' Sophie said. 'He's got a cold and I have the steamer going in his room. You go on and talk. I'll be back in a while.'

Nik looked after her. 'Bathsheba.'

David laughed. 'She comes in the right chronological order.'

'It has nothing to do with chronology.' Nik spoke with his mouth full. 'I just can't help visualizing Bathsheba as being like Sophie.' He pushed his long, thin fingers through his mop of dark curly hair.

It was unfair, Emma thought, that Nik should have luxuriant, lustrous hair, while hers went limp five minutes after it had been washed.

'All the battles—they get boring, and they would be impossible onstage. In a movie, maybe. What about a movie, Dave?'

'I want a play." David was firm. 'I know a movie would be easier, but I agree with you that all the battles are old hat. Let Cecil B. DeMille take care of that kind of stuff. We're interested in David's loves.'

'The women would have seen everything differently from the men. For instance, all of David's wives and concubines would have lived together in a harem. Emma, is there anything in your life which would make you understand that?'

'Sure, I lived in a harem myself for eight years, boarding school and college.'

'How did you feel about it?'

'I loved it. I'm not sure how I'd have felt if I'd been pulled from my stall in the library to go to the bed of some king. I guess a dorm and a harem are alike only in that there are a lot of women under one roof.'

'So you were in more like a convent than a harem?'

'Somewhere in between. There would be a few similarities. Friendship. I had wonderful friends. Some of them I keep up with, though none of my best friends are in New York. I spent part of the summer after Bahama died in Kansas with my roommate, because I knew that as an actress I needed to know more of the country than the East Coast and Seattle. Oh, dear, that sounds calculating, doesn't it?'

'Not necessarily.'

'I was still struggling with grief for Bahama, and my roommate was a supportive person. College was a very productive time for me.'

'Did you all get along together?'

'Most of the time.'

'Did you girls talk a lot about men and sex?'

'Oh, sure. But mostly I was putting it off, waiting to grow up. And I loved the whole academic aura, which you certainly wouldn't find in a harem.'

'Yeah.' Nik nodded.

'So.' David Wheaton sounded impatient. 'Enough of harems. Back to our protagonist, King David.'

'There's no question that he's our protagonist, but there'll be a good many featured roles, such as Zeruiah's sons, Abishai, Joab, and Asahel, who are so important politically, especially Joab.'

'You can manage a cast of thousands with a movie,' David said. 'It's not so easy with a play.'

'Shakespeare managed with *Lear*.'

'So you're the new Shakespeare?'

Nik shouted, 'I'm just saying it can be done!' He banged his fist on the table, so that the silverware clattered on the plates.

Sophie paused on her way through the dining room to the kitchen. 'Something wrong?'

'Everything's fine.' David said. 'Nik's explaining King David's genealogy. It's as complicated as mine. Sorry, Nik, didn't mean to bait you.'

Emma looked at Nik's long, fine fingers, at the dark, soft hairs springing from them, and wondered why he was suddenly jumpy.

'I'm glad you're getting it all straight,' David said.

'I'm not. I'm still just sorting out the characters. Trying to get used to all the names, maybe eliminate a few characters who aren't important to the play. Abigail is the most interesting of David's wives.'

'And of mine,' David said. 'I adore Sophie, but she's not— Well, she's just purely and enchantingly wonderful.'

'Hush!' Emma warned. But Sophie was singing in the kitchen, Noël Coward songs. Sophie could not stay on tune, but she sang with gusto and pleasure, and when she sang onstage the audience laughed and loved her.

'Zeruiah, for instance,' Nik said. 'She was a sensible, pragmatic woman who saw what was going on and had her own point of view about it. My mother was frequently hysterical, but my father goaded her. When she was at her best she was something like Zeruiah. Of course, she wasn't at her best very often, but—'

'You loved her,' David said.

'Yes. I loved her.'

'And your father?' David prodded.

'You mean, did I love him? Yes, I loved him.' He pulled a page from his pad. 'Here. Just take a quick look at this scene between Zeruiah and Asahel.'

'Asahel—Zeruiah's youngest son?' David queried.

'Right.'

David read, picking up one of Zeruiah's lines: 'Samuel was one of those strange babies born after his mother's courses had long ceased, and she was so grateful that she dedicated him to the Lord. I suppose she had to do what she promised, but I know I'd never take one of my little ones, barely able to piss against the wall, and send him to a crotchety old priest to be trained as a prophet.' He looked up. 'Piss against the wall— where'd you get that?'

Nik grinned. 'Right out of the King James Bible. I like it.

How you tell the men from the boys. Or, rather, the babes from the boys.'

'David's not in the scene?' David Wheaton asked.

'Don't worry, Dave, there'll be plenty for you, and more interesting than all the fighting-with-the-Philistines stuff.'

David went out to the kitchen to get more milk, and Emma picked up Nik's pages, reading silently a scene between Zeruiah and Asahel, followed by a scene between Zeruiah and Michal. There was too much talk. The play bogged down. Instead of showing Michal trying to protect David from her father, King Saul, by lowering David from a window and arranging the covers in the bed so they looked like a sleeping form, Zeruiah and Michal talked about it.

•

'Nik, I'm sorry, this scene won't play well.'

His dark eyes seemed to spark. 'What?'

'It won't play well. You usually show what's happening, and here you're telling. I know this is a rough draft, but what I think you're doing here is telling yourself the scene you're going to write.' Surely she should have known better than to criticize that bluntly.

His voice was cold. 'Any decent players could make it work.'

'But, Nik—'

'There is a certain amount of necessary exposition.'

'But, Nik, it isn't interesting.'

'What do you suggest that I do?'

'What I said—show the scene where Michal helps David escape. It's the one place we really see her love for David.'

'If I show everything, the play will last twelve hours. I have to get over a lot of historical information as quickly as possible.'

'It's too much the butler and the maid.'

He had flung the pages down on the table, banged them with his fist, shouted at her. 'You don't understand my play, what I'm trying to do.'

'Nik, stop, please—' She looked up as a burst of giggles came from the kitchen.

He had talked about his explosive temper, but this was the first time she had witnessed it. She felt cold in the pit of her stomach.

David returned, a smudge of lipstick on his nose, a bottle of milk in his hand, asking, 'What's going on?'

Nik stood up. He was shaking. 'I've just been unforgivably rude to your daughter. I'm sorry.' His voice was stiff. Apology did not come easily.

Emma said, 'Okay.' It wasn't okay, but there was nothing else to say.

With a great effort Nik sat down and controlled his voice. 'I don't want to make Zeruiah farcical, but you're right, Em.' He reached across the table and gently touched her fingers. 'These scenes between Zeruiah and Asahel, and Zeruiah and Michal, are dull, and I don't know what to do about them.'

'Do you need to use all of them?' Emma asked carefully. 'I

it, to see the information down on the page, then elf and what you need to

reasonable it was almost cold with shock from his rtly caused by her tact-

t necessary information?' which you can't put on o include how Saul meets goes looking for a seer.'

David asked, 'What's the difference between a seer and a prophet?'

Nik shrugged and looked at Emma, who said, 'Not much. There were prophets who went around in bands, having ecstasies. They got so excited they almost jumped out of their bodies. Ex-stasis: out of body.'

'My darling,' her father asked, 'how do you happen to know so much?'

'Grandpa Bowman and Bahama, of course.'

'And you remember,' her father said proudly, 'like a good actress. Does that bother you, Nik? That Emma knows so much about your subject?'

'You mean, am I jealous? I don't know. Probably. On the other hand, it's extremely helpful. Ecstasies and visions,' he mused, doodling circles on his pad. 'I can hear Zeruiah saying, "Samuel couldn't possibly move fast enough to have an ecstasy, but he claimed to talk personally with God."'

'You'd have to get a good character actress to carry Zeruiah,' David suggested.

'Dave, I thought Emma made it clear—this is embryonic. I'm just trying to work it out.'

'Sorry, Nik. I do tend to jump the gun, and it always gets me in trouble. And with Zeruiah you're working out your own feelings about your mother, aren't you?'

Nik nodded.

'Any particular problem today that's made you so prickly?' David raised his eyebrows, which were still dark despite his whitening hair, and looked at Nik with concern.

Nik laughed. 'Ah, Dave, you're perceptive. Yes. It's my mother's birthday. It would have been her sixtieth.'

Emma reached toward him, barely touching his fingers. 'Nik, I'm sorry.'

'Don't be, Em. I'm the one who's sorry. And yes, I'm working out my own stuff. My mother had that touch of second sight I'm giving Zeruiah. When she said goodbye to me when she and my father went on that last trip, she wept and told me they'd never see me again. My father was furious, and I didn't blame him. We both told her not to be idiotic, always looking for disaster. But she was right.'

'And you're feeling guilty?' David asked.

'Of course.'

'Wipe it out. False guilt, Nik, false. She should not have burdened you with her foresight, if indeed that is what it was. Leave it alone. Let her rest in peace.'

Nik rubbed his face, but when he took his hands down he was calm. 'Thanks, Dave. You're kind.'

'Not kind,' David Wheaton said. 'Truthful, I hope.'

'Yes. That you are. And your daughter is wise and wonderful, like David's Abigail, who won't come in until well into the second act.'

'No, Nik.' Emma shook her head. 'I'm neither wise nor wonderful.' She thought ruefully, —Please love me for what I am, Nik, not what you'd like me to be.

'Let me have my illusions.' Nik's smile was sweet, and in total contrast to his outburst. 'Now here's a scene about some crazy prophets you might like.'

'Those crazy prophets,' Emma suggested, 'were like whirling dervishes?'

'Yeah, pretty much,' Nik agreed.

'Have you ever done it? Whirled?'

He looked at her questioningly.

'When I was in boarding school, in the spring, when the trees were budding and we all had spring fever, we used to whirl, out on the grass of the hockey field. We'd whirl and twirl, round and round, till the sky and grass seemed to meet, and suddenly we were lying on the grass with the sky whirling around us. You never—?'

'I grew up in Brooklyn,' Nik said.

'I grew up in Manhattan. But there are hills in Central Park, and when I was a kid Adair showed me how to roll down them, rolling over and over, and at the bottom he'd pick me up and hold me until I wasn't dizzy, and we laughed, and then we'd do it again . . .'

She stopped as Nik stood up and started twirling himself around.

'No, no, not here,' David warned. 'Go in the living room.'

'You have to twirl faster and faster,' Emma said, 'and you need to be where there's space and if you fall you'll fall on the rug and you won't hit your head on something on the way down.'

Nik went to the living room, where there was a large open expanse on the great Chinese rug.

Nik said, 'I'd like to know what Saul felt like. I feel close to Saul, with his horrible moods.' He began to twirl again.

'Good. Faster, Nik, faster.' Emma, too, began to twirl. 'Just keep turning around,' she ordered. 'Keep your left heel on the floor. Pivot. Keep going. Terrific! Faster!'

The two of them twirled until Nik exclaimed, 'Holy moly! The floor's coming up to meet me!'

Emma fell to the rug beside him. 'I haven't done this in years. I'd forgotten how exciting it is.'

Nik reached for her. 'Ex-stasis. Truly wonderful. But now I'm back in my body.' His lips touched hers. Their mouths opened.

Finally Emma pulled away. 'Papa and Sophie are in the next room . . .'

Nik sat up. 'I'm still dizzy.'

Emma jumped to her feet, held out her hands to Nik, and helped him up.

'Saul,' he said. 'That's a new insight for me about Saul. Maybe about myself, too. Emma, I frightened you, didn't I?'

'Yes.'

'I'm sorry. I'll try not to lose control again. But I do understand Saul, with his ecstasies turning into black depressions, and his violent jealousy over David.'

The dining room was empty. David Wheaton and Sophie were either in the kitchen or had gone to check on Louis. Nik returned to his place at the table and flipped the pages of the Bible. 'Em, bear with me through this rough drafting. I need to move out of comedy, to do something completely new. And even with my comedies I do draft after draft, hacking away at my material until I find out what works and what doesn't. I know a lot of this is even worse than rough, but it's important for me to try to work through it to make it really real.'

·

What is real? They looked for their own reality in doing some of the classic New York excursions. They frequently walked from the theater on Forty-fourth Street to Emma's apartment on Fifty-fifth. She loved her apartment, an unusually large studio room, with a reasonable kitchen and a large dressing room and bath. Etienne had built bookshelves for her on one wall and made a special corner table for her record player. Chantal had given her a silk screen of a Picasso Harlequin for the wall, and Sophie had produced a cover for her bed, and a pile of colorful cushions. On the bed table were her favorite books, Bahama's Bible and Prayer Book, Stanislavsky's *An Actor Prepares* and *My Life in Art*, Arthur Hopkins's *To a Lonely Boy*, Chekhov's letters to his wife. She had a small sofa, a drop-leaf table, and a couple of comfortable chairs. It was a warm, spacious room. She loved her own place.

'But, darling,' Sophie protested, 'you don't need to move away! Louis will be devastated! Isn't your room big enough?'

'It's fine, Sophie, but I'm out of college now and I need to be on my own.'

'It's not that you don't feel welcome—' Sophie's voice was anxious.

'No, Sophie, of course not! And I'll come see you and Papa lots . . .'

And that she had done, always. But moving into her own apartment was a necessary rite of passage.

Adair agreed. 'No matter how grownup you are, you're still a little girl to Sophie, if not to your father.'

Emma had saved money. She could afford her studio—barely, but she could afford it. It was in easy walking distance of most theaters, and not too long a walk to David and Sophie's on Riverside Drive. Emma took Nik down to the Village to Chantal's frequently enough so that he was able to make friends with Chantal and Everard, with Jarvis. She and Nik took Louis to the movies, Inez to Rumpelmayer's for hot cocoa and cakes. 'I love your family,' Nik said. 'I'm an only child. You don't know how lucky you are.'

'Isn't Chantal beautiful?'

'She's so beautiful she terrifies me. I'm happier with your kind of beauty, subtle and surprising.'

They rode the Staten Island ferry. They took the Circle Line boat around Manhattan, becoming friendly with the young un-employed actor who was giving the spiel, and who was in awe when he found out who they were.

'But I saw your show!' he cried to Nik. 'It's amazing.' He turned to Emma. 'I don't think I'd have recognized you—' He broke off.

'It's okay,' Emma reassured him. 'As long as you recognize me onstage, that's enough.'

They rode in the front cars of subway trains, looking for abandoned subway stations, and spotting several. They spent hours in the Egyptian section of the Metropolitan Museum. And wherever they went, they talked about King David and his women.

'There are some amazing parallels,' Emma said, 'between Papa's wives and children and King David's.'

'But many more discrepancies,' Nik pointed out. 'What strikes me is that both Davids are men who love, and men who love are rare.' Nik was walking Emma to her father's apartment. Sophie had promised them fresh asparagus, though she would not tell them where she had found them out of season. He reached for her hand. 'It sounds terrible for me to say that my parents' death has freed me.'

'It isn't terrible,' Emma said, 'because it doesn't mean that you didn't love them.'

Nik groaned, ran his fingers through his tangled hair. No matter how cold it was, he never wore a hat. 'I loved them and I hated them and I loved them.'

'You were bound by them long after it was natural.'

Nik put her hand into the pocket of his new overcoat. 'You were unbound by your parents, long before it was natural. What a pair we are.'

'I think we're wonderful.' Emma's fingers tightened on Nik's, secure in the tweed pocket.

'Emma, do you realize that we couldn't be together the way we are if my parents were still alive? I'm nearly thirty. I've fallen in love before.'

They stopped for a red light, watching some sailors running across the street, dodging traffic, making it safely to the other side. Of course Nik had fallen in love before. It wouldn't be natural if he hadn't. It still made her feel cold. He was a normal man. She was a woman who had never had the dates that the ordinary American girl has. Without Adair, her social life would have been nonexistent. But on Parents' Day at college, when David was usually not free to come to her, Adair would appear, and would be surrounded by a flock of her friends, chattering like birds. 'He's your brother, Em? Wow!' He went out with Emma and two of her friends and their dates, and by the end of the evening their table was filled with other college students, male and female, and Emma suddenly found herself invited to a Dartmouth weekend. That had led to weekends at other colleges. On the whole, she did what she felt was moderately well, though she had not fallen in love, as had so many of her classmates.

'I don't have time to fall in love. I'm playing my second Oedipus, this one in Cocteau's *The Infernal Machine.*'

'Emma'—Nik's voice was urgent—'I know it could easily seem as though I'm pursuing you to get in with your father, but that's only the smallest part of it. It's *you* I'm after, you, Emma. And I'm free to pursue you. See, how my parents got rid of my girls was by drowning them with approval, by shoving them down my throat. The girls couldn't take it, and neither could I. God, Emma, is it too late for me to be my own Nik, not my parents'?'

'It's not too late,' she promised.

'I *still* sometimes think of the phone as a little black monster, compelling me to call, punishing me if I didn't.'

'How were you punished?' she asked gently.

'With love. They were so fearful. They needed to know I was safe. My father's godless world promised no security. My mother's God-filled world was too often filled with *dies irae.* If anything happened to me, it would be to punish her for marrying out of her faith. The phone was a line of safety for them.'

Bahama had taught Emma that the phone was for calling when you were going to be late. It was Bahama's prime rule: 'Go where you want to go after school, but let me know if you're going to be late.' There was no threat in it, no punishment. If Emma called to say that she was having dinner at the apartment of one of her classmates, that was fine. Bahama trusted her. But Emma would not be able to make to Nik the same request Bahama—and then Sophie—had made to her.

'Your father,' Nik asked, 'did he care where you were?'

'Bahama and Sophie did, and Papa knew that.'

'Why did you stay with him instead of with your mother?'

'My mother didn't want me. She was busy with her life in Hollywood.'

'Did she remarry?'

'Once. It was a failure. She wasn't the family type.'

'Do you go visit her?'

'I did, when I was a kid. Once. Some things—it's better to let go.'

'How old were you when your father married Sophie?'

'Not quite eleven.'

'How was it for you?'

'Wonderful. You know Sophie, and how much family means to her.'

'How is it that we manage at all,' Nik asked, 'with our weird backgrounds?'

'Maybe it's a strength?' Emma suggested. 'Maybe it's how we've learned to do what we do.'

.

How well had she learned?

Emma found it difficult not to go to the chart drawers and look for the scenes from Nik's play which her father had put there. When? Recently? Or years ago? The paper was yellowing and turning brittle.

No matter when David had put Nik's work in the chart drawers, this was the summer he was thinking about it. And for his sake Emma would have to call Nik. She did not dare trust the sporadic mail service to get a letter to him in time, so she would have to call him, see him again, here in the enforced intimacy of the *Portia*. She was not sure she could bear it.

·

We bear what we have to bear. Alice had told her that, and she knew it was true.

It was morning, and Emma and Alice sat out on the loading platform of the *Portia*, or what Bahama had called the back porch, sipping coffee. Alice had bathed David and given him breakfast. Ben was puttering about in the engine room before pulling up anchor.

"I'll go fishing this morning." Alice absently swirled the last of the coffee in her mug and put it down on the wide shelf she and Ben used for cleaning fish and other messy chores. A hose was coiled near her feet. "A red snapper would be good. Finish your coffee, Em. It's time we got moving if we're going to get to Bella Bella to meet Abby."

Something in Alice's tone made Emma ask, "Are you nervous?"

"A bit. Yes."

"Don't be. Abby's pure gold."

Alice laughed a little sadly. "Surely it isn't usual for ex-wives to come visit present wives."

"Nowadays it's not that uncommon. But I suppose not many ex-wives are godmothers to their stepdaughters. Abby's been marvelous to me, all my life. She's nearly eighty, though she doesn't look it or seem it. She's done a lot of living and she's learned a lot and she's willing to share. She's wise, and she's forbearing, and I love her."

"I hope she'll approve of me."

"Alice! She'll think you're wonderful. She'll be as grateful as I am for all you're doing for Papa."

Alice was sharp. "I don't want gratitude."

"I'm sorry. Abby'll love you, as I do, and not because of Papa, but for you yourself. When you meet Abby you'll relax. She's that kind of person."

Alice looked at the overcast sky. "David wants me—you— one of us, to call Sophie."

"I will."

"And Jarvis. I'll call him. I've become very fond of Jarvis, though there were times when you'd almost have thought he wrote *King Lear*." She laughed. "He's obviously a very successful producer."

Emma agreed. "Someone certainly has to have made a name for himself before he dares produce *Lear*, even with David Wheaton."

Alice frowned slightly. "Sometimes I thought we saw too much of Jarvis. He does like to run things."

"He runs them well," Emma said, "as long as it's a production of some kind. He's much less successful when it comes to running people. Especially people who don't want to be run."

"David can stand his own against Jarvis, or anybody else. Why hasn't Jarvis ever married?" Alice asked.

"Jarvis tends to adore older women. Papa's first wife, Meredith, for instance, and believe me, Papa did not approve of that, though Meredith put big money in some of Jarvis's early productions. Right now he's adoring Myra Hess—he does have good taste. But Jarvis does not want to make a commitment—except to his work."

Emma had been too young to know when Jarvis first went to Meredith during one of her long summers in the 'cottage,' suggesting that she back a play he was producing. The play was a surprise hit, and Meredith became one of Jarvis's chief 'angels.' David would not allow her to put money in anything he was playing in, and Emma was correct that he was not pleased at Jarvis's association with his first wife. But as long as Jarvis kept Meredith away from him, David let well enough alone.

"Here. Give me the mugs and I'll wash up," Emma said, "and you can get on with your fishing."

"Thanks, Em. We'll putter along for half an hour or so, and I'll look for a likely spot near a bunch of kelp. We should reach Bella Bella around two. I think Abby's plane should come in sometime between three and four, depending on the weather."

During the morning Alice caught a red snapper and a small

halibut, which she cleaned on the back deck, getting soaked as the clouds lowered and rain started to pour down.

"Rain we expect." Alice came into the main cabin, stamping and shaking herself like a dog. "But not the heavens opening. It's a moot point whether or not Abby's plane will be able to land."

"We'll just have to wait, then," Emma said.

"I know. I shouldn't be this nervous about Abby. Sorry. So you'll call Nik. And Sophie—and Louis, of course."

"In Bella Bella?"

Alice considered. "I don't want them coming too soon. Maybe the next time we dock to take on water. I'll call Jarvis. I just— I think we need this quiet time together before—"

·

It was remembering in tranquillity that helped her to understand. Billy. The closest she had come to understanding her eldest brother, Billy, was during her senior year in college when she was home for the Christmas holidays and Etienne, her stagemanager brother, took her to an opening of a play in which Billy had a featured role. It was a delicate role of a young man who felt himself to be a failure and who compensated for his disappointment with alcohol. Many of the lines were laugh lines, but it was a subtle role, and Emma knew enough about acting to know that Billy was not adequate. She knew that she could not compliment him honestly, and she was profoundly uncomfortable.

But after the performance Billy's dressing room was crowded with well-wishers, because Billy knew all the right people, and Etienne and Emma were swept along with the crowd to a private dining room at the Pierre, where the producer was giving the opening-night party. The audience had been wild with applause, and the cast was excited, waiting for the papers with the first reviews.

When they came, it was apparent that the play was a success. But Billy wasn't. He was accused of overacting, of not understanding his role, of not enough sympathy with his character.

'Aw, Billy, forget it.' One of the actresses had her arms about him. 'The guy always picks on someone to demolish in every show. You just happen to be his scapegoat this time.'

But Billy was devastated. He laughed too loudly and—like the character he did not fully comprehend—he drank too much.

Etienne swore. 'Billy doesn't drink and he can't hold it. Let's try to get him home before he makes too big a fool of himself.'

Together they went over to Billy, who was swaying slightly on his feet.

'It's late, Billy,' Etienne said. 'I'm going to take Emma home. Why don't you come along? We'll drop you on the way.'

'I'm on the East Side,' Billy said. 'The pater's on the West. Want to take me down to Chantal's, gorgeous Chantal's?'

'Chantal will have been in bed and asleep for hours.'

'Beautiful girl, your sister,' Billy said. 'Too beautiful. Worry about her.'

'Chantal's fine.' Etienne tried to take Billy's arm.

Billy shook him off. 'But a heathen. All you Mooréans are heathens.'

'Hey, Billy!' Emma was indignant.

Etienne's voice was heavy with patience. 'Billy, you're drunk.'

'Emma.' Billy reached toward her and Emma instinctively pulled away. 'Emma, you're a good girl.'

'Not very.' She was awkward with embarrassment.

'You're a little Miss Priss who's never been kissed. Let's fix that.' He leaned toward her.

Etienne put the flat of his hand against Billy's chest and pushed him away. 'Billy, that's enough.'

Billy sloshed champagne over his shirt. 'You all are mean to me.' Tears came to his eyes.

Etienne put his arm about his half brother. 'Billy. You're okay. Come along.'

'Shit,' Billy said. 'Oh, shit.' He wiped tears away with the back of his hand.

But he came along.

·

'Don't mind Billy,' Etienne said to Emma, after they had delivered him to his apartment. 'He was drunk.'
'I know.'
'He's not subtle. Not in his acting. Not in his life. Poor sod.'
'His reviews were cruel.'
'But deserved.'
'I feel sorry for him,' Emma said.

·

Adair tried to explain Billy to Emma.
'Look, Em, you're bright. And Billy's not. That's something you can't understand. I mean, it's simply not possible for highly intelligent people to understand people who are not. Father is, and Myrlo isn't. Myrlo has smarts, but her brain is below her navel, and Billy's got Myrlo's genes as far as his brain is concerned.'
'Are you being fair?' Emma asked.
'Fair is precisely what I'm trying to be. When I get irritated by Billy I have to try to remember that he just isn't very bright. Myrlo and your father got him through high school with special tutoring, but he didn't go to college.'
'Because he went right to work in the theater.'
'Because he couldn't have got through his freshman year. Don't try to understand it, Em. You can't. But make allowances.'
It was ironic that it should have been Adair who tried to get Emma to make allowances for Billy.
'Billy's stepfather,' Adair said, 'the insurance broker, Wilburton. He's bad for Billy.'
'Why?'
'He buys Billy with his money and makes him want things he can't have.'
'Such as?'
'Oh, being a big financial success like Wilburton.'
'But Billy doesn't want to sell insurance. He's an actor.'

'He's not in Papa's league. And why are we still calling him Billy at his age?'

'Poor Billy.'

'Yes, Emma, poor Billy.'

Emma loved Etienne and Everard, yes, and Jarvis. But Adair was her favorite brother.

·

Adair came to see everything she played in, not just once, but night after night, often taking her to the Russian Tea Room or the Village Vanguard for supper, and making suggestions about her performances which were almost always right. Adair should have been a director.

'No theater for me.' Adair was firm. 'I want to enjoy life, not worry about whether someone's name on the marquee is in letters as large or larger than mine. Anyhow, I don't have the passion for it. The talent, which I probably do have, is not enough. You have both the talent and the passion, Emma, and when you come onstage something happens. It's as though you bring a light on with you.'

Yes, when she stood in the wings waiting to go on, something happened. Emma the shy, the reticent, disappeared. She felt as she thought a race horse must feel at the starting line, waiting for the signal to begin the race. Her blood coursed more swiftly in her veins. She was completely caught up in her role, while at the same time she was distanced, standing, as it were, outside her body, in order to be able to go onstage with confidence. Her adrenaline pumped at just the right rate so that she was completely alert, aware. Excited and joyful.

Adair said, 'If any of my suggestions are helpful to you, I'm happy. I love you, and I want you to be happy, too.'

'I'm happy when I'm working,' Emma said.

'There's more to life than work, Emma. Let's go to Chantal's tonight and make some music.'

Chantal had wanted Emma to share her apartment in the Village, the parlor floor of a brownstone, but once she was out of college, Emma needed her own space, her own privacy. She had had enough of roommates. And Chantal's apartment, now that Marical was living in Connecticut, had become a general gathering place. If Emma hadn't insisted on taking the apartment on Fifty-fifth Street, would things have been different?

—Don't hindsight, Emma, she reprimanded herself.

·

Chantal had hung the walls of her apartment with panels of colored silk instead of pictures. Her living room had little furniture, but gave a sense of graciousness. The largest piece was an old and fine upright piano, over which she had hung a blown-up photograph of Einstein with his violin. Chantal was more serious with her violin than Adair with the piano, practicing at least an hour a day.

'Let me represent you,' Jarvis begged her, one evening when both he and Emma had come down to the Village.

Chantal laughed. 'Jarv, dear, you know perfectly well I'm not a first-class musician.'

'You're good enough. I could at least get you nightclub bookings. My God, Chantal, you're so beautiful, all you'd have to do is walk out on the stage, tuck your violin under your chin, and every heart in the audience would melt.'

Chantal was indeed beautiful. Marical had bequeathed her daughter a regal bearing as well as her Polynesian beauty, and from David, Chantal had flair and sophistication, and gold-green eyes. Her fine, straight black hair fell below her waist. Her beauty had a delicacy beyond that of the women in Gauguin paintings.

'Thank you, Jarvis, but no thank you.'

Jarvis pulled out a long ivory-and-silver holder and inserted a cigarette. When it was lit he turned to Emma. 'What's wrong with you two? Why won't you let me represent you, Emma? You can't pretend you don't have a first-class talent.'

Emma said flatly, 'Jarvis, you're my brother.'

'Only half. I represent Billy.'

'Fine. Good for both of you.'

'Then—'

'No, Jarvis.' Jarvis might push her more quickly up the ladder than she could go without him, but he would want to manage not only her acting career but her whole life. She loved Jarvis, but she never regretted her decision.

The front door burst open and Adair bounced in. 'All hail, siblings! Let's make music.' Adair played the piano rather recklessly for Bach or Beethoven, but he could pick up any Broadway melody. He managed a large and popular music and record store, infecting his customers with his own enthusiasm.

Jarvis hit his hand against his forehead in mock despair. 'You Mooréans! Why can't you be serious?'

Adair continued to play, shifting into a medley of songs from recent Broadway hits. 'Serious? Who's not serious? I manage the best music store in New York. In another few years I'll own it. I have an apartment in Brooklyn Heights with a magnificent view of the harbor—if I lean halfway out my bedroom window. I'm in love with three different girls. What more could any man want?'

'Success?' Jarvis suggested.

'But I am a success.'

'Fame?'

'Hell, no. We've got more than enough fame for any one family. And has it made anyone happy? Is Papa happy?'

'Isn't he? He's in a hit show. Everyone knows he's a great actor.'

Adair said, 'He wasn't happy enough in himself to stay with my mother.'

Jarvis smirked. 'No. He met my mother.'

'Right, the famous ballerina. And then he met Emma's mother—'

'Okay, guys, stop it,' Emma said. 'Here we are, brothers and sisters, with one father and three mothers, but I wouldn't give any one of us up.' She blew Jarvis a kiss. 'Papa is Papa, and I agree with Chantal and Adair, we've got enough fame for one family.'

'We do pretty well.' Jarvis sounded satisfied. 'Your mother's a star in Hollywood, Em, and surely she's pleased that you're making a good beginning in the theater.'

Emma raised her eyebrows and looked skeptical, but Jarvis continued. 'You're going to go far.'

Emma sighed. 'I'm an actress because it's the one thing I know how to do.'

'And you love it,' said Adair.

'Sometimes.'

'Of course you love it,' Jarvis said. 'You'll even love being famous.'

Adair shook his head. 'Fame has too many penalties. But Emma's stuck with being a good actress and has no choice.'

Emma opened her hands in apology, or denial. 'I'm far from being famous. All I want is a chance to act, to bring my roles to life on the stage.'

'And why do you want to do this?' Jarvis demanded. 'If not for fame?'

Emma looked startled. 'It's what I do—it's my talent—'

'But what's it worth?'

Adair interrupted. 'Leave Emma alone. As she said, it's what she does, and it gives pleasure—and hope—to many people.'

Emma added, 'It's a way of giving life—of making real.'

'Playacting.' Jarvis's voice was not unkind. 'Mimicking life.'

'No,' Emma denied. 'It's not mimicking. It's deeper . . .' She was flushed with the intensity of her feeling.

Adair added, 'And if Emma gives the audience this deeper reality, then their ordinary, daily lives take on new meaning. Do you understand that, Jarvis?'

'High-flown sentiment.' Jarvis lit another cigarette.

'But true,' Adair said.

'For some, maybe,' Jarvis conceded. 'Not everybody.'

'Maybe not for people like Billy who want the glamour without the work, but it's true for Emma. She searches for the really real, and that's no small search. Okay, sibs, music. Chantal, where's your violin?'

'Under your nose.' Chantal gestured to the violin case on top of the piano.

But Jarvis wasn't through. 'And what about our little sister, Inez? How's she going to find out who she is, or what she's going to do, if Edith keeps her isolated from the rest of the family?'

Adair laughed ruefully. 'Poor little Inez. She's all legs and knobby knees and elbows. We have a little sister, and she hath no breasts.'

'She's only twelve,' Jarvis said.

'Song of Songs.' Emma smiled at him. 'Adair's quoting from the Song of Solomon.'

Adair banged on the keys. 'Enough! Music! Emma, sing.' He began to play, softly, one of the newly rediscovered folk songs, *Black is the color of my true love's hair*. Emma sang the words in her clear, light voice, and Chantal wove an obbligato on her violin. Jarvis sighed and sat on one of the bright cushions Chantal used for chairs.

When the song was over, Jarvis applauded perfunctorily, then said, 'Chantal, you have a flair for interior decoration. Why don't you take it up?'

Chantal made a face. 'I enjoy doing it for myself, or helping Emma. That's enough.'

'You could be a model, like your mother.'

'I like my job at the Museum of Modern Art.'

'As a secretary.'

'Jarvis, dear, like Adair, I enjoy my life.'

Suddenly Jarvis was defensive. 'I enjoy mine, too. Listen, are all you guys coming to my ma's farewell performance?'

'Of course.' Adair played a series of major chords. 'Wild horses couldn't keep us away.'

'I've asked Billy.' Jarvis stubbed out his cigarette. 'He says he'll come.'

·

They had a box for Harriet's last performance as a prima ballerina. The whole family was there except for David, Sophie, and Louis, who were in Chicago, where David was playing in a revival of *Trelawny of the Wells*.

Harriet was cool and gracious with her stepchildren, unlike Edith, who was cool and ungracious, and would have separated herself and Inez from the family entirely had not Inez been so stubbornly determined to be part of the close-knit group of siblings.

—Everybody except Papa, Sophie, and Louis? Emma asked herself. The absence of Edith and Myrlo was simply taken for granted.

It was an emotional evening, with Harriet performing her most popular roles. At the final curtain the audience erupted into applause. Bouquet after bouquet was brought onto the stage and put in Harriet's arms as she bowed, curtsied, blew kisses to the top balcony. Then, suddenly, the stage was pelted with roses, thrown from all over the theater, from all the boxes and balconies. Inez leaned dangerously out of the box as she threw the flowers Jarvis had provided for her, with Adair holding her back. Tears were streaming down Emma's cheeks as she hugged Jarvis. Chantal kissed him. Adair shouted, 'Brava! Brava!' Etienne and Everard pounded their hands together. Billy thumped Jarvis on the shoulder.

'Well!' There were tears in Jarvis's eyes as the theater slowly quieted, the curtain closed for the final time, and the audience started moving up the aisles to the exits. 'My ma did us proud, didn't she?'

'More than proud,' Adair affirmed.

'We won't go backstage.' Jarvis's voice was rich with pride. 'No point trying to get through the mob.'

'We'll need two Checker cabs,' Chantal said. 'I have champagne in the fridge and I've made sandwiches.'

Billy said, 'Myrlo and Will are waiting for me, and I promised Edith I'd bring Inez home right after the performance.'

Inez pouted. 'It's not fair.'

'Inez, honey.' Billy had his arm about the little girl. 'Come along with big brother Billy. We'll stop in the drugstore and I'll buy you a soda.'

They were being swept along with the crowd. Inez finally let Billy take her off.

After most of the mob had poured out of the theater, they started to walk downtown to get away from the crowd. They had gone nearly ten blocks before Jarvis was able to hail a Checker cab.

As they piled in, Adair said, 'Your ma was splendid, Jarv. What a great evening!'

'What'll she do now?' Etienne asked. 'Won't it be a horrible letdown?'

'Yeah, she'll hit bottom with a bang. But she's going to teach, and she'll dance occasionally for a benefit, or for one of the regional companies. She'd have liked me to be a dancer. It might have been good for my asthma, but I didn't want a career with such an early-age cutoff. If Papa'd been a dancer instead of an actor, he'd have had to retire years ago. And instead he's at the height of his powers.'

Everard and Emma were on the jump seats. Etienne was in front with the driver. Everard said, 'Too bad Billy wouldn't come with us.'

Emma said flatly, 'He said Myrlo and his stepfather were waiting for him.'

'On Park Avenue, in their duplex.' Adair, sitting between Jarvis and Chantal, grinned at Emma.

Everard said, 'I suppose he's a good enough actor, a bit self-indulgent. A lion hunter and ladder climber.'

'Why do you guys always dump on Billy?' Jarvis accused. 'He's been very helpful to me, giving me contacts, letting me represent him.'

Etienne said, 'Here we are. I'll pay, and then we can figure what you all owe me.'

As she put her key in the lock and opened her door, Chantal said, 'Billy's older than the rest of us, and Myrlo and her tycoon think we're pagans and keep him away from us. We're half Mooréan, remember? We're sort of nothings in their eyes.'

Were they? Emma wondered. Or did Billy feel inadequate set against the quicksilver of Marical's children?

'And whose fault is that?' Jarvis pulled out his silver lighter and lit the cigarette he had carefully placed in a new and even longer silver-and-ivory holder. Emma and Chantal looked at each other and repressed grins.

Everard queried, 'Hey, Jarv, is that good for your asthma?'

Ignoring the question, Jarvis said, 'Just because Billy's ambitious, like me—'

Everard spoke quietly. 'Sorry, Jarv. We did sound snide. But you know Billy doesn't bother with us. He prefers being with the rich and famous.'

'Father's not famous enough for him?' Chantal demanded.

'You know what I mean. He just isn't one of us.'

'Because he doesn't want to be,' Etienne said. 'Hey, gang, I have news. I've been accepted by the navy. I start training next week.'

Chantal put her hand to her mouth. 'Oh, God—'

'Etienne—' Emma looked at her brother in shock.

Adair was sitting at the piano; he ran his finger up the keyboard in a long glissando. 'We came here to celebrate with Jarv.' He began to play and sing a Marlene Dietrich song, and Emma joined him.

'See?' Jarvis was triumphant. 'Now Emma is Dietrich. Amazing!'

Adair shifted to 'Stormy Weather,' and Emma leaned against the piano in a sexy position, holding an imaginary cigarette, and singing. In the corner of her mind was fear for Etienne. She had forgotten Billy.

·

'Don't reject Billy,' David Wheaton warned Emma one night when she'd been to see his show and gone backstage afterwards. He was taking off his makeup, and wearing the Chinese robe which Meredith had given him, and which was still beautiful.

'Didn't he reject us when he called himself Wilburton?'

'He was sniping at me,' David said, 'and it wasn't very bright of him. The name Wheaton could open doors.'

'You still help him.'

'When I can. Try to be patient with him.'

'We try.'

'Not very hard. You discount him, you and Marical's kids.'

'Papa, we don't mean to be snobbish about him.'

'Billy's good-looking, but looks aren't everything. He'll do well enough in the theater, but only well enough.'

'I know.'

'He feels inferior to the rest of you.'

'Billy!'

'Yes, Emma, Billy. You outshine him, and he knows it. Inez is the only one of you who doesn't threaten him. Louis is one of the child singers at the Met, and he's done well in the couple of movies Sophie's let him do.'

'I never thought of it that way.'

'Do.' David tightened the cap on his bottle of witch hazel.

'I'm sorry, Papa. We all thought—well, Billy's never tried to be one of us.'

'Because he can't be.'

·

But Nik was. Emma was grateful at how quickly her family had accepted him, how much they seemed to like him. She had been with him at Chantal's one evening after the theater, eating large quantities of spaghetti, and they were walking uptown, needing exercise before they took the subway.

'I'll want to use music as a bridge between scenes. Michal can be a singer, I think. That will help give her role plausibility and depth.' Nik was, as usual, concentrated on his King David play. 'What I'd like, of course, is original music if it could possibly be arranged. Of course, I'm thinking Very Big.'

'Why not?' Emma asked. 'Nothing ventured, nothing gained. Etc.'

They crossed the street. Fifth Avenue was nearly deserted and a cold wind was blowing. They walked west, over to Sixth. 'I don't want your father to think I'm getting too big for my shoes.'

'Write the play you want, Nik, and then you can decide what needs to be cut back.'

'Okay. You're right. Now. We've established Saul as big and strong and handsome and a good warrior.'

Emma grinned. 'Hewing oxen. And Samuel hewed Agag. There was a lot of hewing.' Nik put his arm around her and they laughed. They turned up Sixth Avenue and a half-empty bus wheezed by.

'There needs to be a strong scene where David and Jonathan make vows of friendship. Jonathan gave David his armor, a particular sign of friendship, and that means David has attained full growth. Jonathan, being Saul's son, would not be small.'

'Father's six feet tall. Given good makeup, he can look amazingly young.'

'I'm not worried about that,' Nik said. 'He can carry the early scenes with no trouble.' He stopped and looked around. 'Hey, we're at Twenty-third. Want to take the subway here?'

She held her face up to the night air, faintly stinging, but refreshing. 'I'd just as soon go on walking.'

'Saul's jealousy explains his offering his daughter to David in marriage, and then sending David into the thick of battle, thinking the Philistines will kill him. A nice foreshadowing of what David succeeds in doing later with Uriah the Hittite.'

'Saul does ugly things.' Emma shivered a little, and Nik tightened his arm about her. A taxi slowed down, suggestively, but Nik waved it on. 'But horrible as jealousy is, I do understand it in Saul.'

'Emma?'

'What?'

'What about jealousy in your own family? I'm an only child, but what about you and all your brothers and sisters?'

Emma stopped walking for a moment, then said, 'Oh, Nik, I don't know. Not now. Certainly never with—with Adair and

Etienne. Or Everard or Chantal. You know Ev and Chantal. They like what they're doing, they like their own lives, and they've been marvelous about supporting me.'

'Jarvis?'

'Jarvis likes to run things, to run *us*, but I don't think jealousy comes into it. And darling Louis is still a kid, and whether or not his boy soprano voice will turn into a decent tenor or baritone later is anybody's guess.'

'That's good,' Nik said. 'It makes me wish I'd had the fun of growing up with brothers and sisters.'

'We didn't exactly grow up together,' Emma said, 'but somehow or other, we *were* together.'

'Hey, it's late, and you're tired,' Nik said. 'Let's take the subway here at Twenty-eighth.'

'Okay.'

They stood on the platform, hearing a train in the distance. Two sailors sat on one of the benches, half asleep. A very tall man in a soldier's uniform walked impatiently up and down. The train pulled into the station. The soldier prodded the two sailors to wake them and hurried into the car as the doors opened. 'We're lucky,' Nik said. 'I think they've been waiting for a long time.' They went into the train and sat down.

'Em,' he continued, 'I'm having a hard time making Michal real. Did she love David?' The train swayed, throwing Emma against Nik, and his arm tightened about her to steady her. 'What do you think?'

'I think David was the one bright thing in her life. He was a musician and a poet. All the things Saul was not.'

'And Saul saw and knew that the Lord was with David. And not with him. And I'm sure he was jealous of the way women adored David.' Nik stood up, helping Emma to her feet. The train pulled into the station and the doors opened. They stepped out onto the dimly lit platform smelling of damp and cold.

As they walked up the steps, Emma said, 'David kept on doing everything right because the Lord was with him.' She frowned.

'It bothers me.' The fresh air of the street felt welcome as she breathed it in.

'What, hon?'

'Do you think the Lord chooses one side in a battle and helps that side to win?'

'I haven't the faintest idea.'

Despite the tinge of impatience in his voice, Emma continued. 'But that's what's implied, isn't it? That when David fought, the Lord was with him, and so his enemies were defeated. And I know that there are people now who believe that God is on our side in this horrible war, and God doesn't care how many Germans or Italians or Japanese people are killed. And I hope God *is* on our side—I mean, this is not an equivocal war, I do believe that it has to be fought, and I don't want Adair or Etienne risking their lives in vain, but—'

'But?'

She looked down at her feet. The toes of her kid pumps were slightly scuffed. 'But, Nik—there have to be people in Germany praying that God is on their side. And believing it.'

'Probably. And presumably God, if there is a God, loves the Germans as much as he loves us. War between his children must be painful for God. It's not easy.'

.

—It doesn't get any easier, Emma thought, looking out the *Portia*'s windows at the rain that continued steadily. It was getting on toward evening and they were still waiting for Abby to arrive.

—Back when Nik was working on the David play, Russia was our ally, and now we're terrified of Russia and we're all palsy-walsy with Germany and Japan.

She looked at Alice to ask, "Was war as crazy in King David's day as in ours? Or was it just easier then to think that God was on your side?"

But Alice was sitting with her eyes closed, her hands clasped loosely about her knees.

Emma picked up some of Nik's pages she had brought from the pilothouse to the main cabin and held them loosely. Remembering.

·

Nik said, 'It's not an easy question you're raising, Em. It involves trying to understand right and wrong. Where we sit now, war is always wrong, even when it's inevitable, like this one. The First World War broke the backbone of the century and nothing has been the same since.'

'Grandpa told me, years ago, when I was studying Joan of Arc, that there was a time in the First World War when there was a battle between a small French force and a much bigger German one and there was no way the French soldiers could have won. But they did, and some of the men said that they had seen Joan of Arc and her warriors fighting with them. Do you think something like that is possible?'

'Good heavens, Em, you're in the realm of fantasy. My mother loved stories like that, and my father said they were hogwash. As for me, I don't know.'

'I hate this war. I'm terrified Adair and Etienne will get killed.'

'Of course you hate it, sweetie. I do, too. Here we are. Give me a good-night kiss.'

It was a long kiss.

Then Nik broke away. 'You're so patient with me about my play.'

'Hey, I love it!' —I love you.

'We'll get to Abigail soon, I promise you. She's by far the most complete and complex of David's wives. She'll be a good role for you. A tough one. Michal or Bathsheba would be much easier. But Abigail's got the meat.'

Abigail

❦ ❦ ❦

And it came to pass . . . that the soul of Jonathan was knit with the soul of David, and Jonathan loved him as his own soul.

Then Jonathan and David made a covenant . . . And Jonathan stripped himself of the robe that was upon him, and gave it to David, and his garments, even to his sword, and to his bow, and to his girdle.

I SAMUEL 18:1, 3–4

BEN LOOKED in the cabin. "Abigail is here."

Emma and Alice, roused from their respective reveries, hurried out on deck. An old school bus, which had met Abby's small plane, was pulling up to the dock. Two rough-looking fishermen pushed out, then turned with great deference and helped Abigail Wheaton down the steep step to the ground.

Emma ran toward her. Abby graciously thanked the fishermen, then held out her arms to Emma.

Emma held her godmother closely, smelling the faint, familiar scent of Chypre. "Oh, Abby, Abby, I'm so glad you're here!"

"So am I." Abby pressed her soft cheek against Emma's. "The plane started to land a couple of hours ago and couldn't, and we went all the way back to Vancouver. I didn't think we'd make it this time, either, but there was a sudden opening in the clouds and in we came."

"Come and meet Alice and Ben."

If Alice and Ben found the introductions to David Wheaton's second wife difficult, Abby's graciousness quickly put them at ease. Ben held a large umbrella over her, though the rain had slackened to a drizzle, and helped her up onto the deck and into the main cabin. She turned to Alice, questioning. "David—"

"He's waiting for you, Mrs.—Countess—"

"Abby."

"We've made up the bunk in the pilothouse for him. He's weak and thin, but—"

"Still David."

"Very much so."

"I will go to him." Abby turned and went up the three steps to the pilothouse.

Alice said, "She's brave."

Emma looked after Abby's erect back. "She's had practice."

Ben said, "We won't stay here tonight, even though it's later than we planned. Dave never likes the nights we spend tied up at the dock."

Alice agreed. "He likes the motion of the boat."

"Need any help?" Emma asked Ben.

"Sure. In a bit. I'll need Alice at the wheel, and I don't want to disturb Dave and Abby more than necessary."

Emma checked the oven, where a casserole was keeping warm. She had made salad and had prepared a mixture of leeks and carrots. Everything was ready; there was nothing left to do. She felt an irrational surge of hope that Abby would somehow make everything all right.

Make what all right? David Wheaton was dying.

·

Emma and Alice were in the main cabin, waiting for Abby, who was in the pilothouse with David. Emma put down the scene from Nik's play she had been reading, her eyes bleak. She looked at Alice. "I don't know why I'm reading this stuff after all these years. Papa's dying. It's too late."

"Not for you," Alice said. "You could still play Abigail."

"Nik's not likely to finish it for me. Not now. But you know, Alice, I couldn't play it with Papa. I've played his daughter several times, and I've loved that, even Goneril. But it just wouldn't work for me to play Papa's wife. It would be—oh, sort of Oedipal."

Alice laughed. "Or Electracal—wasn't Electra Oedipus' daughter?"

Emma laughed, too. "No. Antigone was. When Nik was writing the play, well, we were young, and I thought I could do anything. Not now.'

Alice looked at Emma with her straightforward blue gaze. In the soft light the weathering of her face was gentled. The rain had stopped, and long shafts of pale sun slanted in through the starboard windows.

Emma glanced toward the pilothouse, then at her watch. Sighed, then continued. "David escaped from Saul and was with Samuel in Ramah. And here's another of these weird incidents. Saul sent his men to Ramah to kill David, but when they got there, they saw Samuel with a band of wandering prophets, singing and having ecstasies, and the assassins started singing and having ecstasies, too. Alice, what do you think of this religious ecstasy stuff?"

Alice shrugged. "It's not my way."

"You think it's an okay way?"

Alice shrugged again. "So what happened next?"

"Saul joined the prophets and the assassins in singing and dancing, and prophesying. Speaking in tongues, I guess. Grandpa said that 'tongues' is the language of angels, including the fallen ones, and we have to be careful which ones we listen to."

"Did your grandfather speak in tongues?"

"Yes. I heard him once. I was about six, and I'd climbed up into a live-oak tree and the branch I was on broke and I fell and banged my head and had the wind knocked out of me. I thought I was dead, and Grandpa picked me up in his arms and cried out to God, and then the lovely liquid syllables poured over me like water, and the air rushed into my lungs and I breathed again. And then he started to cry. I felt very much loved."

Alice touched her gently on the shoulder. "Yes. Having your wind knocked out is scary if you don't understand what's happened."

"Well, back to Saul"—Emma smiled at Alice—"joining in with the band of prophets. It doesn't make a great deal of sense.

But it might make a good scene if it was properly choreographed. Nik thought Jerry Robbins could do something terrific with it." She looked up as Abby came down the steps from the pilothouse. The older woman was dressed casually in a blue cotton skirt and shirt, with a pale yellow cardigan over her shoulders; she looked very much a countess as she came into the main cabin, pulled out a chair, and sat.

"David says we'll eat up in the pilothouse with him."

"Yes. We'll take up a couple of folding tables," Emma said.

Alice rose. "Ben will want to untie now and move on for the night. He's put your bag down in the lower cabin—but you've been on the *Portia* before, haven't you?"

Abby nodded.

"We've some new flannel sheets for the double bed, so it ought to be cozy."

"Good. Thank you."

"There are some curtains that pull around the bed for privacy," Alice continued.

Emma smiled. "When I sleep there I feel that I'm in a little nest when the curtains are closed. Excuse me for a few minutes, Abby, while I go help Ben."

When she came back Ben had nosed the *Portia* into quiet waters between two islands, and Alice was saying, "Emma's doing all the cooking and making me feel like a lily of the field."

"You're hardly that," Emma said, "and it's therapy for me."

Abby looked steadily at Alice, asking, "How long does David have?"

"A few weeks. Maybe."

"Is it going to be bad? The pain, I mean?"

"Not if I can help it. And I think I can. In a way, I wish his heart wasn't so strong."

"Thank you. I'm grateful beyond words that David has a fine doctor to help him now. But it's not easy when it's your husband who's your patient."

"No."

"I'm glad you and Emma are friends."

"True friends."

Abby spoke gently. "Your father told me you and Nik are not together. I'm sorry."

Best to have it out in the open with Abby, get it over with. "Yes. Well. I'm still struggling with old garbage." Emma looked at her feet. There was a hole in her tennis shoe where her toe poked through. Abby looked at her questioningly. Emma turned on the seawater tap at the sink and ran her hands under the cold water. Then, to Alice, "How about a bottle of wine with dinner?"

Alice glanced swiftly at Emma. "Good idea. I'll get one from the hospitality hole." She rose and opened a large trapdoor, went down a ladder to a storeroom filled with boxes, cans, jars, food that didn't need refrigeration, and returned with a bottle, which she put in the fridge, then lowered the trap. Asked Abby, "Would you like a glass of sherry before dinner?"

"No, thanks. I'm a bit tired from all the traveling, plus the time change, so a glass of wine with dinner will be ample for me." She pulled a small sketchbook out of the canvas bag that hung over her arm. Then she asked, "Do I have time to unpack before we eat? It will take me only a few minutes."

"Sure," Emma said. "There are some hangers on the rod at the foot of the bed, and I've cleared some space in one of the lockers."

"Thanks, that's splendid. And my suitcase will slide easily in and out from under the bed."

"Do you need anything?" Alice asked. "Blue jeans? We have a pile of spares of all sizes."

Abby shook her head. "Thanks, I'm not a jeans person. I brought some winter underwear, if I need it."

Alice looked after Abby as she headed for the lower cabin, holding on to the rail as though her knees were troubling her. "I hated silk stockings and city clothes in New York, and Dave does like me to dress up. He buys most of my clothes for me."

"He loves you and he knows what suits you," Emma said.

"I hope Ben will dock us somewhere soon where there's a laundromat. All my clothes are beginning to smell like fish."

She looked at Emma. "It still strikes me as unusual—that you're her godchild. That she and your father—they love each other very much, don't they?"

Emma agreed. "But it's quite possible to love more than one person. I mean, it doesn't take away any of Papa's love for you."

"I know that," Alice said. "At least, I think I do."

That struck a chord, and Emma remembered a brief scene in Nik's play where Zeruiah is reassuring Abigail that David loves her despite his taking other wives.

And Abigail's reply was the same as Alice's: "I know that. At least, I think I do." Following her own train of thought, Emma said, "Abigail was secure enough in herself—the Abigail in Nik's play—and certain enough of David's love to allow other people to love him."

"Thousands of people love your father," Alice said. "Do you know how many fan letters a week he gets?"

"Don't tell me. Lots. But that's a different kind of love."

Alice laughed. "And not threatening at all, even when women offer to marry him and give him fortunes and even buy him villas." She picked up one of the folding tables and started up to the pilothouse. Emma watched her, then turned as she heard Abigail Wheaton on the steps from the lower cabin. "Alice has just gone to the pilothouse. Why don't you go on up?"

"Anything I can do to help?"

"Everything's all set. I just have to bring up the casserole. Oh, Abby, I'm glad you've come."

"I'm glad I could come. And I'm grateful that your father can die here on the *Portia*, in these beautiful waters where he's spent so many happy times."

"Abby, I know he's old, and I wouldn't want him to live and not be fully himself, but—"

"But it's hard," Abby finished for her. "It's not easy to let go those we love."

"You've had to do a lot of letting go, haven't you?"

"A lot. It's never easy." She held out her hand to Emma and they went up to the pilothouse, where David was talking to Ben.

Alice was sitting in the revolving chair. With five of them, the pilothouse was crowded. Emma put the steaming casserole on the wide shelf above her father's bunk. Alice had already placed the salad and vegetables there, and fresh bread.

"I think the simplest thing is for us to help ourselves," Emma suggested. "You go first, Alice, and fix a plate for Papa."

"When the others come," David said, "you'll have to eat down in the main cabin."

"Meanwhile," Abby said, "this is nice and cozy. Where are we, Ben?"

"I'll show you on the chart after dinner."

"Abby—" David's voice trembled slightly. "I don't want Myrlo to come."

"Don't worry, love. Myrlo's too old, and she has terrible arthritis. Sophie and Louis will want to be with you, of course."

"Dear Sophie," David murmured. "I drove her away with my black despair. I have much to answer for."

"As do we all," Abby said calmly.

David looked quizzically at his daughter. "Your mother, Emma, left the orbit of our lives a long time ago."

Emma returned his look, saying calmly, "She's tied down to her contract in Hollywood."

"Harriet," David continued, "is busy with her ballet school and I wouldn't disturb her for anything. Now, Jarvis—this is a production Jarvis isn't going to want to miss. I think I owe him that small pleasure. Dear Jarvis, he never settles down in his own life, but he does stay in touch with the family, what's left of it. He runs up huge bills—sometimes on my phone—calling Chantal and Everard in Mooréa. Jarvis loves more deeply than he's willing to admit to himself. Alas, that's the lot. I've outlived too many people. Marical. Meredith. Poor little Inez, killed with Edith when that train was blown up. The world isn't any less bloody than it was in King David's day."

"I'll call Nik, Papa," Emma said softly.

"Bless you, my darling. Am I being very primitive? When

Ellis, Norma's husband, died, the whole family was gathered around him."

"It's hardly primitive," Abby said. "It's far more civilized than most of us dare to be."

"King David took his people from the Bronze Age to the Iron Age. What age are we in now? We seem to be moving from metal to plastic." David was eating little, but he was alert, his eyes bright.

Ben cut more bread and offered the breadboard to Abby.

"Thanks, Ben. King David was a luminous man, and so are you, Dave. When you come onstage, it lights up."

"The light is dimming," David said.

"It is still there," Abby assured him. "It has little to do with the body. You will never lose it." She reached out to pat his hand. "They fought a lot, those old tribes. I suppose it's impossible for us, nearly three millennia later, to understand a world of small tribes."

Ben put in, "Maybe they liked fighting, the way people like football today."

David grinned. "Good analogy, Ben, and probably valid."

Emma got up and took their plates. "Fruit and cheese for dessert. I'll be back in a few minutes."

"I'll help." Alice took the serving dishes.

The two women stood in the galley. Alice scraped the plates and rinsed them in seawater, while Emma filled a plastic pan with hot soapy water, another with clear water. "Is it okay for you? Abby's being here?"

Alice nodded slowly. "She brings a kind of serenity with her. And she's good for Dave."

Yes. Emma had noticed that her father's color was better, that he was rallying to Abby's presence. When the dishes were stacked in the rack to dry, she picked up a bowl of fruit.

"I'll be up in a few minutes," Alice said. "Go ahead."

Emma looked at Alice, started to speak, then closed her mouth and went up to the pilothouse. Ben was out on the foredeck, doing something with the anchor chain.

She had left her father talking about football and small, warring tribes. Now Abby was saying, "At least Saul tried to get rid of some of the superstition that abounded."

"You'll never get away from superstition entirely," David said. "Not while the human being is still human. I have my old rabbit's foot in my makeup box. I don't whistle in my dressing room. I spit and say *merde* to my co-players on opening nights."

"I wish on the first star," Emma said.

"But you don't go to fortune-tellers," Abby said.

"Heavens, no, they scare me." Emma shuddered. "What made you think of that?"

Her father laughed grimly. "Myrlo used to go to fortune-tellers the way she now goes to her psychiatrist."

Emma shook her head. "One day at a time is all I can manage. I don't believe in trying to play around with the future."

Her father's mind was back on the King David play. "Saul forbade witches and necromancers and wizards, maybe to try to placate Samuel. I don't think he understood that meddling with the future is a dangerous thing. If I had known when we started rehearsals for *Lear* that I'd never do another play, I wouldn't have enjoyed myself as much as I did."

Abby smiled. "David, you're coming to the end of your days knowing that you've done what you set out to do. Not many people have that honor."

David looked at her lovingly. "I am grateful beyond words. If I had my life to live over again—oh, there are many things I ought to change, and a few that I would, but you're right. I've done what I wanted to do." He put his hand to his mouth to cover a yawn.

Abby rose. "Bedtime for me." She bent down to David and kissed him.

He returned the kiss, took her hand in his, and kissed the palm. "Abby." He smiled at her. "It's a new role for me, this journey into night. I'm eighty-seven, and I've had a good run, and Alice will try to see to it that I die with a semblance of dignity."

Quietly, Emma left the pilothouse and the old man and his second wife.

Alice was sitting at the table in the main cabin. She looked up as Emma came down the steps. "Everything okay?"

"Fine. Abby's just saying good night to Papa."

Alice stirred as Abby came down the steps, holding the rail. "Alice, David's waiting for you. I'll be heading for bed. Good night, my dears."

Emma went to her godmother and embraced her. "Sleep well. See you in the morning."

Abby left them, and they could hear her drawing the curtains around the bed, the curtains that would give her some privacy; Emma and Alice would have to go through the lower cabin to get to their bunks under the pilothouse.

Emma looked at Alice's face, noting the tension about her mouth. "I'm so accustomed to Papa's wives—I didn't realize how hard it was going to be for you."

"It's okay," Alice said. "Really. I'm glad she's here."

Emma used the head in the main cabin, then undressed and climbed into her bunk. When Alice came to bed, Emma was again reading one of Nik's scenes:

Abigail and Zeruiah are on the rooftop of the women's quarters, relaxing, talking. Abigail is weaving, and Zeruiah is folding some embroidered robes.

ZERUIAH: You are not jealous of Jonathan?

ABIGAIL: Jonathan? I love Jonathan.

ZERUIAH: How can you love Jonathan? You don't even know him.

ABIGAIL: (*Smiling*) I do.

ZERUIAH: Abigail, are you getting crazy, like Saul?

ABIGAIL: No, Zeruiah. Jonathan came to David a few nights ago, in secret, warning him of Saul. I served them food and wine, and sat with them while they ate, then left them alone, and in the morning Jonathan had gone. He didn't dare be seen with David, or have anyone know he'd come. He risked everything for David.

ZERUIAH: Because he loves him.

ABIGAIL: Yes, I thank the heavens for Jonathan's love. David might not be alive without it.

ZERUIAH: Oh, you are good. David is blessed to have you, surrounded as he is by men out to get him, some of them as crazy as Saul.

ABIGAIL: (*Sighing*) Aren't most men crazy? My first husband, Nabal, certainly was.

ZERUIAH: And David?

ABIGAIL: Oh, my dear, aren't we all a little crazy, we human creatures, with our wars and our gods and our jostling for power? *She turns as she hears footsteps. David has come up onto the roof, seeking Abigail as well as the cool night breezes. Zeruiah moves away, offstage, left, and David holds out his arms to Abigail.*

Emma had liked this scene and the warmth it gave to Abigail. She sighed as she continued reading the scene between Abigail and David.

ABIGAIL: Ah, David, I wish you and Saul could make peace.

DAVID: So do I. But wishing isn't enough. Saul wants to kill me.

ABIGAIL: You are greater than he is. You will be a greater king. You will unite your people. No wonder he is jealous.

DAVID: (*Leans against Abigail, who holds him*) Oh, my Abigail, I am tired of being hunted.

ABIGAIL: (*Caressing him*) You have cause to fear Saul when his madness comes on him, but remember that you have no cause to fear God. You are the beloved; God has you by the right hand, and shall receive you in glory. God is the strength of your heart and your portion forever.

DAVID: You sound so certain.

ABIGAIL: I am.

·

"Was it a good play?" Alice asked.

"Good material for a play." Emma sighed. "Nik never pulled

it all together. But he had some wise things to say, and some good questions. About friendship, for instance."

"David and Jonathan?" Alice asked.

"Yes. David and Jonathan. Nik really tried to emphasize what he called the friendship of the heart. Well, you and I have talked about that, haven't we?"

"Yes," Alice said. "I wish it were emphasized more, the friendship of the heart. I like that phrase."

"So do I. And all anybody thinks about today is sex."

Alice looked at Emma, raising her eyebrows slightly.

"Remember a couple of years ago—it was a spring evening, the first really warm weather, and we went for a walk in Riverside Park, and we were walking arm in arm, and I was feeling both mothered and sistered by you, and then suddenly some women behind us made nasty remarks?"

"Of course I remember," Alice said. "But it's not wise to take stupidity or viciousness too seriously."

"I know, I know. God knows, in the theater I have plenty of friends who are lesbians or homosexuals, that's not what I'm upset about. It's what you said—the friendship of the heart—people seem to forget that it even exists. Adair—oh, hell, Alice, before—before—well, Billy came to warn me that there were rumors about Adair and me. When people say nasty things often enough, you begin to wonder if you're crazy, and maybe all there is is sex."

"You know that's not all there is." Alice spoke gently. "Your love for your brothers and sisters is beautiful. People can be cruel, but you shouldn't let it get to you."

"I know, but there's so much emphasis on genitalia and expressing oneself and having one's needs met, and that's absolutely idiotic. Nobody's needs are ever met. I do know that."

.

'So, even though he knew a woman—' Nik had asked Emma. 'What do you really think about Jonathan and David?'

Emma had sighed. 'I think we live in a sex-mad society. What's wrong with their just being friends?'

They crossed the street. Fifth Avenue was nearly deserted and a cold wind was blowing. They walked west, over to Sixth. 'I don't want your father to think I'm getting too big for my shoes.'

'Write the play you want, Nik, and then you can decide what needs to be cut back.'

'Okay. You're right. Now. We've established Saul as big and strong and handsome and a good warrior.'

Emma grinned. 'Hewing oxen. And Samuel hewed Agag. There was a lot of hewing.' Nik put his arm around her and they laughed. They turned up Sixth Avenue and a half-empty bus wheezed by.

'There needs to be a strong scene where David and Jonathan make vows of friendship. Jonathan gave David his armor, a particular sign of friendship, and that means David has attained full growth. Jonathan, being Saul's son, would not be small.'

'Father's six feet tall. Given good makeup, he can look amazingly young.'

'I'm not worried about that,' Nik said. 'He can carry the early scenes with no trouble.' He stopped and looked around. 'Hey, we're at Twenty-third. Want to take the subway here?'

She held her face up to the night air, faintly stinging, but refreshing. 'I'd just as soon go on walking.'

'Saul's jealousy explains his offering his daughter to David in marriage, and then sending David into the thick of battle, thinking the Philistines will kill him. A nice foreshadowing of what David succeeds in doing later with Uriah the Hittite.'

'Saul does ugly things.' Emma shivered a little, and Nik tightened his arm about her. A taxi slowed down, suggestively, but Nik waved it on. 'But horrible as jealousy is, I do understand it in Saul.'

'Emma?'

'What?'

'What about jealousy in your own family? I'm an only child, but what about you and all your brothers and sisters?'

Emma stopped walking for a moment, then said, 'Oh, Nik, I don't know. Not now. Certainly never with—with Adair and

Etienne. Or Everard or Chantal. You know Ev and Chantal. They like what they're doing, they like their own lives, and they've been marvelous about supporting me.'

'Jarvis?'

'Jarvis likes to run things, to run *us*, but I don't think jealousy comes into it. And darling Louis is still a kid, and whether or not his boy soprano voice will turn into a decent tenor or baritone later is anybody's guess.'

'That's good,' Nik said. 'It makes me wish I'd had the fun of growing up with brothers and sisters.'

'We didn't exactly grow up together,' Emma said, 'but somehow or other, we *were* together.'

'Hey, it's late, and you're tired,' Nik said. 'Let's take the subway here at Twenty-eighth.'

'Okay.'

They stood on the platform, hearing a train in the distance. Two sailors sat on one of the benches, half asleep. A very tall man in a soldier's uniform walked impatiently up and down. The train pulled into the station. The soldier prodded the two sailors to wake them and hurried into the car as the doors opened. 'We're lucky,' Nik said. 'I think they've been waiting for a long time.' They went into the train and sat down.

'Em,' he continued, 'I'm having a hard time making Michal real. Did she love David?' The train swayed, throwing Emma against Nik, and his arm tightened about her to steady her. 'What do you think?'

'I think David was the one bright thing in her life. He was a musician and a poet. All the things Saul was not.'

'And Saul saw and knew that the Lord was with David. And not with him. And I'm sure he was jealous of the way women adored David.' Nik stood up, helping Emma to her feet. The train pulled into the station and the doors opened. They stepped out onto the dimly lit platform smelling of damp and cold.

As they walked up the steps, Emma said, 'David kept on doing everything right because the Lord was with him.' She frowned.

'Some of the language is pretty strong for friendship.'

'People weren't afraid to use strong language in those days.'

'Oh, my sweet innocent!' Nik softened the words with a gentle smile. 'With your background I don't know how you manage it. I suppose it's Bahama—'

'But, Nik—'

'What I suspect is that you're half right. David, King David, was like your father, with great big uninhibited lusts made comprehensible by the largeness of his heart and his *joie de vivre*. Jonathan, I think, adored him. Was in love with him. And even though Jonathan did have a son, I believe that in his heart he was totally faithful to David.'

'Okay. I'll buy that.'

Nik took her hand and put it in the pocket of his overcoat in a now familiar gesture. They were walking to the Riverside Drive apartment for supper with David and Sophie. 'There's something inexpressibly tender about you that makes me long to protect you. I know you're constantly worried about Etienne and Adair. And there's gossip in the theater about another brother. Something weird about a subway accident when he was on his way to the theater.'

Emma's voice was rigid with control. 'Yes. It was an accident. He fell in front of a subway train.'

'William Wilburton.'

'Yes. Billy. My eldest brother. He didn't use his own name. Papa's name. Wilburton was his stepfather.'

'I'm sorry, Em.'

'Yes.'

'It must have been awful for you.'

'Yes.'

Nik's voice was tender. 'You're still hurting. Did you love him very much?'

The tears started to course down Emma's cheeks. Nik caught her by the shoulders and turned her so that he could hold her as she sobbed, her head against his chest.

Nik patted Emma's back, gently kissed the top of her head. With an effort Emma managed to control the sobs, quench the tears. Her outburst had completely surprised her. And there was no way she could explain to Nik—'Sorry, sorry.' She wiped her face against the rough tweed of his coat.

He took out a handkerchief and wiped her eyes. She took it from him and blew her nose. 'Sorry—' She breathed again.

'Everyone's due a good Aristotelian purge once in a while. Feel better?'

'Yes. But, Nik—'

'You don't have to talk about it. I know it's upsetting. I'm glad I know some of your other brothers. Did I tell you Jarvis is interested in producing one of my plays?'

She swallowed. 'That's Jarvis.' Nik did not want her to talk about it, whatever he thought 'it' was. Sooner or later she would have to. But perhaps not yet? His play had opened in early September, the first hit of the season. It was only mid-November. It was not yet time.

'Are you okay, sweetie? We've got over ten more blocks. Want to take a taxi?'

They were both making good money but they did not ordinarily think in terms of taxis. Emma glanced at Nik, and in the streetlight his face was concerned. 'No, Nik, thanks. Let's go on walking.'

Nik took Emma's arm. 'I went to your father's show last night. God, he's good! I stood at the back of the theater and I could feel affection for him all through the audience, and then, at the curtain calls, there was a great swelling of love, the same kind King David got.'

Emma laughed. 'There are always adoring women crowding the stage door. Poor old Saul never got that, with his dark moods on him again and again, and his jealousy and irrationality.'

'There's a marvelous little scene I want to write,' Nik continued, 'with David coming on Saul asleep in a cave, and it's a perfect opportunity to kill him. David looks down on the old man, and he knows he can't—won't—kill him. And then he takes his sword and cuts off the hem of Saul's garment, and the old king sleeps on, unaware of his danger. Then David leaves him, going as quietly as he came.'

'Wonderful, Nik! That can be a really moving scene. Saul's a sad old man, overcome by madness.'

'David truly believed that although he himself was the Lord's anointed, so was Saul, and the Lord's anointed must not be dishonored.'

'The Lord's anointed,' Emma mused, pressing closer to Nik as a gust of west wind made her stagger slightly. 'Do you believe that?'

'The anointing of kings?' Nik raised his dark brows. The wind from the river was ruffling his hair. 'Maybe, when being a king was a talent and a vocation, not something political.'

'What do you mean?'

'What about your father? Isn't he in a way also the Lord's anointed? Where did his incredible gift of acting come from? Granted, he serves it well, he hasn't wasted or perverted his talent as some artists do, but what about the talent in the first place?'

'Is it maybe genetic?' Emma asked.

Nik shook his head violently. 'I don't want all our gifts relegated to genes and chromosomes. Although I'm sure that would have satisfied my father.'

'And your mother?'

'She believed in gifts. And that I have one as a writer.'

'You do.'

'So all I can do is serve the gift. I'd give anything if I could serve mine as well as your father serves his.'

'He tries,' Emma said slowly. 'When he's working on a role it has nothing to do with his private life.'

Nik hugged her. 'I know he has a reputation. But I've only seen him with Sophie, and they seem to me to be a model of a perfect marriage.'

'I don't think there's any such thing.' Emma shook her head. 'But it's a good marriage.'

'So.' Nik's mind was on the working-out of his play. 'David refused to kill Saul. He was not a killer.'

Emma protested. 'What about "Saul has killed his thousands and David his ten thousands"?'

'That's different. That's war. Hot blood.'

'What about those two hundred foreskins?'

Nik threw back his head and gave one of his rare, joyful laughs. 'Maybe he converted them all before he circumcised them.'

Emma laughed, too, but said, 'No, no, that's hardly likely.'

'It's still different.'

'Why? If David had to bring all those foreskins back to Saul, he certainly had to kill at least a lot of those Philistines, and that's cold blood, isn't it?'

He drew in his breath. 'All I know is that David could not kill Saul. In spite of everything, he loved him.'

In spite of everything. Yes. In spite of everything, her father loved Billy, his first son to survive babyhood. She would always love Adair. No matter what.

'We're here,' Nik said. 'Are you all right, sweetie?'

'Sure.'

He kept his arm about her as they went into the marble lobby. In every way she was his girl. But he did not talk of marriage. Perhaps his parents' example had soured him on marriage.

David had not been a good example, either, but at least he had loved. He loved. And Sophie loved him.

They went up in the elevator. Emma glanced at them in the amber-tinted mirror that lined the back wall. Nik's dark curls were tousled by the wind. She pushed up the striped knitted wool cap which Abby had sent her from Florence, with a scarf to match. Her cheeks were flushed from the cold.

'I'm starved,' Nik said. 'I wonder what treat Sophie will have for us tonight?'

Blinis. Little pancakes with melted butter, sour cream, and caviar. 'Davie's thinking of doing *Uncle Vanya* next season,' Sophie said. 'So I'm being Russian.'

'There might be a nice role for you, Emma,' David said. 'That is, if Nik's play ever closes. You're still drawing full houses, aren't you, Nik?'

'Yes. We're very lucky.'

'Luck shtuck. It's a fine play with a good cast and you've

written a role that's perfect for Emma.' He spooned melted butter onto his pancakes, added caviar and sour cream. 'How's the David play coming?'

'Emma and I were talking about it while we were walking up here. It's coming.'

'You crazies'—Sophie looked at them affectionately—'walking all that way in this weather, with the wind coming across the river from New Jersey.' The way she said 'New Jersey,' it sounded as far off as China.

'We're getting into some really good stuff with David and Saul.' Nik was enthusiastic. 'And then the next thing is that Samuel dies.'

'Onstage?' David Wheaton asked.

'Very off. Not much is made of it. All the Bible says is, "And Samuel died; and all the Israelites were gathered together, and lamented him, and buried him in his house at Ramah." That's all.'

·

'—and then Samuel died.' Grandpa Bowman lowered his voice. 'Right after David had lovingly spared Saul, Samuel died.

'And there was great grief.' Grandpa Bowman winced in anguish. 'For all Samuel's faults and follies, he was a great man. God took a child and shaped him into a prophet, a strange prophet perhaps, a seer, a dervish, but God often uses strange people and seldom has the opportunity to train them from childhood as he did Samuel. When Samuel began to judge the tribes of Israel they were scattered and quarrelsome, united only by their fitful and frequently faithless worship of their God, and by their common enemies, who were always nibbling at their borders. Samuel went a long way toward uniting them into a nation. Samuel, for all his stiff-neckedness, understood that God was more than the tribal god who was greater than the other tribes' gods, but still one god among many. Samuel had fleeting glimpses of the One True Creator, the One God. Samuel was often arrogant and stupid, but he believed that he was being obedient to God, even when he was being obedient only to Samuel.

'Saul was darker, more introverted, understanding neither God nor Samuel. When Saul asked God if he would deliver the enemy into the hand of Israel, God answered him not that day.

'Do you heah that, my people? The Lord does not come and go at our beck and call. The Lord is not a heavenly bellboy. Heah?

'Even Samuel did not understand that, and before full understanding came, he died, and all Israel mourned for him, and Saul wept, and David wept, and Samuel was buried at Ramah, and David rose and went down to the wilderness of Paran. David was more complicated than Samuel, and his vision of God was more complex, less masculine, less patriarchal, more tender and nurturing. But it was Samuel who pointed the way . . .'

·

'I think Grandpa's fond of Samuel, maybe because he's so much like him,' Emma said.

'As opinionated and as stubborn,' her father agreed.

Nik took a swallow of the tea Sophie had prepared, not too strong, and sweetened with a spoonful of marmalade, Russian fashion. 'After Samuel was buried at his house in Ramah, David went down to the wilderness of Paran.'

Sophie poured him more tea. 'What's that all about?'

'Abigail.' Nik grinned. 'At last we come to Abigail and her horrible husband.'

'Nabal,' Emma said.

'The boor. In Hebrew, that's what the name Nabal means. He was a sheep owner, a big one, and shepherds in open country were always in danger from bandits and robbers. David and his men asked Nabal's shepherds for protection money, and the shepherds knew that David had indeed protected them. But Nabal, who should have known better than to confuse David with ordinary marauders, shouted boorishly, "Who is David?

Who is the son of Jesse?" as though David was a nobody. Abigail
was a woman of real wisdom, and she knew that David was going
to be a great king.'

'How did she know?' Sophie asked.

'I suppose stories of David's greatness had gone before him
—Saul has killed his thousands and David his ten thousands,
and so forth. And there were probably rumors of those two
hundred foreskins he paid for Michal. Here.' Nik put his finger
on a passage in the Bible. 'We introduce Abigail into a scene
where David and his men are furious with Nabal. They are in
the background, and Abigail is downstage. A young man rushes
across the stage to her, "Oh, mistress, mistress, quickly!" He
tells her that David is going to kill them all for Nabal's idiocy,
and'—Nik slipped into the role of the messenger—' "But David's men were good to us, and took nothing from us, and guarded
us. Now you will know what to do, mistress, for Nabal has
angered David and he has told all his men to put on their swords
and they are coming to kill us!" Abigail tells him to hush, and
she calls her maids and tells them to gather loaves and wine.
"There are five sheep dressed," she says. "Thank God there is
always feasting at the time of sheepshearing. Get raisins and fig
cakes. Hurry! Put it all on asses and I will go before you." ' Nik
leaned his elbows on the table. 'Abigail goes to David riding on
an ass, but of course that won't work onstage any more than
hewing oxen. So what I plan is for her to slip on a purple-and-
scarlet cloak of soft silk, put flowers in her hair, and she'll walk
upstage to meet David, quickly, but not seeming to hurry. Read
this for us, Em, and modernize it a bit.' He pushed the Bible
over to her.

She read, 'My lord David fights only the battles of the Lord
of Heaven.' Emma stretched her hands out toward Nik. 'No evil
has ever been found in you, so I know that you will shed no
blood today.'

'Good, good. David would take one step toward her, and she'd
say—go on.'

'Mark me, my lord, for I speak the truth. The Lord is with

you, and you will surely be lord over Israel. You are the Lord's anointed.'

'Excellent,' Nik said. 'I think that's enough, don't you? It's a long speech in the Bible. Would you want to carry it all?'

'No, thanks. She makes her point, and that's plenty. David would thank her: "Blessed be the Lord God of Israel which sent thee this day to meet me: And blessed be thy advice, and blessed be thou, which hast kept me this day from coming to shed blood—" '

'He's already in love with her,' Nik said.

'And she with him.'

'And they'd come close to each other, so close they are almost touching, and then they'd break away, and the spotlight would go off them.'

'And then?' Sophie asked eagerly.

'Perhaps we might have a scene with Abigail and Nabal, after the sheepshearing banquet, with Nabal drunk. He'd be even more repellent to her then, after she's seen David.'

'Perhaps we could condense a little here,' Emma suggested. 'Nabal would stagger to his feet to go to Abigail, too drunk even to know what he was doing, and then he could fall to the ground with the stroke that killed him.'

David had taken the Bible and was looking at it. 'He died ten days later.'

'Yes, Papa, but time can be tightened a bit. Give Abigail a scene where Nabal has a fit and dies.'

Nik nodded. 'Then we can have musicians, and servants, everything to indicate that Abigail had all the proper mourners for Nabal, and did all the right ritual things. A musical transition scene.'

Emma smiled. 'Abigail knew David would hear of Nabal's death, and of course he did, and sent for her to be his wife.'

Nik said, 'I visualize a scene between Abigail and David in David's chambers, lying together on his couch. Abigail will go to the window, to look out at the sky, which is that lovely blue that comes just before the stars. This can easily be indicated with a change of gelatins. A Maxfield Parrish or Edmund Dulac scene. I want to show the purple shadows on the hills, and Abigail leaning on the parapet, looking at the mountains and saying—what?'

Emma smiled. 'I will lift up mine eyes unto the hills, from whence cometh my help.'

Nik said, flatly, 'But that's from the Psalms.'

'Yes.'

'But the Psalms are David's.'

'Not all of them,' Emma said calmly. 'Some of them are after the Jews have been driven out of Jerusalem and are in captivity.'

'But why would Abigail know the Psalms?'

'She wouldn't. They were being written. So why'—she smiled across the table at Nik—'why couldn't Abigail have made up some of them? The way you've presented her, she's intelligent and creative. Surely her first speech to David was poetic.'

Nik scowled, then burst into laughter. 'What an idea! I'd never in the world have thought of it! Okay, why not?'

'Why not, indeed,' David Wheaton said. 'That's my glorious Emma. Why couldn't Abigail have made up some of the Psalms and taught them to David?'

'Oh, I like that, Nik,' Sophie said, 'I think that's wonderful.'

'Okay, I'll work on it. Now we come to a problem,' Nik said. 'I mean a problem for Abigail. As soon as David has married Abigail, he marries Ahinoam.'

'Who?' David asked.

Nik answered, 'A-hin-o-am. David married Abigail, and then, immediately, he married Ahinoam.'

'I've never understood that,' Emma said. 'Even Grandpa couldn't make it make sense.'

'Oh, come on, sweetie, you're not thinking,' Nik chided. 'David was constantly fleeing from Saul, who had a big army. Ahinoam was a Jezreelitess, and when David married her, he got all the Jezreelites on his side, and that was no small thing.'

Sophie demanded, 'You mean he married an army, rather than a wife?'

Nik said, 'It was a political match, more than a love one. Abigail brought David Nabal's worldly goods and her five beautiful maidens. But she didn't expand his army, and he needed that.'

'But Ahinoam brought him nothing but trouble,' Emma said.

'It was a mistake,' Nik agreed. 'As much of a mistake as Samuel's anointing Saul in the first place. Yes, Ahinoam was the cause of a lot of David's trouble. As far as I can work out the chronologies, both Ahinoam and Abigail got pregnant fairly quickly, but Ahinoam probably before Abigail, since Ahinoam's son, Amnon, who is the real heavy in this show, is later referred to as David's first son. Poor Abigail's two sons must have died in infancy or early childhood.'

'Poor Abigail,' Emma agreed. 'She probably didn't have an easy pregnancy, and she'd have tried to hide her sickness and her anxiety from David.'

Sophie asked, 'Hide it? Why?' Sophie had bloomed with health while she carried Louis.

'David would not be tolerant of physical weakness.'

'Yeah.' Nik tapped his pen against the table. 'I think you're right, eh, Dave?'

David Wheaton nodded. 'He was a warrior as well as a sweet singer of songs, and Abigail was, as the story suggests, not young. Ahinoam was strong and healthy, and she had a healthy baby.' Abruptly David Wheaton pushed away from the table and left the room.

—Billy. Emma looked after her father. —He's thinking of Amnon as Billy.

She turned to Nik. 'It's okay. He'll be back.'

'Poor Abigail,' Sophie said. 'So hard on her, to be pregnant and sick, with Ahinoam strong and healthy.'

Emma tried not to look toward the door where her father had exited. 'Anyhow, Nik, army or no, I still don't see why David married Ahinoam. I don't remember multiple wives earlier in the Bible.'

Nik thought, eating a cookie. 'The Jews had never had a king before. God and the prophets. No king. So they had no examples at home as to how a king behaves, and I guess a lot of those kings who surrounded them had harems and concubines. It was one of the fringe benefits that went with being a king.'

'And David liked his benefits?'

'Don't we all? Emma—'

'What?'

'You really like what I'm doing with Abigail?'

'Yes. She'll be wonderful to play. She's an admirable person, but I think she has a sense of fun, because that usually goes along with real wisdom.'

David returned, saying, 'Louis was having a nightmare. But he's sweetly asleep again now.'

Emma looked at him, then dropped her gaze. 'We need to go, Papa, it's late.'

Nik said, 'I have to get to the typewriter for an hour or two before I go to sleep. I'll have some more scenes for you tomorrow. Sophie, thanks for a marvelous meal, as usual.'

Rain was misting down when they left the apartment. Nik held out his hand to catch the drops. 'Ugh. It's too cold to walk even to the subway.'

'It's only a few blocks.'

'I don't want my favorite actress catching cold. I'll treat us to a taxi.'

Emma laughed, a bubbling of happiness. 'Save it for worse weather than this.'

He put his arm around her waist, and they walked east, toward Broadway. Suddenly they were silent. As they approached the entrance to the subway he said, 'Emma, you've been hurt, haven't you?'

She tried to laugh. 'Who hasn't?'

They had reached the subway steps, and walked down them. Then Nik turned her so that she faced him. 'I won't hurt you, Emma.'

She raised her face to his, moved fully into his kiss, not even noticing when some soldiers standing farther down the platform sent appreciative whistles in their direction.

.

Chantal asked her, 'Em, are you in love with this guy?'
'I think so. Yes.'
'Does he love you?'
'I don't know. I hope—but he hasn't said—'
'Have you told him about—'
'No. Not until—'
'Emma, you're going to have to tell him.'
'I know, but—'
'But?'
'Maybe he won't want me.'
'Then he's not worth your love. Better you find it out sooner than later.'
'Maybe I'm not worth loving. Maybe it'll never work, not with anybody.'
'Emma, you're going to have to risk it.'
'Why?'
'It's a kind of suicide you can't commit.'
'Oh, Chantal, Chantal, I'm such a mess.'
'Everybody's messed up, one way or another.'
'You?'
'Sure, me. I'm like Jarvis, afraid to commit myself. I go out with guys and I go up to a point and then I get all self-protective and pull away. That's why I can see it in you, see what you're doing, and I don't have your excuse. Emma, we have to take risks.'

Yes, she knew that. But she was afraid.

Alice

*And David said unto Achish, If I have now found grace in
thine eyes, let them give me a place in some town in the
country, that I may dwell there . . . Then Achish gave him
Ziklag that day: wherefore Ziklag pertaineth unto the kings
of Judah unto this day.*

*And it came to pass, when David and his men were come
to Ziklag on the third day, that the Amalekites had invaded
the south, and Ziklag, and smitten Ziklag, and burned it
with fire;*

*And had taken the women captives . . . And David's two
wives were taken captives, Ahinoam the Jezreelitess, and
Abigail the wife of Nabal the Carmelite.*

*And David enquired at the Lord, saying, Shall I pursue
after this troop? shall I overtake them? And he answered
him, Pursue: for thou shalt surely overtake them, and without fail recover all.*

I SAMUEL 27:5–6; 30:1–2, 5, 8

ALICE HAD TAKEN some of Nik's pages from Emma and was reading them, curled up in her bunk. "It's fascinating," she said.

Emma said, "You don't have to read all that stuff, you know."

"I know I don't have to. It's compelling."

"Some of it. It's very uneven."

"I've never read the script of a play-in-the-making before. The world of the theater was like something from another planet to me when I married David, glamorous, I suppose, but completely alien. Watching David work on a role, never losing himself, but somehow finding aspects of himself that were hidden until they were needed for a character—"

"He's taught me," Emma said. "I've learned more from Papa than from everybody else put together."

"Watching you become Goneril—" Alice smiled. "It would have been scary, except I knew that my friend Emma was in there, even if hidden."

Emma sighed. "Goneril's pride and ambition and ruthlessness were at least latent in me; otherwise, I couldn't have played her."

"I'd like to have seen you do Nik's Abigail. This scene I've just read would really be fun, where Abigail talks about how happy David makes her, and Zeruiah asks, 'And David still makes you happy?'" Smiling, she leaned across to Emma's bunk, handing her the pages.

Emma read, aloud, "Yes, David makes me happy." Then she looked down at the page and continued reading, silently.

ZERUIAH: Even when he sends for Ahinoam instead of you?

ABIGAIL: (*Turns her face away*) He's the king.

ZERUIAH: (*Slyly*) Even when he asks you to play the harp for him and Ahinoam?

ABIGAIL: (*Looks at her sharply*) What about it?

ZERUIAH: Don't think there are any secrets in a harem, my dear. Everybody knows.

ABIGAIL: Knows what?

ZERUIAH: That David sent for you to come to him and Ahinoam with your harp, and that after you played for them he threw you out.

ABIGAIL: He did not throw me out. I left.

She raises her hands to pull her thick chestnut hair across her face to hide her smile.

ZERUIAH: What happened?

ABIGAIL: I sang for him. I left.

ZERUIAH: What did you sing?

ABIGAIL: Oh, I sang one of the songs for the defeat of wicked men: Why boastest thou thyself in mischief, O mighty man? the goodness of God endureth continually. Thy tongue deviseth mischiefs; like a sharp razor, working deceitfully. Thou lovest evil more than good . . . God shall likewise destroy thee for ever, he shall take thee away, and pluck thee out of thy dwelling place, and root thee out of the land of the living. Selah!

As she is saying this, she leaves the spotlight that is on her and Zeruiah and walks across the stage to the area for David's chambers. The spot follows her. David is lying on his couch with Ahinoam. Abigail slips on her red-and-purple silken robe and sits on a cushion, taking up her harp.

DAVID: (*Roaring*) Woman! That is not a love song!

ABIGAIL: Oh, did you want a love song, my lord? You merely asked

me for a song. This is a pleasing one about what will happen to
wicked people.

DAVID: To whom are you referring, creature?

ABIGAIL: (*Demurely*) Your enemies, of course, my lord.

Deftly she runs her fingers over the strings of her harp.

DAVID: Are you going to play me a love song?

ABIGAIL: No, my lord, I do not feel like love.

*Abigail picks up her harp, bows to him, and gracefully leaves the
king's chambers, walking slowly across the stage toward Zeruiah as
the light goes down on David and Ahinoam.*

ZERUIAH: He could have you killed for that.

ABIGAIL: But he didn't. And the next night he sent for me, and
we sang together. Love songs.

ZERUIAH: And he still makes you happy?

ABIGAIL: Yes, he still makes me happy.

Emma looked at Alice in the opposite bunk. "Yes. That scene
would have been fun to play. Sometimes Nik made Abigail too
wise and wonderful to be true. Maybe he was writing the ideal
woman he wanted—"

"The one who doesn't exist?" Alice suggested.

"And Abigail was dull in those scenes. Impossible to play.
Well, we ought to go to sleep." She put the papers down,
reached up to turn off her small reading light.

Alice said softly, "Why keep on reading Nik's play if it upsets
you?"

"I don't know. I can't seem to stop myself. It's stupid."

"No." Alice was firm. "I'm not sure what it is, but it's not
stupid."

Whatever it was, it had brought Nik to the forefront of Emma's
consciousness. Sliding half into sleep, she found herself remembering time long gone, when she and Nik were falling in love,
when the future was open and everything was possible.

·

'Nik—' She was a little tentative. 'Sophie called and begged us to come to them after the show tomorrow.'

'Fine. I just don't want to wear out my welcome.'

'Sophie's going to invite you for Thanksgiving dinner.'

Nik's face lit up. 'That's really kind of her.'

'Can you come?'

'Of course. Where else have I got to go? Last Thanksgiving I went to the Automat on Fifty-seventh Street and envied those who could go up the street to the Russian Tea Room. I'd love to be with you on Thanksgiving.'

'Did your parents—'

'They wanted to be proper Americans, so every year my mother cooked an enormous turkey dinner just for the three of us. She didn't have Sophie's talent for making a meal a celebration. Now, back for a minute to King David's sister, Zeruiah. She'd be worried about his marriage to Ahinoam.'

'Why? She's pragmatic enough to understand the political necessity.'

'She also has that touch of second sight. She'll warn Abigail: "Be careful. There will be trouble because of Ahinoam." And she'll tell her that Ahinoam will have a son who will— Em, what's the matter?'

Emma had shuddered convulsively. 'Amnon, Ahinoam's son. He caused all the trouble, didn't he? It must have been terrible for Abigail, having a sickly baby who evidently didn't live very long—'

'Emma.' Nik looked directly at her.

'What?'

'Do you want children?'

'Of course.'

'Not just "of course." Do you really?'

'Yes, Nik.'

'What would it do to your career?'

'Nothing. Lots of other actresses have had children.'

'Did it slow your mother down?'

Emma laughed. 'Not noticeably. But I'm not like my mother

and I do want children.' Whose children? Was Nik thinking of himself as father of Emma's children?

'My mother,' he said, 'was not a good example. She nearly died when I was born, and both my parents made me constantly aware of how much she'd suffered for my sake. If I did anything to displease them, I'd be asked, "How can you do this after all you put your mother through?" I don't have any example in my own life of what good parents are.'

Emma combined a laugh and a sigh. 'I guess I don't, either. Basically, I didn't have a mother. And Papa has certainly never been a typical father. Most fathers don't have a succession of wives.' She looked up as the waiter coughed discreetly. The restaurant had emptied.

'We're going, we're going,' Nik promised, taking the bill. It was not the first time they had closed the restaurant, and their waiter was tolerant.

While he went for their change, Emma continued, 'After David married Ahinoam, he kept right on marrying—Maacah, Haggith, Abital, Eglah.'

'But he loved Abigail the most.' Nik helped her into her coat.

.

Abigail Wheaton was in the pilothouse playing double solitaire with David when Emma came up with the breakfast tray. David's eyes were bright, and he laughed as he slapped down several cards.

"What are you playing?" Emma asked.

Abby smiled. "Spite and Malice. Your father is a most spiteful and malicious player. He's just beaten me by fifteen cards."

"Do you want to break for breakfast?" Emma asked. "Nothing exciting. Just toast."

"From Emma's fresh bread," David said, "with Ben's homemade wild-strawberry jam."

Abby was sorting the cards. "We've finished the game, and the toast smells marvelous."

Alice came up the steps to join them. Emma fixed toast for her father, then poured coffee into her mug, added hot milk. "What's the plan for today?"

"As soon as we finish breakfast we'll pull up anchor and move on."

"Where to?" David asked.

"Ben and I'd like to stop briefly at Whittock Island, show Emma and Abby where we come from. We'll anchor off Whittock for the night, and in the morning we might be able to get some abs."

"Abalone!" Abby exclaimed. "Wonderful! In a good garlic sauce they're delicious."

"The shells aren't as brilliant as those off the California coast"—Alice smiled at Abby—"but they're still quite lovely."

Abby said, "Soft, glowing colors, like mother-of-pearl."

David held out his hand. "I think I'll have another piece of toast if one of you will fix it for me. How lucky I am to be surrounded by such beautiful women."

Abby put the cards away. Emma picked up the coffeepot to refill mugs. Alice put butter and jam on toast for her husband. It was the first time in weeks that David had actually asked for food.

When they had finished, Emma took the tray with the breakfast things and went to the galley. Abby followed her. "Can I help?"

"No, thanks. I'm just going to rinse these and let them air-dry. Papa asked for a second piece of toast. He hasn't been eating well, so I took that as a good sign."

"Is it?"

"Maybe a temporary one. You've brought back his appetite, Abby, but that's not going to stop him from dying."

•

Emma watched her father as he sat at the oval dining table, reading a scene Nik had handed him. David Wheaton's lips were moving, and finally he read aloud: 'Abigail reaches for her harp, not stopping to put on her garments.' He raised his eyebrows, but continued. 'She sits by David's feet, playing and singing. "El Shaddai shall increase you more and more, you and your children. You are blessed of the Power which made heaven and earth. The heaven, even the heavens, are the Maker's, whom we will bless from this time forth and forevermore."'

'It's lovely,' Emma said, 'but you're going to have to let Abigail wear some clothes if I play her.'

Nik groaned, pushing his fingers through his untidy curls. 'Okay, okay. We'll put a light nightdress on her. It's a reaction to my parents—I don't think my father ever saw my mother undressed and they tried to make a prude out of me. Sometimes I go too far in rebelling. Also, I suspect that in David's culture Abigail might well have been nude. Maybe you could check that with your grandpa, Em?'

'Sure.'

'It's also a little hard for our culture to understand, but David slept with Abigail and Ahinoam and the other wives and concubines, too.'

'Lusty,' David Wheaton said. 'One wife at a time is all that's legal nowadays.'

'Davie!' Sophie called from the kitchen. 'Come and put these dishes on the top shelf for your wee wife.'

David sighed in affectionate resignation. 'I'll be back.'

'How tall is Sophie?' Nik asked as David pushed through the swinging door.

'Maybe five two, with heels.'

'Em, what do you think Ahinoam looked like? Was she beautiful?'

Emma shook her head. 'Pretty. That kind of obvious prettiness, big, blue, overly prominent eyes.'

'Why are you whispering?'

Emma looked toward the kitchen door. Spoke in a more normal voice. 'Well, Ahinoam would use whatever beauty aids were available in her day, and I expect there were plenty. Rouge, and eye shadow, and kohl from Egypt. And creams and lotions so the hot sun wouldn't wrinkle her skin. She'd take very good care of her looks, and she'd be terrified of growing old and not being pretty and seductive.'

'Emma, are you talking about someone you know?'

Emma looked again toward the kitchen and heard Sophie and her father laughing. 'Myrlo. Papa's third wife.'

'You evidently don't like her.'

'No. I don't. But I don't want to talk about her in front of Papa.'

'My God,' Nik expostulated. 'When I see your father and Sophie, I can't imagine either of them being married to anyone else. But then, it's only King David and Abigail's marriage that makes any sense to me. Abigail's a wise woman, and she gives him good advice, such as suggesting that he go to the Philistines to hide from Saul. And when he's horrified at the idea of going into enemy territory, she points out to him that it's the one place Saul won't go after him.'

'Pragmatic and intelligent, as you say.'

David Wheaton came in from the kitchen. 'So what next?' he asked.

'David crosses over into Philistine territory,' Nik said. 'And once he and his wives and his retinue are all there, David asks Achish, the Philistine king of Gath, for his own city, and Achish gives him a place called Ziklag.'

'At least Ziklag is easy to pronounce,' David said.

'So David got to Ziklag,' Nik went on, 'and he and all his family and servants made themselves at home there, and then the Amalekites made a raid on the town while David was away, and when David and his men got back they found nothing but devastation, and their wives and their children had all been taken. Gone.'

Sophie came in. 'Everybody okay, my jewels? Need anything more to eat?'

'We're stuffed to the gills.' David pulled her to him. 'Sit down and join us.'

'Nik, you will come for Thanksgiving, won't you? We'll eat at three, so Davie and Emma will be ready to go to the theater for their half-hour call.'

'I'd love to come,' Nik said.

David smiled at him. 'I'm glad you'll be with us. It won't be easy. It will be the first big holiday without the whole family.'

'We have to be brave.' Somehow Sophie managed not to sound trite.

Emma looked at the darkness crossing her father's face.

'Davie,' Sophie said softly. 'We have to make it good for Inez and Louis. They're still too young to be—'

David cut her off. 'It's all right, Sophie. We'll gather together, diminished though we are, and make merry.'

.

Abby called Emma from France the night before Thanksgiving. 'Darling, are you all right?'

'Yes, fine. Abby, it's so good to hear your voice!'

'Yours, too. And I got through to you without any trouble. Amazing. Letters take so long, I just like to check in once in a while. Any news?'

'We had a letter from Etienne a few days ago.'

'Good, oh, that's good. Anything else?'

No word from Adair.

'Not really. Well, Nik Green, the author of the play I'm in, is coming for Thanksgiving dinner.'

'Good. I look forward to meeting him. I love you, Emma.'

'I love you, too, Abby.' She hung up, flushed with pleasure from Abby's call, and wondering how much of her feelings about Nik she had given away to her perceptive godmother. —I do love you, Abby, she said as she turned away from the phone.

.

That love had not diminished, Emma thought, as she got a pair of rubber boots for Abby. Ben had dropped anchor, and they were close enough to row to Whittock Island, but there were too many of them for the little rowboat. Emma had helped Ben get the large rubber Zodiac down from the upper deck, using a system of pulleys, swinging the Zodiac off the deck and lowering it into the water, The sky was a soft grey, cool but gentle.

Ben jumped into the Zodiac with agility, despite his bad leg. Then he had Abby stand at the very edge of the narrow deck and drop into his upraised arms. He was strong and sure and Abby went to him with complete confidence. He seated her on the inflated rubber side of the Zodiac, and then Emma and Alice jumped in.

Emma remembered a rehearsal of a play where her role had been the young Queen Victoria and a footman had pulled out a chair for her to sit in.

'Now, Emma, darling,' the director had said, 'the difference between a queen and a commoner at a time like this is that the commoner looks to see if the chair is there whereas the queen sits. There is no question in her mind that the chair will be there. That is how you will do it. Sit.' Abby had gone to Ben with the assurance of royalty.

Emma held on to the rope that ran around the edge of the Zodiac. "Papa's all right?"

"Emma." Alice's voice was firm. "You don't think I'd leave him if he wasn't, do you? We won't be gone long. Not much more than an hour. I've given him a shot and he should have a good nap. Dave wants you to see where Ben and I grew up."

"It must have been like moving to another planet for you," Abby mused, "when you moved to New York with David."

"Yes. But David was my planet. When I was with him, I was at home."

Ben started the motor and pointed the Zodiac at the island. Abby mused, "David does have that effect. Odd. I don't even remember how many years we've been divorced. Chronology tends to fold in on itself as one gets older."

Emma said, "Papa met Myrlo when the twins—" Her voice trailed off.

"Yes, while my little ones were dying. It threw David into utter darkness. He'd warned me, before we were married, that he had periodic depressions, but I was unprepared— It was a bad time."

Emma looked down at a can of gasoline in the bottom of the Zodiac. "Papa wasn't there for you when he should have been."

"We were very young, and we both learned a lot from our failures, with ourselves, and with each other. We human beings grow through our failures, not our virtues."

"Yes," Emma said. "Sorry." Then she laughed ruefully. "But when I think of you—and then Myrlo—"

Abby's responsive laugh was gentle. "David's darknesses are the abyss for him, and Myrlo was his way of reaching out to life. Dearest Emma, you haven't much more cause to love Myrlo than I have, but you need to take a spiritual dose of salts and get rid of her."

Emma acknowledged this with a smile.

Abby said, "I found it far easier to understand David than I did Myrlo. I was relieved when Marical came on the scene and Myrlo was out. Marical and I were friends until her death, good friends. I did some of my best painting during my visits to her in Mooréa. Now that I'm pushing eighty, I want to concentrate on my friends. David and I are friends." She looked questioningly at Alice, whose strong hands were palms down on the thighs of her jeans. "I hope that doesn't bother you, my dear?"

Alice was slow in replying, saying finally, "It doesn't bother me. I think I'm glad."

"Thank you. It is no longer the custom for those who are dying to call on those they love to say goodbye. David has outlived a great many of those nearest and dearest to him. I still grieve over Etienne going down with his ship when it was torpedoed, and Adair—"

Emma winced with pain.

Abby pursued. "I was so grateful that Everard came home

safely, and that he took Marical and Chantal back to Mooréa as soon as travel was possible."

"It's horribly far away," Emma said. "I've managed only one visit, shortly after Marical died. It's one of the most lavishly beautiful places I've ever seen. I love your painting of Chantal and her babies on the tree-shaded beach, and I was ecstatic when you gave it to Nik and me. But Mooréa is much too far away for Everard or Chantal to come."

"Chantal is happy there, with little ones of her own. It's just as well she not be uprooted and old memories stirred up."

Emma leaned back into the wind as Ben guided the Zodiac toward land. The long summer light shimmered gently against the ripples. Water lapped quietly toward the great silver logs that had washed up on the shore of Whittock Island. Behind the logs, the Douglas firs rose up, dark and secret, the wind against their needles echoing the sound of water. Emma said, "I don't want Jarvis trying to choreograph Papa's deathbed scene."

Abby said quietly, "I don't think Alice will let that happen."

Alice glanced at Abby with a faint smile, and nodded.

"And Jarvis likes Alice more than he should."

Now Alice laughed. "I'm a great deal older than Jarvis, and hardly a femme fatale."

"Jarvis likes older women," Emma said. A small fish leaped out of the water and back in with a splash. Ben nosed the Zodiac toward the shore until the bottom grated against pebbles. He stepped into the water and pulled the Zodiac halfway up onto the beach. Then he turned to help Abby. Emma and Alice splashed in.

Ben bent down and picked up a couple of two-by-fours that had come in on the tide, lost from a lumber barge. He took them up onto a grassy knoll. "Never know when these will come in handy."

Abby sat on one of the great logs, bleached silvery-white by the salt water. "Odd to realize that much of the flotsam and jetsam that washes up here comes from Japanese fishing boats."

"Not much between here and Japan." Ben bent down with a cry of pleasure and picked something up off the beach. "It's a wooden float, an old one. Most of them are plastic nowadays."

He led them along a narrow path that wandered first through low bushes, then trees, until they came to a clearing where there was a weather-beaten house. Inside was a large, high-ceilinged room with a loft at either end. "Those were Alice's and my bedrooms," he said. "I still sleep in mine when I'm ashore. I've put in skylights and a fireplace, and I can lie in bed and look at the stars—when it's clear—or listen to the rain and the crackling of the logs."

"It's charming, Ben." Abby sat in a padded rocking chair. One long wall of the room was full of books.

"Southeast," Ben said, "where the worst of the storms come from. Books are good insulation."

The opposite wall had sliding windows which led out onto a small garden. Ben went to his kitchen, which was similar to the open galley on the *Portia*. "I'll make some coffee," he said. "The generator's not turned on, but the gas still works."

"We don't need anything," Abby said quickly.

"I'd like a cup of coffee." Ben smiled at her. "It won't take long. Powdered or canned milk only, I'm afraid, since I put the cooler away when I'm living on the *Portia*."

"You have a wonderful hi-fi set." Abby was looking around. "All the comforts of civilization in the middle of the wilderness."

"Unfortunately, the hi-fi, too, depends on the generator," Ben said. While the coffee was perking, he went into a small store-room and came out with two glass jars, giving one each to Emma and Abby. "Salal jelly. We learn to make use of whatever grows on the island."

"Wonderful, Ben!" Abby thanked him. "Salal jelly is delicious with meat—strange, and a little exotic."

"You warm enough?" Ben asked her.

"Plenty, thanks." The old woman had on a heavy off-white cardigan and a matching woolen cap. "When I come to the *Portia*, I dress for mid-winter even in mid-July."

"Tide's going to be low early tomorrow morning. We'll spend tonight where we're anchored, hunt for abs in the early morning, and then take off for the Queen Charlottes. Plenty of phones when we get to Masset Inlet."

Alice was curled up on an old leather sofa, behind which was a library table and an oil lamp with two yellow globes. "This was my favorite reading perch in stormy weather. Whittock wasn't a bad place to grow up."

Ben poured coffee into delicate china cups, each different. Emma and Alice took powdered milk; Abby preferred hers black. Alice looked at Abby. "Did Dave talk to you about King David?"

"Oh, yes, my dear," Abby replied. "It's been a continuing obsession with him. And when I was teaching, King David's story was part of my Living Literature course."

"All the wives," Emma said wryly. "He's too old to play David now, but he'd make a marvelous Saul. Sometimes I think he's more like Saul than David, with his depressions coming on him, not unlike Saul's evil spirit."

Abby said, "His depressions are terrible, but clinically atypical."

Alice looked at her questioningly.

"No matter how deep in darkness he sank, he could always rouse himself to go to the theater."

Alice agreed. "Yes. Odd."

"Even after Billy and Adair—" Abby turned to Emma. "Wasn't he playing in a comedy, then, too?"

Emma nodded. "He went to the theater every night and made people laugh and feel happy, and then he came home and sank into the pit again. Sophie sent Louis up to the Cathedral to the Choir School to get him away. The choristers had to be boarders, so Louis was spared it all."

"Why cancer now?" Abby demanded. "Why, at his age, when he's always been so healthy, never a smoker, a moderate drinker, though certainly an immoderate lover—"

"We're living longer, we human beings," Alice said. "Antibiotics have made an enormous difference. If we're not killed in some kind of accident it's likely cancer will get us in the end, particularly as we go on polluting our planet.

"I'm glad Dave's here." Alice put her cup down carefully. "Not just the *Portia*, but this part of the world where death is as accepted as birth. In New York when we were seeing the doctors, when he was having all the tests, there was much more fear in the air. We went to have a drink with one of David's old producer friends. Everybody was given real glasses—except David, who was given plastic."

Abby made a sputter of indignation. Then asked, "There wasn't any kind of treatment to arrest the thing?"

Alice shook her head. "He had some radiation, but it's a very aggressive cancer. There are some new treatments, involving chemicals, but at David's age the cure, if it is a cure, would probably kill him even more painfully than the disease."

"Forgive me—I assume it's inoperable?"

"Yes."

"Thank God for you, Alice. After David dies, will you go back to New York?"

"Whatever for? I went where David went. When David dies, my work is here. I'll go back to doctoring. When Emma's in a show I'll take some time off and come see her. I don't want ever to lose touch with Emma."

"Thanks, Alice. Nor I with you."

"Now that there are planes, the world is a lot smaller," Abby said.

"Yes. I'm glad you're here with us, Abby." Alice looked with her level gaze at David's second wife, at the peace in her face despite the fine network of lines made by all the tragedies and joys of life. "And I guess I'm beginning to understand David's obsession with King David. I'm beginning to see that it's part of his coming to terms with his life before he dies."

Abby nodded. Emma gathered up the coffee cups and took them to the sink.

"Don't bother, Em," Ben said quickly.

"It won't take a minute, and you don't want to find dirty coffee cups whenever you return."

Abby rose. "I'll dry."

When they were back in the Zodiac, they were quiet until a sleek black head lifted from the water and stared at them with ancient liquid eyes. Abby stretched out her hands. "How I love the seals! Alice, you will let David die when the time comes, won't you?"

"Of course."

"There's a terrible tendency nowadays to prolong death. I know you won't do that. It's my own weakness—I'm sorry, Alice." She stopped as Ben pulled the Zodiac to the side of the *Portia*, turned off the outboard motor, stepped out and up onto the deck, securing the Zodiac.

"Abby, let Alice or Emma help you to stand—good, so, right here. Now raise your arms—" As he spoke he reached down, put his hands under her arms, and with one swift lift he had her on the deck.

Emma followed, pulling herself up beside Abby.

"Thanks, Ben," Abby said, slightly breathless. "Old age is a beast, but I'm not going to let it stop me from doing what I want to do—and need to do."

Alice went directly to David in the pilothouse. Abby headed for the lower cabin. "I think I'll take a brief rest."

Emma stood at the galley, wondering what to fix for dinner. From the pilothouse she heard her father laugh. Almost inadvertently, she turned her mind to King David and his wives. That morning she had looked in the drawers for another chart for Ben and had come across more of Nik's sketched-out scenes. Despite herself, Emma kept returning to the script; it was somewhat like pressing a bruise to see if it still hurts.

"How long have these been here?" she asked her father.

"Years, probably. I haven't thought about them till this summer. Might-have-beens can be painful."

"It's not like you to brood over might-have-beens." Emma looked at him in concern.

"Perhaps not," David said. "It could have been a good play."

⋅

'It will be a good play,' David Wheaton said. 'But now Sophie wants us to gather round the table. We're glad you could be with us, Nik. It helps. You've brought happiness back to Emma's eyes.'

'Papa—' Emma whispered.

But he was calling them together, Emma, Nik, Everard, Chantal, Jarvis, Inez, Louis. David Wheaton's children, not his ex-wives. Marical saw Sophie fairly frequently but would not come from Connecticut to any large functions. Harriet stayed in her world of ballet, though occasionally, unlike Edith, she would grace them with an appearance. When they were all seated he held out his hands, and they all clasped hands around the table.

'We give thanks today for this gathering,' David Wheaton said, 'and for the food which Sophie has prepared *mit* so much *Liebe*. We ask for the safe return of Etienne and Adair. We grieve for the loss of Billy from our midst.' There were tears in his eyes, and they were all silent, until David continued, 'As the psalmist said, "Enter not into judgment with thy servant: for in thy sight shall no man living be justified." And again, "In God is my salvation and my glory: the rock of my strength, and my refuge . . . Trust in him at all times." Amen. All right, my darlings, fall to.'

'Everard, are you going to carve?' Sophie asked.

Everard sighed in resignation. 'Why is this job always given to me?'

'Because you're the best at it,' Chantal said.

'See!' Jarvis raised a finger. 'Ev should be a surgeon.'

'Turkeys, yes,' Everard said. 'People, no.'

Sophie had placed bowls of food on the table. David poured wine. 'None for me. I have to work tonight. I'll have ginger ale.'

'Me, too, please,' said Emma.

'No wine for Louis or Inez,' Sophie said.

'I'm old enough! I am!' Inez protested.

'Quiet, child,' her father said firmly. 'Ginger ale. You can have it in a wineglass.'

Conversation became general until after dessert. Sophie, Chantal, and Emma had cleared the table, and they were nibbling at plum pudding.

'As you all know,' David said, 'Nik is writing a play for me.'

'It's going to be a great play. I want to produce it,' Jarvis said.

'There's a good role for Emma, too—'

'I want some more hard sauce, please. And milk.'

'Isn't the chronology confusing?'

'I want wine, not ginger ale.'

'How many wives?'

'Straighten us out, Papa.'

They were all talking at once.

David tried to outline the play as far as Nik had taken it, to the burning of Ziklag.

'Actually,' Nik said, 'between David's move to Ziklag and the sack of the town, Saul goes to see the witch of Endor, but dramatically I think it will work better to have the whole Ziklag story in one scene, and Saul's going to the witch and then his death in another.'

Sophie came in with milk for Louis.

'Can't we help clean up?' Chantal asked.

'No. no. I have my own way of doing things. You talk about Nikkie's play. That makes my Davie happy.'

Nik and David had been excited by the scene that followed the attack on Ziklag. 'Wonderful language,' Nik said, 'with David and his men finding the ruined village and weeping, according to the King James translation, at the loss of their wives and little ones "until they had no more power to weep." '

'They knew how to cry in those days,' Everard said.

'So what happened next, when they'd finished weeping?' Inez asked.

Nik said, 'After he'd finished weeping, David asked God if he should go after the Amalekites. And God told him yes, go after the Amalekites. And he told David he would overtake the Amalekites and recover everything.'

Everard spread his hands out on the damask tablecloth, now spotted with the remains of Thanksgiving dinner. 'We have a nut in my ward who holds long conversations with God about how to run the war.'

Louis protested, 'David wasn't a nut.'

Jarvis laughed. 'In my experience it's mostly nuts who converse with God.'

Inez piped in, 'The Bible is full of nuts, then.'

'Hey, let's get back to Nik's play.' Jarvis let out a stream of smoke through his nostrils.

Nik's play. A safe topic of conversation. It kept them from talking about Billy.

Jarvis continued. 'People didn't have much choice about war in those days. There weren't any conscientious objectors like Ev.' He took another cigarette out of a silver case, saw his father looking at him with disapproval, and put it back. 'Basically, I'm a pacifist, too. Live and let live is my motto.'

'Hitler?' David suggested.

'Ah, Papa, there's the rub.' He finished his wine. 'But I don't talk to God about it. I think it's up to us. So, Nik, did David go after them thar Amalekites?'

'He did.' Nik had his pocket Bible open, his finger marking the place. 'Here, Em, read it, please.'

Emma read, paraphrasing as she did so. 'David reached the Amalekites, who were eating and drinking and dancing, and David in his righteous wrath smote them from the twilight even unto the evening of the next day, and David rescued his two wives, and all the wives and children of his men, and everything that the Amalekites had taken from them.'

'I can see it,' Nik said.

'What?' David asked.

'David going into the camp of the Amalekites. Breaking up the noisy celebration. The stage designer can go wild with colors, flags, tents, costumes. And music! The Amalekites all singing and dancing and making merry, cymbals clashing, tambourines, horns, wine flowing, and then David bursting on the scene. I can hear him bellowing—'

And David Wheaton roared, 'Where are my wives and my children?'

'I'm not, obviously, going to show the battle. I'll just have the music shift into cacophony and then silence, and everybody drifting off until the stage is nearly empty.'

'And then, what do you bet,' Emma suggested, 'Ahinoam would come strolling out of one of the Amalekite tents, cool as a cucumber, with Amnon bouncing on her hip.'

'Good, good,' Nik said. 'Zeruiah—she'd be there, of course, running to David, panting, calling, "Come, David, my lord, come to your wife Abigail, who is waiting for you!" And she'd catch hold of the hem of his garment.'

David asked, 'Why wasn't Abigail there?'

Nik said, 'That's what King David would ask, and Zeruiah will tell him, "Because she would not go into the tents of the enemy, my lord." And Ahinoam will say, defensively, "What would you have me do? I needed to take care of my baby, the king's son." '

David Wheaton asked, 'So where was Abigail?'

'Coming,' Nik said, 'walking slowly toward them, carrying her baby, Chileab, wrapped in her own garment, so that she comes to David naked, her head held high, her eyes proud. And David will leave Ahinoam, take his cloak, and wrap it around Abigail, embracing her.' He stopped, looking at Emma. 'Why are you laughing? It's not a funny scene.'

'No, no,' Emma gasped. 'It's very moving. Truly.'

'Then why are you laughing?'

'You have Abigail naked again.'

'Emma, do you have a thing about this?'

'No, you have.'

Nik got up and stalked out of the dining room, leaving the kitchen door swinging violently.

'Oh, dear.' Emma sighed.

Her father reached out and patted her hand. 'Well, my dear, it wasn't tactful of you.'

'No. I know. I'm sorry.'

'You'll have to learn more about men and our pride.'

'Hey,' Chantal objected, 'what about women and our pride? Do we have to make special exceptions for men?'

Emma fought down her impulse to run after Nik. 'It's okay,' Louis reassured her. 'Ev's gone after him.'

'He really does have too many nude scenes—' Emma said.

David continued, 'I assume David got all the flocks and herds of the Amalekites as his spoil and took them back to Ziklag. At least, that's the usual way of things.'

'Here they come,' Inez said.

'Hush,' Chantal warned.

Emma looked up in relief as Nik came in between Everard and Sophie and returned to his place at the table.

'So, then, Nik,' David went on as though there had been no interruption, 'David took his wives and children home.'

'Right.' Nik made his voice casual. 'And Chileab caught a chill from which he never recovered.'

'Poor Abigail.'

'And Zeruiah would be furious at Ahinoam for being a collaborator, as it were, while Abigail and Chileab had to sleep in the open.'

'Good scene, Nik,' David Wheaton said.

.

Emma, Nik, and David left for the theater together. In the elevator David urged, 'Please come back after the show for a turkey sandwich. Sophie'll be terribly let down, and tired, and it will help if you'll come.'

'But if she's tired—' Nik started.

'She's going to want to sit up with me for a while, anyhow.'

'Okay,' Emma said. 'We'll come for a few minutes.'

·

After the theater Emma, too, was tired. The audience had been heavy Thanksgiving evening. The cast had had to work hard for their laughs. She sat wearily at the table, which Sophie had set with her favorite crocheted mats. She had put fresh candles in the holders, rearranged the flowers.

David Wheaton was returning to thoughts of Nik's play. 'David had an extraordinary sense of community for his day. Tribes of fewer than a hundred people pitted themselves against other tribes, and David was a leader they could all love.'

'You, too, Dave,' Nik said. 'The cast is utterly devoted to you. And we'll need that kind of community if my play is ever to come to life.'

'So what happens next?'

'David, I need to ask you something.'

'Fire away.'

'When you said grace before Thanksgiving dinner this afternoon—I don't mean to pry, but you hinted at things I didn't understand.'

'Yes, Nik, I probably did, and you're due an explanation, but I'd appreciate it if you'd leave it alone for a while. It's something I find very difficult to talk about. When the time comes, it's Emma who should be the one to tell you.'

Emma sat with her hands clenched in her lap, an uneaten turkey sandwich on the plate in front of her.

'Okay,' Nik said. 'I'm sorry. I can see I've touched on something really painful.'

'Nikkie.' Sophie pushed through the kitchen door. 'Another sandwich?'

'Believe it or not, Sophie,' Nik said. 'No.'

'And your David play?' Sophie asked. 'How's it going?'

'Moving along. My next scene will be Saul, going to the witch of Endor. He is frightened and horribly alone. Out of his mind with terror. So he persuades the old witch to bring up Samuel's ghost, and Samuel is outraged at being disturbed from his place among the dead, and he tells Saul that the Lord has rent his kingdom out of his hand and given it to David because Saul disobeyed the Lord in not killing all the Amalekites when the Lord told him to.'

'The story does keep referring back to that. I don't like it,' Emma said.

'But Samuel's ghost spoke true,' Nik said, 'and Saul was killed in battle.'

'What a role for a character actor!' David exclaimed.

'Yeah,' Nik agreed. 'Samuel refused to speak to Saul, and the old king, in anguish, begged God to let him know what was going to happen. But God was silent. God would not speak to Saul.'

.

"It's a tragic story in many ways," Abby said. She was sitting on the long bench in the main cabin, a sheaf of Nik's yellowed pages in her hand. "God's silence. God refusing to talk to Saul. And Saul, old and frightened and knowing that his kingdom was lost—I can but pity him."

Emma nodded. "Nik's made him pitiable. He's made us care about him. Even understand him for going to the witch of Endor, and her familiar spirit, whatever that is."

Abby said, "Someone who's in touch with the spirit world, I suppose."

"With God?"

"Not with God. With the underworld. If you're in touch with God you don't need familiar spirits. Remember, Saul was not in touch with God, not anymore, so it's not surprising he'd think of Samuel." She picked up the next page. Read. "Ah. The death of little Chileab . . ." She put down the page. Her hands were trembling. "After all these years—my babies were both dead long before you were born. Every time I think I'm invulnerable, something happens to tell me I'm not."

"Oh, Abby, I'm sorry, that was insensitive of me, showing you that scene.'

"Nonsense. I've been reading Nik's play right along with you."
She picked up her sketchbook.

.

In the morning, just after six, with David Wheaton and Abby
still asleep, Emma, Alice, and Ben got into the rowboat, Ben
at the oars, and went to the far side of Whittock Island. The
tide was unusually low, and the abalone were stuck to the rocks
above the tide line. Ben pried them loose swiftly and with ease,
and Alice, too, quickly had a small basket full. Emma laughed
at her own futile efforts to get the abs to let go their suction on
the rock. While Ben and Alice filled their baskets, Emma ended
up with two.

"That's plenty," Alice assured her. "We'll never eat this many.
If you can stand garlic at breakfast, I'll fix some to go with the
scrambled eggs."

"I thought I was supposed to cook."

"If you've never cooked abs, you'd better let me do it."

Ben turned the rowboat back toward the *Portia*, skirting
the rocks, pointing out great colonies of sea urchins, a rich
red, with thousands of sharp quills. "Poisonous," Ben reminded
them.

They passed white and green sea anemones, and small, round,
translucent jellyfish opening and closing in rhythmic motions as
they swam.

Emma looked at Alice and Ben. This was their environment,
their home. And yet Alice had appeared wholly contented with
David in New York.

When they got back to the *Portia*, Alice took the baskets of
abs to the sink. The outside of their shells was lumpy and brown-
ish. When Alice had cleaned them of the meat, the inside was
lustrous, gleaming with the colors of mother-of-pearl. While
Alice was cooking, Ben went back to pick up the shrimp traps,
which contained many starfish as well as a plentiful catch of
shrimp. Ben spread the starfish out on the cleaning shelf on the
back deck to show Emma.

"I've never seen starfish with as many colors," she exclaimed. "Red, blue, lavender."

Ben pointed—"Sunflower starfish"—and Emma looked at a strange creature with twenty sun rays of legs. She counted. "What are you going to do with them?"

"Throw them back," Ben said, doing so.

Tamar

✿ ✿ ✿

And David lamented with this lamentation over Saul and
over Jonathan his son:

The beauty of Israel is slain upon thy high places: how
are the mighty fallen!

Tell it not in Gath, publish it not in the streets of Askelon;
lest the daughters of the Philistines rejoice, lest the daughters of the uncircumcised triumph.

Ye mountains of Gilboa, let there be no dew, neither let
there be rain, upon you, nor fields of offerings: for there
the shield of the mighty is vilely cast away, the shield of
Saul, as though he had not been anointed with oil.

From the blood of the slain, from the fat of the mighty,
the bow of Jonathan turned not back, and the sword of
Saul returned not empty.

Saul and Jonathan were lovely and pleasant in their lives,
and in their death they were not divided: they were swifter
than eagles, they were stronger than lions.

How are the mighty fallen in the midst of the battle! O
Jonathan, thou wast slain in thine high places.

I am distressed for thee, my brother Jonathan: very pleasant hast thou been unto me: thy love to me was wonderful,
passing the love of women.

How are the mighty fallen, and the weapons of war
perished!

II SAMUEL 1:17, 19–23, 25–27

BEN PLANNED to make the crossing to the Queen Charlottes that morning. When they had finished breakfast, Emma took the wheel, Alice keeping lookout for logs, or deadheads. It was cloudy, with just enough wind to rock the *Portia*. If they moved about the pilothouse, they held on to the brass rails above the wheel and along the port and starboard sides. Alice grinned. "Just like the subway."

David was asleep, snoring lightly. Abby was in the lower cabin, the curtains pulled around the double bed. Ben, too, was resting, stretched out on the long bunk behind the table. He would relieve Emma at the wheel when they came to open water.

Emma enjoyed being on watch, steering the little craft through the beauty of quiet waters. "It reminds me of the Norwegian fjords," she murmured.

"When were you there?" Alice asked.

"Nik and I took a vacation on a Norwegian mail boat, leaving from Bergen, and going across the Arctic Circle, around the North Cape, and back. We had a lovely, happy time. The scenery was magnificent. Very much like this. Did you miss it terribly when you were in New York?"

"Not terribly," Alice said. Her voice broke. "Watch out for that patch of kelp over there. I think there's a log in the middle."

Emma turned the wheel slightly. Rarely did Alice let her pain show. They held it between them, she thought, Alice and Abby and Ben and Emma, each bearing not only private pain but some of the pain of the others. She steered around a floating log on which sat five birds with dark beaks and bright red feet.

"Oystercatchers," Alice said, following Emma's gaze.

Emma nodded, staring ahead of her at the water, grey under a cloudy sky. They were still in sight of the land on either side, clothed in the deep green of fir trees. Occasionally there was a patch of lighter green where alders had grown up to replace trees which had been logged. Eventually the great conifers would grow and reach above the smaller trees. —Not in my lifetime, Emma thought. —These trees make our life spans seem very short.

"Go to the left of that island," Alice directed, and Emma turned the boat. Alice seldom used nautical terms like port and starboard. She said whatever was simplest. There was silence except for David's breathing and the sound of the *Portia* moving through the water. Alice spoke softly. "I was reading the end of Samuel I and the beginning of Samuel II today. If we're looking for contradictions, there are two completely different stories of Saul's death."

"Two different writers, maybe?"

"Maybe. In the end of Samuel I, Saul's sons were all killed, and Saul himself was wounded, and he begged his armor bearer to take his sword and finish him off so the uncircumcised Philistines would not abuse him."

Although the two women had kept their voices low, David was roused from his nap and joined in. "Saul did not want to be killed by unclean swine."

Alice asked, "Was removing the foreskin that important?"

"Yes," David said. "It was a health measure in a hot and dirty country, very unlike the Pacific Northwest. But circumcision became far more than that. It was a symbol of being God's true people, and those with foreskins were heathens, like me. Nowadays, when we're all compulsive about our daily showers, there's no need to remove a loose and healthy foreskin, is there?"

Alice shook her head.

"And it does add to the woman's pleasure. However, Saul would have cared about the symbol."

"Anyhow," Emma continued, "Saul's armor bearer would not, could not kill the old king. And Saul took his sword and fell on it, and when his armor bearer saw that he was dead he, too, took his sword and fell on it."

"But then," Alice said, "in the first chapter of Samuel II, when David learns of Saul's death, it's from an Amalekite who said that he happened to come to Mount Gilboa and saw Saul leaning on his spear, and there were chariots and horsemen coming after him. So Saul begged the Amalekite to slay him, which the man did. Weren't we just saying that the Amalekites were uncircumcised pigs?"

"We were," David said. "It doesn't ring true that Saul would ask an Amalekite to slay him."

Emma turned the wheel slightly. "I don't give it my willing suspension of disbelief, that the Amalekite would slay him and then take Saul's crown from his head and bracelet from his arm and give them to David."

David Wheaton's voice was strong. "David's response was to ask the man how he dared raise his hand against the Lord's anointed, and then David had him killed."

Emma turned briefly to look at her father's face, thin and drawn, but alive with interest. "In Greek history and drama, doesn't the messenger of bad news usually get killed?"

"Usually. So not many people want to be the bearers of bad news." David held out his hand to Alice, and she came and sat on the side of his bunk, holding his hand in hers. Emma thought she was taking David's pulse, but her face was calm and unreadable.

"There's a logging camp ahead," Alice said, and Emma looked and saw a series of small houses, barely more than wooden huts, plus a big ship with a rig for loading logs, with three little buglike boats nudging the logs into position. Then the camp was behind them and they were alone with water and trees, with an occasional eagle brooding above them on a high tree.

Alice reached for her binoculars. "Two loons," she said, and handed the glasses to Emma.

.

In the water ahead of them Emma and Alice saw an eagle flapping great wings, swimming with massive effort.

"What's the matter?" Emma asked.

"The fish he's caught is too heavy for him. When eagles' wings get too waterlogged they can sink, and sometimes they drown because their claws are trapped in the fish."

Emma turned the *Portia* to move closer to the exhausted eagle, and suddenly it dropped the fish and with an enormous effort raised its wet wings and soared up into the sky, to land on a high tree.

.

David said, "I think I'll snooze again for a few minutes."

"Okay. We'll let you know when there's anything worth seeing." Emma looked ahead at the great expanse of wrinkled sea. They were leaving the islands behind now.

Ben came up to the pilothouse. "Thanks, Em. I'll take the wheel."

Emma nodded, sliding off the revolving chair.

"If all goes well," Ben said, "we'll make Port Clements by evening."

The crossing of the Queen Charlotte Sound was unusually smooth, and full of delights. They saw many ducks, mergansers, scooters, guillemots. The greatest joy was seeing a mother and baby humpback whale playing, slapping flukes on the surface, for a full forty-five minutes.

But even that joy could not stop Emma from projecting. Each minute they were coming nearer and nearer to Port Clements and a public telephone. She would be able to call Nik. She was going to be the bearer of bad news.

The phone, and then a plane, would propel him into the present, whether she wanted him there or not.

·

And whether she wanted to or not, she was drawn back into the past, the past of that Thanksgiving night. They had talked about the two versions of Saul's death, because David did not want to talk about the tensions of that afternoon. And Emma? When would she explain the tensions to Nik?

'The first version of Saul's death rings more true,' she said, turning her concentration to the play. 'That Saul would fall on his sword himself, rather than wait for an Amalekite to kill him. Whatever he was, he was not a coward.'

'You're right,' Nik agreed. 'The other somehow diminishes David's grief.'

'And Abigail's,' Emma said. 'David's grief over Saul and Jonathan would have been so overwhelming that baby Chileab's death would go almost unnoticed. And probably David wouldn't have seen much of his frail little son.'

'You feel for Abigail, don't you?' Nik asked.

'Oh, yes, I empathize. I can hear her with Zeruiah, saying, "I won't tell him about Chileab till later. He will not even hear me now, and I need to be with him in his grief."'

'Um, um.' Nik scribbled on his yellow pad. 'But what do you bet Ahinoam would have spread all over the palace the news that Abigail's puny little son was dead.'

'When David heard about it'—Emma closed her eyes in the intensity of her visualization of the scene—'he'd push Ahinoam and bouncing Amnon out of the way and he'd sweep Abigail into his arms, and they'd weep together, Abigail for her child, David for the dead king, and for Jonathan, his friend Jonathan.'

'Then, when the weeping was spent,' David Wheaton suggested, 'they'd make love, and when that, too, was spent, they'd take their harps and sing.'

Nik smiled. 'Yes. Music would be good here. They'd sing for the baby, for the king, for Jonathan.'

Emma read from Nik's Bible, 'The beauty of Israel is slain upon thy high places: how are the mighty fallen!'

'Wonderful.' David leaned back in his chair. 'It's a great requiem song.'

'Verbose,' Nik said. 'I can't use all of it. David will weep again, and Abigail will hold him, wiping away his tears with her hair.'

Emma continued, her voice gentle, 'Saul and Jonathan were lovely and pleasant in their lives, and in their death they were not divided: they were swifter than eagles, they were stronger than lions. Ye daughters of Israel, weep over Saul, who clothed you in scarlet, with other delights, who put on ornaments of gold upon your apparel. How are the mighty fallen in the midst of the battle! O Jonathan, thou wast slain in thine high places.'

Nik gave her one of his rare sweet smiles. 'Beautiful words of love and exaggeration pouring from David's lips and melody from his harp.'

Emma took up the lament again. 'I am distressed for thee, my brother Jonathan: very pleasant hast thou been unto me: thy love to me was wonderful, passing the love of women.'

At that, Nik laughed, a pealing of merriment. 'And then David presses Abigail down on the bedclothes and tells her, "Passing the love of Michal and Ahinoam, not you, Abigail. Thou hast ravished my heart, my sister, my spouse; thou hast ravished my heart with one of thine eyes, with one chain of thy neck . . ." '

'Song of Songs?' Emma asked. Her flesh was tingling. Were Nik's words only the words of his character, King David, for his character, Abigail? Or was Nik also speaking to Emma? 'Wasn't that attributed to Solomon?'

'If David could get some of the Psalms from Abigail, Solomon could get some of his Song from his father.'

'Why not?' David looked at Nik, who had turned to his pad and was scribbling.

Emma continued, 'David, exhausted from tears and grief—'

'And love,' David said.

'Okay, Papa, but that's not going to be shown onstage.'

'And then,' Nik said, 'David asks God where he should go next. I still find it difficult.'

'What?' David asked, looking up from the script.

'This speaking personally and directly to God.'

'Didn't your father?' Emma asked.

'To a God who wasn't there.'

'Can you speak to someone who isn't there?'

Nik looked at David. 'Dave?'

David Wheaton winced. 'Oh, I speak to God. I beg, I implore that my sons will come home safely. But I'm not sure that's part of the promise. I don't think God interferes with our free will. But I speak. And I know that David did. He had such a conviction that he had been anointed by God that he truly believed that he could talk, ask specific questions, and be answered.'

'But were the answers real, or were they in his head?'

David shrugged and took a swallow of milk.

'But you think it's possible? A direct line? Emma?'

'I don't know.'

'David believed,' Nik said, 'that God told him to go to Hebron. Abigail would offer to go with him, and David would wave his arms grandly and say, "We will all go. All the household." '

.

—It can't be avoided. The household always goes with us, Emma thought. —Nik will always carry the wounds of his parents with him. I will carry my whole crazy family. I will carry forever what I'm going to have to tell Nik—

'Time to go,' Nik said.

'I don't want you walking home in this weather.' David Wheaton shoved a bill into Nik's hand.

'No, Dave—'

'Take Emma home in a taxi, and there should be enough to get you to Brooklyn.'

'Don't argue, Nikkie,' Sophie urged.

'Papa's as stubborn as you are,' Emma added. 'Give in gracefully.'

When the taxi drew up in front of Emma's apartment, Nik asked, 'Okay if I come in for a few minutes?'

'Sure.' Emma opened the door, turned on lights, sat cross-legged on the foot of her bed, waiting. For what?

Nik sat in her most comfortable chair, upright, not relaxed. 'Emma—'

'What is it?'

'Emma, I love your family. But it was very clear today that I am not entirely included, and I understand that. I've been ambiguous about—about us. I love you. But I haven't taken the next step and asked you in any formal way to marry me.'

She made her voice light. 'And informally?'

'Whenever King David makes love to Abigail, I'm making love to you. I don't know what's holding me back. My parents, I suppose. Emma, if I ask you to marry me now, will you misunderstand?'

'Misunderstand?'

'Your family—I want to be part of it. I want to know what was going on when your father said grace. So maybe this isn't a good time for me to ask you to marry me. But I do ask you. Emma, will you marry me?'

She looked at him, slowly nodding her head.

'You will?' He was out of the chair, reaching for her hand.

'Yes, Nik, but there are things we have to talk about—'

He reached in his pocket and pulled out a small box. 'I bought this a week ago. I'd planned to offer it to you today. Then—after dinner—I wasn't sure the timing was right—but I can't wait any longer.' He put the box in her hand.

She opened it, to see a gold band, set with five small stones, three diamonds interspersed with sapphires. 'Oh, Nik—'

'They're not the big jewels I'd like to give you, but—'

'Oh—it's lovely, Nik, lovely—'

He took the box from her, took out the ring, and put it on her finger. Kissed her. Then he drew back. 'Emma! You're crying! What is it, sweetie, what is it?'

She tried to rub away the tears with the heels of her hands. 'It's all out of order—'

'What is?'

'What I have to tell you. I knew—if we ever decided to marry—I'd have to tell you. I didn't know what I'd do if you didn't ask me till—till—'

'Till what, sweetie?'

'Till we'd come to the part in the David story where—'

His voice was very gentle. 'Where what, Emma?'

'You know how Papa tends to—emphasize—the similarities in his life and King David's—when you—when you came to him with your idea for a play about King David and his wives I could hardly believe it—'

'Why, Emma? It just seemed to me to be a good idea.'

'Nik. Be patient with me, please.'

It was out of chronology. It was too soon. But she had his ring on her finger. She opened the Bible, slowly and carefully turning the pages. 'Here. Where Amnon—where he lusts after Tamar —his sister—'

.

Emma was half a year out of college, back in New York and the world of the theater. She had done an Off-Broadway play and a couple of TV dramas. She was beginning to be known as someone to watch. And at last she had her own apartment.

Shortly after Christmas, in the miserable dank weather of early January, she had dinner with friends with whom she was discussing a Molnár play, and then went home, reasonably early, ready for a hot bath and bed and rereading the play and her potential role in it.

As she opened the door to her apartment, the phone rang. It was Chantal.

'Emma, I'm glad I got you.'

'What's up?'

'Nothing earth-shattering. Inez just phoned me.'

.

'So Amnon lay down and made himself sick.' Emma's finger still pointed to the verses in the Bible.

It was an ugly story in Scripture.
Ugly.

·

'Billy called Inez, saying he'd tried to get all of us. Maybe he did. I just got in myself.'

'What did Billy want?'

'He's got the flu, or something, and he told Inez he has a high fever, and he needs one of us to go to the drugstore and get a prescription his doctor called in.'

'Why can't Myrlo go?'

'She's in Florida for the winter.'

'What about Inez herself, then?'

'Edith won't let her go, and she said Billy sounded really sick.'

'Well, it's certainly out of the way for you,' Emma said. 'It's only a few blocks for Inez.'

'It's out of the way for you, too. I'd go, but the thing is, Em, I've got a miserable sore throat, and I really don't want to get sick. It's starting to rain, and I'd have to take two subways.'

'I'll go.' Emma tried not to sound weary. 'It's just across town for me.'

'Oh, Emma, you're an angel. I'll love you forever.'

·

So Amnon lay down, and made himself sick: and when the king was come to see him, Amnon said unto the king, I pray thee, let Tamar my sister come, and make me a couple of cakes in my sight, that I may eat at her hand.

It was like and it was not like. David Wheaton knew nothing about it. It was Inez who called Chantal.

Chantal who called Emma.

If it followed the story, it would have been Chantal, wouldn't it? Chantal would have been Tamar's equivalent. Not Emma. It didn't fit the story at all.

Neither of the Davids knew what their sons were up to. They were pawns in the story. But, as Grandpa Bowman had pointed out, ignorance is not an excuse.

Is it, ever?

At the drugstore the pharmacist looked puzzled. 'No. No one has called in a prescription for William Wilburton. I'm sorry.'

'Could it possibly be under the name of Wheaton?'

'No. I know Mr. Wilburton.'

Emma sighed again. It was indeed raining outside. She wore a raincoat, but it was not quite warm enough. The crosstown bus had been dank and damp.

'I can give you something over the counter, one of the new cold remedies,' the pharmacist suggested.

'I think it was a prescription. Thanks, anyhow.'

Billy was living in his mother's Park Avenue apartment, left her by her rich husband, who had died the summer before. While Myrlo was in Florida, Billy had the apartment to himself, plus Myrlo's cook and maid. Billy liked to live well. Emma went up in the elevator and rang the doorbell. It was answered by the maid, impeccable in grey uniform and white apron. 'Oh, Miss Emma. I think he was expecting Miss Chantal. Never mind. I'm sure he'll be glad to see you. Go on in.'

So Tamar went to her brother Amnon's house . . .

'Oh, it's you,' Billy said. 'I thought Chantal—'

'Chantal lives all the way down in the Village, and all I had to do was take the crosstown bus and walk a few blocks. But, Billy, there wasn't any prescription at the drugstore.'

'Never mind.' Billy pushed himself up against the pillows. 'You're as good as a prescription any day.' He patted the side of his bed. 'Sit down, puss.'

She sat, and put the back of her hand against his forehead. 'You don't feel hot.'

'I have a raging fever,' Billy said. 'Feel my chest.'

And Amnon raped Tamar.

'Billy, what are you doing? Billy, no! Billy, don't!'
He was strong. She fought, but he was much stronger than she.

Then Amnon called his servant . . . and said, Put now this woman out from me, and bolt the door after her.

'You're not Chantal,' Billy said. 'Get out. I wanted Chantal. You're an ugly cunt.'
Emma struggled to button her blouse where Billy had torn it open.
'You're no better than a whore,' Billy said. 'Emma. What a stupid, Victorian name. If you want to be an actress, you should change it to Emily.'
Emma struggled to her feet.
'You can't even act, you bitch,' Billy said. 'Get out.'
Blindly, Emma left. Went down in the elevator. Did not have enough money for a cab.
On the bus a woman asked her, 'Miss, are you all right?'
—My brother has raped me. 'Yes. Thank you.'
'Miss, there's blood on your coat.'
'Oh. I'm sorry.'
She got off at the next stop. Thank God the bus had already crossed the Park. It was only one block west to Sixth Avenue, one long block and half a block more . . .

Chantal called her. 'Emma, did you get the medicine for Billy? Is everything okay?'
Emma could not speak. Could only moan. She had answered the phone out of instinct, not thinking.
'Emma, what is it?'
'D-don't—don't—'
'Don't what?'

'I can't—I can't—'
'Emma?'
'No. No.'
'Emma, I'm coming. Adair's here. We're coming.'

They held her, bathed her, sobbed with her. 'I should have been the one,' Chantal cried. 'You went instead of me. Oh, Emma, Emma!'
'How's your sore throat?' Emma asked.
'I'll kill him,' Adair said.

And King David was angry with Amnon. But he did nothing.

'I don't want anyone to know,' Emma said.
'We ought to call the police.'
'No! No!'
'Hush.'
'I tried to fight him, but he's so big. I hit him and it just seemed to make him more strong.'
Chantal blew her nose. 'Papa has to know,' she said grimly.
'Why?'
Adair's hands were clenched. 'Billy can't get away with this.'

Memory was hazy. David and Sophie were in her room with Chantal and Adair. There were phone calls, Sophie trying to call the obstetrician she had had for Louis. He was away. Another doctor was taking his calls.
Emma curled up inside her own mind like a very small snail retreating into its shell.
Arms around her. A taxi ride and then blazing, painful lights. A hospital. Sophie and Chantal with her.
'No,' she heard Chantal say. 'We're not leaving her. We're staying.' An argument, and Chantal insisting, 'We're staying with Emma.'
She was put on a table, examined. Billy's violence had torn her. There were stitches. And a cold, male voice telling her,

telling Chantal and Sophie, that she would be all right, that no permanent damage had been done.

'She should be more careful next time,' the voice said.

Sophie swore at the man. 'You arrogant bastard. Get out.' She had never before heard Sophie swear.

And then she was in the Riverside Drive apartment, in her old room, with Sophie and Chantal. David and Adair hovered in the doorway.

'Leave her alone for now,' Sophie ordered. 'Let her sleep.'

She drank hot milk which must have had a sedative in it, because her eyes began to droop, her ears to buzz.

She heard Adair's voice. 'Papa, you can't let Billy get away with this.'

'What do you want me to do?'

'Put him in jail.'

'Do you want that kind of publicity? Does Emma?'

Chantal said, 'Billy's a pervert, a sick pervert. He should at least be put in a mental hospital.'

Their words were lost in the buzzing in her ears. She slid into darkness.

Sophie was in the room when she drifted into wakefulness, a thin winter sun coming through the windows. Sophie hugged her, kissed her gently on the forehead. 'Darling love, you're all right. You're all right.'

She stayed with Sophie and her father for a week. Sophie would have kept her indefinitely, but Emma said, 'Things have to get back to normal as soon as possible.' There was too much talking going on around her in the apartment, David talking to Myrlo, trying to get her to get Billy to a psychiatrist. Myrlo shouting. Emma heard Myrlo's 'She asked for it!' before a door was slammed. Chantal called her daily, sounding miserable with the terrible cold she had tried to avoid and which developed into flu.

Chantal said, sneezing, 'Edith came to see Papa. She wanted him to know Inez had nothing to do with it.'

'With what?'

'Billy's wanting one of us to come bring him medicine. All Papa's doing is trying to get him to see a doctor, and Myrlo refuses. Adair says Papa can override her. Billy's dangerous. Adair thinks Billy still might—with me— One of my friends is staying with me so I won't be alone.'

King David spoke to Amnon. To Ahinoam. But he did nothing definitive.

During a crowded rush hour when Adair and Billy were standing on the subway platform, Billy fell and went under an oncoming subway train.

It was an accident it was an accident it was an accident

Myrlo blamed Adair, wanted him in the electric chair. Myrlo, still grieving for her insurance-executive husband, was insane with grief over Billy. David managed to keep her mouth shut, keep reporters at bay. It was an accident. Prosecuting Adair would not bring Billy back. Any revenge she tried to take would only smear Billy.

Myrlo screamed, 'It was Adair who seduced Emma, not Billy, not my baby, sweet Jesus, it was not my baby Billy!'

David stood unmoving and let her shriek herself out. Finally she turned her energies to Billy's funeral, held in a church near Times Square.

Sophie came to Emma. 'You don't have to go to Billy's funeral.'

Emma said dryly, 'I hadn't planned to.'

'It's going to be awful,' Sophie said. 'But I promised Davie I'd go with him. Emmelie, what are you doing with yourself? You've got purple shadows under your eyes.'

'I'm starting rehearsal for a TV show tomorrow. I'll be all right, Sophie. I just wish I'd get a job in China.'

Tears came to Sophie's eyes. 'Sometimes we hurt you just by loving you, don't we?'

—Adair, Emma thought. Where is Adair?

Adair withdrew completely from the family. Refused to talk to his father.

Absalom, Absalom, oh, my son, Absalom. Would I had died for thee, Absalom, my son.

But Adair was not Absalom.

.

Finally, unexpectedly, without warning, he came to Emma. Came at night to her apartment on Fifty-fifth Street. Held out his arms.
'Go to Georgia, Emma,' Adair said. 'Go to your grand-father.'

.

Chantal told her father and Sophie, 'Adair thinks Emma should go South to see her grandfather.'
'Oh, how right! How right of Adair!' Sophie exclaimed.
She helped Emma pack. 'Listen, Emma, darling. Nothing in you has changed. You're still the pure young woman you always were.'
'I feel soiled.'
'Oh, I know, I know, sweetheart. But you're not. It's Billy who's soiled. He should have had psychiatric help years ago, but Myrlo wouldn't hear of it. Emma, don't let this turn you against men. One day you'll meet a man who loves you purely, the way Davie loves me.'

.

In Georgia, winter was over. The Judas trees were in full rosy bloom. Dogwood and azaleas were budding. Emma sat on the screened porch with Grandpa Bowman and listened to a mockingbird singing its loveliest song.

'Are you angry?' Grandpa Bowman asked.

'I don't know.'

'You have every right to be angry. The fact that Billy is dead does not change what he did. Don't keep putting your anger off. Until you go through it, you can't get out of it.'

'Myrlo says I asked for it.'

'Since when have you started paying attention to what Myrlo says?'

'Grandpa, I didn't.'

'You don't have to persuade me. I know that.'

'He took me completely by surprise.'

'Emma, Emma, stop trying to blame yourself.'

'Maybe I shouldn't have been surprised. When I was little, he used to kiss me on the lips and I hated it.'

'When your father married Myrlo, he made a very expensive mistake.'

'Grandpa, I don't like feeling hate.'

'It is a destructive emotion, you are right. Anger is better, rightful anger. Have you cried?'

'I've cried for Adair.'

Grandpa Bowman put his arms around her. His beard scratched against her face. And then she felt his tears.

.

Life continues. Somehow.

Emma went back to New York. She took a role in a play in a small, experimental theater.

Adair was gone. He had enlisted in the army and been sent overseas.

There was no news of Etienne, or what waters his battleship plied. Marical wept, wept.

But as long as Adair and Etienne were alive, there was hope.

Everard came to the city, to Emma. He could not stay away
from his duties at the hospital late enough in the evening to take
her for supper after the show at the little theater down in the
Village, so he met her at Chantal's.

After Chantal had put out soup and sandwiches, Everard
looked at Emma carefully. 'You're better.'

'Yes.'

'Did going to Grandpa Bowman help?'

'Yes. I have a wonderful grandfather. But I wish I'd had a
chance to say goodbye to Adair.'

'Nobody did. Adair just left.'

Chantal added, 'Papa's very broken about it. Maman is praying
that Adair will come back safely.'

Emma looked at Everard. 'Why would anybody want to rape
someone? Take what wasn't being given?'

Everard grimaced. 'What I think is that it's a sort of through-
back.'

'How?'

'In the beginning of human history the planet was very
sparsely populated. Men got killed by each other, or wild animals, or earthquakes, or other natural disasters. Keeping the
population from dying out was a big priority. So men were
programmed genetically with an enormously strong sex drive.
Then, when the population increased and it wasn't necessary
anymore, the strong sex drive was still programmed in—'

'Hey, wait!' Chantal broke in.

Everard looked at his sister with his gentle gaze.

'Rape is not aggressive sexuality,' Chantal said. 'It's sexualized
aggression.'

Everard sighed. 'Right. You're right. I guess I was trying to
let Billy off the hook by making him a Neanderthal.'

'Billy may be dead,' Chantal said, 'but that doesn't change
who he was or what he did. He wasn't a Neanderthal trying to
propagate the species. Rape is hate. It would still have been
hate if I had gone to Billy, instead of Emma.'

'Is lust hate?' Everard asked.

'Yes.' Chantal was definite.

·

In early June, Sophie came to Emma. 'Are you set for stock this summer?'

'For July and August.'

'Emma, will you go to the West Coast with Davie, to be with him on the boat? For a few weeks? He's afraid to ask you.'

Emma sighed. 'I can't do anything with Papa when he's depressed.'

'You don't have to do anything. He's trying hard to pull himself up. Louis's going to a day camp and I can't leave him. And I know you love the *Portia* and being on the water. Emma, I'm asking a lot of you, when it's you I should be thinking of, not Davie, but Davie's my husband, and I think it would do you both good.'

Reluctantly, Emma went. Once they were away from the city and the crowded boatyards, she found the quiet of the water and the forests healing. David, too, was quieter.

They stopped at Norma's village. Norma came out onto the dock to greet them.

'Come,' David said, and led the way onto the boat. 'Emma. Wait.' He headed for the pilothouse, gesturing to Norma to follow him. Emma sat on a bench on the dock, letting the sun warm her. Waited. Waited. At last Norma came back to Emma, took her in her arms. 'Your father told me.'

Norma took Emma home to her village, to her house. There she bathed her like a baby, washing every area of skin, every orifice. And then she rubbed Emma's body with pungent, healing oils. When Emma was clean and dry, Norma rocked her, speaking slowly in her deep voice. 'You will stay here with me for a few days.'

Emma nodded drowsily, then asked, 'Papa told you—'

'He told me everything.'

'That Billy is dead?'

'Yes. There was an accident.'

Norma waited.

'There is more. Billy was with Adair—the brother I have always loved the most—I don't know whether or not Adair was—whether or not—somehow—responsible.'

.

At the end of three days, Norma took Emma up the hill behind her house, sat with her on a sun-warmed rock. 'Emma, you must make a decision.'

Emma looked at her, not understanding. 'What decision?'

'To come back to life. To love, and laugh.'

Emma wrapped her arms about her knees, put her head down. Norma's hand was warm against her head.

'When I was younger than you, only sixteen, I went to see cousins in—a city which need not be named. It was over the border. I was sent out to buy some groceries and when I left the store five men jumped on me, knocking the bag out of my hand. Everything spilled. A bottle of milk broke. I didn't realize what was going on, and I bent over and tried to pick things up.' Emma looked at the dark eyes, at the face which revealed nothing. 'They raped me,' Norma said in her level voice. 'All of them, and more than once, and some other men just stood looking on.'

'Oh, my God!'

'I was made pregnant by God knows which of the men.'

'Norma, the police—'

'I was an Indian, a girl, the police were not interested in me. They said I asked for it. My cousins brought me home, back here, to my village. I drank some tea which usually helps a baby such as mine to abort, but nothing happened. I carried the baby for seven months and then it came, premature, deformed. I wept for it, poor little thing who had no part in its own conception. I nursed it, cared for it, with little stumps for arms and legs which never would have carried it. When it died I felt that I had died, too. No one told me that the baby and I were both better off for this death, and I was grateful for that. And then I nearly died, as well, of a strange fever that raged through my veins. The women in the village took turns sitting with me, nursing me, caring for me. When I was well they told me that I was at a crossroads, and I did not know what they meant.'

Norma continued, her voice still quiet, devoid of emotion. 'The elder of the village, our wise woman, came to me. She was old, over one hundred years of age, and she smiled at me and repeated that I was at a crossroads. I asked her, "Where do the roads go?" '

'Where?' Emma asked.

'She told me that one road led to a wedding and the other to a funeral, and that it was up to me which road I chose. It's up to you, too, Emma.'

Emma looked for a long time at Norma, who returned her gaze with luminous dark eyes that emphasized the smile on her lips. 'You chose the wedding. If you can, then I can,' Emma said.

'It was after I had chosen that I met Ellis. Not before. My only sadness is that I was not able to have children. Something about my poor little deformed baby and the fever burned out my ability to have babies. But I have a good life, Emma, a life of great joy.' She rose, standing tall and straight on the rock, looking out to sea. 'You can still have children.'

Emma nodded. 'The doctor said I'm okay as far as that's concerned.'

'That is good. Joy will return, Emma, and then, one day, happiness. Now it is time that you and your father move on.'

'Papa—'

'He has a wound, a darkness that is beyond his control. You do not have this wound. Go and love him now.'

·

Emma read from Nik's Bible. 'So Tamar remained desolate . . . But Absalom fled . . . And David mourned for his son every day . . .

·

'Emma, Emma, Emma—' Nik's arms were around her, his tears mingling with hers.

'I didn't know how I'd tell you—when we came to that part in the play—'

'No—no—' Nik gently pushed Emma away so that he could look at her. 'So there are certain resemblances between your father and King David, between their wives, but as you pointed out yourself, you're not a twentieth-century equivalent of Tamar. Sure, I can see the parallels, but there's no preordained necessity.'

She leaned her forehead against his chest. 'I know.'

'Free will, Emma, sweetie, not predestination. For instance, where do I come into the story?' He kissed her gently, pushing her hair back from her forehead.

After a while she said, 'You don't. Thank God.'

'And we belong together, you and I.'

'Yes.'

'And if we're looking for coincidences, what about Henry VIII? He had eight wives.'

'No—' Emma laughed shakily. 'I think it was only six.'

'Six—eight. I could see you as Queen Elizabeth, Anne Boleyn's daughter.'

Emma laughed again, 'Neither King David nor Papa killed off their wives.'

Nik took her hands, held up the left one, touched his ring on her finger. 'You're a marvel, Emma. Norma didn't make you choose the wedding at that crossroads. It wasn't just Grandpa Bowman and Norma who healed you. You had to heal yourself.'

'For a while I took baths three and sometimes four times a day. Then, when I went on the boat with Papa, that had to stop. We don't carry that kind of water. And Norma's cleansing did help. When we came back to New York I could look at my body and accept it as mine, and okay.'

•

'My sweetie, my sweetie.' Again Nik held her close. 'You know how to love. I only hope I'll be able to love as well as you. I love you, Emma, I love you.'

·

On Saturday Emma went down to Chantal's between the matinee and the evening performance. Her sister was alone.

'I thought maybe you could give me a quick bite to eat,' Emma said. Chantal put down her violin, which she had been playing. 'It sounded good. But sad,' Emma commented.

'It's a sad piece. I was feeling broody. How about some salad? And I have a little smoked salmon.'

'Perfect.' Emma tried not to hold out her left hand too obviously.

But Chantal saw. 'What's this? What's this?'

'A ring.'

'What kind of a ring?'

'An engagement ring.'

Chantal took Emma's hand, studied it. 'Um. Nice. Not ostentatious, but nice. It came from Niklaas Green?'

'Yes.'

'When?'

'Thanksgiving night. Late. Or early the next morning.'

'And you've taken this long to tell me?'

'I've been—absorbing it. Absorbing that I'm happy.'

·

She called Georgia. Yes, Grandpa Bowman said, yes, he would manage to make the trip. He needed to meet this Niklaas Green, and certainly nobody else was going to perform Emma's wedding ceremony.

Emma tried to call Abby, but, as often happened, could not get her call through, so she sent a telegram. She tried not to look too often at the ring finger of her left hand.

Sophie was ecstatic, full of hugs and little squeals of joy.

David shook Nik's hand, kissed his daughter. 'But don't expect me to act surprised. The writing was on the wall if not in the stars. It is good to welcome you formally to the family, Nik.' He held out his arms and gave Nik a bear hug.

'Champagne!' Sophie cried. 'We should have champagne.'

'Later,' David said, 'when we gather together—as many as can—to celebrate, and I have a chance to buy some champagne and get it chilled.'

'Food, then. I've made some lovely—' Sophie's words were muffled as she went to the kitchen.

'It's a good thing I metabolize my food easily and stay thin,' David said affectionately. 'Sophie's going to have to watch it. Forgive me if I seem selfish, children, but I'd like to get back to the play. I *am* selfish when it comes to a great role. We couldn't get it ready for next season, but—'

'Wait till I finish it, Dave.'

David grinned. 'Don't take as long as you did to ask Emma to marry you.'

.

"What's the matter?" Abby asked. She and Emma were in the main cabin; Alice and Ben were in the pilothouse. They were nearing Port Clements, and the wind was rising, rocking the little craft.

Emma put down the scene she had been looking at. "I don't know why I'm reading this. It brings up too many bad memories. When Nik was writing about Ahinoam and Amnon he might just as well have been writing about Myrlo and Billy. God knows I don't have much good to say of either Myrlo or Billy, but it's my fault if Nik's made Ahinoam and Amnon into flat villains."

"Emma, love, can't you let it go?"

"Most of the time I can. I thought I had. Coming across all these scenes from Nik's play, reading them—it brings it back."

"For David, too, do you think?"

Emma shook her head. "I don't think so. Except during his horrible glooms, Papa's always had the ability to remember the good things and let the bad ones go."

"Not a bad ability."

Emma paused. Then said, "I'm not sure. I think we have to remember it all before we can forgive it."

Sophie

❦ ❦ ❦

Abner . . . captain of Saul's host, took Ishbosheth the son
of Saul . . . And made him king over . . . all Israel.

Ishbosheth Saul's son was forty years old when he began
to reign over Israel, and reigned two years. But the house
of Judah followed David.

And Abner . . . and the servants of Ishbosheth the son
of Saul, went out from Mahanaim to Gibeon.

And Joab the son of Zeruiah, and the servants of David,
went out, and met together . . . And there was a very sore
battle that day; and Abner was beaten, and the men of
Israel, before the servants of David.

And there were three sons of Zeruiah, Joab, and Abishai,
and Asahel: and Asahel was as light of foot as a wild roe.

And Asahel pursued after Abner; and in going he turned
not to the right hand nor to the left from following Abner.

Then Abner looked behind him, and said, Art thou Asahel? And he answered, I am.

And Abner said to him . . . Turn thee aside from following
me: wherefore should I smite thee to the ground? how then
should I hold up my face to Joab thy brother?

Howbeit he refused to turn aside: wherefore Abner with
the hinder end of the spear smote him under the fifth rib,
that the spear came out behind him; and he fell down there,
and died in the same place.

II SAMUEL 2:8–10, 12–13, 17–23

ABBY WAS in France. There was no way she could leave. 'And even if travel was possible,' she wrote, 'it would be better for me not to come. Let Sophie have the pleasure of this wedding. Darling, I will be with you in spirit, every minute. I am more happy for you than I can say, and you must send me pictures, and when this terrible war is over, then we will be together. Give my love to everybody, and especially to your Nik.'

Jarvis took Emma and Nik to the Blue Angel for supper, inviting Chantal, too.

'Have the wedding soon,' he urged.

Chantal agreed. 'Right, Jarv. Emma and Nik should get married as soon as possible. It would give Maman something pleasant to think about.'

'So get married,' Jarvis urged Emma and Nik. 'The world is falling apart around us. You're sleeping together, aren't you? So why delay?'

Nik kept his voice low. 'Jarvis, you've no right to jump to conclusions!'

'You're in the theater, aren't you? Not Sioux Falls, South Dakota.'

'Shut up, Jarvis.' Emma's voice was cold.

'Just trying to be helpful.'

The lights went down in the restaurant and a spotlight came

up on Madame Claude Alphond, whose simple voice and French love songs brought tears to Emma's eyes. *Les filles de Saint-Malo ont les yeux le couleur de l'eau.* Emma bit her lip to try to stop from crying. Chantal reached out and took her hand, pressing it gently.

'So where?' Jarvis asked as the songs were over and the lights came up.

'Where what?' Nik asked.

'Where will you be married?'

Chantal said, 'Sophie loves the Cathedral, and so did Bahama.'

'It's so big—' Emma demurred. 'Nik—would you mind being married in church?'

'What I want is whatever you want,' Nik affirmed, reaching for her hand.

'There are all those little chapels,' Chantal suggested.

When they talked about it with David Wheaton, he agreed with Chantal. 'St. Ambrose Chapel behind the high altar would be just right for a small wedding.'

'But I want Grandpa.' Emma was anxious. 'Do we have to get permission or something for him to marry me—I mean, he's not an Episcopalian—'

'I'll speak to Tom Tallis,' David said. 'He's one of the young canons there, a friend.'

'Okay, Nik?' Emma asked.

'Hey,' Nik said softly, 'I want to meet your grandpa, and if it's okay with him for the wedding to be in a big cathedral, it's fine with me.'

.

Grandpa came; grunting, groaning, complaining about the dangers of travel in wartime, he came to New York. He was staying with David and Sophie, but he met Emma and Nik for supper after the theater. 'Niklaas, thank you for writing such a wonderful role for Emma.'

'Emma's wonderful for the role, sir.'

Grandpa Bowman snorted. '*Sir* doesn't sit well with me.

Call me Grandpa. I'm giving you my bed for a wedding present. It will just about fit in your apartment, Emma. David and Sophie tell me that's where you're going to live.'

'Yes. Apartments are impossible to find right now, and my one room is bigger than Nik's two, and more convenient. But not your bed, Grandpa—'

'Oh, yes. Oak isn't fashionable right now, but it will come back into style, and it may be worth something one day.'

'It's a gorgeous bed,' Emma told Nik, 'with a great carved headboard that reaches almost to the ceiling. Oh, Grandpa—'

'I'll also give you enough money to buy a decent box spring and mattress. Right now the bed sags in the middle and it suits me, but it wouldn't do for the two of you. It may be a little big, but you're not going to stay in a one-room apartment forever.'

'We'll need someplace a bit larger,' Emma said, 'particularly with children, and maybe there'll be more apartments available in a few years—but your bed, Grandpa—you can't—'

'I can,' Grandpa Bowman said firmly. 'It's already crated and on its way to you.' He turned to Nik. 'You are in complete earnest about this marriage?'

'Yes, Grandpa, I am.'

'I'm old. I'd like to be sure that I can trust you to take care of Emma.'

Emma said, 'This is the twentieth century. I can take care of myself.'

'I love Emma.' Nik and Emma were sitting side by side on a banquette in their usual restaurant, opposite the old man, and he took her hand, holding it tight, under the table. 'And she loves me.'

The old man sighed. 'Bless you, then, my children.' He looked at his watch. 'Theater hours are hard on this old body. I need to get back to David and Sophie.' He heaved himself to his feet. Sat again, snapping his fingers as though remembering something. Looked at Nik. 'Where are you and God?'

Nik smiled. 'Barely nodding acquaintances. My mother was a devout Catholic and my father was Jewish and atheist and I'm caught somewhere between. I hope that doesn't disqualify me.'

'I saw your play last night. For all its laughter, it makes a brave attempt to deal with reality. And you, Emma?'

'I'm caught someplace between you and Bahama, Grandpa, and that's not a bad place to be.'

The old man nodded, satisfied.

•

The upcoming wedding filled Sophie with delight. She insisted on shopping with Emma, buying her the silkiest underclothes to be had in wartime, and a white satin nightgown. 'Now, about a wedding dress—' Sophie said.

'Sophie, please, I don't want a real wedding dress. We're being married Saturday morning, and then we have a matinee and an evening performance—'

'And then you have till Monday evening for a honeymoon.'

Emma laughed. 'You and Papa—thank you!'

'It's little enough,' Sophie said. 'Two nights in the Plaza—'

'In the bridal suite—'

'For your whole honeymoon.'

'It's wonderful. We'd never have thought of it. Travel is almost impossible and there was nowhere particular we wanted to go, and we were just going back to my apartment.'

'Here, look!' Sophie took a white wool dress from a small rack of clothes. 'It's simple enough for morning, and I'll give you my pearls to wear that Davie gave me when we were married, so you'll have something borrowed.'

Emma looked at her engagement ring. 'And the two sapphires are something blue.' Around her neck was a small gold cross that had belonged to Bahama. 'Something old.'

'And the dress can be something new.'

Emma looked at the price tag. 'No, Sophie, it's much too expensive!'

Sophie fingered the soft wool. 'It's good material, and it's well cut. Let's try it on. Come on, Emmelie, try it.'

It fit perfectly, as though made for Emma's figure. 'Your father and I don't expect you to get married more than once, so make me happy by wearing this.'

'Oh, Sophie, we're so lucky Papa found you!'

.

The wedding was, as David had suggested, in St. Ambrose, a small, charming Italianate chapel behind the high altar of the Cathedral. All of Emma's available family were there. She stood between her father and Sophie, with Louis by them. Jarvis was dashingly out of place in a morning suit, looking more like Diaghilev than like a Broadway agent and producer. Chantal was Emma's maid of honor; Everard, Nik's best man. Marical had come from her small house in Connecticut, and when Emma stepped forward to stand by Nik, Sophie pulled Marical between herself and David.

Wesley Bowman rather grudgingly read the great words of the Episcopal wedding service, interpolating a few thoughts of his own. Canon Tallis, a shy, bald young man, was there to see to whatever were the legal necessities. It was a grey winter morning, and the Cathedral was dark, but the glow from the candles pushed away the shadows, and Emma felt bathed in light.

.

When Emma and Nik reached their suite in the Plaza after the play that evening, the lights were on and David and Sophie had ordered sandwiches and champagne to be waiting for them. Everard had sent flowers from himself and Chantal, and had written on the card, 'These are from Etienne and Adair, too.' There was a note from Jarvis saying that breakfast had been ordered brought to their room and all they had to do was call room service in the morning. Emma and Nik had tried to keep their plans quiet, but there was a large box from Tiffany and in it was a silver goblet from the company, with a card signed by players, stagehands, costume woman—everybody connected with Nik's play. They felt surrounded by love.

Emma bathed slowly, luxuriously, trying to still the anxiety that made her heart beat rapidly. She dried, powdered herself, put on the nightgown and robe Sophie and David had given her. Walked slowly to the living room of the suite. As she entered, Nik poured her a glass of champagne. 'Sit on the sofa, my sweetie, and relax for a few minutes.'

She sat, sipped the champagne, sneezed as the bubbles went up her nose. Laughed, shakily. Nik sat beside her, his arm about her. When she had finished the glass of champagne he bent toward her, kissed her gently, on the lips, eyes, neck, opening the robe, kissing the hollow at the base of her neck. He was slow, gentle, patient. Nik stroked her, tasted her lips, her breasts, stroking her, sensing when the tension in her body, the tension of terror, began to leave her. Finally he lifted her from the sofa, took her to the large, waiting bed.

She began to cry.

He kissed the tears. 'Sweetie, sweetie. Don't be afraid. I won't hurt you. The hurting has been done. But if you want me to stop, just say so.'

'No, no—don't stop.'

'Emma, I love you. I come to you with love.'

'I love you, too, Nik, I love you . . .'

·

The two nights at the Plaza, away from everything familiar, away from memories, helped Emma begin the process of relaxing, of, ultimately, moving into pleasure. It did not happen at first, but she believed Nik's gentle promises. In her urgent desire to please, she slowly learned how to be pleased. When it happened, it was indeed pleasure.

·

Grandpa Bowman's great oaken bedstead took up nearly half of Emma's studio. But there was still room for a sofa and a couple of easy chairs, and a small table to eat from. Emma moved her desk into the dressing room off the bathroom, and for a wedding present she gave Nik an old rolltop desk which she had found in an antique shop near Chantal's apartment in the Village.

Emma and Nik loved going home to their nest after the theater, fixing sandwiches or soup, simply being quietly together. But David and Sophie continued to urge them to come for supper.

'You keep Davie alive with his interest in your play, Nikkie,' Sophie said. 'I'm so afraid he'll slip back into that darkness of last year. Now that he's happy about Emma, and the David play, it helps stop it from happening again.'

So they went at least once a week to David and Sophie for supper, and Nik brought his current scenes.

'Maybe I could do something with projections,' he suggested. 'I really don't want any fighting onstage.'

David Wheaton laughed. 'It's as bad as *Hamlet*, isn't it? All those dead bodies, and finally Fortinbras coming onto a stage running with blood. What about Abner?'

'Abner tried to carry on Saul's war against David. At this point in the play, Zeruiah's sons really come into the picture. Abishai, and Joab, who will be a featured role. If Abner was captain of Saul's forces, Joab was captain of David's.'

'Abishai, Joab, and then there's the youngest, Asahel,' Emma said, 'and you've already made us fond of this kid, in his early scenes with Zeruiah.'

'The three of them were foremost in battle,' Nik said.

'Which battle?' David Wheaton demanded. 'Who was fighting whom, and for what?'

'Okay, Dave. Abner was continuing Saul's war against David, and David was trying to unite the two kingdoms, Judah and Israel. So it was a civil war. David fought Abner, with Zeruiah's sons, Abishai, Joab, and Asahel, right beside him.'

'And Asahel, who's young and fleet as a deer, chases after Abner, and Abner has to kill him.'

'Has to?' Sophie asked.

Nik answered, 'Abner tries to get Asahel to go back, and the kid won't, and Abner is older and bigger and a much better fighter and Abner kills him, and the Bible makes it very clear that Joab was not likely to forgive or forget. Em, read this scene for your father and Sophie. I scrawled it out on the subway, but I think you can read my writing.'

Emma took the page he handed her, glanced at it swiftly, then read aloud:

Act IV, scene vii

The scene is a shallow grave in the desert, with the white, hot light glaring down on Abishai and Joab, who are finishing the digging. Zeruiah is sitting back on her heels on the sand, holding her dead young son in her arms. Abigail is kneeling beside her. There is silence except for the sound of the spades, which occasionally hit rock with a clang like a gong.

Asahel's servant stands rear left and blows the long, strange horn, the shofar, with its terrible, haunting sound. Then silence again.

The light is so fierce it seems to flicker.

Joab puts down his shovel, bends, and takes Asahel's body from Zeruiah, and with Abishai's help wraps it in a white linen cloth; they then carefully place it in the grave. Zeruiah remains kneeling, Abigail holding her as the brothers cover the body with sand, then place stones at the head and foot to mark the place.

Again the shofar sounds.

Blackout.

'Nikkie, Nikkie!' Sophie exclaimed. 'That gives me the shivers.'

'It's a good scene.' David applauded.

Emma handed the page back to Nik. 'I know war was totally different then, but I keep thinking about my brothers. I know Ev isn't actually fighting, but driving an ambulance isn't exactly safe.' She swallowed. 'Poor Zeruiah. Asahel was her baby.'

David Wheaton closed his eyes. Both Emma and Sophie looked at him anxiously, but David Wheaton flung off his mood, laughed, and sang:

King David and King Solomon
Led merry, merry lives.
They had many, many mansions,
And many, many wives.
But old age came upon them
And with many, many qualms
King Solomon wrote the Proverbs
And King David wrote the Psalms.

Emma, too, laughed. 'You used to sing that to me when I was little. And I sang it for Grandpa Bowman.'

Nik reached for the Bible, reading out loud: 'Now there was long war between the house of Saul and the house of David: but David waxed stronger and stronger, and the house of Saul waxed weaker and weaker.'

'I like that word, *waxed,*' Emma said, 'like the moon waxing. Abner knew he was losing, so he made overtures to David, suggesting that he and David get together, and he'd give David all of Israel.'

'Not a bad deal,' David Wheaton said.

'But,' Emma said, 'David made a condition about making peace with Joab. He demanded the return of his first wife, Michal, Saul's daughter, so they took her away from her husband, Phalti. He came along with her, weeping all the way.'

'So somebody actually loved Michal,' Sophie said.

Emma said, 'I feel sorry for Phalti. He and Michal were happy together. He loved her, and expected to spend the rest of his life with her, quietly, away from court politics. They were caught in the middle of a political ploy, and there wasn't a thing they could do about it. They weren't asked so much as a by your leave, and suddenly Abner and the king tore them apart.'

'Did King David love Michal?' Sophie asked.

Emma said, 'It was David's power play against Joab, rather than Michal.'

'Right,' Nik agreed. 'But power came into it with Michal, too, didn't it?'

· 237 ·

'I think power had a lot to do with it.' Emma frowned. 'I mean, look at our various politicians who get caught with their pants down. You said it yourself, Papa. You said it's power, not sex.'

'Really?' Sophie asked. 'Is it really nothing but power?'

'Sometimes,' Emma said. 'Not always. It doesn't have to be. Two people can love each other without one of them wanting to have power over the other.'

'But David—King David—what do you think, Dave?'

David Wheaton laughed. 'Do you think I'm a good one to ask, with my reputation and my wives? Six of one, half a dozen of the other. Meredith: power. For both of us. Abby: love. Myrlo: power. Marical: I loved Marical. Harriet: It was a mistake, a one-night stand. I wanted to be true to Marical. Harriet and I agreed that it would never happen again, but lo and behold, Jarvis. Elizabeth: your mother, Emma. We were in competition and that's never good. Edith: power. Nothing but power. Sophie—' He laughed tenderly. 'Blessed Sophie.' He put his arm around her and hugged her. 'The power of love, maybe, and that's something entirely different. But, back to David: it strikes me that when David called Michal back, he did it more for power than for love.'

'It must have been strange for the women—the other wives,' Emma speculated, 'when Michal came back.'

'A good scene.' Nik picked up one of his soft black pencils and pulled his yellow pad toward him. 'When Michal comes back it'll be a great opportunity for the costume designer. Michal would dress in her most royal clothes, to show the other women that she's the daughter of a king and the wife of a king. Brilliant colors, red, purple, green, embroidered in gold and silver.'

'Maacah, who was Absalom and Tamar's mother, was the daughter of a king, too,' Emma reminded him. 'She'd probably have put on her royal garments and maybe even a crown. The women would all have dressed their very best for Michal's coming. Let me have the Bible, please, Nik. I think I remember a Psalm that—here it is.' She read, ' "Kings' daughters were among thy honourable women: upon thy right hand did stand the queen in gold of Ophir. Hearken, O daughter, and consider, and incline thine ear; forget also thine own people, and thy father's house." '

'Hey, I really like that,' Nik said. 'Perfect.'

'The other wives must have been nervous about Michal's coming.'

'I never met Meredith,' Sophie said. 'But Marical is my friend.'

'King David's wives all lived together, Sophie,' David Wheaton reminded her. 'They already had their pecking order, and Michal's coming would have shifted everything.'

'Abigail?' Emma asked.

Nik said, 'I think Abigail would have been pretty secure in her position.'

Emma picked up the Bible and read on: ' "So shall the king greatly desire thy beauty: for he is thy Lord; and worship thou him . . . The king's daughter is all glorious within: her clothing is of wrought gold. She shall be brought unto the king in raiment of needlework: the virgins her companions that follow her shall be brought unto thee. With gladness and rejoicing shall they be brought: they shall enter into the king's palace." ' She looked up. 'Abigail and Maacah might have felt secure, but it would really have been tough on the other wives.'

David laughed. 'Maybe I was wise to marry at a time when polygamy is no longer permissible.' Gently he tousled Sophie's curly, taffy-colored hair.

'You're glad you married me, Davie?' she asked.

'Sophie, I adore you.'

'That's nice, but I think I'd rather be loved.'

'I love you.'

'And you want me?'

'I want you.'

'And I want you, too,' Sophie said. 'Lust and love don't have to be two separate things. In my oven is a wonderful fresh peach pie, which I am just going to take out and bring in here. How about a slice, with cream?'

Nik smiled at Sophie. 'You're a marvel. We need a break.'

Sophie moved away from David and went into the kitchen.

Emma said, 'Hey, Nik, aren't you being much too hard on Michal?'

'Are you sorry for her because she was passed around—'

'Like a property,' Emma said. 'Yes.'

'Em, sweet, women *were* property in those days. Not like today when women go to college. Women vote. Women handle their own money and have their own bank accounts. Did you know that not so long ago a man could marry a woman of property, divorce her, and keep all her property?'

'What!'

'Don't you remember? Clemence Dane wrote that famous play about it, *A Bill of Divorcement*. It was a big hit, right after the First World War, I think. Women have come a long way in this century.'

'Men, too?' Emma asked.

'Men, too. And hey, did you know that in the early years of this century an actor could not be buried in consecrated ground?'

Sophie pushed through the swinging door, bearing her fragrant pie. 'Any ground Davie is buried in will automatically be consecrated.'

'Don't bury me yet, please.'

'Not for hundreds and hundreds of years.' Sophie passed them slices of pie, handed around a pitcher of cream.

'So,' David said, 'David got Michal back, Abner gave him his kingdom—'

'And everybody lived happily ever after?' Sophie suggested.

Nik closed the Bible. 'No, Sophie. Joab killed Abner, because Abner had killed Joab's brother, Asahel.'

David pulled Sophie onto his lap. 'Revenge. It's a dangerous, damaging emotion.'

'After that'—Emma looked at her father, then picked up the Bible—'Saul's son Ishbosheth, the one Joab made king, was murdered in his sleep by two of his own men—'

'Enough!' Sophie pushed off David's lap and slid to the floor.

'I hate all this talk of killing and useless bloodshed. I hate war.'

'So did David,' Nik reassured her. 'And in the end he made peace and became king of Israel and Judah, and united the kingdom.'

'And how long did that last?' Sophie demanded. 'Enough. I have joined a class at a gym. I go and exercise. All this cooking and I am getting plump.'

Emma slowly turned the pages of the Bible. 'After David took Jerusalem, it was known as the city of David.' Then she began to laugh, partly as a release, and she continued to laugh until Sophie asked, 'What's the joke?'

Emma gasped. 'I don't know why it strikes me as hilarious, but after King Hiram of Tyre sent David cedar logs and carpenters and stone masons to build him a palace in Jerusalem, David realized that God had indeed established him as king, and he took more concubines and wives and had more sons and daughters. The children born to him in Jerusalem were Shammuah, Shobab, Nathan, Solomon, Ibhar, Elishua, Nepheg, Japhia, Elishama, Eliada, and Eliphelet. And of the eleven of these, only Solomon really comes into the story.' She burst again into laughter. 'He leaves you in the pale, Papa.'

Bathsheba

ꙮ ꙮ ꙮ

And it came to pass, after the year was expired, at the time
when kings go forth to battle, that David sent Joab, and
his servants with him, and all Israel; and they destroyed
the children of Ammon, and besieged Rabbah. But David
tarried still at Jerusalem.

And it came to pass in an eveningtide, that David arose
from off his bed, and walked upon the roof of the king's
house: and from the roof he saw a woman washing herself;
and the woman was very beautiful to look upon.

And David sent and enquired after the woman. And one
said, Is not this Bath-sheba, the daughter of Eliam, the wife
of Uriah the Hittite?

And David sent messengers, and took her; and she came
in unto him, and he lay with her . . .

And the woman conceived, and sent and told David, and
said, I am with child.

II SAMUEL 11:1–5

AT PORT CLEMENTS Ben docked the *Portia* between a large white yacht and a small, functional fishing boat. Dogs ran up and down, barking in excitement. Sea gulls sat on pilings. Children chased the dogs. It was crowded and noisy after their nights of anchoring in solitary inlets.

Emma left the *Portia* and walked along the dock, lined on either side by boats of all kinds, until she found a pay phone. Five in the afternoon in Port Clements is eight in the evening in New York. Nik would probably not be home. She could leave a message with his answering service.

But he was there. "Nik."

"Emma. What's the matter?"

"Papa."

"What—"

"I told you he had cancer—?"

"Yes."

"Nik, he's dying. I didn't tell you how bad it was. I didn't want to know how bad it was. He has only a few more weeks, Alice says. He wants to see you. Can you come?"

"Of course."

"When can you leave?"

"Tomorrow. Tell me how to get to you."

· 245 ·

"I guess the quickest thing would be to fly to Vancouver, and then get a seaplane to Port Clements."

"Okay," Nik said. "Can I call you back?"

Emma looked at her watch. "I'm at a public phone booth on the dock. I could be back here in an hour and call you, if that would give you enough time."

"Sure. I've just got to find out about flights. Talk to you in an hour."

It was all very civilized. And Emma was shaking. Her right hand cradled her left, covering the finger where Nik's rings had been. She had not told him about reading his David play, that, with her father, she had been reliving the past. No. She had wanted to cry out to him, "I'm terrified of airplanes! Be careful!" Flying was still not the way Emma automatically thought of travel.

Why hadn't she urged him to take the train? Put off seeing him as long as possible. Alice had said a few weeks . . .

She raised her hands to her face, trying not to cry, then walked away from the phone booth.

When she returned to the *Portia*, Ben and Alice were peeling shrimp.

"Nik's coming tomorrow. I've got to call him back in an hour to see if he was able to make plane reservations, so dinner may be a little late."

"We'll fix a shrimp curry," Alice said. "Don't worry about it. Go tell your father."

Emma went to the pilothouse and found David and Abby playing double solitaire. There was no question that Abby was good for David.

When Emma told them, Abby said, "Then perhaps I'd better leave."

"No," David said, and reached across the small table for her hand.

"There's an extra sleeping bag," Emma said. "Nik can use that, and sleep up in the main cabin with Ben. The seat is more than long enough for two tall men."

"Good," David said. "That's settled, then."

"Darling." Abby pressed his hand. "I'm going to have to leave in a few days. When Sophie comes, she'll need the bed. And when everybody goes—and we all must go—then it will be your time with Alice. Your most special time."

Emma left them and went to her bunk. Lay there on her back with her hands under her head, staring at the ceiling. Their love both warmed and pained her.

She looked at her watch. Fifty minutes before time to go back to the phone booth.

Nik's pages were in the main cabin, and in the chart drawers. She did not need them. In a strange way Nik was more present with her in memory than he might be when he came and she was in his physical presence. They had both changed. Nik's hair was shot with white, turning early, as dark hair often did.

The Nik of her thoughts had tousled black hair, and if it was longer than most men's hair in the forties, she liked it that way, and seldom reminded him to go to the barber.

·

It had needed cutting the weekend she and Nik boarded the night train to Savannah after the show, and spent Sunday with Grandpa Bowman. They would get back on the sleeper that evening so that Emma would have time for a rest before the performance Monday evening.

They arrived in time to eat a large breakfast with Grandpa Bowman before church, and sat in the old, musty dining room, talking. Nik had brought his current scenes with him, and Grandpa Bowman read them eagerly, his big Bible beside him.

' "The ark of God," ' Grandpa Bowman read, ' "whose name is called by the name of the Lord of hosts that dwelleth between the cherubims." '

' "The ark of God," ' Emma repeated. 'Bahama said it was a symbol. A metaphor for God.'

'Yes,' Grandpa Bowman agreed, 'but portable shrines were common in those days.'

Nik shook his head, 'Grandpa, sir, you know it was more than a portable shrine. It had intrinsic power. God's power.'

'And David, now that he was safe, and his kingdom established, wanted it back?'

'Yes. He wanted it back. He was the anointed of God, and it was only proper that the ark be returned to Jerusalem. But in a way it's peripheral to my play. In fact, I think it's another play, just about the ark. It's that important. It can't be just a secondary scene.'

'Your instinct is right.' Grandpa Bowman pulled out his pocket watch, then heaved himself out of his chair. 'You'll have to put in Michal's reaction to David's dancing around the ark, won't you? Now, children. I have to leave for church. If you want to wait for me, it's cooler out on the porch.'

'Nonsense, Grandpa, sir,' Nik said. 'We're coming with you.'

•

' . . . when at last David brought the ark into Jerusalem, into his city, the city of David, he danced before the Lord, honoring the Lord with his joy. He wore only a linen ephod as he danced, but he was not thinking of revealing his nakedness as he leaped before the Lord, he was fully rejoicing in his Creator.' Grandpa's voice rang with triumph. Then it was lowered.

'And Michal, Saul's daughter, looked from her window and saw her husband dancing and she—oh, poor king's daughter, poorer king's wife—did not understand that where true joy is, there God is, and she despised David in her heart.

'David did not see Michal and her mean-mindedness and he offered burnt offerings and peace offerings before the Lord, and he blessed the people, and gave to everyone bread and meat and wine. Then he returned to bless his household, and Michal, Saul's daughter, came out to meet him, and poured her scorn on him: "How glorious was the king of Israel to day, who uncovered himself to day in the eyes of the handmaids of his servants."

'And David told Michal that his dancing was to honor the

Lord. "I will play before the Lord," he told Michal, "and the handmaids of whom you have spoken will honor me."

'Joyless Michal did not understand that joy honors the Lord. And she was barren for it.'

.

After church Emma and Nik cleaned up the breakfast dishes, then joined Grandpa Bowman on the porch. A mockingbird was singing in the chinaberry tree. It was still winter in New York, but there was the freshness of spring in Georgia, with new leaves pushing off the old.

'Grandpa,' Emma asked, 'did you imply that after that scene where Michal scorned David, they never made love again?'

'That would be my reading of it,' Nik said. 'It wasn't a good marriage, David and Michal's. He was much happier with Abigail.'

'And then all those other wives,' Emma said. 'When does Bathsheba come in?'

'Soon. First I've got to get in some information about Nathan the prophet, who appears out of the blue, like so many characters in this story.'

Grandpa Bowman huffed slightly. 'The Biblical narrator leaves out all nonessentials. Nathan comes when he's needed.'

'He isn't a copy of Samuel. He's much too cerebral. He isn't one of those whirling-dervish-type prophets. But he was like Samuel in that he changed his mind, and attributed the change to God. When David had the ark safely in the city, he wanted to build a temple for it. He said it wasn't suitable for him to live in a palace and for the ark of God to be in a tent. At first Nathan said that was a great idea, but then God spoke to Nathan and said no.'

'Slow to understand, as always,' Grandpa Bowman said. 'God told Nathan to tell David that God wanted to have a people, a nation, for his own, and that God has never lived in a house, but has always traveled with his people. The entire universe is the home of the Lord. We need church buildings for our sakes, not God's.'

Nik, as usual, had his Bible with him. 'Nathan told David that God promised him that his dynasty would never end.'

'A rash promise,' Grandpa Bowman said. 'But, then, God has never been known for playing it safe.'

Nik made a face. 'That rash promise was one of the many reasons my father was an atheist. My mother said God kept his promise in Jesus. My father said Jesus didn't have any children, so what was she talking about? It was one of their battlegrounds.'

'God always keeps promises,' Grandpa Bowman said, 'but often in ways that are unexpected and surprising.'

.

It was a good visit. Emma was grateful that Nik had had a chance to see her grandfather in his own setting. After the play that evening they went to the Riverside Drive apartment to tell David and Sophie all about it.

Sophie greeted them with hugs. 'I've made chicken à la king. It's better than what you'd get at the Algonquin, that's what my Davie says.'

'Thanks, Sophie. Grandpa Bowman was right; the food on the train was cardboard.'

Sophie served them, then sat by David. 'Davie's play's closing in a couple of months. They decided not to run it through the summer. They're going on the road with it, starting in early September, and I'm going along. Louis's happy in Choir School, and Davie needs me.'

'Nik's play'll be going on the road, too,' Emma said. 'Most of the cast is going, so it should be fun.'

'I'll come to Em whenever I can,' Nik said, 'Chicago, for instance, where they'll run for at least a month.'

'Maybe we'll be there at the same time,' David said. 'We'll be at the Blackstone.'

'And I think we're at the Shubert,' Emma said.

'I'll miss these evenings with Nik's play. King David is definitely on my mind.'

Nik had his Bible open. 'Lots of battles for David, and lots of victories. He beat the Philistines again, and then the Moabites—'

Sophie interrupted. 'One of Jesus' ancestors was Ruth, the Moabitess.'

'Yes, thanks, Sophie. David was a terrifically successful fighter. Successful at everything.'

'Including love,' Sophie said. 'Just like my own Davie.'

Perhaps while Sophie believed it, it was true.

.

'. . . and he was generous, was David,' Grandpa Bowman had preached. 'Once he moved to Jerusalem, to his own city'— Grandpa Bowman's voice was quiet, and the people in the pews leaned forward to listen—'and was settled in his palace and had won many battles, he thought of his friend Jonathan. We do not forget our friends after their deaths. They remain part of the fabric of our lives, influencing our thoughts and actions. So David remembered Jonathan.

' "Is there anyone left of Saul's family?" he asked. "If there is, I would like to show him kindness for Jonathan's sake."

'And there was, indeed, Mephibosheth, Jonathan's son. When the news came of Saul's and Jonathan's deaths, Mephibosheth's nurse took him and fled in terror for his safety, but in escaping she dropped him, and he was lame in both feet. But David sent for him, and treated the young man kindly, and gave him lands, and servants to farm them, and Mephibosheth lived in Jerusalem and ate at the king's table.

'But there was no peace for David. Other rulers wanted his land. His sister Zeruiah's sons, Abishai and Joab, fought with him and for him, and together they drove the Syrian army back, and the Syrians made peace with Israel. Then David sent out Joab with his officers and the Israelite army, but David himself stayed in Jerusalem.

'Why, my people, why? Why did David stay in Jerusalem, instead of going out with his army? On such small incidents does history depend. Had David not stayed in Jerusalem, had he not risen from his nap in the early evening and walked upon his roof, he would not have seen Bathsheba.'

.

'So come on,' Sophie urged Nik. 'How are you going to bring Bathsheba into the play?'

Nik laughed. 'I am not going to have David spying on her in her bath.'

'She was beautiful.' Sophie was pleased, and her pleasure eradicated what would otherwise have been smugness.

'She was beautiful, indeed,' Nik said. 'Do you think she knew David could see her when she bathed?'

'She was no dummy,' Sophie said. 'She must have known that she would be visible from the palace roof. She probably wanted her David as much as I did mine.'

'How *did* you meet Dave?' Nik asked.

'In a movie. I didn't have a talking part, but I needed the money. Any money. And I *was* in a bathtub.' She giggled infectiously. 'There were lots of bubbles, so it was all quite proper. David opened the bathroom door by mistake—the character he was playing, that is—and apologized. I let out a little squeak and that was my scene. But for some reason the director couldn't get it right. He kept saying that Davie and I were fine, but he wasn't satisfied, so we did it over and over. Then Davie asked me out to dinner.'

'And the rest is history,' David said.

'So there again,' Nik pointed out, 'there aren't any real parallels. You didn't have a husband, and Dave didn't have to use foul means to get rid of him.'

'I had a sort of boyfriend,' Sophie said.

'But no husband, and no murder. We aren't acting out some inevitable Greek tragedy.'

David poured himself another glass of milk, looking into it as though for an answer.

'Hey, Sophie,' Nik said. 'I wrote a big scene for Bathsheba last night. Want to see it?'

'Of course. Maybe we could read it aloud and I could do Bathsheba?'

'All the wives are in it, all the eight named ones. Too many for a reading.'

'It's a terrific scene,' Emma said. 'I read it last night, hot off the typewriter.' It would play well, she thought, as Nik handed a sheaf of pages to Sophie. Emma got up and stood behind Sophie's chair, to read along with her.

Sophie murmured as she read:

David's wives, along with several maidservants, are on the roof of the women's wing of the palace. Abigail is weaving. Maacah is in a large tub, bathing, with two maidservants pouring fresh water over her shoulders.

'Maacah?' she asked. 'Who is Maacah?'

'She's the daughter of a king, and she's Tamar and Absalom's mother, so she's important,' Nik explained.

Some of the women are folding embroidered cloths. Others are relaxing, enjoying the freshness of evening.

EGLAH: Zeruiah was never the same after Asahel was killed by Abner.

ABIGAIL: There's been too much death.

BATHSHEBA: (*Gently*) I'm sorry about your baby, your little Daniel. It must have been terrible for you, to give David two sons and lose them both.

'I'm glad she cares,' Sophie said. 'I'm glad she and Abigail like each other.'

ABIGAIL: You're kind, Bathsheba. Thank you. (*She goes on weaving*)

MAACAH: It's a lovely night. Look at the moon, just coming up behind the olive trees, so tiny, like a fingernail paring.

ABITAL: I like it when it's just us women together, and we can forget war.

HAGGITH: And men.

EGLAH: Yes, it's good to be together, the children all in bed or being taken care of by the nursemaids. No matter how they squabble during the day, they're like angels when they sleep.

Childless Michal sighs.

AHINOAM: (*To Bathsheba*) It's wonderful, how you can go on being so happy.

BATHSHEBA: I love David. I'm carrying his child.

AHINOAM: Don't you grieve for Uriah?

Abigail stops weaving and looks at Ahinoam, sensing trouble.

BATHSHEBA: I wept for him when he was killed in battle. He was a good husband, and I was fond of him. He was kind, and much older than I. He died an honorable death.

AHINOAM: Did he?

ABIGAIL: Ahinoam, stop.

AHINOAM: But she knows, doesn't she?

MICHAL: How can she help knowing?

BATHSHEBA: Know what?

ABIGAIL: (*To Ahinoam*) Stop now, before you cause grief.

AHINOAM: She'll hear, sooner or later. Better she hear it from us.

MAACAH: Better she not hear at all.

BATHSHEBA: Hear what? What's Ahinoam talking about?

MAACAH: Nothing.

MICHAL: Leave well enough alone.

BATHSHEBA: No, it's something. What is it? (*The women draw back, silently. Maacah gestures to the maids, who withdraw discreetly*) Tell me.

AHINOAM: Uriah. Your husband.

'She's a stinker, that Ahinoam.' Sophie looked across the table at Nik. 'A real heavy.'

'I don't want to make her too heavy,' Nik said.

'Go on.' David was impatient. 'Hurry. I want to read it, too.'

BATHSHEBA: David is my husband. I'm carrying his child.

AHINOAM: You were carrying his child before Uriah was killed. Don't you ever wonder how—or why—he was killed?

BATHSHEBA: (*Trembling. Near tears*) In battle.

AHINOAM: Have you spoken to Joab?

BATHSHEBA: Why would I speak to Joab?

MAACAH: Ahinoam, why are you doing this?

ABITAL: She can't bear to see anybody else happy.

BATHSHEBA: Abigail! What is this all about? Tell me!

Abigail leaves the loom and sits on the parapet. Bathsheba runs over to her and sits at her feet. Abigail strokes the girl's hair.

ABITAL: (*She is troubled, and speaks gently*) Bathsheba, dear, you *were* pregnant before Uriah died.

BATHSHEBA: Yes, I know, but—

AHINOAM: So don't pretend it wasn't a relief.

BATHSHEBA: No, no, I could have told Uriah it was his baby.

MICHAL: Uriah can count. He'd been away for many months.

BATHSHEBA: But—but—David sent for him. He took him out of battle and brought him to me.

AHINOAM: Did he lie with you?

Bathsheba covers her face, weeps. Abigail holds the girl as though she were a small child. Crooning softly.

ABITAL: He was an honorable and loyal man. He knew he had to go back into the army.

EGLAH: And a man cannot fight for three days after he's lain with a woman.

HAGGITH: It's a stupid law. I wouldn't think much of a husband who didn't break it.

'Me either,' Sophie said.

HAGGITH: We don't know what Uriah really did, after all.

MAACAH: So we don't know what really happened. It's private between Bathsheba and Uriah.

MICHAL: It's the law. Uriah did what was right. So he wouldn't have been able to think the baby was his, would he?

BATHSHEBA: I don't know. I'd have—have—

AHINOAM: There wasn't anything you could have done.

MICHAL: So David took care of it.

BATHSHEBA: (*Her voice rises frantically*) What do you mean?

AHINOAM: Ask Joab.

ABIGAIL: Be quiet. All of you. (*To Bathsheba*) My dear, you and David were in a terrible position. David did everything he could to make Uriah come to you.

BATHSHEBA: But Uriah always obeyed the laws . . .

MICHAL: Had he been less obedient—

HAGGITH: And more of a man—

MICHAL: He might still be alive.

BATHSHEBA: No—no—

AHINOAM: David told Joab to send him to the front of the battle lines where he'd be sure to be killed.

BATHSHEBA: No! (*She is screaming now*) No!

ABIGAIL: Hush, my dear.

BATHSHEBA: David wouldn't—

AHINOAM: I thought you knew, or I'd never have mentioned it.

MICHAL: It was certainly the only way out for David.

EGLAH: It was what he had to do, that's plain. So why get so upset?

Bathsheba sobs while Abigail holds her, murmuring endearments but saying nothing.

AHINOAM: It wasn't exactly murder. It's certainly possible he might not have been killed.

MAACAH: Or he may have been killed the way any man may be killed when he goes into battle.

ABITAL: He could have come home safely.

MICHAL: After all, my father tried to kill David the same way, sending him into battle against the Philistines. And David came home.

HAGGITH: So David thought Uriah could have come home safely, too.

AHINOAM: It just happened that he didn't.
MICHAL: Perhaps you're better off this way.
ABITAL: Hush. She's really upset. She didn't know.

'I wish I weren't too old to play Bathsheba,' Sophie said. 'That's a wonderful scene, Nikkie, wonderful.' She handed the scene to David, then turned to Nik. 'After Bathsheba comes into the story, what happens next?'

'Nathan the prophet again,' Nik said. 'I suppose I have to have him in the play, but somehow he irritates me. He always has to be right. He didn't like what King David did, either, and he made that quite clear with his famous story of the poor man and the rich man.'

'What story?' Sophie asked eagerly.

Nik smiled. 'There was a poor man who had no possessions at all except a tiny little ewe lamb, and he treated it just like his child and loved it dearly. And there was a rich man who had many flocks and herds, but when an important traveler came by, the rich man did not take one of his own animals but took the poor man's little lamb and had it killed and dressed and cooked and served it to the traveler.'

Sophie held her nose. 'That stinks.'

'David thought that, too, when Nathan told him the story.'

'So what happened?' Sophie asked.

'David said the rich man deserved to be killed. And Nathan said to David, "You are the man." '

'Oh, no!'

'David never denied that he had sinned,' Nik said. He looked at Emma. 'What would he have said? Anything from the Psalms?'

She nodded, leafing through the Bible.

David looked up from the scene, which he had skimmed. 'It's good, Nik. But David's not in it—' Then he laughed at himself. 'I do tend to megalomania on occasion. It's an excellent scene.'

'Here.' Emma had the Bible open and read aloud, 'Have mercy upon me, O God, according to thy loving kindness: according unto the multitude of thy tender mercies blot out my transgressions. Wash me thoroughly from mine iniquity, and cleanse me from my sin. For I acknowledge my transgressions: and my sin is ever before me. Against thee, thee only, have I sinned, and done this evil in thy sight.' She looked up.

'That's it!' Nik cried. 'And it's one of the great things about David, that he never tried to rationalize or justify what he'd done. But Nathan was as harsh as Samuel, and as certain that he spoke for God. Nathan told David that God was angry, and that David's own house would turn against him, and other men would take his wives openly, because David had killed secretly.'

David said, 'Nathan and Samuel were alike in presuming to speak for God.'

'David took Nathan at his word,' Nik said. 'He cried out in an agony of repentance, "I have sinned against the Lord." '

Sophie put her hands to her face. 'Poor David. Poor Bathsheba.'

David asked, 'Was David truly sorry? Nik, what do you think?'

'I think David suddenly saw himself as an ordinary human being who sinned,' Nik replied slowly, 'like other human beings, and that's when he truly began to love God, and to understand that he was God's anointed, not because he was sinless, but because God had chosen him and he didn't have to understand why. Yes, I think he was sorry. That he repented.'

'Metanoia,' David murmured. 'That's what your grandfather calls it, Em—turning completely around.'

Emma nodded. 'Grandpa said that metanoia is the opposite of paranoia, which is turning in on oneself.'

Sophie put her arms around her husband's neck. 'So it was murder that was wrong, not wanting Bathsheba?'

David Wheaton held her. 'Does this come a little close to home, Sophie?'

'You never killed anybody.'

'I committed adultery. For lust for you, I left a wife and an innocent child.'

'But did you love Edith, Davie? Did you?'

He shook his head. 'But that was no excuse.'

'But Edith was unkind to Emma—'

'And that made it easier. I could blame Edith. But if she'd been the perfect stepmother I'd probably have fallen for you anyway, Sophie. So I do not excuse myself.'

Sophie said, 'I think Edith was just looking for an excuse to get rid of you.'

Emma looked at her father. He had never committed a physical crime to get his own way. Nevertheless, he had hurt many people. This was the first time he had referred to the breakup of his marriage to Edith with any indication of contrition.

Nik was doodling on his yellow pad. 'David's repentance pleased God. Nathan said, "The Lord also hath put away thy sin; thou shalt not die." Nevertheless, Nathan insisted that, because of what David had done, the child Bathsheba was carrying would die.'

'No, no.' Sophie pushed away from David.

He said gently, 'Bathsheba sinned, too. She committed adultery.'

Slow color suffused Sophie's fair face and tears came back to her eyes. 'My God, if anything happened to Louis—'

'Calm down,' her husband said. 'Louis is fine. And you aren't Bathsheba, and I'm an actor, not a king.'

'The baby was born,' Nik continued, 'and it was beautiful, but in a few days it ran a high fever and—'

'Stop.' Sophie put her fingers in her ears. 'I don't want to hear any more.'

'Okay, Sophie, it's late.' Emma hugged her stepmother.

'You're a good girl, Emmelie.' Sophie rubbed her cheek against Emma's shoulder. 'You don't believe God would kill a baby, do you?'

'No, I don't.' She gave Sophie another hug. 'It's late, and Nik and I have to go.'

.

Nik and Emma walked home. It was cold, and she walked as usual with her left hand plunged into his right-hand coat pocket, his fingers clasped around hers.

'It *was* hard on Bathsheba,' Emma said, 'having the baby be a scapegoat for David's wrongdoing.'

'David and Bathsheba's,' Nik reminded her.

'Okay. Yes.'

'Putting sins on a scapegoat is an ancient idea. The sin has to be got rid of. David could repent and receive God's forgiveness, but the sin was still there.' Emma sighed. He held her hand tightly. 'Look what's happening in the war right now, innocent people being slaughtered in the bombings—from us, too, Em, not just the Germans. Sorry, love, I know you're terribly worried about Etienne and Adair, and Ev going overseas.'

Emma's pace quickened. 'Are the innocent people who are being killed in the bombings paying for other people's sins?'

'Some people would think so.'

'Do you?'

'No, but I'm a heathen.'

Emma's fingers clasped his more tightly. 'For a heathen, my darling love, you have your characters talk a lot about God.'

Nik pulled his fingers out of hers, then took her hand again. 'Yeah, they do, don't they? Their idea, not mine. I have to let my characters say what they say.'

'What I think,' Emma said, 'is that you don't like what institutions and establishments have done about God.'

'They think they know everything,' Nik growled.

'They don't, and we don't. But I think your characters know a lot, and you're a good writer because you listen to them.'

'Yes. I listen to my characters better than I listen to anybody else. That's not good.' They had reached their building and he let go of Emma's hand to reach for his key.

'No, it's not good, but I think maybe it's true of all artists. When I'm working on a role I listen to my character. And I listen better than I listen to myself. Or to you.'

'Is it a fatal flaw?' Nik opened the door.

'No,' Emma said as they went into the apartment. 'The fatal

flaw is hubris, pride against the gods. Maybe as we listen to our characters we'll learn to listen to each other.'

Nik turned on the lights, threw his battered briefcase on the bed. 'Good enough. Maybe that's why you're an actress and I'm a writer. If we need to have a reason.'

Marical

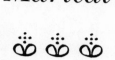

Amnon . . . is dead: for by the appointment of Absalom this hath been determined from the day that he forced his sister Tamar.

But Absalom fled . . . And David mourned for his son every day . . . And the soul of king David longed to go forth unto Absalom.

II SAMUEL 13:32, 34, 37, 39

EMMA WALKED slowly along the wooden planks of the dock, not seeing the vessels tied up on either side, not seeing a child who almost ran into her, not hearing the noise of sea gulls. She was thinking not of Nik but of Chantal, Chantal who was far away in Mooréa, busy with her own life, her marriage, her children, a life far from the stresses of the mid-twentieth century. It was a kind of peace Emma had known for a few weeks during her one visit to Mooréa, and while it had been wonderful for a few weeks, she had been happy to get home to New York, the theater, the work she loved.

She and Chantal wrote regularly, phoned on birthdays and Christmas. Chantal knew that David Wheaton was dying, had offered to come. Emma and Alice had talked it over; Emma had called Abby for further confirmation of her feeling that Chantal should stay home with her family. Desperately as she would have liked to have Chantal with her now, she still thought she and Alice and Abby had been right.

Everard, too, had offered to make the long, hard journey. Everard, too, had been willing to accept their advice and to stay in Mooréa. It was another world. It was almost another time. David was married to Alice. He loved Alice. If Chantal or Everard had come, old wounds would inevitably have been opened. Adair, Emma thought. Let Adair rest in peace.

She walked, looking down at her feet in old socks and sneakers, looking at the worn planks with their occasional knots and scars, until she got to the phone booth. She stopped, feeling in her pockets. She had used up her change in the first call; this one would have to be collect.

She gave the number to the operator and waited while it went through, and then her heart lurched as she got a busy signal. "Please try again," the operator told her. She walked up and down the dock. Three minutes. Nik did not like to waste time on long phone calls. Surely the line would be clear.

Busy again. Why was she so upset? What did it matter? She was no longer part of Nik's life. It could be anybody. Another woman.

She made herself wait five minutes, walking up and down, back and forth, before she could tell the operator again that she wanted to make a collect call.

This time the phone rang and was answered at once by Nik, who accepted her call. "Em, did you try me a few minutes ago? I'm sorry, I tried to keep the line clear, but it was a producer —someone who may be interested in my new play."

"Oh, Nik, I'm glad, and I'm sorry I had to call collect—"

"No problem. I'm taking an early plane tomorrow morning, one of those new jets, and I should be in Port Clements by late afternoon, what with the three-hour time difference. How is Dave? Is he—"

"Physically, he's thin and weak," Emma said. "Thank you for coming."

"Of course I'm coming. See you tomorrow." He hung up.

She left the phone booth and turned back toward the *Portia*, breathing slowly and deeply, trying to calm the racing of her heart. Would she feel differently about seeing Nik if she had not spent these days deep in the past of his King David play? Did it make it easier or more difficult? She stepped up onto the wooden milk box Ben used as a step, and onto the deck.

Abby was in the main cabin, playing solitaire, her sketch pad beside her. "Everything all right?"

"He's coming tomorrow. He should be here in time for dinner." Automatically, she walked to the stove. Alice had rice steaming in a colander. The curried shrimp were keeping warm in a *bain marie* which Abby had brought from France one year to give to David for Christmas. "It's good of Alice to have fixed dinner. Is she in the pilothouse?"

"Yes. She gave David a shot a few minutes ago. I'll take the table up in a moment so she'll know we're ready. Emma, sit down. You're pale."

Emma pulled out one of the captain's chairs. "It's absurd. I'm sorry."

"It's not absurd. Nik's arrival has to be a great emotional drain on you."

"I don't know—I don't know what to do."

"Do you have to do anything?"

"I can't huddle up in my sleeping bag and hide."

"Do you still love him?"

Emma stood at the stove, staring out at the dock, not seeing. Said, at last, "You still love Papa."

"Yes, Emma, though when Myrlo came into the picture I had no emotion left for a long time. But it comes back, Emma, and when it does, the pain has become bearable."

"Thanks, Abby. I'm sorry.'

"No, Emma. Just give yourself time. I know that Nik's coming is too soon, but sometimes too soon isn't too soon after all. I agree with Bahama that there is a time that has little to do with our ordinary chronology and which is more true. *Eh bien.* Enough philosophizing."

"Thanks, Abby, and thanks for reminding me of Bahama."

Abby's pencil moved carefully on the page of her sketchbook. "You've managed to allow your father to be human, faulted and flawed like all human beings, and to love him, anyhow, haven't you?"

Emma sighed. Nodded.

Abby continued to sketch. "We'd all like people to be what we want them to be, instead of what they are."

"Your marriage to Yekshek—that was terrific, wasn't it?"

Abby laughed. "Terrific, but highly imperfect."

"I don't think I'm looking for perfection . . ."

"I'm sure you're not, my love. Whatever your problems with Nik have been, I know they're real."

They turned as they heard a movement, and Alice stood at the head of the pilothouse steps. "Emma. You're back."

Emma rose. "Nik will get to Port Clements sometime late tomorrow afternoon."

Abby rose, too, putting cards, sketch pad, pencil, into her bag. "It will be good to be able to leave this dock."

Alice smiled. "Dave says the wonderful thing about the *Portia* is that we can be someplace different every night, but he can sleep in the same bed, not like one-night stands when he went on tour with a play."

．

Emma's tour started in late August. Her father would not be leaving the city till well into the autumn. Nik went with Emma to Boston, where they would be playing for two weeks. Opening night went well. The audience was appreciative; all the laughs came, and she heard several sniffles at just the right moment when tears were needed to balance the laughter.

Emma was being starred on the tour, rather than featured, her name for the first time above the title of the play. Nik was waiting for her in her dressing room, where there were several bouquets of flowers from well-wishers, and a crowd of people hovering in the doorway.

'My God,' Nik exclaimed when the dressing room emptied, 'I'm married to a star. Okay, love, we're going to go back to the hotel—the Ritz, we *have* come up in the world!—and order supper sent to our room.'

'Oh, Nik, are you sure we should—'

'Of course I'm sure. We won't do it every night, and we do need to put money in the bank so our kids can go to college, at least six children, I hope. But once in a while it's good for our souls to splurge, and I want to do a little brain-picking about Bathsheba and the baby. I plan to do a good bit of writing while we're here. Okay?'

Emma grinned. 'Sure.' Her fingers moved softly against the palm of his hand.

The stage manager knocked at the dressing-room door. 'Hey, Em, good performance. This tour's going to be fun.'

Nik was holding out her light jacket. 'Come on, sweetie. It's late.'

When they reached their hotel room she undressed and bathed while Nik ordered up sandwiches. By the time she was dried and in her nightgown, Nik was waiting, having eaten most of the sandwiches. 'But we can order more.'

'No, this is plenty.'

'Em, sweetie, I'm glad we're having this time together. Now that we know the play's going to go well, we can relax. Your father'll be starting rehearsals for the tour—when?'

'In about a month. He and Sophie are off in the Poconos for a few days together, now that Louis's back in Choir School.'

'When I'm writing lines for Bathsheba I can't help hearing Sophie's voice. And it's made me love Bathsheba.'

'I'm glad,' Emma said. 'I think she should be lovable.'

'And David.' He put his hand on the Bible. 'All the while the baby is dying, David is praying, importuning God, begging for mercy. And when the baby dies—'

'What the Bible tells us,' Emma said, 'is that David called for his servants and asked for meat and wine.'

Nik looked over her shoulder at the open page. 'And the servants were incredulous, asking, "Now? Now? When your baby has just died?"'

'And David said—'

Nik took over. 'Why should I cry to God now? The child is dead. I can do no more. I had hoped that God would repent. While the child was alive I could hope. But the Lord did not repent. And I need something to eat and drink.'

'Pragmatic,' Emma said.

'He had to be, to survive as a king.'

'But he did believe in God.'

'Yes.' He turned to her with sudden vehemence. 'You still do?'

'Bahama and Grandpa have had their influence. But I come closest to a glimpse of God-who-cares when I'm working on a role—the way I'm already working on Abigail—suddenly understanding what a character wants, feeling love and pity even when I have to play someone I'd hate in real life. I know it isn't going to work until that happens.'

'Ha!' Nik said. 'That's why you aren't good at first readings.'

'That's right. When I get a script, at first it's as though I'm trying to read in the dark, and it's a while before the light comes on.'

'Does the light always come on?'

Emma pondered. 'Sometimes it's brighter than others.'

Nik took the last sandwich off the platter. 'Bathsheba would at least have had Abigail, Abigail who understood and loved both David and Bathsheba, and Abigail would weep with Bathsheba,' Nik said, sitting on the edge of the bed.

'Your Abigail,' Emma said, 'the one you created out of that one glimpse when she stopped David from revenge and blood guilt over Nabal's stupidity.'

'Your Abigail, I've drawn her from you.'

'*Your* Abigail,' Emma said firmly. 'A delicious role. The Biblical Abigail must have been pretty old by the time Bathsheba had the baby.'

'Old enough to hold the girl like a mother and weep with her, for Bathsheba's babe, and for her own two dead sons.'

'I love Abigail,' Emma said. 'She'll be wonderful to play.'

'You're the actress for her. It's a wonderful story.'

'Abigail's?'

'Yours. And mine.'

·

Was she still part of Nik's story? Or had he ripped her out of the typewriter and flung her into the wastepaper basket?

She had left Nik, not the other way around. She thought she had cause. But was she being like Papa, who had not been able to make a marriage last?

She and Abby were in the pilothouse with David, sipping herbal tea. Ben looked in. "Since we can take on water here, why don't you ladies take baths and wash your hair tomorrow? You can take turns, a good hour apart, to give the water time to warm up between baths. The tank's not very big."

Abby laughed. "I'm used to cool baths on the *Portia*."

Emma ran her fingers through her hair. "It needs washing. At home I wash it every day."

"Home?" Her father asked. "Where is home for you, child?"

"New York. And I'm not a child, Papa."

He put his hands to his sides, as if in pain. "Forgive me, Emma, forgive me."

Emma's voice was low. "Papa, I love you. Let the past be past."

"People's lives should be consistent with what they do," David said, "at least to some extent. My life has been—"

"It's been your life, Papa, nobody else's. What's right for you—"

"It isn't right for you, Emma, and whether or not it was right for me, God only knows. But it isn't right for you."

"I know that."

"I let you down. You had just cause to be angry."

"I *was* angry. Don't you remember? I really let you have it."

"God, Emma, you were like an avenging angel. That's when I knew you should play Joan of Arc. And you were wonderful."

"It was a really great idea of Josh Logan's, alternating Shaw and Anouilh, really stretching. Playing both Joans was one of the most exciting challenges I ever had onstage."

.

From Boston the road company of Nik's comedy went to New Haven. The two weeks in Boston had been good, a beautiful memory, except that Emma's period had come, nearly two weeks late, dashing their hopes that she was pregnant.

But the review of Nik's play, Emma's reviews, and the reviews in general, had been all that they could have hoped for. Chantal, who came up to Boston to see the play, marveled at a new quality in Emma's acting. 'You've always been good, but there's a sort of compassion—I can't explain it. It isn't just Nik, your marriage, and your love and your happiness.'

Emma knew that there was a difference in her acting, a deepening that was beyond technique. Whatever had caused it, she was grateful.

The last night in Boston they again had sandwiches sent to their room, and Nik sat cross-legged on the bed writing on his lined pad while Emma bathed.

When she came out of the bathroom, wrapped in two towels, Nik was sitting staring at the tray of uneaten sandwiches.

'Nik, what's wrong?'

He put his arms around her, breathing in her fragrance. 'Emma, I can't write this play.'

'What?' She pulled away from him, unbelieving.

'I can't write the King David play. I should have known it the night we got engaged. The night you told me about Billy. I did know it, but my vanity wouldn't accept it. A play starring your father would have made me an important playwright. And I want to be important. Serious.'

'Nik, have I—I mean, I want you to write this play. You've made me know I'm not Tamar. Have I been getting in your way?' She had tried not to, to leave him free to write whatever he wanted. But was that even possible?

'You've supported me in every way,' Nik said. 'But I've come to the Tamar, Amnon, Absalom scenes, and I can't do it to you.'

'No, Nik.' To her surprise, tears began streaming down her cheeks. 'I can't bear it if you stop because of me.'

His lips wiped away her tears. He no longer tried to hold back his own tears. 'I can't do it, Em, I just can't do it. It isn't only Tamar. The play's not working.'

'Because of Tamar—'

'I don't know. I've hit a blank wall. I can't get through it.'

They held each other.

'Don't decide anything tonight,' she said at last. 'Give it time.'

'There's so much anger,' he said. 'Joab kills Abner for killing Asahel. And Absalom never forgave Amnon for what he did to Tamar, even after he'd had Amnon killed. And his rage turned into ambition. He wanted to be king. Ambition and anger were all tied up. He wanted to punish his father. Everard told me that when Adair left he was still angry. He wanted to punish your father.'

Emma shuddered. 'He's succeeded in punishing if that's what he really wants. He's punishing Sophie, too. She sent Louis to Choir School only to protect him from Papa's darknesses.'

'Oh, Em, sweetie.' Nik reached into his bathrobe pocket for his handkerchief and blew his nose. 'Maybe later. Maybe after everything stabilizes. After your brothers come home and you and I have our family. Maybe I can write it then. Not now.'

'Nik, you've written such marvelous scenes—'

'But they don't hang together. Maybe it's not my kind of play. Maybe I'm just kidding myself, the clown wanting to play Hamlet.'

'No, Nik—'

'I'll write it someday, Emma. Someday.' He picked up the tray of uneaten sandwiches and put it out the door for the waiter to pick up.

·

Nik returned to New York, to catch up on mail which would have accumulated while they were in Boston, to check in with his agent.

In New Haven Emma had a small room, but at least it was her own. In Boston she had been with Nik, almost as though they were on their honeymoon. In New Haven she was with the company, going out for supper after the show with two or three, depending on who had plans.

One night she was having supper at an Italian restaurant with a group from the company, plus some of their friends, sitting at a large, happily noisy table. They were eating pizza, a new discovery perfect for after-theater supper. The rough white tablecloths were still damp. Someone ordered a bottle of "red ink"—Chianti. Emma turned away from the person she was talking to as she heard her name called, and an older actress who had decided against joining them hurried across the crowded room. 'Emma—'

'What's up?'

'Your mother—Sophie—she's trying to get you. I heard you being paged when I went into the lobby, so I took the call, in case—Emma, I don't know what's happened, but whatever it is, she's terribly upset, and I think you'd better call—'

Emma rose. 'Of course. Thanks, thanks for coming to get me.'

'It sounded desperately urgent.'

Emma put some money on the table—'I think that's okay for my share—sorry I have to leave'— and hurried out of the restaurant.

Her room was on the fourth floor and she did not wait for the elevator but panted up the stairs, fumbled for her key, and ran to the telephone, turning on the light.

—Calm down, Emma. If Sophie is hysterical, you have to be calm.

Deliberately she slowed her breathing, waited for her heart to stop pounding.

Dialed.

Sophie answered.

'Sophie, it's Emma.'

'Oh God, Emma, oh, two, both in one day, two, only an hour apart, two, both of them—' Sophie's words were barely distinguishable through her sobs.

'Two what, Sophie? Slow down. Tell me.'

'Telegrams. An hour apart. Both of them.'

'Sophie. Tell me.'

'Etienne. And an hour later, Adair.'

'Etienne and Adair—'

'Dead. Killed.'

Emma's heart felt cold and heavy as stone.

'Both of them. David won't speak to me. He's sitting. Like marble. He won't speak. Oh, Emma—'

'Louis? Does Louis know?'

'He's at school—he's safe—I don't want to tell him yet, not till David—'

'Chantal—'

'Marical got telegrams, too. Chantal is with her.'

Everard was overseas, driving an ambulance. Someone would tell Everard.

'Emma—'

'Oh, Sophie, Sophie—I'll call you in the morning, first thing.' She could not think. Her mind had gone dead. Automatically she reached out to dial Nik, but before she could touch the phone, it rang.

It was Chantal, cold and quiet. 'Emma?'

'Yes. I've just been speaking with Sophie.'

'I'm with Maman in Connecticut.'

'Good.'

'Emma, if you can—if it's possible—I think Papa needs you.'

'How is it possible? I can't leave the show.'

'No, but—New Haven's not that far. There are lots of trains. You could be back tomorrow afternoon in plenty of time for half hour. Emma, I think you need Papa. I don't think you should be alone.'

'I was just going to call Nik.'

'Emma, please go to Papa and Sophie. Please.'

'Does Nik know?'

'I'll call him. Ask him to meet you there.'

'But—'

Chantal had hung up. Emma looked at her watch. Nearly one in the morning. Surely there were not many trains between New Haven and New York during the small hours.

Nevertheless, she left the hotel, went to the railroad station. To her surprise, a train was leaving in thirty-five minutes. She

walked up and down the platform. Not thinking. Not accepting.
No. Not Etienne and Adair.

Not Adair.

•

Her father was as Sophie had said. Sitting. Dry-eyed. Sophie was for the moment wept out, but her face was blotched
and puffy, her eyes rimmed with red, her blond curls moist,
limp. Emma hugged her and could feel Sophie's chest heave
with dry sobs. 'Ah, Em, I didn't think you'd be able to come—
I'm so glad—'

Jarvis was there, sitting by his father. Looked up at Emma,
his face haggard. 'He won't speak.'

Emma looked around the living room, dim and dull with only
one lamp lit. Her father was sitting upright in a wing chair, his
hands on the arms, staring into nothing. Emma pulled up a stool
and sat at his feet. 'Papa.'

No response.

She looked at Jarvis, who shook his head.

Emma pulled her stool closer, put her head down on her
father's knees. Stayed there, unmoving, eyes closed. After a
while she felt his hand on her head. Still she did not move.

She did not know how long it was before she felt herself gently
being pulled to her feet, and Nik had his arms around her.

•

She took the train back to New Haven, giving herself an hour
to rest before going to the theater.

After the show Saturday evening, the stagehands broke the
set. They would be opening in Baltimore on Monday for a two-
night stand, then on to Washington. Emma took the train from
New Haven to New York. She would have Sunday with her
father—

She should see Marical, surely she should see Marical, old
wounds opened again.

She got off the train in Greenwich and took a taxi to Marical's house, dark and closed up at three o'clock in the morning. Huddled in her sweater, she curled up on a wicker love seat on the porch and dozed until she heard sounds a little before six. Cold, stiff, she got up and knocked on the door.

Marical and Chantal greeted her. Hugged. Wept. Made coffee and tea. Gave her breakfast. Marical's face was pale with grief, but she was able to go through the motions of living, offer Emma more toast, jam, coffee.

Chantal said, 'I'll drive you into the city. The train service is awful on Sunday.'

'Thanks. Thanks, Chantal.'

There was silence on the drive until Chantal said, 'Emma, you have to forgive Adair.'

Emma looked at her in surprise. 'I have, oh, I have. There was never a question in my heart about forgiving Adair.'

'Do you think Adair was ever able to forgive himself?'

Emma looked out the window. The leaves were turning. Chrysanthemums were blooming in front of many of the houses. The roadsides were full of goldenrod. 'Perhaps,' she suggested tentatively, 'we have to do the forgiving? If Adair can't, well, we can.'

'Can we?'

'We have to.'

'Does that mean forgiving Billy?'

Emma did not answer.

Chantal spoke in a small, chill voice. 'If we have to do the forgiving for Adair, then we have to forgive Billy, too.'

Emma closed her eyes. There was a terrible empty space where Etienne and Adair should have been. 'What is forgiveness?'

Chantal's long fingers gripped the steering wheel. 'It's not forgetting. That's repression, not forgiveness.'

Emma looked over at her sister.

'Remembering,' Chantal said, 'but not hurting anymore.'

·

The company was tender with Emma, seeing that she had someone to eat with after the show, between matinee and evening performance. They went from Baltimore to Washington to Philadelphia. Nik called her every night. He would join her in Chicago.

'Your father's in rehearsal.'

'How's it going?'

'They've done some recasting. Sophie has a small role. Louis's at school, so she's free to go on tour. It's one way for her to keep close to your father, and it's a funny little part and she's quite good.'

'Papa?'

'I went to rehearsal yesterday. Sophie asked me to. It's amazing, Em. Your father stands in the wings like a dead man and then he goes onstage and comes to life.'

She would see her father in Chicago. His play was dark on Monday, hers on Sunday, so she could go to the Blackstone Sunday night.

She had not yet faced her own grief. Her heart was still a cold stone inside her.

Abby

❦ ❦ ❦

My God, my God, why hast thou forsaken me? why art thou so far from helping me, and from the words of my roaring?

O my God, I cry in the daytime, but thou hearest not; and in the night season, and am not silent.

But thou art holy, O thou that inhabitest the praises of Israel.

Our fathers trusted in thee: they trusted, and thou didst deliver them.

They cried unto thee, and were delivered: they trusted in thee, and were not confounded.

But I am a worm, and no man; a reproach of men, and despised of the people.

PSALM 22:1–6

ABBY WAS in France when Etienne and Adair were killed. She had been in France when Billy went in front of the subway train. The war separated people by distance as well as death. Emma had tried and tried to reach Abby by phone after the two telegrams, but could not get through. Wrote. Had no response. Evidently her letter hadn't made it across the ocean, past the censors (was death censurable?), to the Auvergne. The only reason Abby could make her occasional phone calls, Emma learned later, was that she and Yekshek were friends of the mayor and she could call from his office.

From Chicago she wrote Abby again, this time receiving a reply full of warmth and love and compassion. But an ocean separated them. A war separated them. Emma's own pain separated them.

She turned to Nik, to her husband, to assuage her grief, grief not only for her brothers but for her father, lost in his own pain.

.

They weren't the only family with multiple griefs.

Nik had never met Adair, had never met Etienne.

Often when they were alone together she could let her pain ease, could relax in her love for Nik. But Nik had his own grief. He was deep in a play based on Everard's army hospital experiences, but putting the David play away had been a death for him, a different kind of death from the one that took Adair and Etienne, but, nevertheless, a death.

They were staying at the Croydon on the Near North, in a room that had a Murphy bed, a couch, and two sagging chairs; a bathroom, a kitchenette, where she cooked for the two of them, and sometimes for other members of their company, or other friends in Chicago. Emma had never done much cooking; she was not like Sophie. But in their tiny, inadequate kitchen she found she enjoyed it, that she had a flair for it. Friends brought her a decent paring knife, a good colander. Puttering, making sauces, goulashes, salads, she was close to being contented.

When they went to see David's play, her father seemed almost himself onstage; but Emma missed something in his acting, something only she would notice, an almost invisible drop in vitality. Sophie was indeed charming in her small role.

Emma had not seen her father for three weeks. When she went backstage she was shocked. Suddenly he looked old. He had lost weight. He looked at Emma and tears flowed down his cheeks. 'Emma. Emma.' She pressed her face against his, and their tears mingled.

'Adair wanted Billy dead. And he hated me. He didn't have to go into the army and get killed, a horrible death, he did it to punish me.'

Nik was sitting on a chair in the corner. He stood up, as though to intervene or to leave, then sat again.

'Stop,' Sophie said. 'Emma is grieving, too. You aren't the only one.' She sounded unutterably weary.

David stretched out his hands in supplication, first to Sophie, then to Emma. 'Why am I doing this to you, my daughter? I'm acting, even now . . . but I'm true when I'm acting. And then I'm emptied, drained, and I come home no more than a shell. Oh, Sophie. If only Adair had come home. If only he had forgiven me.'

Emma sat at her father's feet. 'Listen, Papa, please. We none of us knew what Adair was thinking before he died. Adair had a volatile temper, we all know that. But it hurt him to stay angry.'

'It hurt everybody.'

'I think he didn't, Papa. I think he didn't stay angry. I think when he got in the army and went overseas and saw all the horrors of war, things fell into perspective for him. I do not believe that he died with anger in his heart.'

David let out a long, slow breath. 'You knew him better than anybody.'

Sophie said, 'And even if Adair did die angry, Davie, that anger can be released and redeemed now. That's what Bahama would say.'

'My mother.' David relaxed for a moment. 'She had enough faith for all the rest of us poor sinners.'

Sophie turned to Emma and Nik. 'Will you come to the Drake and have supper with us?'

'No,' Nik said. 'Not tonight. Emma's tired. Are you coming to our show tomorrow? Maybe we could have supper then.'

.

They walked back to the hotel through the crisp, autumnal air. 'Em, I wanted to get you away.'

'I know. Poor Sophie. Papa's hard to reach when you have to grope through the dark.'

'Everard told me that Jarvis was in there pitching, trying to reconcile Adair and your father. In the King David story it was Joab, but the animosity between David and Absalom over Tamar's rape was too deep, and the civil war was started in earnest, Absalom fighting against his father and almost succeeding, so that David had to flee his holy city of Jerusalem.'

Emma realized she was holding her breath. She said, softly, 'You're still thinking about the David play.'

'Well.' He shrugged. 'Has your father forgiven Adair?'

'I don't think that even comes into it with Papa. He's totally preoccupied with whether or not Adair has forgiven him.'

'For what?'

'For not doing something strong and definite about Billy, maybe putting him in a mental hospital.'

'Did he belong in one?'

'Not all rapists are insane. But it might have helped.'

'Would it have helped you?'

'I don't know. He might be alive now. Adair might be alive. But we can't—we can't rewrite the past.'

Nik walked, head down, finally saying, 'It's hard for me to let this play go, Em.'

'Do you have to?'

'I have to. But—it's been such a habit, thinking about it, talking—'

'I wish you'd go back to it.'

'I can't, Em.'

'But you keep thinking about it.'

'I woke up last night wondering what would happen when Abigail died. She's older than David.'

'Like most of the women,' Emma said, 'she just sort of gets dropped.'

'It must have been a terrible blow for David when she died. I can see him rushing through the servants' quarters after the servants have called him, and flinging himself on her. What would he say? Something from the Psalms?'

'My God, my God, why have you forsaken me?'

Nik looked at her. 'I thought that's what Jesus said on the cross.'

'It was. But King David himself said it long before, in the Twenty-second Psalm.'

'I don't remember that—if I ever knew it.'

'It's there. David's son Absalom has turned against him, taken his throne, his holy city of Jerusalem, raped his concubines, as Nathan the prophet said would happen. And David still loves Absalom, in spite of it all. He's begged Joab to deal gently with Absalom, but Joab kills him, and David is wild with grief. So those lines are there, but maybe they're too familiar to too many people as part of the crucifixion.'

Nik shrugged. 'It doesn't matter now, does it?'

'It does matter. It's the kind of scene you'd really plunge into.'

'No, Em. I'm happy working on the army hospital play. It's going well.'

'I'm glad, then.'

'But I'm worried about your father.'

'So am I. Oh, Nik, if Abby were here, maybe she could help Papa.'

'But she's not here,' Nik said. 'And she's not his wife any longer. Sophie is. And Sophie's doing all anybody can possibly do.'

'Yes, I know. I just want—I just want someone to wave a magic wand and make everything all right.'

'Many magic wands in your life?' Nik asked.

'I used to think Adair—' She felt a great sob welling up in her chest and barely managed to force it down.

Nik put his arm around her, but she did not relax against it or she would have broken into a torrent of weeping.

As they walked, her breathing slowed, regularized. They stopped on the bridge over the Chicago River and looked down at the dark water.

Nik said, 'You're strong, my Em, don't you know that? You've steadfastly refused to wallow in being a victim. You're living your own life and living it well.'

'You make it easy.'

'You were already doing it long before I came into the picture. You make the audience feel you've been in the hard places with them, and that gives them courage to go on living their own lives. It's what I hope to do as a playwright.'

'You do. Without the lines, a player can't do anything.'

'Mostly life's not very funny. The irony of it is, I write about tragedy best in comedy.'

They had reached the hotel. Went up in the elevator to their floor. Nik opened the door and turned on the lights, pulled the Murphy bed out of the wall.

—Tragedy in comedy, Emma thought, as she went into the bathroom to draw her bath. —Where's the comedy?

·

When the news came of the train explosion that killed Edith and Inez it was more than could be comprehended. It was,

Emma thought, somewhat like Abigail's son Chileab's death being overwhelmed by Saul's and Jonathan's. She cried for Inez. She cried for Etienne and Adair and for herself. For everybody.

One evening when Emma was lying in the Murphy bed waiting for Nik, looking with what was still amazed awe at his rings on her finger, he said, 'It's time for me to go home. I've overstayed the two weeks I gave myself.'

She did not want him to go. She fingered the sheet and the rather worn blanket.

'Day after tomorrow, I'd better go back to New York.'

He was right. He had planned to be in Chicago with her for only two weeks. It was part of theater life, that there would be many times when their work would keep them apart. It would be hard for Nik alone in New York. If Emma would miss Nik, he would also miss her.

Finally she brought herself to say, 'Go home and write your comedy, Nik. If there was ever a need for laughter, it's now.'

.

Nik's comedy was always compassionate, never cynical. What Nik had to say about the dark complexities of human relations he said with laughter, and audiences laughed and loved him. The play he wrote back in New York was based on Everard's experiences, but Nik somehow managed to fill the lines with laughter without losing the depths. It was a passionate anti-war statement clothed in comedy. It was probably the best work he had done.

But when it opened it was not a success. Patriotism was still high, and people were not ready for a call to turn swords into ploughshares.

Emma was back in New York, in rehearsal for Chekhov's *The Three Sisters*. 'Your play's good, Nik, it's more than just good. The critics pointed out that the timing wasn't right. Brooks Atkinson said that the play was so fine it should be revived in a few years when public opinion has changed.'

'You're my loyal supporter,' Nik said.

'I'm not just loyal. I'm truthful.'

'I know. Thank you. Emma, when I graduated from high school I was third from the top in my class. So I was neither valedictorian nor salutatorian. From my father's reaction, you'd have thought I came in the dunce at the bottom. Third was not good enough.' They were in bed, their pillows propped up against the great oaken bedstead. Nik leaned his head back, looking, she thought, like Hamlet.

'Seems to me third was pretty good.'

'My father thought I was a failure who'd come to no good. That's what the critics think.'

'Nonsense. You know that's absurd. What about your mother? Didn't she count on you to be a writer?'

'Dostoevsky. At the very least. Not light comedies which don't make it.'

'Hey, Nik, stop it.'

For a while he was silent. Emma picked up Chekhov's *Letters* and read a page.

Finally Nik said, 'You think it's self-flagellation, eh? Masochism?'

'I don't think you need to accept anybody else's assessment of you and your work. It's a good play. You're a fine writer.'

'You believe that?'

'I do.'

'You're prejudiced.'

'Probably. I'm also intelligent enough to know good work when I see it. Nik, I think I'm glad I never knew your parents. But you're not whoever it was they wanted you to be, and who no son could possibly be; you're yourself. Don't be hung up on their fantasies.'

Nik reached out for her hand. 'You're right, my Em, you're right. We mustn't do this to our children. We have to let them be who they are.'

Emma was again three weeks late for her period, but she was seldom regular. She did not want to be too hopeful.

'I'll try not to take my disappointment out on you,' Nik promised.

He did try, though he was not entirely successful.

Emma threw herself into her role, spending hours reading Chekhov's letters to his wife, and his instructions as to how Masha was to be played—against the lines, against the darkness, lightly, with laughter.

They spent a weekend with Marical, but Nik was restless. He tried to be sociable, and perhaps it was good for Marical to turn from her own grief and worry about Nik.

When Nik went for a walk, Emma sat in the kitchen with Marical. 'His play got stupid reviews,' Emma said.

'I read them. Unfair.'

'Very. But they stirred up all Nik's old self-doubts. He's working on another play now, a serious drama about Bramwell Brontë.'

'Why doesn't he do another comedy?'

'He wants to be taken as a serious playwright.'

'I think his comedies are serious plays,' Marical said.

'So do I.'

'Emma, are you all right? You look a little washed out.'

'I got my period this morning. This time I really hoped I was pregnant.'

'You worry about it too much,' Marical said. 'That's not good.'

'I know it's not good.'

Marical looked slowly around her kitchen, at the pot of geraniums on the table, the fuchsia in a hanging basket in the window, the bird feeder outside. 'I had a letter from Everard today. My one living son. I'm learning to let go, to move back into life. It isn't just worries about not conceiving that you're hanging on to, Emma.'

Emma smiled at her stepmother. 'If you can let go, I should be able to, shouldn't I? And I have a husband I love. Why haven't you ever married again, Marical?'

Marical returned Emma's smile. 'I've thought about it a couple of times. But everybody seems pale, after David. Despite all his faults, his selfishness, what I love is his *élan vital*.'

'He doesn't have it now.'

'I have two sons to grieve for. David has three. His *joie* will return. It will take time, but it will return.'

.

Emma believed Marical, but her own vitality was at a low ebb. For Nik she tried to be lighthearted, and working on *The Three Sisters* helped. It was a good cast, a good director. She could be proud of what they were doing.

It opened to distinguished reviews. Emma's 'unusual' conception of Masha was remarked on and generally approved.

'It's not unusual,' Emma said. 'I'm just playing it the way Chekhov wanted his wife, Olga, to play it.'

Sophie had come backstage to see Emma, waiting until other well-wishers had left and the two of them were alone in the dressing room. 'You're marvelous,' Sophie said. 'You make me believe utterly in Masha, and care.' She was nervously fingering the hem of her silk coat.

'Sophie, what's the matter?'

Sophie's eyes brimmed with tears. 'Emma, I didn't want you to hear this from anybody else. I'm going to marry Ulysses.'

'Who?' Emma looked at her stepmother in shock.

'He owns the gym where I exercise. I can't stand it any longer, Davie's darkness. He's pulling me into it with him. Louis's voice is changing. He's an acolyte now, but he'll be leaving the Choir School at the end of the semester, and I can't have him come home to Davie's gloom. Ulysses—he isn't the gorgeous lover that Davie can be, but at least he's more consistent. And consistency is what Louis needs.'

'And you?' Emma asked.

'Oh, Em, are you angry?'

'I'm just—surprised. Maybe I shouldn't be. I've been like Papa, preoccupied with my own griefs and problems. I know it must be impossible for you.'

'That's it,' Sophie said. 'Impossible. I wish it weren't. Davie's going into rehearsal for *Uncle Vanya* next week, or I wouldn't

—oh, Emma, Emma, I'm sorry, sorry, sorry . . .' Her words dissolved into sobs, and she flung her arms around Emma.

·

Sorry sorry sorry

Emma left the theater, took a cab, went to her father's apartment. He was sitting at a small table in the living room, playing cards with a blondined actress who had been cast in a small role in *Uncle Vanya*.

Emma flung her handbag on the floor in a rage. Stalked over to her father. 'No wonder Sophie left you. What do you think you're doing?'

He stood up, knocking half the cards on the floor. The blonde bent and started picking them up.

'Just go,' Emma said.

'Who the hell do you think you are?' the blonde asked.

'Go,' Emma ordered. 'Get out.' She was smaller than the other woman, but she approached her fiercely.

The actress shrugged, dropping some cards on the table. 'Okay, I'm off. See ya, Dave.'

Emma followed her to the door, bolted it, turned back to her father. 'I came to be with you because Sophie told me she was leaving. I don't know why she stayed with you as long as she did. Why can't you work your problems out instead of dumping them down the drain and turning to some new female to fix it all for you?'

David looked at his daughter, his mouth opening in astonishment.

'I'm not as forbearing as Abby.' Emma's voice cracked. 'But she's in France and can't see you ruining your life and everybody else's, too. Are you planning to marry this dame? She's even worse than Edith.'

'She's not—' David started, but Emma overrode him.

'Or Myrlo. Don't you realize Myrlo was a disaster for us all? What is it that blinds you to what you're doing? Why on earth did you throw Sophie into this gym character's arms? Don't you know she loves you? Don't you realize what a treasure you had? Don't you even care?"

.

"Sorry," David Wheaton said. "I have been a selfish bastard all my life. I've done what I wanted, even when it's hurt other people."

Emma sat on the revolving seat, her hands lightly on the wheel, looking out over the water. She had gone to comfort her father and instead had shouted her rage at him. She could not now remember all that she had said, about his gloom, his giving in. She had ordered him to get back into life, not lust.

David continued. "If I hadn't given in to the horrors of my darkness after Adair and Etienne were killed, Sophie might not have left me. It was a mistake, her marrying Ulysses, and I just let her do it."

"Hey, Papa," Emma said. "Sophie has some free will of her own, you know. It was her mistake, not yours, and so was Gino."

"But if she hadn't left me—"

"Where would Alice be?" Emma asked, as Alice came up the steps to the pilothouse.

"You mean," David asked with a smile, "that I'm trying to be the author of the play, not just an actor?"

"Maybe. We all make mistakes."

"Sounds like a heavy conversation," Alice said.

David moved restlessly. "It's noisy here, kids yelling and screaming, dogs barking—"

"It hurts you, doesn't it?" Alice asked.

"Yes."

"As soon as Nik comes, we'll leave the dock and head for a quiet inlet. You'll be better away from the confusion."

"Am I being selfish again?" The question was earnest.

Emma said, "None of us likes the noise at the dock. We'll all be happier when we get back in the wilderness."

When Nik comes—

.

Nik had felt real pain for Abigail, for Bathsheba. For the characters in Everard's hospital. For all his imaginary people. As a writer, he went deep into the emotions of his characters.

Emma's fists clenched. For his characters, yes, Nik empathized. But what about real life? And what did she expect?

Ups and downs, which is how life usually runs along, over hills, into valleys, occasionally into dark holes, up again into the light. They had been married five years when Emma became pregnant.

Well into the fifth month she felt the first lovely flutterings of life. The baby was very real to them. They were ecstatic. Nik's Brontë play had failed, but he now had a successful comedy on Broadway. Emma was in a play of Marlowe's with a limited run, closing in another week, which was why she had been able to accept the job. Her costume had been let out a little in order to disguise the gentle swelling of her belly. At bedtime Nik loved to put his ear against her stomach, listening, feeling for the little movements of the life within.

It was winter, cold, raw. And, one night, icy. Nik came to call for Emma after her show. When they left the theater it was sleeting, and the iron stage-door stairs were slick with ice. Emma slipped and fell. Nik, trying frantically to hold her, fell, too.

Members of the cast huddled around her, frightened, not knowing what to do. Finally they took her into the emptied theater. Called a doctor. Before he came she had started into premature labor.

'Get a taxi,' Nik said. 'I've got to get her to the hospital.'

.

Nik was not allowed into the delivery room with her. A nurse held her hand during the contractions. And then the baby came.

The doctor said reluctantly, 'He's dead, Mrs. Green.'

'I want to see him.'

'Better not.'

'Please.'

So tiny. He had been barely a bulge in Emma's womb. Tiny, a baby boy, tiny, dead.

'It's over, Mrs. Green,' the doctor said. 'Let it go.'

Let *it* go? It? He was a lost life. And they expected Emma just to let it—him—go? To get on with it. They were briskly kind. Called her Mrs. Green. Which of course she was. But she was also Emma Wheaton. That was not only her stage name, it was her identity. Mrs. Green was Nik's mother.

'Now cheer up, Mrs. Green. See? Here are some lovely flowers.'

.

Nik turned his grief into rage. Rage against fate, rage against Emma for falling, for losing the baby. Emma was too full of her own grief to understand that Nik's rage was his defense against anguish. She needed him and he wasn't there. He came dutifully to the hospital each day, bearing flowers or lavender water, stayed five minutes, and left.

David sent roses. He was in Boston, trying out a new play.

The cast of Emma's play sent a great basket of fruit. Some of the women came to see her, to commiserate. 'We'll all be out of work again at the end of the week,' someone said. 'We're having good houses. I don't know why they can't let it run a little longer.'

'So what's new? We'll be making the rounds again.'

'We'll see you, Em. You'll probably get a job soon.'

'If we pick up any news about casting at the Astor, we'll let you know.'

They were trying to draw her back into life, and she felt dead, as dead as her baby.

Sophie, divorced from David but still in touch, sat on the edge of Emma's hospital bed. 'It's men,' she said. 'They simply can't cope. When men hurt, they get mad, or they run away.' Then she started to cry. 'I shouldn't dump on men. I ran away when Davie needed me most. He was dragging me down into the pit

with him, and I had to climb out or die.' She wiped her eyes.
'But forgive Nik, Emma, forgive him. He can't help it. It's too
much for him.'

—What about me? Emma thought, but was silent. The words
were self-pitying and her feelings ugly as well as wounded.

·

She woke up from a dream sobbing, and calling out, 'Adair!
Adair!'

But Adair could not come to her.

·

Canon Tallis from the Cathedral came, the bald young priest
who had been in the background when Grandpa Bowman married Emma and Nik. He stood shyly in the doorway. Asked
diffidently if he could come in. He pulled a chair up to her bed
and sat there quietly, not saying anything, looking at her with
sorrowing brown eyes. Canon Tallis was a friend of her father's,
she remembered, an admirer of his work.

'Your father is a great actor,' he said, 'and you, too, Miss
Wheaton, it's evidently in your genes. I saw *The Three Sisters*.
Your interpretation of Masha was subtle, but every nuance was
clear. It will help when you can go back to work.'

'I suppose. If I get a job.'

The priest cleared his throat. 'I talked with your grandfather
last night.'

'Grandpa!'

'He called me. He believes that the baby should have had a
funeral.'

Emma said bitterly, 'That's not scientific nowadays. Just some
dead tissue.'

'A little boy. Did he have a name?'

'If it was a boy we were going to name him after my grandfather, Wesley Bowman. Grandpa was happy about that. And
now—'

'He is still honored,' the canon said. 'Tomorrow morning I

will celebrate the 7:15 Eucharist. I will make baby Wesley my intention. I wish you could be there, but your doctor says you are still running a little fever. However—do you have a Prayer Book?'

Emma indicated a pile of books on the shelf of her bed table. 'I have my grandmother's. Sophie brought it.'

He picked it up, opened it, and gave it to her. 'You can follow along. I know that the doctor told you to let your baby go. I, too, tell you to let him go, but with a difference. I know where he is going.'

That helped. Emma went home. The world was still strange, but she went to auditions and got a role in a revival of an Oscar Wilde comedy. Nik's play was doing well, and he was working on a new one. The David play, if he thought of it at all, had long been shoved in the back of his filing cabinet.

.

Grandpa Bowman died of a heart attack while he was preaching, only a few weeks after Emma lost the baby. It was a quick death, the way he would have wanted to go, doing the work he loved. Emma missed him fiercely.

.

"Grandpa Bowman died suddenly, with no time for preparations," David Wheaton said. They were sitting in the pilothouse, drinking a late cup of tea. Emma had a casserole waiting in the oven; it would be ready no matter when Nik arrived.

"Grandpa was prepared," Emma said.

"Yes, I believe he was. He had less to answer for than I. My children. At least Everard came home safely. He took over, pulled strings, got his mother and Chantal to Mooréa. I'm repeating myself. I don't like that. I do love my children."

Emma looked at him with concern. "We know you love us."

"You are very special to me, my daughter. Not many actors have the joy I have had in working with you. In many ways you have kept me going. You and Louis—and Jarvis—are all I have left. I won't see Chantal or Everard again. Mooréa is far, far away."

"But they love you, Papa." Emma's voice was firm. "Chantal sends you pictures of her French husband and her children. Everard sends you pictures of his pineapple plantation."

"Marical wouldn't let them hate me. But there were things she would not tolerate. The first slip I made—" He sighed. "So I married Harriet because I didn't know what else to do. People tended to get married in those days, even in the wicked world of the theater, and Harriet had a prima donna's cool beauty. Jarvis was an accident—she didn't want children. How kind Marical's boys—and Chantal—were to Jarvis, never seeing him as the cause of Marical's and my divorce, but treating him as a brother. Jarvis is both Adonijah and Joab to me. And my son. Has anybody called him?"

"I will, Papa," Emma said, "or I'll get Nik to, as soon as he goes home."

"When's Nik coming?" the old actor asked impatiently, wincing, shifting position. Alice looked at him sharply.

Emma said, "If all goes well and he makes his connections, it could be any time now." She went down the steps, through the main cabin, and out onto the deck, as though looking for Nik on the dock. Ben followed her.

"Em, I'm sorry."

"It's okay."

"No, it's not. I'd give anything if I could help and I know I can't." He reached his strong hands toward her, then dropped them to his side, helplessly. "You gave me such joy, that summer when you and I—"

Emma sat in one of the folding chairs. "It should never have happened. I'm sorry."

"I'm not."

"I am. It wasn't fair to you."

"It was my fault."

"No, Ben. Ours."

"You were hurting," Ben said. "You'd lost your baby, and Nik—"

"It was hell for Nik, too." Emma clasped her hands tightly.

"You were in need." Ben's voice was stubborn. "And it was beautiful. Rowing you to that little island, with the birds still singing, as though just for us."

.

When Emma had come to the *Portia* for a few days' rest, Nik was, she was certain, having an affair with another actress. Emma was still full of grief for the lost baby. She felt that Nik had turned away from her because her body had failed him. She had stood in front of the bathroom mirror, shining wet from her bath, and looked at her body with misery, not quite understanding that her feeling of sadness as she looked at her breasts, her belly, still slightly swollen, was residual sadness not only for the miscarriage but the violation of her body by rape.

Ben had pulled the rowboat up to a small, round jewel of an island crowned by trees, picked Emma up and carried her to a soft bed of sweet green moss, undressed her gently, slowly, then undressed himself. Slowly, tenderly, Ben explored her body, affirming it, returning it to health and beauty.

.

Emma sighed. "Yes. It was beautiful. But it shouldn't have happened."

"You were in need," Ben repeated.

Emma sighed again. "Ben, one thing I have learned is that all our needs do not have to be fulfilled."

"Okay, Emma, I honor that. But if you ever—"

"Ah, Ben, you're my friend, my good, true friend. But right now I'm not fit for anybody. I have too much to work through. What's left of me has to be for Papa."

"I just want you to know I'm here." Ben reached across the table and loosened her clenched fingers.

"Thank you. Thank you, Ben." Emma gently withdrew her

hands. Ben nodded, watched after her as she went back into the main cabin.

.

Emma opened the door to the fridge. Automatically she drew out the crab Ben had cleaned earlier in the day. He had shaken her. She did not want to think about Ben. How different was she, in essence, from her father? The evening with Ben may have been the only time she had—she did not like the words —committed adultery. But that, in fact, was what she had done. And if Ben had helped her at a time when her self-esteem was almost nonexistent, she had hurt Ben.

"We all hurt each other," Nik had said, once. "It's part of the human predicament."

She shut the fridge door, returned to the pilothouse, hearing her father saying, as she came up the steps, "Emma, I'm glad you're here. I want you to know that I know that God has forgiven me. I'm not sure whether or not I've forgiven myself. God doesn't have false expectations of us human creatures, but we do. And if I can believe that God has forgiven me, then I can believe that Adair has forgiven me, too."

"Yes, Papa, believe it."

"I needed to hear it again. I'll try not to be too repetitive. I miss your grandfather after all these years. How I wish he was here, to argue, shout, stimulate. When he died—remember— that church could have been filled a dozen times over for his funeral. I've never seen so many people, weeping, moaning. And speak of funeral baked meats! I've never seen so much food."

.

When she came back to New York after the funeral, Emma missed her grandfather more than she could ever express.

.

There were other sorrows, the ordinary sorrows of daily living, of two artists struggling to serve their work.

There was something missing after Nik put the David play away and they no longer had the intimate working together, the discussions of character, period, ideas. Instead of balancing Nik's glooms, Emma fell into moods of sadness, continued to grieve for Grandpa Bowman, tended to weep when she remembered his sermons, irritated Nik because both their lights were dim.

Weeping for Grandpa Bowman was also weeping for Billy's abuse of her. For Adair's and Etienne's deaths. For her lost baby. She needed the tears, but Nik did not understand all they were for.

'Your grandpa was a great man and he had a long life. Don't be so inordinate.'

Was it inordinate?

Only after a brilliant dream in which she saw Grandpa Bowman and Bahama sailing together on a great river, golden with sunlight, did Emma's grief begin to abate.

Sometimes, to compensate for the darkness, Emma and Nik quarreled noisily, but the quarrels weren't the problem. Nik's new play wasn't going well. He was blocked. Emma offered to improvise with him, and that helped, but he felt that his juices had dried up. He wrote some scripts for TV which brought him in some money.

'But I'm making enough, Nik.'

'I won't live on your money.'

'It's our money. Whatever either of us makes, it's our money.'

Nik gritted his teeth. 'So you say.'

'It's true. And you're getting royalties from little theaters and summer-stock companies.'

He was. But it was, to him, money for old work and therefore devalued.

That night, while they were in bed reading, Emma looked up from her book. 'Hey, listen to this.'

Nik lowered his copy of *Variety*.

Emma read aloud, 'This is Ibsen, writing of himself: "Your soul is like the dry bed of a mountain stream, in which the singing waters of poetry have ceased to flow. If a faint sound comes rustling down the empty channel, do not imagine that it portends the return of the waters—it is only the dry leaves eddying before the autumn wind, and pattering among the barren stones." '

'Why are you reading that to me?' Nik asked.

'I thought it was interesting. I mean, Ibsen was a really terrific playwright, and yet he got frightened and discouraged.'

Nik said heavily, 'Emma, your sermonizing doesn't help.'

'I'm not sermonizing. All really good artists get discouraged.'

'Okay, okay, so I'm discouraged, but I don't need you to try to be Bahama and Grandpa rolled into one. Can't you get out of their shadow?'

She knew that he was being unreasonable and couldn't help it. She said, 'I don't think I want to.'

'And I'm not Ibsen.'

'You're a fine playwright.'

'At the moment it doesn't seem so. I've hardly made a nickel in the past six months.'

'Nik, darling. Can't you relax? We're not tight for money. And I'm working.'

'Yeah, you're in a show now. When it closes, who knows when you'll get another job?'

'Who knows? Like all actors I'll be convinced that I'll never work again. But I'm putting plenty in the bank every week. You don't have to kill yourself writing stuff you don't want to write.'

'I do.'

Emma did not know how to be wise with Nik. She was wiser with Louis, her youngest sibling.

.

She came home after the theater one evening to find Louis waiting in her doorway, looking distressed.

'Emma, excuse me, I need to talk to you.' He was in high school now, a handsome if somewhat stocky young man with a mop of curly blond hair the color of wheat. His voice was a warm baritone, and he still loved to sing.

'Sure, Louis, come on in.'

'Where's Nik?' he asked.

'In New Haven with a new play.'

'I like your new show,' he said, 'and I think you're really exciting in it.'

'Sam Behrman has given me some wonderful lines.' She took out her keys and let them in. She hung up her coat and hat in silence, took Louis's coat. 'What's wrong?'

'Oh, Emma, I went to see Papa.'

She sat down on the bed. 'That's good. He's lonely without you and Sophie.'

'So am I. I mean, I miss being there, with Papa and Mom. I like Ulysses—what a crazy name for a health freak, and he adores Mom, and she's pregnant and they're ecstatic—but I certainly wouldn't choose him over Papa.'

'So what happened to upset you when you went to see Papa?'

Louis collapsed into her most comfortable chair. 'I still have keys to the apartment, and of course the doorman knows me, so I just went in. I hadn't called ahead or anything. I didn't think it was necessary.'

'It wasn't, was it?' Then she wondered: had Louis come across their father with some new woman?

'Emma, he was lying on the floor of the living room. Emma, he was crying, I mean, really crying. I've never seen Papa except—well, like Papa, full of life. And there he was, on the floor, broken. I can't bear it, not Papa!'

Sophie had succeeded in protecting Louis, in keeping his image of his father bright. 'Oh, Louis, I'm sorry.'

'I left—and I walked around until I knew you'd be coming home—and then I came running to you. I didn't let Papa know I was there, I couldn't embarrass him, I just left.'

'Listen, Louis, when I was in college we studied Kierke-gaard—'

Louis interrupted, 'Emma, I came to tell you about Papa.'

'Yes, and I'm not changing the subject. Kierkegaard wrote about Solomon hearing a noise one night in his father's sleeping quarters. He was terrified that one of David's enemies had come in and was trying to murder him. He went into David's bed-chamber and he saw King David just the way you saw Papa. I still remember it, vividly, what Kierkegaard told about Solomon, who never got over seeing David broken apart by grief. So Solomon was never really a great king, in that he was never quite complete. He had more wives and concubines than David did, and he lived much more lavishly, but he was never able to accept that David was a human being, or that he himself was human. Don't let that happen to you, Louis. Solomon couldn't stand having the image of his father broken, the great king always in control, always the great hero, always perfect. He never got over it.'

'Nor will I,' Louis said.

Emma sighed. 'Listen. Even if Solomon couldn't, you must. Didn't Solomon ever listen to the Psalms his father and Abigail sang? *A broken and a contrite heart, O God, thou wilt not despise.*'

'Emma, I saw Papa in agony.'

'Yes, little brother,' Emma said gently. 'That's part of life. No agony, no joy. Papa has an amazing sense of *joie de vivre*, and maybe that's because he's able to see himself as he is, and accept himself.'

'Emma, what went wrong, that Mom left Papa?'

She looked down. 'Papa grieved so over Adair and Billy and Etienne—'

'But Mom should have understood that. I keep thinking that if I'd been home instead of up at Choir School I could have helped keep them together.'

'For heavens' sake, don't blame yourself.'

'I love Mom, but I don't think she should have left Papa, particularly when he was full of grief.'

'Marriage is complicated. You'll understand more when you're married yourself. Louis, does Sophie know where you are? It's late, and you have school tomorrow, don't you?'

'Yes. Can I spend the night here?'

'If you don't mind sleeping on the couch.'

'I'll sleep on the floor if you want me to.'

'The couch will do. Here's a blanket and a pillow. Go call your mother.'

·

'Call your mother.' That was Bahama's influence. Go where you need to go, but let me know where you are.

It was also Bahama's influence, even more than Grandpa's, that kept Emma going to church on Sundays. Sometimes she wondered why she went. If there was time, she took the subway up to the Cathedral, especially if Canon Tallis was preaching. His sermons challenged and stimulated her. Often what she heard in other churches seemed rigid and unloving and unforgiving and made her hackles rise. He always gave her something new to think about.

She came home from church one Sunday to find Nik tense and edgy. She fixed lunch, and while they were eating she asked, 'What's the matter?'

'Does something have to be the matter?'

'No, but I think something is.'

He shrugged, then said, 'I wish you weren't so churchy.'

Surprised, she took a bite, then said, 'I enjoy Canon Tallis's sermons, and I got in the habit of going to church with Bahama.'

'Habits can be broken.'

'I don't see this as a particularly bad habit. Does it bother you?'

'I don't want to go to church.'

'Fine. Have I ever asked you to?'

'No.'

'Then give me the same freedom.'

They finished eating, and she picked up the papers and climbed onto the bed to read in comfort. Suddenly she put down the paper, shocked, chilled. In a gossip column she read: *Playwright Niklaas Green is often seen in the company of a certain redheaded actress.* She looked at him. 'Nik?'

'What?'

'What's this about?' She held out the paper.

'Oh, that. I hoped you wouldn't see it.'

'I've seen it.'

'It isn't anything, Em, just vicious gossip. You know good news isn't news. If there isn't anything available, the gossip-mongers make something up.'

Was that why he was so prickly? 'I'm certainly not a redheaded actress,' she said.

'No, and I don't give a damn about any redheaded actress. Please, Em, don't pay any attention to it. It's a lie.'

It probably was a lie. Nevertheless, it hurt.

She returned to the paper, holding it to hide behind.

Suddenly he was sitting on the bed beside her. 'Em, sweetie, I'm sorry. I'm a bastard, taking my insecurities out on you. Let's go out to dinner, someplace nice.'

·

For better for worse, for richer for poorer, in sickness and in health . . .

They were solemn promises and she had made them solemnly and she believed that Nik had, too. It wasn't that things were actively bad between them, or that they hit out at each other, or that they were particularly unhappy. It was just that there was a kind of greyness.

It was better when they had a chance to work together. Emma was rehearsing in an Off-Broadway production of Chekhov's *The Sea Gull*. The director was a friend of Nik's, who was invited to a rehearsal; they went out to a coffeehouse together afterwards.

'You're trying to make it too complicated,' Nik said to the director. 'I don't think Chekhov's trying to be highly symbolical. And I don't think the play's any more symbolical than—than—'

'*Hamlet* or *Winnie-the-Pooh*,' Emma supplied.

'Chekhov's people are complex, four-dimensional people, I know that,' the director said, 'but—'

'No buts.' Nik had ordered milk rather than coffee, and smiled at the director over his glass. 'They aren't Maeterlincky symbols. As for the sea gull itself, it seems to me to stand only for beauty carelessly destroyed.'

Emma nodded agreement. 'It means more to Nina personally in her grief than it did to Chekhov or needs to mean to the audience.'

'Yeah, but,' the director said, 'audiences are used to either the typical Broadway comedy or problem play where they find nothing but types, or the Shavian play where each character stands for an aspect of the author's argument.'

'Chekhov simply wrote about people—' Nik said.

'The way you do,' Emma said.

'—and his characters are inconsistent with the terrible inconsistency of people. Sometimes those who go around saying how clear everything is are the most confused.'

Emma laughed, adding, 'Or they laugh when they are sad, and cry when they are happy. If you live with a Chekhov play, really live with it, if you look at it simply, like a child, you'll find there's nothing confusing in the play; it's as simple as life; but on the other hand that's the most confusing thing in the world!'

'Okay, okay,' the director said. 'I concede.'

'If Chekhov's plays need to be categorized,' Nik said, '*prophetic* is better than *symbolic*.'

'You're right, you're right,' the director said. 'But do you think it's going to work?'

'Of course it's going to work,' Nik said. 'With Chekhov and Emma, how can you go wrong?'

'Very easily, as you just pointed out.'

'It's going to be a hit,' Nik said.

That was good, that mutual understanding between Emma and Nik. The production was well received, and the play settled down to a fair run.

·

Then there was an unexpected blow. The building in which they lived was being sold. It would be torn down, along with several others on the block, to make way for a large apartment complex. Leaving was a wrench.

'It was inevitable,' Nik said, 'and maybe it's just as well. When you get pregnant again, when we have children, there's no way we can stay here.'

They found a comfortable two-bedroom apartment on 116th Street in Morningside Heights. There was no reason Emma should not get pregnant again, the doctor said. But she didn't. Perhaps she wanted a baby too badly. Nik was a good lover, giving as well as taking. Their bodies meshed in rhythm. Even in Nik's worst moods, Emma was subject, not object. But nothing happened.

And she felt she was failing him.

.

Nik's play which had not made it to Broadway from New Haven had a chance for a two-week run in Miami. Nik went down to Florida with a new cast. The lead was now being played by a well-known comedienne, and Nik had real hopes that this time it would work.

He called Emma from the hotel. 'The weather's terrible. It's pouring rain and it's in the fifties. The set isn't working. The turntable sticks.'

'You have a week before you open.' Emma tried to be encouraging. 'And the cast is good.'

'They're okay. But everything's heavy, like the weather. Nothing bubbles.'

'When the weather clears up, you'll feel better. Call me tomorrow?'

'If the play flops again, I can't afford to.'

'Hey, Nik, we can afford a few long-distance calls.'

'Okay.' He did not call her for three nights. Then, the next night, he sounded more than depressed.

'Nik, what's wrong?' Emma asked.

'Everything. The play stinks. I've rewritten the whole last act and it still sags. We're doing a preview tomorrow.'

The weather changed, but nothing else improved. It was obvious from the preview that the play was not reaching the audience, that it would not make it to New York no matter how much work he and the cast and the director did on it.

When Nik came home after the two-week run he was more depressed than Emma had ever seen him. Depressed in a different way from his ordinary depression over bad reviews, over plays that did not work.

Finally Emma said, 'What's really wrong, Nik?'

'What do you mean, what's really wrong? I had a hell of a time in Miami. Nothing went well. Some of my rewriting was good and they couldn't get it. The timing was awful.'

'But it's more than that.'

He was belligerent. 'Isn't that enough?' Suddenly he seemed to wilt. 'I don't want you to read about it in a gossip column.'

She felt suddenly cold. 'Read what?'

It seemed that Nik and the comedienne had gone out drinking the last night of the play to drown their sorrows. They drank too much, much too much, evidently, because they were picked up for being drunk and disorderly and they spent the night in jail.

'Oh, Nik, I'm sorry—' He was obviously in terrible distress. She felt no anger, only a kind of anguish.

'You know I'm not a heavy drinker—'

'I know.'

'We were just so damn depressed.' He came to her, kneeling beside her, putting his head in her lap. 'I don't know why it happened. I don't even know what happened. I know it will never happen again. I promise. I'm glad my mother's dead. If she'd seen something like that in the papers, it would have killed her.'

Emma did not look at him. It would not kill her, certainly, but it hurt. And why? Why would having it in the paper hurt more than the fact that Nik had been in jail for drunk-and-disorderly behavior? If other people knew about it, would that make it more real?

She had been rocking him like a child, but suddenly he reached up and kissed her fiercely. Then he pushed away. Stood up. Went to his briefcase and pulled out some pages.

'Em—'

'What?' She was still numb, her feelings anesthetized by shock.

'That night in the hotel—the night after I'd been in jail—the play sagged. I knew it wasn't working. I couldn't sleep. And suddenly—I don't know why—I rewrote a scene from my David play. Actually, it was one of those scenes that wrote itself. Between David and Abigail. After—would you read it with me?'

She did not feel like playing a part, even in a simple reading between herself and Nik. But she could not say no to him. 'Sure.' Emma sat on their bed, leaning back against the great head-board, and Nik got up beside her, holding the pages so they could both see them. He read:

The scene is the king's chambers. David is lying on the floor. Abigail comes in, bends over him, touches his shoulder gently.

Emma cleared her throat, read:

David, you ought to be with Bathsheba.

Nik continued as David, groaning as though in pain:

No. I need you, to make myself a man again, not a quivering bowl of jelly. I cannot go to Bathsheba like this, with my tears out of control.

'David should give a deep sob here,' Nik said. 'I'm no actor, but I can just hear your father doing it.' Emma looked down at the script, reading Abigail's words.

ABIGAIL: Let her see you cry. She will not love you less.
DAVID: Nathan said the child will die.
ABIGAIL: Nathan said. Do you believe everything that Nathan says?

DAVID: Nathan said that it was God, that God has forgiven my sin—Abigail, which sin?

ABIGAIL: Are they separate, David? You lusted after Bathsheba when you knew she was Uriah's wife. You took what was not yours to take, and getting rid of Uriah followed on the heels of the first wrong.

DAVID: (*Reaching for her*) But if God has forgiven my sin, why does Nathan say that the child Bathsheba carries will die?

ABIGAIL: David, David, how many babies born in the summer months die, their little bowels cramping and emptying until there is no life left in them? Did not our own little Daniel die thus?

DAVID: (*Tired. Resigned*) It is true.

ABIGAIL: If Bathsheba's baby dies, then Nathan's prediction comes true. And if the baby lives, then Nathan can tell you that God has relented and granted his forgiveness. Whatever happens, Nathan will not be in the wrong.

DAVID: (*With sudden hope*) Then it may be that the baby—

ABIGAIL: I do not know, David. The baby may die, as our Daniel died. The baby may live, as Amnon and your other sons have lived. What I do know, David, is that if the baby dies, this death does not come from God.

DAVID: But Nathan—

ABIGAIL: Nathan's god is Nathan, an angry father-god who enjoys using the rod. Would you, David, condemn to death an unborn child?

DAVID: I? No!

ABIGAIL: Nathan's god and Samuel's are alike. Perhaps a father would punish by killing an innocent babe. Not a mother.

DAVID: But will God forgive—

ABIGAIL: It is the nature of God to forgive. If the child dies, it will not be because God has not forgiven. It will be because these things happen—

Tears were streaming down Emma's face. 'Nik—'

'Emma, it was so strange, writing that scene. Abigail—you told me what to say. It's Abigail's dialogue, not mine.'

'Do you believe it?' Emma reached for a tissue, blew her nose, but the tears were still sliding down her cheeks.

'Abigail believes it. Em, I couldn't have written it before—before—'

'Before our baby. Wesley.'

'Maybe it's taken me this long to come to it, to get over my anger.' Now they were holding each other, Nik's tears mingling with Emma's. 'Em—maybe it took a night in jail—seeing myself as the bastard I am—before I could listen to Abigail.'

'I wish you'd go back to the David play. Will you?'

'I don't think I can.' Nik's face was buried in her shoulder. 'If a scene comes, I'll write it. But I don't have any sense of the whole.'

'Maybe that would come while you wrote. Isn't that how it sometimes works?'

'Sometimes. Not always. Sweetie, I've been such a lousy husband.'

'I've been a pretty lousy wife.'

'Maybe we're just human,' Nik said. 'At least we're still together. You put up with me. Emma, you'll go on putting up with me?'

'As long as you put up with me.'

'My mother used to quote something about Jesus giving life, and life more abundantly, but she didn't have it. Do you think we can?'

She was still sore and numb. The scene between Abigail and David had broken through, made her feel again, and feeling hurt. —Life hurts, she thought. She said, 'Yes, Nik.'

·

They read the gossip columns carefully for several days. Divorces. Romances. Adulteries. Nothing about Nik in Miami. They heaved a breath of relief.

'Let's not talk about it,' Emma said. 'It's over.'

·

"I've talked too much," David Wheaton said. "I've talked when I shouldn't have talked, and I've been silent when I should have spoken."

"Hush, Papa," Emma said. "We all do the same."

He smiled at her. "Nik's really coming?"

"Yes, Papa. Any time, now."

"I asked you that before. Just like a child. When are we going to get there? How much longer? The same questions over and over."

"It's okay, Papa."

"Is this asking too much of you, Emma?" His eyes questioned her anxiously.

"I don't know. I think we're supposed to ask too much of each other; otherwise, nothing would ever get done. I've got to check dinner. It's a venison casserole, and I don't want it to burn."

Ben hunted, not so much for sport as from necessity. During the winter it was often impossible for him to get to the mainland. He kept the boat's freezer well stocked with all the food that would be needed when it was not easy for them to get to a market. They were able to eat well on the *Portia*.

Emma checked her casserole, then closed the oven door, stood up, and looked out the window. She stiffened as she saw not one but two men in business suits walking along the dock toward the *Portia*.

Jarvis had come with Nik.

Emma

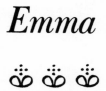

And David spake unto the Lord the words of this song in the day that the Lord had delivered him out of the hand of all his enemies, and out of the hand of Saul.

And he said, The Lord is my rock, and my fortress, and my deliverer;

The God of my rock; in him will I trust: he is my shield, and the horn of my salvation, my high tower, and my refuge, my saviour; thou savest me from violence.

And he rode upon a cherub, and did fly: and he was seen upon the wings of the wind.

He delivered me from my strong enemy, and from them that hated me: for they were too strong for me.

He brought me forth also into a large place: he delivered me, because he delighted in me.

II SAMUEL 22:1–3, 11, 18, 20

"THEY'RE HERE!" Emma called.

Abby emerged from the lower cabin. "They?"

"Jarvis."

Abby, too, looked through the window. Sighed.

Alice hurried down from the pilothouse, and the three women went out onto the dock to meet the men, Alice helping Abby with the wooden milk-box step.

"Why was I not told?" Jarvis demanded without greeting.

"Jarvis, we were both told about the cancer," Nik said.

"But not that Papa was dying. Imminently."

Alice took Jarvis's hand in hers. "You were the next to be called, Jarvis. I'm not sure I can say welcome to you right now. The *Portia* isn't a yacht, there's very little space, and we were going to bring you all in to see David in relays. And, Jarvis, you must not smoke."

"I gave it up three years ago," Jarvis said indignantly.

"I'm glad to hear it. But I don't know where we're going to put you."

"I'll stay in a hotel," Jarvis said, "though I can see there isn't one my style in this backwater."

Nik said, with some embarrassment, "Jarvis happened to call me last night." He looked at Emma.

She returned the look. Plunged her hands into her cardigan pockets.

Jarvis said, "Hi, little sis. Glad you're here, Abby. Not surprised. Alice, you're as beautiful as ever. But I wish you'd paid me the honor of calling me."

"As I said, you were next on the list. And don't forget Sophie and Louis. Let's go aboard. There's no point standing out on the dock."

"But why was Nik called before I was?" Jarvis followed Alice into the boat, sat down on the long seat.

"He's Emma's husband," Alice said calmly.

Jarvis looked around the cabin, sniffed the delectable odor of Emma's casserole. "I'm David Wheaton's son. Basically his only son at this point, with Everard in Mooréa."

"You forget Louis." Emma opened the oven, looked into it, then sat at the table.

"Louis? He's only a child."

Alice went quietly up the steps to the pilothouse.

Nik said, "You underestimate Louis, Jarvis."

"Okay, you two," Emma started, then stopped as Alice came down from the pilothouse.

"Dave would like to see you," Alice said, "but one at a time, please."

Jarvis nodded at Nik. "You're the one he expected."

Nik pushed back his chair and stood up. "Coming, Emma?"

"Do you want me?"

He looked directly at her. "Oh, yes, I want you very much."

.

'I don't want you,' Nik said, 'or need you.'

'What's that supposed to mean?'

'If you think I'm dependent on you or your salary, you're crazy.'

'Nik, we've had this out a thousand times. Any money we make is our money. I just happen at this moment to be in a successful play.'

'And my last play was a flop.'

'I've been in flops, too.'

'You didn't write them.'

'Nik, I know you're hurt.' She had gone, after her own performance, to the cast party opening night, waiting for the first reviews to come out. They had met upstairs at Sardi's, hopeful, not knowing what to expect. The audience, Emma was told, had been friendly, enthusiastic. And then someone came in with the first paper. There was a hush of expectancy. And then the blow. Heavy-handed humor. Inadequate theme. Flabby acting. All the bubbles deflated. Voices which had been high and excited dropped. Emma went to stand beside Nik. And the second paper came in.

.

'It was badly cast,' Nik said, 'and you refused to be in it.'

'I didn't refuse. I was already in a play. I was under contract.'

'Contracts can be broken.'

'No, Nik, you know I had to honor it. And the role you wanted me for wasn't right for me.' She tried to put her arms about him and he shook her off.

'You don't know anything about fidelity. How could you, with your father with all his wives.'

'Please. Leave Papa out of it.'

'The truth hurts, doesn't it? Maybe that's why you have such unreal expectations of what a marriage ought to be.'

'As you pointed out,' Emma said, 'it ought to be faithful.'

There was a distance between them that slowly grew wider and deeper. Nik's anxiety about money was surely what he himself would call inordinate. He had saved and invested money from his successful plays. But three consecutive plays which failed, plus producers becoming wary, had him close to despair. Emma understood his depression but could not alleviate it. She knew that if she had nine good reviews and one bad one, it was the bad one, criticizing her acting, that stuck in her mind. She knew how demoralizing destructive criticism can be.

She thought of staying home and not going to auditions or readings, but her presence seemed to increase Nik's irritability.

Ironically, the quarrel which precipitated their breakup came after an Off-Broadway revival of Nik's hospital play, which this time was a glowing success, so successful that it was moving uptown. But something in Emma broke. She herself did not understand completely why suddenly she found it intolerable to live under the same roof as Nik.

'You're being totally irrational.'

'I know. I'm sorry.'

'Don't be sorry. Just tell me what the hell this is all about.'

'I can't live with you anymore.'

'Why now, when at last things are going well for me?'

'I don't know.' She did not.

'Listen, why don't you go to Mooréa and stay awhile with Chantal?'

'Leave *King Lear*? Leave Papa? You're crazy.'

'You love your father more than you love me.'

'Don't be silly.'

'You're in love with him.'

She looked at him and laughed. 'My father is eighty-seven years old. He's a wonderful actor. I love working with him.'

'Incest,' Nik said. 'It runs in the family.'

Emma went into the bathroom and fell on her knees by the toilet and threw up.

·

When she could stand without getting dizzy, she walked out of the apartment, letting the door slam behind her, took the subway downtown, and booked a room at the Algonquin for the night.

Because of the size of the cast, only David Wheaton had a private dressing room. Emma shared a large room with the actresses playing Regan and Cordelia, and Regan had sensed that Emma and Nik were having trouble.

'Em, I happened to have supper at the Algonquin with friends and I saw you standing at the elevator. Something wrong?'

Emma shrugged. 'I guess you could call it that.'

'Even you can't afford the Algonquin for more than a night or two. Come home with me till you pull yourself together. My apartment's not big, but it's in walking distance of the theater, and I have a good pullout couch in the living room.'

Emma accepted gratefully. She felt so numb that it was all she could do to make herself eat, go to the theater, open the couch, fall into bed. She had been living with Regan for over a week before she noticed one of the understudies going through the living room, past the pullout couch, and into the bedroom.

Regan, noting her surprise, remarked casually, 'I broke up with my fellow a few months ago. Now I'm having fun playing the field. I'll find someone I like enough to settle down with sooner or later. I'm not ready to marry.'

That night after the theater she fixed Emma a bowl of home-made vegetable soup and sat at the foot of the couch. 'I do take an occasional night off. Emma, do you know what an innocent you are?'

Emma laughed. 'That would hardly be my definition of myself. I'm at least ten years older than you are.'

'And innocent. It's something about being born in New York.'

'What?'

'I was born in a small town in Mississippi. When we walked down the street we spoke to everybody. "Hey, how yawl doin'?" We looked at people. If someone new came to town, we all knew it in an hour. If a girl got a new dress, or a new boyfriend, we knew that, too. But you New Yorkers are trained not to see. I've watched you slither through a mob on Broadway so quickly you're almost invisible, but you don't see anybody. They're just bodies.'

'No—' Emma started to protest.

'It's self-defense for you, Em. That's how you're trained to protect yourself from supersaturation. But you miss a lot. I bet you don't know that the guy who plays Edmund has half a dozen lovers a night, that he goes from bar to bathhouse to bar, looking for God knows what. I bet you don't know that the guy who plays the Fool is living with his mother, who's dying by inches, and he goes home from the theater and nurses her. Gloucester is terrified of something, but I haven't yet figured out what. If you grow up in a small town, that's the kind of thing you notice. Gossip is a way of life. There isn't anything else to do. Maybe it isn't always nice, but you, Em, you miss a lot.'

'I never thought of it that way.'

Regan grinned. 'You're a good actress because it's bred in your bones. Your fairy godmother touched you with her magic wand. I'm a good actress because I learned to observe. People are a mess of genes and chromosomes and hormones run wild. Nik, your ex—'

'Not yet.'

'—sees all that and laughs at it affectionately. That's why his dialogue is so good. But you've shut something off, Emma. It opens when you're onstage and closes at the last curtain call. Is it just the native New Yorker syndrome?'

'I don't know.'

Regan's slightly bantering tone sobered. 'Emma, have you talked with your father lately—I mean, really talked?'

'Papa—'

'He's lost weight, Emma. His energy barely carries him through the performance.'

Emma looked at Regan with shock.

'Breaking up with a husband must take everything you've got, and I don't want to worry you, but—'

.

Louis saw what Emma had not seen. He came backstage to see Emma. 'I'm worried about Papa.'

'Why? What's the matter?'

'When I went to his dressing room, he was just standing and letting his dresser take off his costume.'

'That's one of the fringe benefits that go with being the star.'

'Emma, he looked exhausted.'

'He gives an exhausting performance. You know that.'

'I don't know, Em, he didn't seem well.' Then he looked at her. 'What about you?'

She did not want to accept that both Regan and Louis were seeing more than she had seen. 'I'm fine. I just have a sort of virus. It's good to see you. How's your show?'

Louis's green eyes sparked from the pleasure of his success in his first good role. 'Going well. But my show's lots shorter than Shakespeare. We break more than half an hour before you.' Then he looked at her shrewdly. 'You're sure you're okay?'

'Sure.'

'You're my only available sister. I don't want you to be unhappy.'

'That's life, isn't it?'

'Is it? I'm happy.'

'That's wonderful. You got marvelous notices.'

'I'm good,' Louis said, with the same kind of unselfconscious pleasure as his mother. Both Sophie and Louis could accept their talent and take joy in talking about it, unlike Emma, who still found it difficult to accept praise. 'Can I take you out for a bite to eat?'

'That would be fun.' But she felt cold. Papa. No. Nothing should be wrong with Papa.

'Will Nik join us?'

'No.'

'Where is he?'

She did not know exactly where Nik was. 'Busy with his own play.'

'Well, give him my love, then.'

·

Emma went to Alice.

'Yes, I'm worried,' Alice acknowledged. 'You haven't noticed anything wrong?'

Emma said bitterly, 'Papa's a consummate actor. And I've been preoccupied with myself. I'm sorry, Alice. I should have seen. What do you think is wrong?'

'We're running some tests.'

'For what? Tests for what?'

'Cancer.'

'You don't think—'

'We won't know until the results come in.'

Alice, involved with fear for her husband's life, had not seen Emma's pain. Emma, involved with the dissolution of her marriage, had not seen anything outside her immediate anguish until it was pointed out to her.

'Hey, Em,' Regan said in the dressing room that night. 'Don't beat yourself. We all get lost in our own lives. You've just joined the human race.'

For the first time? Where had she been before?

'Sure. Thanks.'

'And you miss your fellow.'

Yes. She could not live with Nik, but she missed him.

.

"Emma—"

"I'm here, Nik."

They went up the steps to the pilothouse. Nik braced himself as he turned to greet his father-in-law. "Dave." He bent down to kiss the old man.

"Thanks, Nik. In New York I was untouchable because I had cancer. People are more realistic about life and death out here."

"I don't want you to die. I want you to live forever."

"No, you don't. It would be a horrible idea, like a play running year after year with the same cast, losing all freshness, becoming routine and dull. I've come to the end of this role, and whether or not there's another role ready for me on the other side of death, I'll have to wait and see."

Nik sat down on the side of the bunk and took David's hand. "Dave, I want you to know that I'm back on the David play for you."

David Wheaton raised his eyebrows. Emma, who had been looking out at the water, swiveled slightly to look at Nik.

"I know how to do it now. It will indeed be the David play, but King David himself will not be in it. It will be a one-woman play for Emma, from the point of view of all of David's women, from Zeruiah and Michal, Abigail and Bathsheba, to the concubines raped by Absalom, to Abishag, lusted after by Adonijah."

"Abishag," David murmured, "sent to keep David warm in his old age. I know Alice is no Abishag, but she's still an attractive woman. I want her to be happy. I don't want her to spend the rest of her life carrying the torch for me."

"Dave, leave it up to Alice. Trust her to do whatever's best. My hunch is that Alice misses medicine."

David pressed Nik's hand. "You can be wise for me, can't you?"

"And less wise for myself?" He looked to Emma, then back to David. "Theater is changing. The big play I had in mind in the forties is no longer financially feasible now that we've reached the sixties. Small-cast plays will be the norm, and the one-man or -woman show is definitely the wave of the future. Times Square is changing. It's no longer the Great White Way. Porn movies and massage parlors and all kinds of perversity are on the upsurge. Things need to be said about men and women and love that I think I can say in this play."

"You say you're doing this for Emma?" He looked toward his daughter.

"For myself. Emma is the actress to do it. And it's my tribute to you. I would never have been able to understand King David if I hadn't known and loved David Wheaton."

"Emma?"

"I don't know, Papa."

"It's going to be a great role," Nik said. "I hope it will tempt Emma. I know she—" He looked at Emma. "You—can turn it down. I hope you won't."

"Nik, I can't even think about it now."

Nik spoke not to Emma but to David. "I've been horrible to Emma. I said unpardonable things. I took out my nerves, my failures, on her. I've done everything my father did to my mother, and I hated my father for it. But Emma's not like my mother."

"No." David shifted position. He was in pain. "Why is Jarvis here? I did hear his voice, didn't I?"

Nik said, "He's your son, and he insisted on coming with me. He says he'll stay in a hotel.'

"The Golden Spruce is hardly what Jarvis is accustomed to." David sounded irritable.

Emma laughed. "It's also next door to a laundromat that runs all night."

But David was distracted and not amused. "Ben plans to pick up anchor at any time now. Ben! Ben!"

As Emma started to slide off the stool, Nik said quickly, "I'll get him."

"Of course I want to see Jarvis—" David again shifted position.

"Now, or after you've spoken to Ben?"

"Now."

"I'll get him," Emma said.

.

Together they went to the main cabin, where the others were seated around the table.

"Jarvis," Emma said, "Papa wants you."

Nik asked, "Where's Ben? Dave wants him, too."

Alice said, "He's tinkering with the pulley for the Zodiac." She went out onto the aft deck.

Emma had noticed that increasingly her father wanted to know where everybody was, needing that security. Alice, particularly Alice, he needed to be able to call, to see, to know that she would be there for him—a final holding on to that which he was going to have to leave forever.

She watched her brother as he went up the steps to the pilothouse, rather hesitantly, without his usual brash authority. "What are we going to do with him?" she demanded. "I can't imagine Jarvis in a sleeping bag, and there isn't room for him."

Alice, returning to the main cabin, laughed, then quickly sobered. "Dave needs to get away from all this confusion. It is, quite literally, causing him pain. He needed to see Nik, so it was worth staying here at Port Clements overnight, but now we must get away to some peace and quiet."

Abby asked, "How far away is peace and quiet?"

"Oh, not that far, really. The problem is Jarvis."

Nik offered, reluctantly, "I could go now, if that would ease matters. I've seen Dave, and Jarvis can sleep wherever you were going to put me."

Alice pointed to the long seat. "Here, with Ben, in a sleeping bag. I don't think it will do for Jarvis."

"Well, that's good." Nik sounded relieved. "At least for me." He stopped abruptly. He was sitting on the far end of the window seat and he reached out for some sheets of yellow paper with his own strong handwriting. "What's this?"

Emma answered with absolute calm. "Scenes from your King David play."

"What on earth are they doing here?"

"They were in the pilothouse between the charts in one of the drawers. Papa had them there."

Nik picked up a page. Read aloud: "And even though David was victorious, he kept weeping for Absalom, and the victory was turning into mourning, with the king crying out in a loud voice, 'O my son Absalom, O Absalom, my son, my son!'"

Emma took the page from Nik, and read: "Again the scene is indicated by a scrim, with a projection of Absalom, David's son, caught in an oak tree by his hair. He is hanging there, helpless, when Joab enters, and stabs Absalom through the heart. 'And ten young men that bare Joab's armour compassed about and smote Absalom, and slew him.'

"They take Absalom's body, and leave with it. The lights go off the scrim, and we see David in his chambers, weeping bitterly." She put the page down and looked at Nik. "Then we have the famous 'O my son Absalom' speech. Nik, you must have written this long after you'd put the play away and I thought you'd forgotten it."

"I was like a mouse, keeping on nibbling at a piece of cheese much too big and tough for him. Em, why—why is your father—"

"Why is he rereading your play?"

"Yes. He can't be reading it just as a play. It's tied in with too much pain—"

"It's pain that has to be exorcised. I think that talking about the play has helped."

"And you?"

Emma clasped her hands together tightly. "We've talked, whenever he's wanted to. He's said some amazing things."

Nik looked at her questioningly.

"He said that it was only after David lusted after Bathsheba, caused Uriah's death, only after he had failed utterly with Tamar and Amnon and Absalom, only after he was fleeing his enemies, fleeing his holy city of Jerusalem, that he truly became a king."

Nik looked down at his hands clenched on the yellowed pages of his play. "Maybe we have to sin, to know ourselves human, faulty, and flawed, before there is any possibility of greatness. I think your father's right. David did become great only after he'd lost everything."

"Is it always the hard way?" Emma asked.

"Isn't it?" Nik unclenched his fists. "David's grief over Absalom—it was grief over his own failure as a father."

"Oh, Nik—yes—Papa, too. He believes that he failed all of us."

Nik's voice was calm. "Parents always fail their children. If we'd had children, we'd have failed ours. That's simply how it is, and the kids have to get along as best they can. My parents were who they were. Dave is Dave."

"And I love him," Emma said. She reached out and took the pages from Nik, reading silently, her lips moving. "And Joab had to speak fiercely to David about his continuing grief, telling him that he was shaming all his friends who had saved his life and put him back on the throne."

·

And Jarvis told his father to get back on the stage. He had living children he should be thinking about, who loved him, and were being hurt by his behavior.

.

Emma looked bleakly at Nik. "There really isn't a happy ending, or an ending at all. David stopped grieving for the sake of his friends, and he took up his crown again, and returned to his holy city, and Israel and Judah were united, briefly, but there's still a lot of fighting and confusion and—"

"Hey, sweetie, that's the old play, remember? I'm on a new one now. Look. Here's the opening."

"Nik—you still have your old briefcase."

"And will, as long as it lasts. Here, Em, look at this."

She took a page from his hand.

The stage is bare, bathed in a soft evening light. We see the roof of King David's parapet, the whiteness of the low wall shining with a moonlike glow.

Then we see a projection of eight women, standing hand in hand. King David's eight named wives.

Behind them are other women, the other wives, the concubines, the friends.

Then the projection fades out. The spotlight moves center stage as Abigail steps into it.

"Nik—I like it, I like it."

"There's more," Nik said. "I didn't bring it. I'll have to show it to you later."

"Children." Abby's voice was gentle but firm. She was coming up from the lower cabin, Alice following her. Emma had not noticed when they had left her and Nik alone. "There are certain plans we have to make. Alice is right. We need to get Dave away."

Ben came down from the pilothouse. "I'll take the *Portia* to a place less than an hour from here, and we can drop anchor near Wathus or Wiah. Jarvis can stay for dinner—I assume he'll want to do that—and then I'll bring him back to Port Clements in the Zodiac and he can stay at the hotel, and I'll pick him up again in the morning."

"Oh, Ben, you're wonderful!" Emma cried.

"No problem," Ben said. "Abby and I worked it out. We'll have to lend Jarvis some rain gear."

Emma laughed. "I can just imagine what would happen with his city suit in a Zodiac ride. Where is he? Still with Papa?"

"No. He's gone to the Golden Spruce to make a reservation for tonight."

"I didn't see him go—" She had been too drawn into Nik and the play to notice Jarvis leaving. She had been plunged back into all the joys of collaboration, and all the sorrows that had caused Nik to put his play aside.

"As soon as Jarvis comes back, we'll take off." Ben went down the steps to the lower cabin and into the engine room.

"It's as good a solution as any," Alice said. "I don't want Dave upset."

"It's all right," Abby assured her. "We'll keep things quiet."

.

The sky was moving into the long, slow dusk when Ben dropped anchor. They were in a narrow inlet where they saw no sign of life except the dark sleek heads of seals looking at them timidly, and a watchful eagle sitting high up on the topmost branch of an ancient fir tree. A small waterfall tumbled down between rocks and trees. At the far end of the inlet was a half-moon of sandy beach.

"Bear territory," Alice said.

Jarvis shuddered. "I'm not excited about wild life."

"If we see a bear, which isn't likely," Alice said, "it will ignore us. Jarvis, your father is tired, and I'm going to take him his dinner on a tray. We'll eat in here."

"I've come a long way to see Papa," Jarvis said. "I don't plan to be exiled."

"You haven't been exiled." Abby spoke swiftly. "We'll have a pleasant meal and then, after you've had a good night's sleep, you can look forward to seeing David tomorrow."

Emma rose and went to the oven. "Jarvis and Nik, will you set the table, please?" She got a tray which slid between stove and refrigerator and started preparing a plate for her father. There were too many of them for the pilothouse and the confusion would not be good for the old actor; he would be better off alone. But she did not like it. She gave the plate to Alice.

Alice took it, saying, "You all start. I'll sit with Dave for a few minutes."

As soon as Alice had gone up the steps, Jarvis, with a handful of knives in his hand, said, "I want to get Papa somewhere—at least Vancouver—where he can have proper medical attention."

Emma banged a wooden spoon against the stove. "Alice is a doctor."

"A backwoods doctor."

Emma's voice was stiff with anger. "Alice was trained at Johns Hopkins. Isn't that good enough for you? She did her residency at NIH in Washington, D.C. You could hardly find anyone more qualified."

Jarvis was equally stiff. "I'm beginning to understand why I was not consulted. Papa ought to be in a hospital where—"

Abby interrupted. "David does not want to be in a hospital to die away from everything and everyone he loves. Alice is doing everything that needs to be done."

"Is he in pain?"

"To a certain extent, but Alice is controlling that. Don't worry, Jarvis. David saw all the specialists in New York. He knows what he's doing. He loves the *Portia* and the Pacific Northwest. He needs to be here, surrounded by the land and water which sustain him."

Jarvis frowned. "I hate nature."

"That's your privilege. Let David be where he is happy."

"Is he happy?"

Abby answered carefully, "He is acknowledging and accepting

his life, and that is preparing him for his death. When we've all visited him, then we must all leave him and Alice alone."

Emma nodded, her eyes filling with tears. These days on the *Portia* had been days out of time and therefore days without end. Jarvis's coming had precipitated her awareness of ending.

"We'd better eat." Emma tried to keep her voice from trembling. She put the casserole on the table, and Jarvis finished handing around the knives. He said nothing more about getting David away from the *Portia*.

Ben came up from the engine room, stopped, and washed his hands. He was about to sit down at the table when his head went up, listening. He held up his hand for silence.

From the radio in the pilothouse Emma could hear, "The *Portia*, the *Portia*, the *Portia*."

Ben leapt up the steps to the pilothouse and the radio, saying, "*Portia* here. Over."

"Stop." Abby stood with her hands out, holding back, as it were, Nik and Jarvis, who were following Ben. "Don't crowd up to the pilothouse. Ben will tell us whatever it's about."

Emma strained her ears, but Ben had evidently turned down the volume. She heard a muffled expletive.

"What's going on?" Jarvis demanded.

"The Coast Guard's calling us on the ship's radio," Alice said. "Wait."

Ben came down the steps. "Alice, go up to Dave." Then, to the others, "That was a message from Sophie. She and Louis are arriving at Port Clements tomorrow."

"How on earth—" Emma started, then turned to her brother. "Jarvis?"

"I happened to mention to Sophie that I was coming."

"It's too much!" Emma expostulated. "We were going to call everybody, one at a time. You know the *Portia*'s a little boat, we don't have room—"

"Emma." Abby's voice was quiet. "Hush."

"I'll book them rooms at the hotel." Jarvis's voice was smooth. "It will all work out beautifully, you'll see."

"Jarvis, Father's death is not a production for you to stage—"

Jarvis reached across the table for Emma's hand. "Sorry, sis. Staging it is my way of not falling apart. Sorry. I shouldn't have spoken to Sophie."

"She had to know, sooner or later," Nik said. "Maybe it isn't bad to have us all here, get it done with, give Dave some peace."

"He can't be overwhelmed—" Emma started.

"We won't overwhelm him," Nik promised. "One at a time, and for whenever and however long Alice decides."

Alice came down the steps from the pilothouse, her face calm. "I have Dave quieted down now for the night. If you'll look out on that little patch of sand, there's a bear, beachcombing."

Emma and Nik went eagerly to the windows and there, indeed, grubbing about on the sand, was a black bear, ignoring, if he was aware of, their presence. The long evening light slanted against his fur, giving it golden lights.

Alice asked, "Jarvis, are you through with dinner?"

"It's a good thing I eat quickly."

"Ben will take you to Port Clements. What time do you want him to come for you in the morning?"

"I get up at ten," Jarvis said. "Eleven would be good." Then he added, "If that's convenient."

Abby asked, "Are Sophie and Louis coming in at the same time that Nik and Jarvis did?"

"Weather holding," Ben said, "they should be on the same plane. I'll get the Zodiac ready."

"Need any help?" Nik asked.

"Sure. I can always use a hand."

Emma watched them go out to the back porch. She was not sure what she was feeling. Far past and near past were running together. Nik was the Nik of their youth, when Adair and Etienne were alive, and the King David play was new and growing, and Bathsheba was Sophie—time again dissolving. But Nik was also the Nik of the near past from which she had fled.

Abby had pulled out her sketchbook and was drawing swiftly.

Emma was able to glance at the pad and saw that with a few strokes Abby had put Jarvis on the page.

Jarvis looked at Emma. "How do you find Nik?"

Emma replied coolly, "Tired from all the travel, just as you are."

"He's written a good new play."

"I'm glad."

"I'm producing it."

"Good."

"What about you, Emma?"

"I'm here for Papa. That's all. I don't want to talk about anything else."

"Jarvis!" Nik called. "Your limousine is ready."

Jarvis rose. "I guess I'm a lot of trouble." No one spoke. He added, "I don't really like being on boats—except one like the *France*. I'm better off in the hotel with my own bathroom. I'll be more use if I get my creature comforts."

"It's all right, Jarvis." Abby smiled, closing her sketchbook. "We're all made the way we are. Have a good night's sleep and we'll see you for lunch."

"Shall I bring anything? I assume there are available grocery stores."

"We could do with more milk and eggs," Emma said.

"And I'll get a bottle of wine for dinner. Thanks, all of you. Good night." He waved, an insouciant Jarvis wave, and went out on the loading dock.

·

Emma went to the pilothouse to say good night to her father. He was drowsy but held out his arms to her. "Ah, Em, Em. Are you all right?"

"Yes, Papa, fine."

"They'll all be here tomorrow, all the available ones."

"Yes."

"I'll make my peace with Billy and Adair and Etienne later."

She pressed his hand gently.

"Everard and Chantal. Good children. You'll say goodbye for me?"

"Yes, Papa. I will."

"Goodbyes are not easy, but I'm ready to move on. I'm not reluctant, Emma, not holding back. I don't have answers to the questions, at least not yet, but I have some good questions. I have loved life, and I believe that life is to be loved, because it is a gift."

Again, she pressed his hand.

"Love it, Emma."

"I do. Most of the time."

"You can love it even when you're in anguish."

"I know."

"When you're onstage, you love. We both love well when we're onstage. You're better offstage than I've been. But I'm not beating my breast. I'm not saying what I want to. What I want is for you to be happy."

"I know, Papa. Thank you. Mostly I am. Good night."

"Emma, you don't have to make the mistakes I have made."

"I know."

"Good night, my sweet child."

There were tears in her eyes when she left him. She got ready for bed and was using the upper head when Ben returned in the Zodiac, which he simply tied by the side of the boat, since he would be using it again the next day.

Emma came out, her warm bathrobe belted round her.

"Emma?"

She looked at him questioningly.

"Emma, if I could, I'd do anything to get you away from Nik. But you're an actress, a city person. You wouldn't be happy out here. And I'm not like Alice. I couldn't transplant to New York. Anyhow, you're still in love with Nik."

She looked down at her feet in fleece-lined slippers. "Yes, Ben."

"Why don't you go back to him?"

"I'm not sure. It's complicated."

"I know it's been painful for you, the way Dave's been going on and on about the King David play, but it's also brought you back to Nik, hasn't it?"

"In a way."

"Don't be like your father's wives, Emma. I know you've had lousy examples, but marriage has to be worked at."

"Why haven't you ever married again, Ben?"

"I'm a loner. I loved my wife, and since her death I've learned to live comfortably with my memories and myself. I'm married to the land, the sea. I'm like a great blue. I love my friends, but ultimately I need to live alone. So who am I to give you advice?"

"It's good advice, Ben. Generous."

"Will you take it?"

"I'll think about it. I promise."

Think. It was hard to think with her father lying on the bunk in the pilothouse, with the entire family, at least the entire remnant of the family, arriving to say goodbye. Despite the fact that she was in her nightclothes, she went out onto the loading dock, let down the rowboat, and got in, rowing quietly away from the *Portia*. She was not heading in any particular direction. She merely needed to be alone with the water and mountains and sky.

She was not like Ben. Life in the theater is, at its best, life in community, and she needed community. Seeing Nik again had been both painful and joyful. Nik was Nik, and that was not going to change. Emma was Emma. Was she strong enough to allow both of them to be themselves? Bahama had instilled in her an honoring of promises, but she could not keep her promise unless she was willing to allow Nik to be Nik, not a projection of someone who could fill all her empty spaces, heal all her wounds.

A late-night bird sang a sleepy song, and she rested her oars, listening. Her father and his wives had not been able to do that, to allow each other to be who they were. Sophie had come close. Alice—Alice, she thought, was unique. She had learned much about wisdom and maturity from Alice. We are all wounded, and we will never heal until we accept our wounds, whether they be wounds of glamour, like David's, or—as Regan had called it—naïveté, like hers. Her father had blundered over and over again, had, perhaps, let her down over Billy. But she had let him down in not noticing that he, like King Lear, was moving toward death. Yet, ultimately, their love had been stronger than their human flaws.

If Nik had committed adultery, so had she, and both of them in more ways than physical. If Nik was no further from accepting his wounds than she was, he had made it quite clear that if she was willing to accept their marriage, so was he. She did not want to go back to him because he could dazzle her with his bright good looks and mind. She needed to accept his darknesses, too. And her own. For if there is no darkness for the light to shine against, we cannot see the light.

She looked up at the sky, still luminous with a soft, pearly light. She would be in her bunk before it was dark enough for stars.

She turned the rowboat and headed back toward the *Portia*.

·

Abby already had the curtains drawn around her bed. Emma walked past quietly and on into the forward cabin under the pilothouse. Alice was in her sleeping bag, reading. Emma said, "I don't know why it's thrown me so, everybody arriving all at once this way." She spoke softly, trying not to disturb Abby in the double bed, or Nik and Ben up in the main cabin.

"It's brought death close," Alice said. "They've all come to say goodbye to Dave, and that's made us face our own goodbyes. We've been living so much in the moment, even with Abby here making her farewells, that we haven't projected into the future."

"And now Nik and Jarvis, Sophie and Louis, are making us project?"

"Yes, Em." For a moment Alice's voice quivered. "It's hit me, too. I'm so in the routine of taking care of Dave that I've forgotten the routine is going to end."

There was a long silence between them. Emma looked around

the cabin, at Ben's books, at the lingering light showing through the portholes. "The *Portia*—"

"Dave wants Ben to keep it."

"Oh, good. That's good."

"But Ben will have to find other work. David pays him, and generously, for what he does."

"Nobody could really pay Ben for what he does," Emma said. "Like Sophie, he does it *mit Liebe*."

"Emma, Nik wants to talk to you. You, alone."

"I know."

"You've seemed—amazingly welcoming, considering everything."

Emma laughed softly. "We ought to stop talking. I'm sure we're disturbing Abby." She lay down, pulling the sleeping bag about her shoulders.

·

Ben was, as always, up early. Nik, used to theater hours, like Jarvis, and with a three-hour time lag, was still in his sleeping bag when Emma came up to the galley to start the coffee. She tried to be quiet, but Nik stirred.

"Hi."

"Nik, sorry. I didn't mean to wake you."

"I'm eminently wakable. So, you've been looking through some old scenes from my long-defunct David play."

"It's not defunct if you're still working on it."

"What I'm doing now is a different play, completely different."

"The old one—"

"It was doomed. Not because of you, Em, or the things that tore us all apart. I never ended it."

"No."

"David won all those battles and went back to his holy city. And there were the ten concubines Absalom had shamed. And David treated them well, 'and put them in ward . . . but went not in to them.'"

"He went not in to them because they were defiled?" Emma demanded.

"That was how they thought, in those days."

"The ones who are defiled are the ones who are punished, rather than the one who did the defiling?"

"Hey, Emma, that was one of the reasons I was writing the play, writing about David's women and women in general, and trying to get over some of my own male chauvinism."

She laughed. "Sorry, Nik. My skin's like tissue paper right now. And that hit close to home."

"I know. I'm sorry. And I take your point about the concubines. That attitude still prevails, to some extent."

"It was Myrlo's attitude. I asked for it, she said."

"Sweetie." Nik's voice was gentle. "Myrlo paid, and Billy, and Adair. And so did Absalom. Heavily."

"And you paid," Emma said, "for what—"

Nik cut her off. "We all paid. We don't live in isolation. When wrong is done, everybody pays. Eventually we have to realize it's all been paid for."

Emma let her breath out slowly, not quite a sigh.

"It's time to stop thinking about blame and guilt. Actions have consequences, and they have to be played out."

"And then we have to let them go," Emma said.

"Can we?" Nik demanded. "Are we both damaged goods? So damaged that we simply can't make it in an ordinary human way?"

Emma turned on the flame under the coffeepot. "I was in a show once with an actor who'd had TB, and when I was concerned about his going out in a horrible rainstorm, he told me not to worry, that his TB was cured, and that scar tissue is the strongest tissue in the human body. I suspect that spiritual scar tissue is strong, too, and that it should make us more able to be human, rather than less."

"It's made you stronger," Nik said. "I'm not sure about me. Am I still using my background as an excuse for all my horrible behavior?"

"No, Nik, I agree with you that we have more free will than that. We can hang on to our scars, forgetting that they are healed, or we can get on with life." She smiled, then turned her attention to the galley, taking bacon from the undercounter fridge, putting strips in a large frying pan.

"Hey," Nik said, "what would be really good would be if you'd cut up the bacon the way you used to do, and crisp it, and then scramble eggs into it."

"Okay. We may have just enough eggs. Norma brought us some, and I haven't quite used them all up."

"Norma?"

"She's an Indian, an old friend of Papa's. And of mine."

—Norma, Norma, she thought. —Papa's dying. How will you see him again?

The eggs were in a wire basket on the windowsill. Half a dozen left. Barely enough. Jarvis, she hoped, would remember to bring more. She broke Norma's eggs into a bowl, added milk, seasonings. Ben had pots of herbs on the windowsills, and she cut chives, summer savory, thyme.

"You're a wonderful cook."

"I learned to cook in that funny old Croyden Hotel in Chicago."

"What I said about incest—I was lashing out, using whatever weapon I could to hurt you. You love your father as his daughter, and you loved Adair as his sister."

"How do brothers and sisters love? We were half brothers and sisters. We didn't have a normal family life."

To her relief, Alice came up the steps then, but did not stop. She greeted Emma and Nik on her way to her husband.

"Emma." Nik spoke in a low voice. "I know I've said some unpardonable things. Beyond apology. But please come back to me."

She took a whisk from the drawer and began to beat the eggs. "Emma?"

"Maybe I'm the one who needs to change. Look at the way I rose to your bait over King David's concubines. I thought I was long healed from Billy, but—"

"You didn't rise to the bait," Nik said. "You had a point to make, a valid point."

Emma smiled, looking at the crisping bacon. "You've changed, I think, Nik. You wouldn't have given me a point, not even a valid one, a few months ago."

"A few months ago I didn't know how much I had to lose. Maybe we can't change, either of us. But maybe we can modify."

Emma reached out to touch his sleeve. "I don't think I want you overmodified."

"Just slightly modified, then." Nik got out of his sleeping bag, stood up. He was wearing a pair of Ben's flannel pajamas. He took his jeans and a flannel shirt and went into the head.

Emma drained the bacon fat into an empty coffee can, dried the bacon between paper towels. Turned off the heat under the coffee.

Alice, sniffing, came down the steps. "Dave says it smells wonderful. That's good."

"Alice, are you worried? I mean, especially?"

"I'm concerned about his kidneys."

"You don't think he ought to be in a hospital or anything, do you?"

"No. In a hospital we could check his creatinine level, but knowing just how badly his kidneys are affected wouldn't make me do anything I'm not already doing. He's hungry this morning, and that's a good sign."

Emma put the bacon-and-egg mixture into the frying pan. "We'll let Abby sleep. If she can. Where's Ben?"

"He went off in the rowboat. He needs to be alone for a while."

Emma stirred the eggs gently. "It's not easy to be alone with six people on a fifty-foot boat. And when we add Jarvis and Sophie and Louis—"

"The main thing," Alice said, "is for Dave not to feel crowded. Abby has been wonderful for him. Whatever he and Nik talked about was good. Jarvis is upsetting. Sophie and Louis—I don't know."

"Sophie's emotional." Emma turned the flame as low as she could get it. "Life has been rough for her. Even after she left

Papa, she always turned to him for advice. I don't know how she'll be with him now."

Alice sighed. "I don't want to be overprotective. That's not what Dave needs. We'll just have to take it as it comes."

Emma fixed a plate of her egg-and-bacon mixture for her father, added two blueberry muffins which had been warming in the oven, and set a cup of coffee and a pot of warm milk on the tray.

Alice took it. "I'll be back. I'll bathe Dave after breakfast."

She left, carrying the tray, just as Nik came out of the head. He rolled the pajamas up in the sleeping bag. while Emma fixed him a plate. "It's starting to rain," he said, "but it's a soft rain, and I don't think it should cause any delay for Sophie and Louis."

Their coming or not coming would neither hasten nor delay David Wheaton's death. Or would it? Was David waiting to make his final farewells before letting go? Emma shuddered. She wished that Jarvis had not come, that Sophie and Louis would not come.

Nik? Alone in the rowboat the night before, she had made her decision.

.

While Alice was bathing David and readying him for the day, a radio message came through that Jarvis would stay in Port Clements until Sophie and Louis arrived, so that Ben would have only one trip to make with the Zodiac. It was pouring. He was better off staying dry in the hotel until the rain stopped.

"Typical," Emma said. "He says he's being thoughtful of Ben, but he's really thinking of Jarvis."

Abby looked at her inquiringly.

"I'm being horrid about Jarvis, aren't I? Oh, Abby, I'm feeling horrid." She and Abby were in the main cabin. Alice was in the pilothouse. She did not know where Nik was. Probably some-where with Ben. "I suppose I've been in a make-believe world, really thinking that this summer would go on and on forever, that I'd do the cooking, and Alice would take care of Papa, and the curtain would never come down. And I've somehow been counting on Norma. Norma's Haida and Athabascan and has a good bit of others in her mix, and she has senses that ordinary people don't have, and she said she'd see Papa again. There's no way Papa's going to be anywhere near Norma's village again until next summer. That is, if he lived, he'd be going to see Norma again next summer."

"Emma." Abby's voice was gentle. "I know Norma and I, too, trust her. But Dave is dying. There isn't going to be any next summer for him. Whatever Norma meant, she didn't mean that there's going to be some kind of miracle."

"Well, there have been miracles, haven't there? Cures at Lourdes, and so forth . . . and so on . . ." Her voice trailed off.

"Oh, yes, there have been miracles, genuine miracles. And I suppose it is not outside the realm of possibility that Dave's cancer might remit. But, Emma, dearest, I don't think it's going to."

Emma reached across the table for Abby's hand. "I know. I don't think so, either."

.

Toward noon the rain stopped and a soft yellow sun began to burn through the clouds. After lunch Abby retired to the lower cabin to rest. Ben headed for the Zodiac. "I'm off to Port Clements. We're not exactly sure when they'll get in. I'd better be there early."

Emma asked, "Ben, please make sure that Jarvis got milk and eggs."

"Okay."

She had stuffed a small turkey for dinner, taking it out of the big freezer below-decks the night before. It seemed the simplest thing for that many people. She prepared brown and wild rice, and threw in some hazelnuts. She creamed onions and steamed a mixture of vegetables. When there was nothing left for her to do, nothing to occupy her mind, she went up to the pilothouse.

Nik was there with her father, and the two men were laughing.

"It was hilarious," Nik said. "Here was Emma with the great Ethel Barrymore, and Barrymore was playing a nun. It was a scene in a Boston mansion at night, and Emma wore white silk pajamas, and the wardrobe mistress hadn't checked the buttons, and right in the middle of the scene the waistband button went, and Emma's pajamas dropped to the stage, revealing her very skimpy scarlet undies (I'd given them to her for Christmas). Barrymore just stepped in front of Emma, spreading out her nun's skirts, until Emma had her pajamas up again, holding them by hand until the scene was finished. Only a few people in the audience noticed anything at all."

Emma perched on the foot of her father's bunk. "It was horribly embarrassing at the time, and taught me to check my own buttons. It's funny, now."

David said, "Did you hear about Louis and last New Year's Eve?"

"I didn't," Nik said.

"He was playing in that political show, remember, and on New Year's Eve he borrowed a big white towel and got a wide white satin ribbon with the date on it to go across his chest, and when Mel Douglas, who was playing the lead, opened the set door expecting to greet his stage wife, instead he was met by Louis in towel and ribbon and otherwise as naked as the day he was born."

"Marvelous Louis," Emma said. "He's really growing up. It took a long time before he developed that uninhibited kind of humor."

"There's a good role for him in my new play," Nik said. "No leading lady, Emma. No women, in fact, just a gaggle of idiotic little ingenues. But it's fun. I think you'll like it."

"I'm sure I will."

David Wheaton shifted position. "Do you remember that summer of stock we did in Westport, and we were doing Agatha Christie's *Ten Little Indians*?"

"Oh, indeed, yes." Emma laughed. "Remember that wonderful old character actor playing the judge? And he thought

he'd found the murderer, a guy called Seton. And he was supposed to say, 'I'll cook Seton's goose.' "

"And he said"—David Wheaton picked up the cue—" 'I'll
goose Seton's cook,' and he had no idea why we were all trying
not to break up."

Alice came in with mugs of tea. "Tea time. What did I miss?
Are you telling theater stories again?"

"We are," David said. "We have an endless supply. Did you
hear about the time Emma played Queen Elizabeth I, and one
of her strands of pearls broke, and pearls went bouncing across
the stage, and somehow or other the actor playing Essex got
one up his nose—"

"And couldn't get it out," Emma said. "He kept putting one
finger to his nose and trying to blow it out, and I had a terrible
time to keep from laughing, and the audience couldn't figure
out what was happening—"

It was a good afternoon of laughter, healing laughter.

·

The rain started again and it was expected that Sophie and
Louis would be delayed. It was six by the time Ben returned
with them and with Jarvis. Alice was there to greet them. "One
at a time, please. David gets very tired if there's any confusion.
Sophie, will you—?"

"Of course." Sophie sounded and looked very composed.
Emma had thought that she might fall apart, weep, but she
seemed to be in control of her emotions. She wore a grey flannel pants suit, and silver jewelry, and her mop of hair had
turned from gold to silver. "He's in the pilothouse? I know the
way."

"She's changed," Emma mused. "She's still Sophie, but
there's a sense of quiet."

Louis had his arms around Emma. "Alice, I'm so glad you're
here for Papa. And I'm glad Mom and I got here. I wasn't sure
about that last plane we took, the one that only seated four
people. And I'm glad Papa knows I'm making it in the theater.

Maybe I'll never be as big as he is, and maybe I'll do more musicals than serious theater—"

"Hey, Louis," Nik corrected, "musicals are serious theater."

"Oh, sure, I know, I'm sorry," Louis said. "I guess I just don't want to compare myself to Papa, but I want him to know I'm doing okay."

"He knows it." Emma took the turkey out of the oven. "He knows it, and he's glad. How are you at carving, Louis?"

"Not bad. Gino taught me."

"I'll carve," Jarvis said. "I claim seniority."

"Get to it, then, please," Emma ordered, "and by the time Sophie comes down we'll be ready." She helped put bowls of rice, onions, vegetables, on the table.

When Jarvis had finished carving, Louis said, "I'll get Mom."

"No, Louis, dear," Emma said. "I'll get her. Then you can visit with Papa later."

When they were all seated, Louis said, "I think we should hold hands and sing grace, the way we used to when we all got together."

"What grace?" Jarvis looked sour.

"The one I brought back from summer camp, Johnny Appleseed."

Emma held out her hands. She was sitting at the end of the table, where she could easily reach the galley, one hand holding Louis's; the other, Abby's. They sang the happy and robust melody. It was not the kind of music that plucked the chords of emotion. Thank heavens.

When everybody was served and Alice had taken a tray up to David, Jarvis looked at all of them around the table. "We're all sitting here as though everything's normal. And it isn't. Papa's death is going to change all our lives."

"Hold it, Jarvis," Louis said. "Papa's still alive."

"But we're all here to say goodbye to him. When we leave, we'll leave knowing that we're never going to see him again."

"We're at a crossroads," Sophie said softly, "and we must be careful which road we choose. I haven't always been careful."

Emma gasped, putting her hand to her mouth. At a crossroads. Surely a common expression, but it brought back uncommon memories. She looked around the table. "Do you remember Norma?"

"Sure," Sophie said. "That magnificent Indian woman. Has Davie seen her this summer?"

"Yes," Emma assured her. "We stopped at Norma's village and she and Papa had a good visit."

"Oh, I'm so glad. Norma's always been good for Davie. She's a tough old bird. No Indian's life is easy, thanks to us, I guess."

Abby looked at her godchild. "Is there something about Norma and a crossroads?"

Emma nodded gravely. "When Norma was young, she had a terrible time—she nearly died. I spent several days with her after—after a very bad time in my own life. Norma told me that when she was well and able to think again, the wise woman of her tribe told her that she was at a crossroads."

Sophie looked across the table inquiringly.

Emma smiled at Sophie. "The wise old woman said that one road led to a funeral and the other to a wedding. Norma said, 'I chose the wedding.'"

There were tears in Sophie's eyes. "Davie has always chosen the wedding. He's choosing it even now."

"You can say that, Sophie, after seeing Papa's depressions?" Emma asked.

"Davie's depressions weren't the real Davie. I know that now." She looked around the table. "Yes, we are all at a crossroads." She looked at Emma. At Nik.

"I have usually chosen the funeral," he said, "and this has been disaster for everybody I have loved. I can't blame it on the fact that my parents always chose the funeral. I made my own choices."

"And now?" Abby asked.

"I choose the wedding. No matter what"—he looked at Emma—"I will still choose the wedding. I've had too many funerals."

"But when Papa dies"—Louis's voice was choked—"how can we choose the wedding?"

Sophie laughed. "By giving him an enormous great grand glorious funeral at the Cathedral, a real show for all his family and friends and fans. And by going on living, living better because we've been part of his life than if we'd never known him."

.

After dinner Louis went to see his father, and Sophie insisted on doing the dishes. Nik said, "I'll dry and put. There's nowhere on this boat big enough for all these dishes except in their own places in the cupboards."

As they were finishing, Ben came in. "Last call for the ferry to Port Clements."

Jarvis said, "I haven't seen Papa today. You'll have to wait a few minutes."

"Not long," Alice said. "It's late."

"Louis has been with him for half an hour. I came all these thousands of miles to—"

"Not long, Jarvis," Sophie reiterated. "I'll get Louis."

"No." Jarvis was firm. "I'll go to the pilothouse and send Louis down."

After fifteen minutes Alice said, "Enough," and went after Jarvis.

When Jarvis, Sophie, and Louis had gone off with Ben in the Zodiac, Abby looked at Alice. "You're very concerned about David?"

"I think his kidneys are going."

Abby nodded. "Then it's time for all of us to leave. We can go from Port Clements tomorrow. Emma?"

Emma closed her eyes, sighing deeply. "You're right, Abby. It's time. It's too much confusion for Papa." Then she looked around. "But it's too much confusion for me, too, leaving with everybody."

"You're very close to your father," Abby said. "But not too long, Emma. As you said, you have to let go."

"If you leave tomorrow, I'll leave the next day."

"Alone?"

"With Nik."

.

She and Nik got into the dinghy in order to have a few minutes alone, Emma taking the oars and pushing away from the *Portia*.

"You really mean it?" Nik asked.

"As long as you really mean it about choosing the wedding. No. I'm sorry. That won't work. No qualifications. I love you, I'm your wife. I won't walk out on you again. But, Nik, you mustn't walk out on me."

"Emma, I'm not your father. You aren't any of his wives." He watched her as she rowed away from the *Portia* and toward one of the small islands. "Sweetie. I may regress. You may have to pull me away from the funeral. But I'll try."

"We'll try together," Emma said.

"Em?"

"Yes?"

"Why?"

"Why what?"

"Coming back to me—"

"I don't know. I'm not sure. Going over the David play, talking about it with Papa, with Abby and Alice—I did some reassessing. And then—seeing Abby, and now Sophie, and knowing how close they came to—well, if it hadn't been for Papa falling for Myrlo, Abby and Papa would still be married. And Marical— Adair thought she should have stayed with Papa. And Sophie— I know she's sorry she left when things were rough. I don't think I want to give up."

"I'm glad you don't. Neither do I."

.

That night in the lower cabin Emma watched while Alice got ready for bed. "I'm going back to Nik."

· 347 ·

"Yes. I'm glad."

"I may be crazy. But when I left Nik three months ago I wasn't the same person I am now."

"No." Alice climbed up onto her bunk, sat there looking at Emma. Finally she asked, "Emma—forgive me—when did you last have a period?"

Emma looked at her in surprise. "I don't know. I haven't thought. So much has been happening."

"Think."

"Well. Not for a while."

Alice continued to look at Emma with her cool blue gaze. "I think you're pregnant."

"Preg—why on earth?"

"You were sick in the morning the first few days you were here, for instance."

"I had that virus that was going around. It hit me just when I left Nik, and all my defenses were down. Everyone said it lasted forever—" She stopped. "Morning sickness?"

"Well?"

Emma started to laugh. "That would be choosing the wedding, all right. I'm nearly forty."

"Well?" Alice asked again.

Emma continued to laugh. "I'd given up all thought of ever getting pregnant again. I haven't bothered to keep track of my periods. They've never been very regular. Oh, Alice, I think maybe you're right. I think maybe I am pregnant— But at my age—"

"There's no reason you shouldn't be fine, and the baby, too."

Emma's laughter dissolved into tears. "Oh, God, it would explain a lot of little things. I hope—I hope it's true."

"I suspect it is," Alice said gently.

"When did you—"

"For quite a while. It didn't seem appropriate to mention it when you'd just left Nik."

"No. Well. I'm glad I decided to go back to Nik before—it wouldn't have been for the right reason if I'd gone back to him because I'm pregnant. I wish I could have my baby here, with you."

"No, you'll be better off in New York. I'll do some research and find the right obstetrician for you. There are some good women coming along in the field."

"I want to tell Nik," Emma said.

"Wait till morning," Alice advised. "Wait till the others go."

·

Ben took Abby, Sophie, Louis, and Jarvis to Port Clements in the Zodiac. When Abby left David, she looked white and shaken. David had clung to her. Leaving was not easy.

Sophie, Louis, and Jarvis did not have a final farewell visit. "It's been done," Sophie agreed.

"But Abby did—" Jarvis started.

"Jarvis, hush. You produced David Wheaton's last play."

Louis was silent, trying to control tears.

The *Portia* seemed empty when the Zodiac left.

"Emma!" David Wheaton called. "Alice!"

Alice went up to the pilothouse.

Nik was sitting on the long bench in the main cabin. Emma went over and sat beside him, reaching for his hands.

"Nik. Something I never expected."

He looked at her, reaching to clasp her hand. "What, sweetie?"

She was suddenly tongue-tied.

"What?" Nik asked again.

"Well, it seems—well, last night Alice told me she thinks I'm pregnant." The words came out in a burst.

"What?"

"Alice thinks I'm pregnant."

"Do you think—"

"Well, yes. I do."

"Oh, Emma, sweetie, sweetie—"

"I didn't know—I didn't have any idea—so much has been going on and I thought I had one of those intestinal things—

I've been sick in the morning—but I thought I'd never get pregnant again, it just never occurred to me, and my mind has been so on Papa—" She ran out of breath.

He put his arms around her, holding her close, murmuring his pleasure. "Your father'll be ecstatic."

"He won't ever see the baby. And we have to leave tomorrow."

"Yes, love. He'll still be happy. Emma, sweetie, you've had some wonderful, unique times with your father, onstage, playing together. Nobody can ever take that away from you."

"I know. And it's right for Alice to be with him now, just the two of them."

"Very right. The analogies break down here. Alice is no Abishag. She's a mature woman who's known your father, fully, deeply, all the way. Jarvis is no Adonijah, either, and Adonijah is not going to get the throne. Neither is Solomon."

"What?" Emma was startled. "I thought Louis—he's turning into a fine actor."

"He's good. I really want him in my new play. But you—when you walk onstage, every person in the audience chooses the wedding."

•

The rest of that last day on the *Portia* was quiet. They ate lunch with David in the pilothouse. He received the news of the coming baby with delight. But it was obvious that he was unusually tired, and he slept most of the afternoon. Emma made a turkey hash for dinner, and David ate little, but seemed calm and collected, talking about various productions he had enjoyed.

"I'm glad you're going to finish the David play, Nik, and sorry I won't be in it."

"David himself won't be in it," Nik reminded him. "Just Abigail."

"You're right, that the theater is changing," David said. "If *Lear* hadn't been a success, Jarvis would have lost his socks."

"But it was a success," Nik said. "For you, and for Emma. For the two of you together."

"Yes. A good play for my curtain call." His voice strengthened. "Now these be the last words of David, the sweet psalmist of Israel. He said, 'The Spirit of the Lord spake by me, and his word was in my tongue.' That was a good scene, Nik. I memorized it when we were working on the play and I still remember it. 'The Rock of Israel spake to me, He that ruleth over men must be just, ruling in the fear of God. And he shall be as the light of the morning, when the sun riseth, even a morning without clouds; as the tender grass springing out of the earth by clear shining after rain.' " He opened his eyes and smiled at them. "Good words, David's. He had a powerful vision of God. Like Grandpa Bowman, eh, Emma?"

"Very like."

"There went up a smoke out of his nostrils, and fire out of his mouth . . . He bowed the heavens also . . . and darkness was under his feet. And he rode upon a cherub, and did fly: and he was seen upon the wings of the wind . . . He drew me out of many waters, and brought me forth also into a large place . . ." He laughed. "That takes me back to my childhood. I memorized a lot of the Psalms for my mother. I remember standing in front of her on Sundays looking like Little Lord Fauntleroy and reciting Psalms. I haven't got it quite right, but it's close enough. I suppose you won't have David speak in the new play—"

"Who knows, Dave? I'm simply going to listen to the play and see what happens."

"You'll listen well. Won't he, Emma?"

"Yes, Papa, I believe he will." —He's returning to his childhood, she thought, and her heart was heavy. Wasn't this kind of returning to early memories a sign that death was near?

.

Emma and Nik left the next morning, turning from the pilothouse; hugging Alice. Getting into the Zodiac. Holding back emotion that otherwise would have overwhelmed them.

Ben started the outboard motor. They rode in silence, the little rubber craft moving with the swells of the water. Nik had his feet around an orange can of fuel. Emma looked back at the *Portia* as it began to recede in the distance. Then, deliberately, she turned away, looking out to sea. Almost stood up.

"Nik—Ben—"

They looked at her.

"Norma," she breathed.

Coming toward them was an old fishing boat with eyes painted on either side of the prow. It drew level with them, heading for the *Portia*. The tall woman at the wheel waved, a solemn raising of her arm and hand in what could be either greeting or farewell.